TWO KN

A Novel of Canadian Summer Life

By J CAWDOR BELL

PUBLISHERS' NOTE.

The Publishers have extreme pleasure in placing this novel, by a new and promising native author, before the reading public of Canada. They will be greatly disappointed if it does not at once take its place among the best products of Canadian writers. While the work has peculiar interest for Torontonians and dwellers in the districts so graphically described, its admirable character drawings of many "sorts and conditions" of our people—its extremely clever dialect, representing Irish, Scotch, English, Canadian, French, Southern and Negro speech, and the working out of its story, which is done in such a way as would credit an experienced romancer—should insure the book a welcome in very many homes. The literary flavour is all that can be desired; the author evidencing a quite remarkable acquaintance with English Literature, especially with Wordsworth, the Poet of the Lake Country.

[Pg 5]

TWO KNAPSACKS:
A Novel of Canadian Summer Life.

BY J. CAWDOR BELL.

CHAPTER I.

The Friends—The Knapsacks—The Queen's Wharf—The Northern Railway—Belle Ewart—The *Susan Thomas*, Captain and Crew—Musical Performance—The Sly Dog—Misunderstanding—Kempenfeldt Bay.

Eugene Coristine and Farquhar Wilkinson were youngish bachelors and fellow members of the Victoria and Albert Literary Society. Thither, on Wednesday evenings, when respectable church-members were wending their way to weekly service, they hastened regularly, to meet with a band of like-minded young men, and spend a literary hour or two. In various degrees of fluency they debated the questions of the day; they read essays with a wide range of style and topic; they gave readings from popular authors, and contributed airy creations in prose and in verse to the Society's manuscript magazine. Wilkinson, the older and more sedate of the two, who wore a tightly-buttoned blue frock coat and an eyeglass, was a schoolmaster, pretty well up in the Toronto Public Schools. Coristine was a lawyer in full practice, but his name did not appear on the card of the firm which profited by his services. He was taller than his friend, more jauntily dressed, and was of a more mercurial temperament than the schoolmaster, for whom, however, he entertained a profound respect. Different as they were, they were linked together by an ardent love of literature, especially poetry, by scientific pursuits, Coristine as a botanist, and Wilkin[Pg 6]son as a dabbler in geology, and by a firm determination to resist, or rather to shun, the allurements of female society. Many lady teachers wielded the pointer in rooms not far removed from those in which Mr. Wilkinson held sway, but he did not condescend to be on terms even of bowing acquaintance with any one of them. There were several young lady typewriters of respectable city connections in the offices of Messrs. Tyler, Woodruff and White, but the young Irish lawyer passed them by without a glance. These bachelors were of the opinion that women were bringing the dignity of law and education to the dogs.

It was a Wednesday evening in the beginning of July, and the heat was still great in the city. Few people ventured out to the evening services, and fewer still found their way to the Victoria and Albert hall; in fact, there was not a quorum, and, as the constitution stated that, in such a case, the meeting should be adjourned, it was adjourned accordingly. Coristine lit a cigar in the porch, and Wilkinson, who did not smoke, but said he liked the odour of good tobacco, took his arm for a walk along the well-lit streets. They agreed that it was time to be out of town. Coristine said: "Let us go together; I'll see one of the old duffers and get a fortnight's leave." Wilkinson had his holidays, so he eagerly answered: "Done! but where shall we go? Oh, not to any female fashion resort." At this Coristine put on the best misanthropic air he could call up, with a cigar between his lips, and then, as if struck by a happy thought, dug his elbow into his companion's side and ejaculated: "Some quiet country place where there's good fishing." Wilkinson demurred, for he was no fisherman. The sound of a military band stopped the conversation. It came into sight, the bandsmen with torches in their headgear, and, after it, surrounded and accompanied by all the small boys and shop-girls in the town, came the Royals, in heavy marching order. The friends stood in a shop doorway until the crowd passed by, and then, just as soon as a voice could be distinctly heard, the schoolmaster clapped his companion on the shoulder and cried, "Eureka!" Coristine thought the music had been too much for his usually staid and deliberate friend. "Well, old Archimedes, and what is it you've found? Not any new geometrical problems, I hope." "Listen to [Pg 7]me," said the dominie, in a tone of accustomed authority, and the lawyer listened.

"You've heard Napoleon or somebody else say that every soldier of France carries a marshal's baton in his knapsack?"

"Never heard the gentleman in my life, and don't believe it, either."

"Well, well, never mind about that; but I got my idea out of a knapsack."

"Now, what's the use of your saying that, when its myself knows that you haven't got such a thing to bless yourself with?"

"I got it out of a soldier's—a volunteer's knapsack, man."

"O, you thief of the world! And where have you got it hid away?"

"In my head."

"O rubbish and nonsense—a knapsack in your head!"

"No, but the idea."

"And where's the knapsack?"

"On the grenadier's back."

"Then the grenadier has the knapsack, and you the idea: I thought you said the idea was in the knapsack."

"So it was; but I took it out, don't you see? My idea is the idea of a knapsack on a man's back—on two men's backs—on your back and on mine."

"With a marshal's baton inside?"

"No; with an extra flannel shirt inside—and some socks, and a flask, and some little book to read by the way; that's what I want."

"It'll be mortal heavy and hot this boiling weather."

"Not a bit. You can make one out of cardboard and patent cloth, just as light as a feather, and costing you next to nothing."

"And where will you be going with your knapsack? Will it be parading through the streets with the volunteers you would be after?"

"Go? We will go on a pedestrian tour through the finest scenery available." This was said correctly and with great dignity. It had the effect of sobering the incredulous Coristine, who said: "I tell ye, Farquhar, my boy, that's a fine idea of yours, barring the heat; but [Pg 8]I suppose we can rest where we like and go when we like, and, if the knapsacks get to be a nuisance, express 'em through, C.O.D. Well, I'll sleep over it, and let you know to-morrow when I can get away." So the pair separated, to retire for the night and dream a knapsack nightmare.

Coristine's leave did not come till the following Tuesday, so that Friday, Saturday and Monday—or parts of them, at least—could be devoted to the work of preparation. Good, strong, but not too heavy, tweed walking suits were ordered, and a couple of elegant flannel shirts that would not show the dirt were laid in; a pair of stout, easy boots was picked out, and a comfortable felt hat, with brim enough to keep off the sun. Then the lawyer bought his cardboard and his patent cloth and straps, and spent Saturday evening with his friend and a sharp penknife, bringing the knapsacks into shape. The scientists made a mistake in producing black and shiny articles, well calculated to attract the heat. White canvas would have been far better. But Wilkinson had taken his model from the military, hence it had to be black. The folded ends of the patent cloth, which looked like leather, were next to the wearer's back, so that what was visible to the general public was a very respectable looking flat surface, fastened round the shoulders with becoming straps, equally dark in hue. "Sure, Farquhar, it's pack-men the ignorant hayseeds will be taking us for," said Coristine, when the prospective pedestrians had strapped on their shiny baggage holders. "I do not agree with you there," replied the schoolmaster; "Oxford and Cambridgemen, and the best *litterateurs* of

England, do Wales and Cornwall, the Lakes and the Trossachs, to say nothing of Europe, dressed just as we are." "All right, old man, but I'm thinking I'll add a bandanna handkerchief and a blackthorn. They'll come in handy to carry the fossils over your shoulder. There now, I've forgot the printers' paper and the strap flower press for my specimens. True, there's Monday for that; but I'm afraid I'll have to shave the boards of the flower press down, or it'll be a sorry burden for a poor, tired botanist. Good night to you, my bouchal boy, and it's a pack you might throw into a corner of your sack." "Cards!" replied Wilkinson; "no sir, but [Pg 9]my pocket chess box will be at your service." "Chess be hanged," said the lawyer; "but, see here, are they checkers when you turn them upside down? If they are, it's I'm your man."

On Tuesday morning, about eight o'clock, there appeared at the Brock Street Station of the Northern Railway, two well-dressed men with shiny knapsacks on their shoulders. They had no blackthorns, for Wilkinson had said it would be much more romantic to cut their own sticks in the bush, to which Coristine had replied that, if the bush was as full of mosquitos as one he had known, he would cut his stick fast enough. They were the astonishment, rather than the admiration, of all beholders, who regarded them as agents, and characterized the way in which they carried their samples as the latest thing from the States. For a commencement, this was humiliating, so that the jaunty lawyer twisted his moustache fiercely, and felt inclined to quarrel with the self-possessed, clean-shaven space between Wilkinson's elaborate side-whiskers. But the pedagogue, in his suavest manner, remarked that Cicero, in his *De Natura Deorum*, makes Cotta call the common herd both fools and lunatics, whose opinion is of no moment whatever. "Why, then," he asked, "should we trouble our minds with what it pleases them to think? It is for us to educate public opinion—to enlighten the darkness of the masses. Besides, if you look about, you will see that those who are doing the giggling are girls, sir, positively girls."

"Your hand on that, Farquhar, my boy; if it keeps the hussies off, I'll wear a knapsack every day of my life."

Coristine did not know where he was going, being subject to the superior wisdom and topographical knowledge of his companion, who appeared in the row that besieged the window of the ticket office. "Two for Belle Ewart," he demanded, when his turn came.

"Trains don't run to Belle Ewart now; you had better take Lefroy, the nearest point."

"All right; two for Lefroy."

The ticket agent looked at the attire of the speaker, and was about to produce the cardboard slips, then hesitated as he glanced at the straps and the top of the black erection on Wilkinson's shoulders, and enquired, "Second [Pg 10]class, eh?" The dominie was angry, his face crimsoned, his hand shook with indignation. Being a moral man, he would not use bad language, but he roared in his most stentorian academic tone, a tone which appalled the young agent with rapid visions of unfortunate school days, "Second Tom-cats! Does the company put you there to insult gentlemen?" It was the agent's turn to redden, and then to apologize, as he mildly laid the tickets down, without the usual slap, and fumbled over their money. The feminine giggling redoubled, and Coristine, who had regained his equilibrium, met his friend with a hearty laugh, and the loud greeting, "O Lord, Wilks, didn't I tell you the fools would be taking us for bagmen?" But Wilkinson's irritation was deep, and he marched to the incoming train, ejaculating, "Fool, idiot, puppy; I shall report him for incivility, according to the printed invitation of the company. Second! ach! I was never so insulted in my life."

There was room enough inside the car to give the travellers a double seat, half for themselves and the other for their knapsacks. These impedimenta being removed the occupants of the carriage became aware that they were in the company of two good-looking men, of refined features, and in plain but gentlemanly attire. The lady passengers glanced at them, from time to time, with approbation not unmingled with amusement, but no responsive glance came from the bachelors. Wilkinson had opened his knapsack, and had taken out his pocket Wordsworth, the true poet, he said, for an excursion. Coristine had a volume of Browning in his kit, but left it there, and went into the smoking-car for an after breakfast whiff. The car had been swept out that morning by the joint efforts of a brakesman and the newsagent, so that it was less hideously repulsive than at a later stage in the day, when tobacco juice, orange peel, and scraps of newspapers made it unfit for a decent pig. The lawyer took out his plug, more easily carried than cut tobacco, and whittled it down with his knife to fill his handsome Turk's head meerschaum. When all was ready, he discovered, to his infinite disgust, that he had no matches nor pipe-lights of any description. The news agent, Frank, a well-known character on the road, supplied him with a box of Eddy's [Pg 11]manufacture, for which he declined to receive payment. However, he pressed his wares upon the grateful Coristine, recommending warmly the Samantha books and Frank Stockton's stories. "Are there any women in them?" asked the smoker. "Full of them," replied Frank; "Why, Samantha is a woman." "Take them away, and bring me something different." The news agent returned with a volume made up of cartoons and other illustrations from *Puck*, and soon the Irishman was shaking his sides over the adventures of Brudder Sunrise Waterbury and similar fictitious characters. So absorbed was he in this trivial literature that he failed to notice the entrance of an old man, respectably dressed who took a seat on the opposite side of the aisle, and was preparing to smoke his three inches of clay. He was aroused by the salutation and request:—

"Good marnin', Sor, an' moight Oi be afther thrubblin' yeez for a loight to my poipe?"

"Certainly, with pleasure; glad to be of any use to a fellow countryman," replied Coristine, looking up, and perceiving that his new acquaintance, though old and stooped, had a soldierly air. "You have been in service?" he continued.

"Troth I have, puff, puff, now she's goin' aisy. Oi was in the Furren Laygion in South Ameriky, an' my cornel was the foinest man you iver see. It was Frinch he was by his anshesters, an' his name it was Jewplesshy. Wan toime we was foightin' wid the Spanyerds an' the poor deluded haythen Injuns, when a shpint bullet rickyshayed an' jumped into my mouth, knockin' out the toot' ye'll percaive is missin' here. Will, now, the cornel he was lookin' at me, an', fwhen Oi shput out the bullet and the broken toot' on the ground, he roides up to me, and says, says he, 'It's a brave bhoy, yeez are, Moikle Terry, an' here's a' suverin to get a new toot' put in whin the war is over, says he. Oh, that suverin wint to kape company wid a lot more that Oi'd be proud to see the face av in my owld age. But, sorra a toot' did the dintist put in for me, for fwhere wud the nate hole for the poipe have been thin, till me that, now?"

Mr. Coristine failed to answer this conundrum, but continued the conversation with the old soldier. He [Pg 12]learnt that Michael had accompanied his colonel to Canada, and, after serving him faithfully for many years, had wept over his grave. One of the old man's sons was a sergeant in the Royal Artillery, and his daughter was married to a Scotch farmer named Carruthers, up in the County of Grey.

"She was a good gyurl, as nate an' swate as a picter, whin she lift the cornel's lady's sarvice, an' wint an' tuk up wid Carruthers, a foine man an' a sponsible, not a bit loike the common Scotch. Carruthers and her, they axed me wud Oi go an' pay thim a visit, an' say to the comfort av her young lady on the way."

"What young lady?" asked Coristine, and immediately repented the question.

"Miss Jewplesshy, to be sure, the cornel's darter, and an illigant wan she is, av she has to make her livin' by the wroitin'."

At this juncture, the lawyer, with lively satisfaction, hailed the arrival of Frank, who came straight towards him.

"Are you Mr. Coristine, the lawyer?" he half whispered. "Yes; that's my name," his victim replied, thinking that Wilkinson had sent him a message.

"Well, there's a lady in the rear car wanted to know, and I said I'd find out."

"Fwhat's that you'll be sayin' av a lady in the rare car, my lad?" questioned the old soldier, who had overheard part of the conversation.

"It's the tall girl in the travelling duster and the blue ribbons that wants to know if Mr. Coristine is here."

"Fwhat? my own dare young mishtress, Miss Ceshile Jewplesshy; shure it's her that do have the blue ribbins, an' the dushter. Do yeez know that swate young crathur, Sor?"

"I do not," replied Coristine abruptly, and added, *sotto voce*, "thank goodness!" Then he relit his pipe, and buried his head in the Puck book, from the contemplation of which the

Irish veteran was too polite to seek to withdraw his attention. In a few minutes, the door opened and closed with a slam, and Wilkinson, pale and trembling, stood before him.

"Eugene, my dear friend," he stammered, "I'll never forgive myself for leading you and me into a trap, a con[Pg 13]founded, diabolical, deep-laid trap, sir, a gin, a snare, a woman's wile. Let us get off anywhere, at Aurora, Newmarket, Holland Landing, Scanlans, anywhere to escape these harpies."

"What's the matter, old man?" enquired Coristine, with a poor attempt at calmness.

"Matter!" replied Wilkinson, "it's this matter, that they have found us out, and the girl with the cream coloured ribbons and crimson wrapper has asked that villainous news-agent if my name is not Wilkinson, and if I don't teach in the Sacheverell Street School. The rascal says her name is Miss Marjorie Carmichael, the daughter of old Dr. Carmichael, that was member for Vaughan, and that her friend, the long girl with the blue ribbons, knows you. O, my dear friend, this is awful. Better be back in Toronto than shut up in a railway car with two unblushing women."

"Stay here," said Coristine, making way for his friend, "they'll never dare come into this car after us." Yet his eye followed the retreating form of the South American warrior with apprehension. What if he should bring his 'dare young misthress' and her friend into the atmosphere of stale tobacco after their lawful game? Wilkinson sat down despairingly and coughed. "I feel very like the least little nip," he said faintly, "but it's in my knapsack, and I will not enter that car of foul conspiracy again for all the knapsacks and flasks in the world."

Now, Coristine had smoked two big pipes, and felt that it was dry work, but loyalty to his friend made him braver than any personal necessity would have done. "It's sick you're looking, Farquhar, my dear," he said, "and it's no friend of your's I'd be, and leave you without comfort in such a time of trouble. Here's for the knapsack, and woe betide the man or woman that stops me." So up he rose, and strode out of the car, glowering fiercely at the second-class passengers and all the rest, till he reached the vacated seats, from which he silently, and in deep inward wrath, gathered up the creations of cardboard and patent cloth, and retreated, grinding his teeth as he heard the veteran call out behind him, "Would yeez moind comin' this way a bit, Mishter?" He paid no attention to that officious old man, but hurried back to [Pg 14]the smoking-car, where he extracted Wilkinson's flask from its flannel surroundings, removed the metal cup, poured out a stiff horn, and diluted it at the filter. "Take this, old man," he said sternly, pressing it to the lips of the sufferer, "it'll set you up like a new pin." So the schoolmaster drank and was comforted, and Coristine took a nip also, and they felt better, and laughed and joked, and said simultaneously, "It's really too absurd about these girls, ha, ha!"

Apprehension made the time seem long to the travellers, who gazed out of the windows upon a fine agricultural country, with rolling fields of grain, well-kept orchards and substantial houses and barns. They admired the church on the hill at Holland Landing, and the schoolmaster told his friend of a big anchor that had got stuck fast there on its way to the Georgian Bay in 1812. "I bet you the sailors wouldn't have left it behind if it had been an anchor of Hollands," said Coristine, whereupon Wilkinson remarked that his puns were intolerable. At Bradford the track crossed the Holland River, hardly flowing between its flat, marshy banks towards Lake Simcoe. "This," said the schoolmaster, "is early Tennysonian scenery, a Canadian edition of the fens of Lincolnshire," but he regretted uttering the words when the lawyer agreed with him that it was an of-fens-ive looking scene. But Lake Simcoe began to show up in the distance to the right, and soon the gentlemanly conductor took their tickets. "Leefroy," shouted the brakesman. They gathered up their knapsacks, dropped off the smoker, and sped inside the station, out of the windows of which they peered cautiously to see that no attempt at a pursuit was made by the ladies and their military protector. The train sped on its way northward, and feeling that, for a time, they were safe, the pedestrians faced each other with a deep-drawn sigh of relief. The station-master told them to walk back along the track till they met the old side-line that used to go to Belle Ewart. So they helped each other to strap on their knapsacks, and virtually began their pedestrian tour. The station-master would have liked to detain them for explanations, but they were unwilling to expose themselves to further misunderstanding. Walking on a railway track is never very pleasant [Pg 15]exercise, but this old Belle Ewart track was an abomination of sand and broken rails and irregular sleepers. Coristine tried to step in time over the rotting cedar and hemlock ties, but, at the seventh step, stumbled and slid down the gravel bank of the road-bed. "Where did the seven sleepers do their sleeping, Wilks?" he enquired. "At Ephesus," was the curt reply. "Well, if they didn't efface us both, they nearly did for one of us." "Coristine, if you are going to talk in that childish way, we had better take opposite ends of the track; there are limits, sir."

"That's just what's troubling me; there are far too many limits. If this is what you call pedestrianizing, I say, give me a good sidewalk or the loan of an uneven pair of legs. It's dislocation of the hip or inflammatory rheumatism of the knee-joint I'll be getting with this hop and carry one navigation." Wilkinson plodded on in dignified silence, till the sawmills of the deserted village came in sight, and, beyond it, the blue green waters of Lake Simcoe. "Now," he said, "we shall take to the water." "What?" enquired Coristine, "on our knapsacks?" to which his companion answered, "No, on the excellent steamer *Emily May*."

There was no excellent steamer *Emily May*; there had not been for a long time; it was a memory of the past. The railway had ruined navigation. What was to be done? It would never do to retrace their steps over the railroad ties, and the roads about Belle Ewart led nowhere, while to track it along the hot lake shore was not to be thought of. Wilkinson's plans had broken down; so Coristine left him at the village hostelry, and sallied forth on exploration bent. In the course of his wanderings he came to a lumber wharf, alongside which lay an ancient schooner.

"Schooner ahoy!" he shouted, when a shock-headed man of uncertain middle age poked his head up through a hatchway, and answered: "Ahoy yourself, and see how you like it." This was discouraging, but not to a limb of the law. Coristine half removed his wide awake, and said: "I have the pleasure of addressing the captain of the ship *Susan Thomas*," the name he had seen painted in gold letters on the stern.

[Pg 16]"Not adzackly," replied the shock headed mariner, much mollified; "he's my mate, and he'll be along as soon as he's made up his bundle. I'm waitin' for him to sail this yere schooner."

"Where is the *Susan Thomas* bound for?"

"For Kempenfeldt Bay, leastways Barrie."

"Could you take a couple of passengers, willing to pay properly for their passage?"

"Dassent; it's agin the law; not but what I'd like to have yer, fer its lonesome, times. Here comes the old man hisself; try him."

A stout grizzled man of between fifty and sixty came walking along the wharf, with his bundle over his shoulder, and Coristine tried him. The Captain was a man of few words, so, when the situation was explained, he remarked: "Law don't allow freight boats to take money off passengers, but law don't say how many hands I have to have, nor what I'm to pay 'em or not to pay 'em. If you and your friend want to ship for the trip to Barrie, you'd better hurry up, for we're going to start right away."

Coristine was filled with the wildest enthusiasm. He dashed back to the hotel, the bar of which was covered with maps and old guide-books, partly the property of Wilkinson, partly of mine host, who was lazily helping him to lay out a route. "Hurry, hurry!" cried the excited lawyer, as he swept the maps into his friend's open knapsack. Then he yelled "hurroo!" and sang:—

For the ship, it is ready, and the wind is fair,
And I am bound for the sea, Mary Ann.

Like a whirlwind he swept Wilkinson and the two knapsacks out of the hotel door, along the sawdust paths and on to the wharf just in time to see the first sail set. "What in the name of common sense is the meaning of this conduct?" asked the amazed schoolmaster as soon as he got his breath.

"Meaning! why, we're indentured, you and I, as apprentice mariners on board the good ship *Susan Thomas*, bound for Kempenfeldt Bay.

Brave Kempenfeldt is gone,
His victories are o'er;
And he and his eight hundred
Shall plough the waves no more.

6

[Pg 17]But we'll plough them, Wilks, my boy. We'll splice the spanker boom, and port the helm to starboard, and ship the taffrail on to the lee scuppers of the after hatch, and dance hornpipes on the mizzen peak. Hulloa, captain, here's my mate, up to all sorts of sea larks; he can box the compass and do logarithm sums, and work navigation by single or double entry." The schoolmaster blushed for his companion, at whose exuberant spirits the sedate captain smiled, while the shock-headed man, whom Coristine named The Crew, displayed a large set of fairly preserved yellowish teeth, and guffawed loud and long.

"Do I understand, Captain, that you are willing to take us to Barrie in your—ah—vessel?" asked Wilkinson, politely.

"Aye, aye, my man," answered the ancient mariner, "get your leg aboard, for we're going to sail right away. Hi, you, Sylvanus there, give another haul on them halliards afore you're too mighty ready to belay, with your stupid cackle."

So the indentured apprentices and their knapsacks got on board, while Sylvanus,*alias* The Crew, stopped laughing, and put a pound or two extra on to the halliards. "Wilks," said Coristine, "it'll puzzle the women to find us out on our ocean home."

Wilkinson saw the captain hauling at the halliards of the after-mainsail and went to his assistance, while Coristine, doffing his coat, lent a hand to The Crew, when, by their combined efforts, the sails were all hoisted and the schooner floated away from the pier. The lawyer walked over the deck with a nautical air, picking up all loose ends of rope and coiling them neatly over his left arm. The coils he deposited carefully about the feet of the masts, to the astonishment of Wilkinson, who regarded his friend as a born seaman, and to the admiration of the captain and The Crew. The schoolmaster felt that Wordsworth was not the thing for the water; he should have brought Falconer or Byron. So he stuck to the captain, who was a very intelligent man of his class, and discussed with him the perils and advantages of lake navigation. They neither of them smoked, nor, said the captain, did he often drink; when he did, he liked to have it good. Thereupon Wilkinson produced what remained in his flask, which his [Pg 18]commanding officer took down neat at a gulp, signifying, as he ruefully gazed upon the depleted vessel, that a man might go long before he'd get such stuff as that. Then the conversation turned on the prohibitory Scott Act, which opened the vials of the old man's wrath, for making "the biggest lot of hypocrites and law-breakers and unlicensed shebeens and drunkards the country had ever seen." The schoolmaster, as in duty bound, tried to defend the Act, but all in vain, so he was glad to change the subject and discuss the crops, politics, and education. This conversation took place at what the captain called "the hellum", against the tiller of which he occasionally allowed his apprentice to lean his back while he attended to other work. Wilkinson was proud. This was genuine navigation, this steering a large vessel with your back; any mere landsman, he now saw, could coil up ropes like Coristine. The subject of this reflection was quite happy in the bow, chumming with The Crew. Smoking their pipes together, Sylvanus confided to his apprentice that a sailor's life was the lonesomest life out of jail, when the cap'n was that quiet and stand off like as one he knowed that wasn't far away, nuther. Coristine sympathized with him. "The bossest time that ever was on this yere old *Susan Thomas*," he continued, "was last summer wonst when the cap'n's niece, she come along fer a trip. There was another gal along with her, a regular stunner, she was. Wot her name was I raley can't tell, 'cos that old owl of a cap'n, whenever he'd speak to her, allers said Miss Do Please. I reckon that's what she used to say to him, coaxin' like, and he kep' it up on her. Well, we was becalmed three days right out on the lake, and I had to row the blessed dingy in the bilin' sun over to Snake Island to get bread and meat from the Snakes."

"From the snakes!" ejaculated Coristine, "why this beats Elijah's ravens all to nothing."

"Oh, the Snakes is Injuns, and Miss Carmichael, that's the cap'n's gal, says their rale name is Kinapick."

"Look here, Sylvanus, what did you say the captain's name is?"

"Oh, the old pill's name is Thomas, like the schooner, but, you see, he married one of the pretty Carruthers gals, and a good match it was; for, I tell ye, them Carruthers[Pg 19]gals hold their heads mighty high. Why, the ansomest of them married Dr. Carmichael that was member, and, of they did say he married below him, there wasn't a prouder nor a handsomer woman in all the country. There's a brother of the Carruthers gals lives on a farm out in Grey, and he took up with a good lookin' Irish gal that was lady's maid or some such truck. That's marryin' below yourself ef you like, but, bless you, Miss Carmichael don't bear him no spite for it. She goes and stays with him times in the holidays, just like she does along o' the old man here. My! what a three days o' singin' and fun it was when them two gals was aboard; never see nothing like it afore nor sence."

"By George!" groaned the lawyer.

"What's up, Mister? turned sick, eh? smell o' the tar too much fer your narves? It do make some city folks a bit squarmish. Wish I'd a drop o' stuff for you, but we don't carry none; wouldn't do, you know." Coristine was touched by the good fellow's kindness, and opened his flask for their joint benefit, after which he felt better, and The Crew said it made him like a four-year-old.

"Hi, Sylvanus, come aft here to your dog watch," cried the captain, and The Crew retired, while his superior officer and Wilkinson came forward. The former went down into the hold, leaving the dominie free for conversation with his friend. "It's all up again, Wilks," said Coristine sadly; "those two girls were on board this very schooner, no later than last summer, and the one that spotted you is the captain's niece."

"I know," groaned Wilkinson; "did he not tell me that he had a niece, a wonderfully fine girl, if he did say it, in the public schools, and made me promise to look her up when I go back to town! This kind of thing will be the death of me, Corry. Tell me, is your friend at the helm another uncle?"

"Oh, no," laughed Coristine, "he's a simple-hearted, humble sort of creature, who worships the boards these girls trod upon. He has a tremendous respect for the Carmichaels. What a lucky thing it is they didn't come on board at Belle Ewart! Do you think they'll be on hand at Barrie?"

"I shouldn't wonder."

[Pg 20]"Then, Wilks, I tell you what it is, we must slope. When it gets dark, I'll slip over the stern into the dingy and bring her round to the side for you; then we'll sail away for parts unknown."

"Corry, I am ashamed of you for imagining that I would lend myself to base treachery, and robbery, or piracy rather, on the high seas, laying us open, as you, a lawyer, must know, to penalties that would blast our reputations and ruin our lives. No, sir, we must face our misfortune like men. In the meanwhile, I will find out, from the captain, where his niece and her friend are likely to be."

Coristine walked aft to The Crew, and served his apprenticeship to sitting on the tiller and propelling the rudder thereby in the desired direction. When he went wrong, while The Crew was lighting his pipe, the flapping of the sails warned him to back the tiller to its proper place. When hauling at the halliards, he had sung to his admiring companion in toil the "Sailor's Shanty":—

My Polly said she'd marry me when I came home,
Yo hee, yo ho, haul all together;
But when I came I found she'd been and took my messmate Tom,
Yo hee, yo ho, haul all together.

Now, therefore, The Crew was urgent for a song to cheer up the lonesomeness a bit, and the lawyer, nothing loath, sang with genuine pathos:—

A baby was sleeping;
Its mother was weeping.
For her husband was far on the wide rolling sea.

When he came to the sea-ee-ee-ee-ee at the end of the third line, The Crew, who had been keeping time with one foot on the deck and with one hand on the tiller, aided him in rolling it forth, and, when the singing was over, he characterized it as "pooty and suitin' like," by which he meant that the references to the howling tempest and the raging billow were appropriate to the present nautical circumstances. After much persuasion The Crew was induced to add to the harmony of the evening. His voice was strong, but, like many strong things, under imperfect control; his tune was nowhere, and his intended pathetic unction was simply maudlin. Coristine could recall but little of the long ballad to which he listened, the story of a niggardly and irate father, who followed and fought [Pg 21]with the young knight that had carried off his daughter. Two verses, however, could not escape his memory, on account of the disinterested and filial light in which they made the young lady appear:—

"O stay your hand," the old man cried,
A-lying on the ground,
"And you shall have my daughter,
And twenty thousand pound."
"Don't let him up, dear sweetheart,
The portion is too small."
"O stay your hand," the old man said,
"And you shall have it all."

The lawyer was loud in his admiration of this classical piece, and what he afterwards found was The Crew's original and only tune. "That was the kind of wife for a poor man," remarked Sylvanus, meditatively; "but she was mighty hard on her old dad."

"They're a poor lot, the whole pack of them," said the lawyer, savagely, thinking of the quandary in which he and his friend were placed.

"Who is?" asked The Crew.

"Why, the women, to be sure."

"Look here, Mister, my name may be Sylvanus, but I know I'm pretty rough, for all that. But, rough as I am, I don't sit quiet and let any man, no, not as good friends as you and me has been, say a word agin the wimmen. When I think o' these yere gals as was in this blessed schooner last summer, I feel it my juty, bein' I'm one o' them as helped to sail her then, to stand up fer all wimmen kind, and, no offence meant. I guess your own mother's one o' the good sort, now wasn't she?"

"I should say she is," replied Coristine; "there are splendid women in the world, but they're all married."

"That don't stand to reason, nohow," said The Crew, with gravity, "'cos there was a time wonst when they wasn't married, and if they was good arter they was good afore. And, moreover, what was, is, and ever shall be, Amen!"

"All right, Sylvanus, we won't quarrel over them, and to show I bear no malice, I'll sing a song about the sex," whereupon he trolled out: "Here's to the Maiden of Bashful Fifteen." Wilkinson came running aft when he [Pg 22]heard the strain, and cried: "Good heavens! Coristine, whatever has got into you, are you mad or intoxicated?"

"I'll bet you your boots and your bottom dollar that he ain't that, Mister," interposed The Crew, "fer you couldn't scare up liquor enough on this yere *Susan Thomas* to turn the head of a canary."

"We are exchanging musical treats," said Coristine in defence. "Sylvanus here favoured me with an old ballad, not in the Percy collection, and I have been giving him one of the songs from the dramatists."

"But about women!" protested the dominie.

"There ain't no songs that ain't got somethin' about women in 'em that's wuth a cent," indignantly replied The Crew, and Wilkinson sullenly retired to the bow.

When the captain emerged from the hold he was hardly recognizable. Instead of his common sleeved waist coat and overalls, he was attired in a dark blue suit of broadcloth, the vest and frock coat of which were resplendent with gilt buttons. These clothes, with a befitting peaked cap and a pair of polished boots, had evidently come out of the large bundle he had brought from Belle Ewart, where the garments had probably done Sunday duty, for a smaller bundle, which he now threw upon the deck, contained his discarded working dress. Wilkinson was confirmed, by the spectacle presented, in his dire suspicion that the captain's niece would appear at Barrie, and, then and there, begin an acquaintance with him that might have the most disastrous consequences. But hope springs eternal in the human breast, as the poet says, so the schoolmaster tackled the commander, congratulated him on his fine appearance, and began to pump him as to the whereabouts of Miss Carmichael. The old gentleman, for such he looked now, was somewhat vain in an off-hand sort of way, and felt that he was quite the dominie's equal. He was cheerful, even jovial, in spite of the contrary assertions of The Crew, as he replied to Wilkinson's interrogations.

9

"Ah, you sly young dog," he said, "I see what you're at now. You'd like to hear that the pair of them are waiting for us at Barrie; but they're not. They've gone to stay with my brother-in-law, Carruthers, in the County of Grey, where I'll go and see their pretty faces myself in a few days."

[Pg 23]Wilkinson swallowed the "sly young dog" for the sake of the consolation, and, hurriedly making his way aft, communicated the joyful news to Coristine. That gentleman much amused The Crew by throwing an arm round the schoolmaster's waist and waltzing his unwilling partner over the deck. All went merry as a marriage bell till the waltzers struck a rope coil, when, owing to the dominie's struggles, they went down together. Recovering themselves, they sat on deck glaring at each other.

"You're a perfect idiot, Coristine."

"You're a regular old muff, Wilkinson."

The Crew, thinking this was a special pantomime got up impromptu for his benefit, roared with laughter, and applauded on the tiller. He was about to execute a hoedown within tiller limits to testify his sympathy with the fun, when the captain appeared in all his Sunday finery.

"Let her away, you laughing hyena," he yelled to the unlucky Sylvanus, who regained his mental balance and laid his back to the tiller the other way.

"Sorry I've no chairs for you gentlemen," he remarked to the seated travellers; "but I guess the deck's as soft as the wooden kind."

"Don't mention it, my dear captain," said Coristine, as he sprang to his feet; "we were only taking the latitude and longitude, but it's hard work on the bones."

"You allow yourself too much latitude, sir, both in your actions and in your unjustifiable remarks," muttered the pedagogue, more slowly assuming the perpendicular.

"Now, captain," cried the lawyer, "I leave it you, sir, as a judge of language, good and bad. What is the worst thing to call a man, a muff or an idiot!"

The captain toyed with the lanyard of his tortoise shell rimmed glasses, then put them deliberately across his nose, coughed judiciously, and gave his opinion:—

"An ijit is a man that's born without sense and can't keep himself, d'ye see? But a muff is that stupid, like Sylvanus here, that he can't use the sense he's got. That being the case, a muff is worse than an ijit."

"Mr. Wilkinson, I bow, as in duty bound, to the verdict of the court, and humbly apologize for having called you something worse than an idiot. In my poor opinion, sir, you are not worse than the unfortunate creature thus described."

[Pg 24]Wilkinson was about to retort, when The Crew called out that the schooner was in the Bay, and that the lights of Barrie could be seen in the distance.

"Keep to your helm, Sylvanus," growled the captain; "there's three pair of eyes here as good as yourn, and I hope with more sense abaft 'em."

Sylvanus relapsed into silence of a modified kind, merely whistling in a soft way his original copyright tune. As the travellers had never seen Kempenfeldt Bay before, they admired it very much, and forgot their little misunderstanding, while arm in arm they leaned over the bulwarks, and quoted little snatches of poetry in one another's ears. The twinkling lights of the town upon the cliffs suggested many a pleasing passage, so that Wilkinson told his dear Corry he was more than repaid for the trouble incident on their expedition by the sweet satisfaction of gazing on such a scene in company with a kindred spirit of poesy. To this his comrade replied, "Wilks, my dear boy, next to my mother you're the best friend I ever hope to have."

"Let us cherish these sentiments for one another, kind friend, and the cloud on the horizon of our tour will never rise to darken its happy future," after which the learned dominie recited the words of Ducis:—

"*Noble et tendre amitié, je te chante en mes vers.*"

"Murder!" cried Coristine, "Do you know that that Miss Jewplesshy, or Do Please, or whatever her name is, is French?"

"O, Corry, Corry, how could you break in upon a scene of purest friendship and nature worship like this with your wretched misses? O, Corry, be a man!"

"The anchor's agoin' out," remarked The Crew, as he passed by; so the travellers rushed to the capstan and got hold of the spikes. Out went the cable, as Coristine sang:—

Do! my Johnny Boker,
I'm a poo-er sailor,
Do! my Johnny Boker,
Do!!!

The ship made fast, the captain said, "Sylvanus will take you gentlemen ashore in the dingy. It only holds three, so I'll wait till he comes back." The pedestrians protested, but in vain. Sylvanus should take them ashore [Pg 25]first. So they bade the captain good-bye with many thanks and good wishes, and tumbled down into the dingy, which The Crew brought round. The captain shouted from the bulwarks in an insinuating way, "I'll keep my eye on you, Mr Wilkinson, trying to steal an old man's niece away from him," at which the victim shuddered. Away went the dingy some fifty yards or more, when Coristine called out, "Have you got the knapsacks, Farquhar, my dear?"

"Why, bless me, no," he answered. "I thought you had them." "Row back for your life, Sylvanus, to get the blessed knapsacks;" and Sylvanus, patient creature, did as he was told. The captain threw them over the side with another farewell speech, and then the dingy made for the bank, while Coristine sang in a rich voice:—

Pull for the shore, sailor,
Pull for the shore.

They landed, and, much against The Crew's will, he was compelled to receive a dollar from each of his passengers.

"I'll see you again," he said, as he rowed back for the captain. "I'll see you again up in Grey, along of the old man and the gals, mark my word if I don't."

"Glad to see you, Sylvy, old fresh (he was going to say 'old salt,' but corrected himself in time), glad to see you anywhere," bawled the lawyer, "but we've made a vow to dispense with female society in our travels. Ta, ta!"

[Pg 26]

CHAPTER II.

Barrie—Next of Kin—Nightmare—On the Road—Strawberries and Botany—Poetry and Sentiment—The Virago—Luncheon and Wordsworth—Waterplants, Leeches and Verse—Cutting Sticks—Rain, Muggins and Rawdon.

The travellers carried their knapsacks in their hands by the straps, to the nearest hotel, where, after brief delay, a special supper was set for them. Having discussed the frugal meal, they repaired to the combined reading and smoking room, separate from the roughish crowd at the bar. Wilkinson glanced over a Toronto paper, while his companion, professing an interest in local news, picked up an organ of the town and read it through, advertisements and all, in which painstaking effort he was helped by his pipe. Suddenly he grasped the paper, and, holding it away from his face, exclaimed, "Is it possible that they are the same?"

"Who, who?" ejaculated Wilkinson; "do not tell me that the captain was mistaken, that they are really here."

"Do you know old Carmichael's initials, the doctor's, that was member for Vaughan?" his friend asked, paying no attention to the schoolmaster's question.

"James D.," replied that authority; "I remember, because I once made the boys get up the members' names along with their constituencies, so as to give the latter a living interest."

"Now, listen to this: 'Next of kin; information wanted concerning the whereabouts of James Douglas Carmichael, or his heirs at law. He left the University of Edinburgh, where he was in attendance on the Faculty of Medicine, in the spring of 1848, being at the time twenty-one years of age. The only trace of his farther life is a fragment of a letter written by him to a friend two years later, when he was serving as a soldier in the military station of Barrief, Upper Canada. Reward offered for the same by P.R. MacSmaill, W.S., 19 Clavers Row, Edinburgh.' If James Douglas Carmichael, ex-medical [Pg 27]student, wasn't the member and the father of that girl of yours, I'm a Dutchman."

11

"Mr. Coristine, I insist, sir, before another word passes between us, that you withdraw and apologize for the deeply offensive expression, which must surely have escaped your lips unperceived, 'that girl of yours.'"

"Oh, there, now, I'm always putting my foot in it. I meant the girl you are interested in—no, it isn't that other—the girl that's interested in you—oh, wirra wisha! it's not that at all—it's the girl the captain was joking you about."

"A joke from a comparatively illiterate man like the captain of the schooner, to whom we were under travelling obligations, and a joke from my equal, a scholar and a gentleman, are two distinct things. I wish the expression, 'that girl of yours,' absolutely and forever withdrawn."

"Well, well, I consent to withdraw it absolutely and apologize for saying it, but that 'forever' clause goes against my legal judgment. If the late Dr. Carmichael's heiress comes in for a fortune, we might repent that 'forever.'"

"What has that to do with me, sir, fortune or no fortune? Your insinuations are even more insulting than your open charges of infidelity to our solemn compact."

It was Coristine's turn to be angry. He rose from the table at which he had been sitting, with the paper still in his hand, and said: "You make mountains out of molehills, Wilkinson. I've made you a fair and full apology, and shall do no more, if you sulk your head off." So saying, he stalked out of the room, and Wilkinson was too much angered to try to stop him.

The lawyer asked the landlord if he would spare him the newspaper for an hour and supply him with pen and ink and a few sheets of paper. Then he took his lamp and retired to his room. "Poor old Farquhar," he soliloquized, as he arranged his writing materials; "he'll feel mighty bad at being left all alone, but it's good for his health, and business is business. Let me see, now. Barrie was never a military station, besides the letter had Barrief on it, a name that doesn't exist. But the letter was torn there, or the corner worn away in a man's pocket. By the powers, it's Barriefield at Kingston, and there's the [Pg 28]military station for you. I'll write our correspondent there, and I'll set one of the juniors to work up Dr. Carmichael's record in Vaughan County, and I'll notify MacSmaill, W.S., that I am on the track, and—shall I write the girl, there's the rub?" The three letters were written with great care and circumspection, but not the fourth. When carefully sealed, directed and stamped, he carried them to the post-office and personally deposited them in the slit for drop-letters. Returning to the hotel, he restored the newspaper to the table of the reading-room, minus the clipped advertisement to the next of kin, which he stowed away in his pocketbook. This late work filled the lawyer with a satisfaction that crowned the pleasures of the day, and he longed to communicate some of it to his friend, but that gentleman, the landlord said, had retired for the night, looking a bit put out—he hoped supper had been to his liking. Coristine said the supper was good. "What was the number of Mr. Wilkinson's room?"

Mine host replied that it was No. 32, the next to his own. Before retiring, Coristine looked at the fanlight over the door of No. 32; it was dark. Nevertheless he knocked, but failed to evoke a response. "Farquhar, my dear," he whispered in an audible tone, but still there was no answer. So he heaved a sigh, and, returning to his apartment, read a few words out of his pocket prayer-book, and went to bed. There he had an awful dream, of the old captain leading Wilkinson by the collar and tail of his coat up to the altar, where Miss Carmichael stood, resplendent in pearls and diamonds, betokening untold wealth; of an attempt at rescue by himself and The Crew, which was nipped in the bud by the advent of the veteran, his daughter and Miss Jewplesshy. The daughter laid violent hands upon The Crew and waltzed him out of the church door, while the veteran took Coristine's palsied arm and placed that of his young mistress upon it, ordering them, with military words of command, to accompany the victims, as bridesmaid and groomsman. When the dreamer recovered sufficiently to look the officiating clergyman full in the face, he saw that this personage was no other than Frank, the news-agent, whereupon he laughed immediately and awoke.

[Pg 29]"Corry, Corry, my dear fellow, are you able to get up, or shall I break the door in?" were the words that greeted his ear on awaking.

12

"The omadhaun!" he said to himself under the bedclothes; "it would be a good thing to serve him with the sauce of silence, as he did me last night." But better counsels prevailed in his warm Irish heart, and he arose to unlock the door, when suddenly it flew open, and Wilkinson, with nothing but a pair of trousers added to his night attire, fell backwards into his arms. It was broad daylight as each looked into the other's face for explanations.

"But you're strong, Wilks!" said the lawyer with admiration.

"Corry, when I heard you groan that way, I was sure you were in a fit."

"Oh, it was nothing," replied his friend, who found it hard to keep from laughing, "only a bad nightmare."

"What were you dreaming about to bring it on?"

Now, this was just what Coristine dared not tell, for the truth would bring up all last night's misunderstanding. So he made up a story of Wilkinson's teaching The Crew navigation and the use of the globes, when the captain interfered and threatened to kick master and pupil overboard. Then he, Coristine, interposed, and the captain fell upon him. "And you know, Wilks, he's a heavy man."

"Well, I am heartily glad it is no worse. Get a wash and get your clothes on, and come down to breakfast, like a good boy, for I hear the bell ringing."

Over their coffee and toast, eggs and sausages, the two were as kind and attentive to one another's wants, as if no dispute had ever marred their friendship. The dominie got out his sketch map of a route and opened it between them. "We shall start straight for the bush road into the north, if that suits you," he said, "and travel by easy stages towards Collingwood, where we shall again behold one of our inland seas. But, as it may be sometime before we reach a house of entertainment, it may be as well to fill the odd corners of our knapsacks with provisions for the way."

"I say amen to that idea," replied the lawyer, and the travellers arose, paid their bill, including the price of [Pg 30]the door-lock, seized their knapsacks by the straps and sallied forth. They laid in a small stock of captain's biscuits, a piece of good cheese, and some gingersnaps for Wilkinson's sweet tooth; they also had their flask refilled, and Coristine invested in some pipe-lights. Then they sallied forth, not into the north as Wilkinson had said, it being a phrase he was fond of, but, at first, in a westerly, and, on the whole, in a north-westerly direction.

When the last house on the outskirts was left behind them, they helped each other on with their knapsacks, and felt like real pedestrians. The bush enclosed them on either side of the sandy road, so that they had shade whenever they wanted it. Occasionally a wayfarer would pass them with a curt "good morning," or a team would rattle by, its driver bestowing a similar salutation. The surface of the country was flat, but this did not hinder Wilkinson reciting:—

Mount slowly, sun! and may our journey lie
Awhile within the shadow of this hill,
This friendly hill, a shelter from thy beams!

"That reminds me," said Coristine, "of a fellow we had in the office once, whose name was Hill. He was a black-faced, solemn-looking genius, and the look of him would sink the spirits of a skylark down to zero. 'What's come over you?' said Woodruff to me one fine afternoon, when I was feeling a bit bilious. 'Oh,' said I, 'I've been within the shadow of this Hill,' and he laughed till he was black in the face."

"Corry, if I were not ashamed of making a pun, or, as we say in academic circles, being guilty of antanaclasis, I would say that you are in-corri-gible."

Coristine laughed, and then remarked seriously, "Here am I, with a strap-press full of printing paper in my knapsack, and paying no attention to science at all. We must begin to take life in airnest now, Wilks, my boy, and keep our eyes skinned for specimens. Sorry I am I didn't call and pay my respects to my botanical friend at the Barrie High School. He could have given us a pointer or two about the flowers that grow round here."

"Flowers are scarce in July," said the schoolmaster, "they seem to take a rest in the hot weather. The spring [Pg 31]is their best time. Of course you know that song about the flowers in spring?"

"Never heard it in my life; sing it to us, Farquhar, like a darlin'."

Now, the dominie was not given to singing, but thus adjured, and the road being clear, he sang in a very fair voice:—

We are the flowers,
The fair young flowers
That come with the voice of Spring,
Tra la la, la la la, la la,
Tra la, tra la a a a.

Coristine revelled in the chorus, which, at the "a a a," went up to the extreme higher compass of the human voice and beyond it. He made his friend repeat the performance, called him a daisy, and tra la la'd to his heart's content. Then he sat down on a grassy bank by the wayside and laughed loud and long. "Oh, it's a nice pair of fair young flowers we are, coming with the voice of spring; but we're not hayseeds, anyway." When the lawyer turned himself round to rise, Wilkinson asked seriously, "Did you hurt yourself then, Corry?"

"Never a bit, except that I'm weak with the laughing; and for why?"

"Because there is some red on your trousers, and I thought it might be blood—that you had sat down on some sharp thing."

"It'll be strawberry blite, I'll wager, *Blitum capitatum*, and a fine thing it is. Mrs. Marsh, that keeps our boarding house, has a garden where it grows wild in among the peas. She wanted some colouring for the icing of a cake, and hadn't a bit of cochineal or anything of the kind in the house. She was telling me her trouble, for it was a holiday and the shops were shut, and she's always that friendly with me; when, says I, 'There is no trouble about that.' So I went to the garden and got two lovely stalks of *Blitum capitatum*. 'Is it poison?' said she. 'Poison!' said I; 'and it belonging to the *Chenopodiaceæ*, the order that owns beets and spinach, and all the rest of them. Trust a botanist, ma'am,' I said. It made the sweetest pink icing you ever saw, and Mrs. Marsh is for ever deeply grateful, and rears that *Blitum* with fond and anxious care."

[Pg 32]"I would like to see that plant," said Wilkinson. So they retraced their steps to the bank, over which Coristine leaned tenderly, picking something which he put into his mouth. "Come on, Wilks," he cried; "it isn't blite, but something better. It's wild strawberries themselves, and lashings of them. Sure any fool might have known them by the leaves, even if he was a herald, the worst fool of all, and only knew them from a duke's coronet."

For a time there was silence, for the berries were numerous, and, although small, sweet and of delicate flavour.

"Corry, they are luscious; this is Arcadia and Elysium."

"Foine, Wilks, foine," mumbled the lawyer, with his mouth full of berries.

"This folly of mine, sitting down on the blessings of Providence—turning my back upon them, so to speak," he remarked, after the first hunger was over, "reminds me of a man who took the gold medal in natural science. He had got his botany off by rote, so, when he was travelling between Toronto and Hamilton, a friend that was sitting beside him said, 'Johnson, what's in that field out there?' Johnson looked a bit put out, but said boldly, 'It's turnips.' There was an old farmer in the seat behind him, and he spoke up and said, 'Turmuts!' said he, 'them's hoats—ha, ha, ha!'"

As they tramped along, the botanist found some specimens: two lilies, the orange and the Turk's cap; the willow herb, the showy ladies' slipper, and three kinds of milkweed. He opened his knapsack, took out the strap press, and carefully bestowed his floral treasures between sheets of unglazed printers' paper. Wilkinson took a friendly interest in these proceedings, and insisted on being furnished with the botanical names of all the specimens.

"That willow-herb, now, *Epilobium angustifolium*, is called fire-weed," said the botanist, "and is an awful nuisance on burnt ground. There was a Scotchman out here once, about this time of the year, and he thought it was such a pretty pink flower that he would take some home with him. So, when the downy-winged seeds came, he gathered a lot, and, when he got back to Scotland, [Pg 33]planted them. Lord! the whole country about Perth got full of the stuff, till the farmers cursed him for introducing the American Saugh."

"The American what?" demanded Wilkinson.

"Saugh; it's an old Scotch word for willow, and comes from the French *saule*, I suppose."

"I am not sorry for them," said Wilkinson; "they say that pest, the Canada thistle, came from the Old Country."

"Yes, that's true; and so did Pusley, which Warner compares with original sin; and a host of other plants. Why, on part of the Hamilton mountain you won't find a single native plant. It is perfectly covered, from top to bottom, with dusty, unwholesome-looking weeds from Europe and the Southern States. But we paid them back."

"How was that?"

"You know, a good many years ago, sailing vessels began to go from the Toronto harbour across the Atlantic to British ports. There's a little water-plant that grows in Ashbridge's Bay, called the Anacharis, and this little weed got on to the bottom of the ocean vessels. Salt water didn't kill it, but it lived till the ships got to the Severn, and there it fell off and took root, and blocked up the canals with a solid mass of subaqueous vegetation that made the English canal men dredge night and day to get rid of it. I tell you we've got some pretty hardy things out here in Canada."

"Do you not think," asked Wilkinson, "that our talk is getting too like that of Charles and his learned father in Gosse's 'Canadian Naturalist'?"

"All right, my boy, I'll oppress you no longer with a tender father's scientific lore, but, with your favourite poet, say:—

"To me the meanest flower that blows can give
Thoughts that do often lie too deep for tears."

"That is because of their associations, a merely relative reason," said the dominie.

"It isn't though, at least not altogether. Listen, now, to what Tennyson says, or to something like what he says:—

[Pg 34]
Little flower in the crannied wall,
Peeping out of the crannies,
I hold you, root and all, in my hand;
Little flower, if I could understand
What you are, root and all, and all in all,
I should know what God and man is.

There's no association nor relation in that; the flower brings you at once face to face with infinite life. Do you know what these strawberries brought to me?"

"A pleasant feast I should say."

"No, they made me think how much better it would have been if I had had somebody to gather them for; I don't say a woman, because that's tabooed between us, but say a child, a little boy or girl. There's no association or relation there at all; the strawberries called up love, which is better than a pleasant feast."

"According to Wordsworth, the flower in the crannied wall and the strawberry teach the same lesson, for does he not say:—

That life is love and immortality.
Life, I repeat, is energy of love,
Divine or human, exercised in pain,
In strife and tribulation, and ordained,
If so approved and sanctified, to pass
Through shades and silent rest, to endless joy?

At any rate, that is what he puts into his Parson's lips.

"Farquhar, my boy, I think we'd better stop, for I'm weakening fast. It's sentimental the flowers and the fruit are making me. I mind, when I was a little fellow in the old sod, my mother gathering wild flowers from the hedges and putting them all round the ribbon of my straw hat. I can't pay her the debt of that mark of love the same way, but I feel I should pay it to somebody. You never told me about your mother."

"No, because she is dead and gone long ago, and my father married again, and brought a vixen, with two trollops of girls, to take the place of an angel. These three women turned my stomach at all the sex. Look, there's a pretty woman for you!"

They had reached a clearing in the bush, consisting of a corn patch and a potato field, in which a woman, with a man's hat on her head and a pair of top-boots upon her nether

15

extremities, looking a veritable guy, was sprink[Pg 35]ling the potato plants with well-diluted Paris green. The shanty pertaining to the clearing was some little distance from the road, and, hoping to get a drink of water there, Coristine prepared to jump the rail fence and make his way towards it. The woman, seeing what he was about, called: 'Hi, Jack, Jack!' and immediately a big mongrel bull-dog came tearing towards the travellers, barking as he ran.

"Come back, Corry, for heaven's sake, or he'll bite you!" cried Wilkinson.

"Never a fear," answered the lately sentimental botanist; "barking dogs don't bite as a rule." So he jumped the fence in earnest, and said soothingly, as if he were an old friend: "Hullo, Jack, good dog!" whereupon the perfidious Jack grovelled at his feet and then jumped up for a caress. But the woman came striding along, picking up a grubbing hoe by the way to take the place of the treacherous defender of the house.

"Hi, git out o' that, quick as yer legs'll take yer; git out now! we don't want no seeds, ner fruit trees, ner sewin' machines, ner fambly Bibles. My man's jist down in the next patch, an' if yer don't git, I'll set him on yer."

"Madam," said Coristine, lifting his hat, "permit me to explain—"

"Go 'long, I tell yer; that's the way they all begin, with yer madam an' explainin'; I'll explain this hoe on yer if yer take another step."

"We are not agents, nor tramps, nor tract distributors, nor collectors for missions," cried Coristine, as soon as he had a chance to speak. "My friend, here, is a gentleman engaged in education, and I am a lawyer, and all we want is a glass of water."

"A liyer, eh?" said the Amazon, in a very much reduced tone; "Why didn't yer say so at wonst, an' not have me settin' that good for nuthin' brute on yer? I never see liyers with a pack on their backs afore. Ef yer wants a drink, why don't yer both come on to the house?"

Wilkinson, at this not too cordial invitation, vaulted over the fence beside his companion, and they walked housewards, the woman striding on ahead, and the dog sniffing at Wilkinson's heels in the rear. A rather pretty red-haired girl of about fifteen was washing dishes, evi[Pg 36]dently in preparation for the mid-day meal. Her the woman addressed as Anna Maria, and ordered her to go and get a pail of fresh water for the gentlemen. But Wilkinson, who felt he must do something to restore his credit, offered to get the water if Anna Maria would show him the well or pump that contained it. The girl gave him a tin pail, and he accompanied her to the back of the house, where the well and a bucket with a rope were. In vain he tried to sink that bucket; it would not sink. At last the girl took it out of his hands, turned the bucket upside down, and, letting it fall with a vicious splash, brought it up full of deliciously cool water, which she transferred to the pail.

"You are very clever to do that the first time," remarked the schoolmaster, wishing to be polite to the girl, who looked quite pleasant and comely, in spite of her bare feet and arms.

"There ain't no cleverness about it," she replied, with a harsh nasal accent; "any fool most could do as much." Wilkinson carried the tin pail to the shanty disillusioned, took his drink out of a cup that seemed clean enough, joined his friend in thanking mother and daughter for their hospitality, and retired to the road.

"Do you find your respect for the fair sex rising?" he asked Coristine, cynically.

"The mother's an awful old harridan—"

"Yes, and when the daughter is her age she will be a harridan, too, the gentle rustic beauties have gone out of date, like the old poets. The schoolmaster is much needed here to teach young women not to compare gentlemen even if they are pedestrianizing, to 'any fool most.'"

"Oh, Wilks, is that where you're hit? I thought you and she were long enough over that water business for a case of Jacob and Rachel at the well, ha, ha!"

"Come, cease this folly, Coristine, and let us get along."

Sentiment had received a rude shock. It met with a second when Coristine remarked "I'm hungry." Still, he kept on for another mile or so, when the travellers sighted a little brook of clear water rippling over stones. A short distance to the left of the road it was shaded by trees and tall bushes, not too close together, but presenting, here and [Pg 37]there, little patches of grass and the leaves of woodland flowers. Selecting one of these patches, they unstrapped their knapsacks, and extracted from them a sufficiency of biscuits and cheese for luncheon. Then one of the packs, as they had irreverently been called, was turned over to make a table. The biscuits and cheese were moistened with small portions from the contents of the flasks, diluted with the cool water of the brook. The meal ended, Wilkinson took to nibbling ginger snaps and reading Wordsworth. The day was hot, so that a passing cloud which came over the face of the sun was grateful, but it was grateful to beast as well as to man, for immediately a swarm of mosquitoes and other flies came forth to do battle with the reposing pedestrians. Coristine's pipe kept them from attacking him in force, but Wilkinson got all the more in consequence. He struck savagely at them with Wordsworth, anathematized them in choice but not profane language, and, at last, rose to his feet, switching his pocket handkerchief fiercely about his head. Coristine picked up the deserted Wordsworth, and laughed till the smoke of his pipe choked him and the tears came into his eyes.

"I see no cause for levity in the sufferings of a fellow creature," said the schoolmaster, curtly.

"Wilks, my darling boy, it's not you I'm laughing at; it's that old omadhaun of a Wordsworth. Hark to this, now:—

He said, "'Tis now the hour of deepest noon.
At this still season of repose and peace,
This hour, when all things which are not at rest
Are cheerful; while this multitude of flies
Is filling all the air with melody;
Why should a tear be in an old man's eye?'

O Wilks, but this beats cock-fighting; 'Why should a tear be in an old man's eye?' Sorra a bit do I know, barring it's the multitude of flies. O Wordy, Wordy, bard of Rydal Mount, it's sick with laughing you'll be making me. All things not at rest are cheerful. Dad, if he means the flies, they're cheerful enough, but if it's my dear friend, Farquhar Wilkinson, it's a mistake the old gentleman is making. See, this is more like it, at the very beginning of 'The Excursion':—

Nor could my weak arm disperse
The host of insects gathering round my face,
And ever with me as I paced along.

[Pg 38]That's you, Wilks, you to a dot. What a grand thing poetic instinct is, that looks away seventy years into the future and across the Atlantic Ocean, to find a humble admirer in the wilds of Canada, and tell how he looked among the flies. 'Why should a tear be in an old man's eye?' O, holy Moses, that's the finest line I've sighted in a dog's age. Cheer up, old man, and wipe that tear away, for I see the clouds have rolled by, Jenny."

"Man, clod, profaner of the shrine of poesy, cease your ignorant cackle," cried the irate dominie. Silently they bathed faces and hands in the brook, donned their knapsacks, and took to the road once more.

The clouds had not all passed by as the pedestrians found to their cost, for, where there are clouds over the bush in July, there also are mosquitoes. Physically as well as psychically, Wilkinson was thin-skinned, and afforded a ready and appetizing feast to the blood-suckers. His companion still smoked his pipe in defence, but for a long time in silence. "The multitude of flies" made him gurgle occasionally, as he gazed upon the schoolmaster, whose blue and yellow silk handkerchief was spread over the back of his head and tied under his chin. To quote Wordsworth then would have been like putting a match to a powder magazine. The flies were worst on the margin of a pond formed by the extension of a sluggish black stream. "Go on, Wilks, my boy, out of the pests, while I add some water plants to my collection;" but this, Wilkinson's chivalrous notions of friendship would not allow him to do. He broke off a leafy branch from a young maple, and slashed it about him, while the botanist ran along the edge of the pond looking for flowers within reach. As usual, they were just out of reach and no more. So he had to take off shoes and socks, turn up the legs of his trousers, and wade in after them. "Look at that now!" he said with pride as he returned with his booty, "Nymphæa odorata, Nuphar advena, and Brasenia peltata; aren't they beauties?"

"What is that black object on your leg?" the dominie managed to gasp.

17

"I'm thankful to you for saying that, my kind friend, for it's a murdering leech."

"Salt is the only thing to take them off with," [Pg 39]remarked Wilkinson really interested; "and that is just what we are deficient in."

"I say, Wilks, try a drop of the crater on him; don't waste the blessings of Providence, but just let the least particle fall on his nose, while I scrape him off."

The surgical operation succeeded, and the schoolmaster half forgot his own troubles in doing good to his friend. While the latter was reclothing his feet, and pressing his specimens, the maple branch ceased working, and its owner finely apostrophized the field of white and yellow blossoms.

There sits the water lily like a sovereign,
Her little empire is a fairy world,
The purple dragon-fly above it hovering,
As when her fragile ivory uncurled,
A thousand years ago.

"Bravo, Wilks, if you are poaching on my preserves; but I wish that same purple dragon-fly would hover round here in thousands for a minute. It's a pleasure to see them sail along and gobble up the mosquitoes."

The dominie continued:—

To-day I saw the dragon-fly
Come from the wells where he did lie.
An inner impulse rent the veil
Of his old husk; from head to tail
Came out clear plates of sapphire mail.
He dried his wings: like gauze they grew,
Thro' crofts and pastures wet with dew
A living flash of light he flew.

"Hurroo!" cried Coristine, as with knapsack readjusted, he took his companion by the arm and resumed the journey; "Hurroo again, I say, it's into the very heart of nature we're getting now. Bless the mosquito and the leech for opening the well of English undefiled."

Wilkinson was wound up to go, and repeated with fine conversational effect:—

But now, perplexed by what th' old man had said,
My question eagerly did I renew
How is it that you live, and what is it you do?
He, with a smile, did then his words repeat;
And said, that, gathering leeches far and wide,
He travell'd; stirring thus about his feet
The waters of the ponds where they abide.
"Once I could meet with them on every side;
But they have dwindled long by slow decay;
Yet still I persevere, and find them where I may."

[Pg 40]"Dad, if the old man had been here, he might have made his fortune by this time. 'Stirring thus about his feet the waters of the ponds where they abide' may be fine employment, but the law's good enough for me, seeing they're bound to dwindle long by slow decay. You don't happen to have a scrap on a botanist, do you?"

"Yes," replied the schoolmaster, "and on a blind one, too:—

And he knows all shapes of flowers: the heath, the fox-glove with its bells,
The palmy fern's green elegance, fanned in soft woodland smells;
The milkwort on the mossy turf his nice touch fingers trace,
And the eye-bright, though he sees it not, he finds it in its place."

"A blind botanist, and in the Old Country, too; well that's strange! True, a blind man could know the lovely wallflowers and hyacinths and violets and all these sweet-scented things by their smell. But to know the little blue milkwort and the Euphrasia by touch, bangs me. If it was our fine, big pitcher plant, or the ladies' slipper, or the giant-fringed orchis, or the May apple, I could understand it; but perhaps he knew the flowers before he got to be blind. I think I could find my way blindfolded to some spots about Toronto where special plants grow. I believe, Wilks, that a man couldn't name a subject you wouldn't have a quotation for; you're wonderful!"

Wilkinson was delighted. This flattery was meat and drink to him. Holding the arm of his admiring friend, he poured out his soul in verse, allowing his companion, from time to time, the opportunity of contributing a little to the poetic feast. The two virtually forgot to notice the level, sandy road and tame scenery, the clouded sun, the troublesome flies. For the time being, they were everything, the one to the other. By their own spirits were they deified, or thought they were, at the moment.

Though the schoolmaster was revelling in the appreciation of his friend, he could not fail to perceive that he limped a little. "You have hurt your foot, Corry, my dear fellow, and never told me."

"Oh, it's nothing," replied the light-hearted lawyer; "I trod on a stick in that pond where I got the Brasenia and things, and my big toe's a bit sore, that's all."

"Corry, we have forgotten the blackthorns. Now, in [Pg 41]this calm hour, sacred to friendship, let us present each other with nature's staff, a walking-stick cut from the bush, humble tokens of our mutual esteem."

Coristine agreed, and the result was a separation and careful scrutiny of the underbrush on both sides of the road, which ended in the finding of a dogwood by the lawyer, and of a striped maple by the dominie—both straight above and curled at the root. These, having removed from the bush, they brought into shape with their pocket-knives. Then Coristine carved "F.W." on the handle of his, while Wilkinson engraved "E.C." on the one he carried. This being done, each presented his fellow with "this utterly inadequate expression of sincere friendship," which was accepted "not for its intrinsic worth, but because of the generous spirit which prompted the gift." "Whenever my eye rests on these letters by friendship traced," said the dominie, "my pleasant companion of this happy day will be held in remembrance."

"And when my fingers feel 'E.C.' on the handle," retorted the lawyer, "I'll be wishing that my dear friend's lot, that gave it me, may be easy too. Faith but that's a hard pun on an Irishman."

"Seriously, now, Corry, does it give you any satisfaction to be guilty of these—ah—rhetorical figures?"

"All the delight in the world, Wilks, my boy."

"But it lowers the tone of your conversation; it puts you on a level with common men; it grieves me."

"If that last is the case, Farquhar, I'll do my best to fight against my besetting sin. You'll admit I've been very tender of your feelings with them."

"How's your foot now?"

"Oh, splendid! This stick of yours is a powerful help to it.

Jog on, jog on, the footpath way,
And merrily hent the stile-a:
A merry heart goes all the day,
Your sad tires in a mile-a.

Shakespeare's songs remind me of young Witherspoon. There was a party at old Tylor's, and a lady was singing 'Tell me where is fancy bred?' when young Witherspoon comes up to the piano in a hurry, and says: 'Why, don't you know?—at Nasmith's and Webb's.'

[Pg 42]"Lord! how savage old Tylor was! I thought he would have kicked the young ass out."

"That is just what we lovers of literature have to endure from the Philistines. But, Corry, my dear fellow, here is the rain!"

The rain fell, at first drop by drop, but afterwards more smartly, forcing the pedestrians to take refuge under some leafy pines. There they sat quietly for a time, till their interest was excited by a deep growl, which seemed to come round a jog in the road just ahead.

"Is that a bear or a wolf, Corry?" the dominie asked in a whisper.

"More like a wild cat or a lynx," cheerfully responded his friend.

The growl was repeated, and then a human like voice was heard which quieted the ferocious animal.

"Whatever it is, it's got a keeper," whispered Coristine, "so we needn't be afraid."

Then the sun shone forth brightly and a rainbow spanned the sky.

"The rainbow comes and goes," said the lawyer, which gave the schoolmaster occasion to recite:—

My heart leaps up when I behold
A rainbow in the sky.
So was it when my life began;
So is it now I am a man;
So be it when I shall grow old
Or let me die!
The child is father of the man;
And I could wish my days to be
Bound each to each by natural piety.

"Brayvo, well done, ancore!" cried a cheery and cheeky voice coming round the jog; "oo'd a thought of meetin' a play hactor 'ere in the bush! Down, Muggins, down," the latter to a largish and wiry-looking terrier, the author of the ominous growls.

"I beg your pardon, sir," said Wilkinson with dignity, "I have nothing to do with the stage, beyond admiring the ancient ornaments of the English drama."

"Hall right, no hoffence meant and none taken, I 'ope. But you did it well, sir, devilish well, I tell you. My name is Rawdon, and I'm a workin' geologist and minerologist hon the tramp."

[Pg 43]The stranger, who had thus introduced himself, was short, about five feet five, fairly stout, with a large head covered with curly reddish hair, his whiskers and goatee of the same hue, his eyes pale grayish, his nose retroussé, and his mouth like a half-moon lying on its back. He was dressed in a tweed suit of a very broad check; his head was crowned with a pith hat, almost too large even for it; and he wore gaiters. But, what endeared him to the pedestrians was his knapsack made of some kind of ribbed brown waterproof cloth.

"Either of you gents take any hinterest in science?" he asked affably, whereupon the schoolmaster took it upon himself to reply.

"I, as an educationist, dabble a little in geology, mineralogy, and palæontology. My friend is a botanist. You are Mr. Rawdon. Allow me, Mr. Rawdon, to introduce my friend Mr. Eugene Coristine, of Osgood Hall, Barrister, and my humble self, Farquhar Wilkinson, of the Toronto Schools."

Mr. Rawdon bowed and shook hands, then threw himself into a stage attitude, and said: "His it possible that I am face to face with Farquhar Wilkinson, the describer of a hentirely new species of Favosites? Sir, this is a perroud day for a workin' geologist. Your servant, Dr. Coristine!"

"I'm no doctor, Mr. Rawdon," replied the lawyer, a bit angrily; "I passed all my examinations in the regular way."

"Hif it's a fair question, gents, ware are you a goin'"? asked the working geologist.

"We intend, if nothing intervenes, to spend the night at the village of Peskiwanchow," answered Wilkinson, whose heart warmed to the knapsack man that knew his great discovery.

"Beastly 'ole!" remarked Mr. Rawdon; "but, as I'm a long way hoff Barrie, I'll go there with you, if Mr. Currystone is hagreeable. I don't want to miss the hopportunity of making your better hacquaintance, Dr. Wilkinson."

"I am sure that my friend and I will be charmed with your excellent society, as a man, a fellow pedestrian and a lover of science," the dominie effusively replied.

[Pg 44]"Well, Muggins, we're a-goin' back, hold dog, along o' two gents as haint above keepin' company wi' you and me," whereat Muggins barked and sought to make friends with his new companions. Coristine liked Muggins, but he did not love Muggins' master. Sotto voce, he said: "A cheeky little cad!"

Mr. Rawdon and Wilkinson forged on ahead. Coristine and Muggins brought up the rear.

20

"What are you working at now, Mr. Rawdon?" asked the schoolmaster.

"I'm workin' hup the Trenton and Utica, the Udson River and Medina formations. They hall crop hup between 'ere and Collin'wood. It's the limestone I'm hafter, you know," he said, sinking his voice to a whisper, "the limestone grits, dolomites, and all that sort of thing. Wen I can get a good grinstun quarry, I'll be a made man."

"Grinstun?" queried Wilkinson, helplessly.

"Yes, you know, g, r, i, n, d, s, t, o, n, e, grinstun, for sharpenin' tools on; turn 'em with a handle and pour water on top. Now, sir, hevery farm 'ouse 'as got to 'ave a grinstun, and there's 'ow many farm 'ouses in Canidy? wy, 'undreds of thousands. You see, there's money in it. Let me find a grinstun quarry and I'm a made man. And wot's more, I've found the grinstun quarry."

"You have? Where?" asked the dominie.

The working geologist drew off, and playfully planted the forefinger of his right hand on the side of his upturned nose, saying "Walker!" Then he relented, and, reapproaching his companion, said: "Honour bright, now, you're no workin' geologist, lookin' out for the blunt? You're a collector of Favosites Wilkinsoma, Stenopora fibrosa, Asaphus Canadensis, Ambonychia radiata, Heliopora fragilis, and all that rot, ain't you now?"

"I certainly seek to make no money out of science, and am a lover of the fossil records of ancient life in our planet, but, above all, I assure you that I would no more think of betraying your confidence than of picking your pocket. If you have any doubts, do not make me your confidant."

"Hall right, hold cock, I mean, my dear sir. You're safe has a church. There's a 'undred hacre lot hup in the [Pg 45]township of Flanders, has full of grinstuns as a hegg's full of meat. It belongs to a Miss Do Please-us, but who the dooce she is, I dunno. That's just wot I'm a-goin' to find hout. If she hain't paid her taxes, bein' hon the non-resident roll, I maybe hable to pick hup the land for less than ten dollars, and it'll bring me hin tens of thousands. Then I'll skip back to hold Hingland and cut it fat."

Coristine was not so taken up with Muggins that he failed to overhear the conversation. He did not catch it all, but he learned that a lady, a maiden lady, whose name mediated between Jewplesshy and Do Please, owned valuable mineral lands, of which the working geologist intended to deprive her by unfair means. Miss Do-Please-us was nothing to him, but justice was something, and the man Rawdon was an unutterable cad. How Wilkinson could take any pleasure in his society he could not understand. He had a good mind to chuck the dominie's stick into the next creek and let it float to Jericho. He did throw it away along the road, but Muggins brought it back. Deserted by his bosom friend for a common, low down cad like that; Oh, by Jove! He strode along in silence, while Muggins, his only friend, came and rubbed himself against his leg. No, he would not give in to fate in the shape of a Rawdon. He had important secrets regarding the welfare of two women, that Providence seemed to have thrown in his way, in his possession. If Wilks turned traitor, he could break the pact, and make one of these women happy. Pity he wasn't a Turk to take care of the pair of them. Night had fallen, but the moon shone out and the stars, and it was very pleasant walking, if only Wilkinson would give the least hint that he was conscious of his friend's existence. But the schoolmaster was happy with the mining adventurer, who knew his man well enough to mix a few fossils with the grinstuns.

[Pg 46]
CHAPTER III.

Peskiwanchow Tavern—Bad Water—A Scrimmage and Timotheus—The Wigglers—Pure Water and Philosophy—Archæology and Muggins—Mrs. Thomas and Marjorie—Dromore—Rawdon's Insolence and Checks—On the Road and Tramp's Song—Maguffin and the Pole-cart.

"Ere's this beastly 'ole of a Peskiwanchow," said Mr. Rawdon as the pedestrians came to a rather larger clearing than usual, prominent in which was the traditional country tavern.

"Is it clean?" asked Wilkinson.

"Well, there hain't hany pestilence that walketh hin darkness there, not to my knowledge; though they say hif you keep your lamp lit hall night, they won't come near you; but then, the blessed lamp brings the mosquitoes, don't you see?"

Mr. Wilkinson did see, but was glad of the information, as the look of the hotel was not reassuring.

"Ullo, Matt!" cried his new friend to the coatless landlord. "I'm back, you see, hand 'ave brought you a couple of guests. Look sharp with supper, for we're hall 'ungry as 'awks."

The ham which they partook of, with accompanying eggs and lukewarm potatoes, was very salt, so that in spite of his three cups of tea Wilkinson was thirsty. He went to the bar, situated in the only common room, except the dining-room, in the house, and asked for a glass of water. A thick, greenish fluid was handed to him, at which, as he held it to the light, he looked aghast. Adjusting his eye-glass, he looked again, and saw not only vegetable and minute animal organisms, but also unmistakable hairs.

"Where do you get this water?" he asked in a very serious tone.

"Out of the well," was the answer.

"Are you aware that it is one mass of animal and vegetable impurities, and that you are liable to typhoid and every other kind of disease as the natural effect of drinking such filth?"

[Pg 47]The landlord stared, and then stammered that he would have the well cleaned out in the morning, not knowing what sort of a health officer was before him. But the crowd at the bar said it was good enough for them, as long as the critters were well killed off with a good drop of rye or malt. Wilkinson asked for a glass of beer, which came out sour and flat. "See me put a head on that," said the landlord, dropping a pinch of soda into the glass and stirring it in with a spoon. The schoolmaster tried to drink the mixture, but in vain; it did not quench the thirst, but produced a sickening effect. He felt like a man in a strange land, like a wanderer in the desert, a shipwrecked mariner. Oh, to be on the *Susan Thomas*, with miles of pure water all round! Or even at home, where the turning of a tap brought all Lake Ontario to one's necessities.

"Is there no other water than this about?" he asked in despair.

"Wy, yees," answered Matt; "thay's the crick a ways down the track, but it's that black and masshy I guess you wouldn't like it no better."

"Well, get us some from there, like a good man, to wash with if we cannot drink it, and have it taken up to our room," for it had appeared that the two pedestrians were to inhabit a double-bedded apartment.

"'Ere, you Timotheus, look spry and go down to the crick and fetch a pail of water for No. 6."

A shambling man, almost a hobbledehoy, of about twenty five, ran out to obey the command, and, when he returned from No. 6, informed Wilkinson civilly that the water was in his room. Something in his homely but pleasant face, in his shock head and in his voice, seemed familiar to the dominie, yet he could not place his man; when Coristine came along and said, "You've got a brother on the *Susan Thomas*, haven't you, and his name is Sylvanus?" The young man shuffled with his feet, opened a mouth the very counterpart of "The Crew's," and answered: "Yes, mister, he's my oldest brother, is Sylvanus; do you happen to know Sylvanus?"

"Know him?" said the unblushing lawyer, "like a brother; sailed all over Lake Simcoe with him."

The lad was proud, and went to his menial tasks with [Pg 48]a new sense of the dignity of his family. He was called for on all sides, and appeared to be the only member of the household in perpetual request; but, though many liberties were taken with him personally, none were taken with his name, which was always given in full, "Ti-mo-thé-us!" Wilkinson was too tired, thirsty and generally disgusted to do anything but sit, as he never would have sat elsewhere, on a chair tilted against the wall. Coristine would fain have had a talk with "The Crew's" brother, but that worthy was ever flitting about from bar-room to kitchen, and from well to stable; always busy and always cheerful.

The Grinstun man came swaggering up after treating all hands at the bar to whisky, in which treat the pedestrians were included by invitation, declined with thanks, and suggested

22

a game of cards—any game they liked—stakes to be drinks; or, if the gents preferred it, cigars. Coristine somewhat haughtily refused, and Wilkinson, true to his principles, but in a more conciliatory tone, said that he did not play them. He was obliged, therefore, to get the landlord, Matt, and a couple of bar-room loafers to take hands with him.

"Wilks, my dear boy, get out your draft-board and I'll play you a game," said Coristine.

The board was produced, the flat, cardboard chessmen turned upside down, and the corner of a table, on which a few well-thumbed newspapers lay, utilized for the game. The players were so interested in making moves and getting kings that, at first, they did not notice the talk of the card players which was directed against them; for Matt, being called away to his bar, was replaced by a third loafer. Gradually there came to their ears the words, "conceited, offish, up-settin', pedlars, tramps, pious scum," with condemnatory and other adjectives prefixed, and then they knew that their characters and occupations were undergoing unfavourable review. Mr. Rawdon was too "hail fellow well met" with the loafers to offer any protest. He joined in the laugh that greeted each new sally of vulgar abuse, and occasionally helped his neighbours on by such remarks as, "We musn't be too 'ard on 'em, they hain't used to such company as hus," which was followed by a loud guffaw. Wilkinson was playing badly, for he [Pg 49]felt uncomfortable. Coristine chewed his moustache and became red in the face. The landlord looked calmly on. At last the card players, having had their third drink since the game began, came over to the little table. One of the roughest and worst-tongued of the three picked up a pile of dirty newspapers, looked at one of them for a moment, pshawed as if there was nothing in them, and threw the pile down with a twist of his hand fair on to the draft-board, sweeping it half off the table and all the cardboard men to the floor. In a moment Coristine was up, and laid hold of the fellow by the shoulder. Pale but resolute, the schoolmaster, who had done physical duty by unruly boys, stood beside him. The working geologist and the landlord, Matt, looked on to see the fun of a fight between two city men and three country bullies.

"Get down there," said Coristine to his man, trembling with indignation, "get down there, and pick up all these chessmen, or I'll wring your neck for you." The fellow made a blow at him with his free hand, a blow that Coristine parried, and then the Irishman, letting go of his antagonist's arm, gave him a sounding whack with all the might of his right fist, that sent him sprawling to the ground.

"Pile in on 'im, boys!" cried the prostrate ruffian, who had lost a tooth and bled freely at the nose. The other two prepared to pile, when the schoolmaster faced one of them, and kept him off. It is hard to say how matters would have gone, had not a tornado entered the bar room in the shape of Timotheus. How he did it, no one could tell, but, in less than two minutes, the two standing bullies and the prostrate one were all outside the tavern door, which was locked behind them. Peace once more reigned in the hotel, and it was in order for Matt and the Grinstun man to congratulate Coristine on his knock down blow. He showed no desire for their commendation, but, with his friend, whom Timotheus helped to pick up the chessmen, retired to his room. The Crew's brother had disappeared before he had had a chance to thank him.

Before retiring for the night, the lawyer was determined to be upsides with Mr. Rawdon. He asked his roomfellow if he had any writing materials, and was at once provided with paper, envelopes, and a fountain pen.

[Pg 50]"I hope I'm not depriving you of these, Wilks, my dear," he said, when the party thus addressed almost threw himself upon his neck, saying, "Corry, my splendid, brave fellow, everything I have is at your absolute disposal, 'supreme of heroes—bravest, noblest, best!'" for he could not forget his Wordsworth. Coristine wrote to the clerk of the municipality of Flanders, to know where Miss Jewplesshy or Do Please-us had a lot, and whether the taxes on it had been paid. He directed him to answer to his office in Toronto, and also wrote to his junior, instructing him how to act upon this reply. These letters being written and prepared for the post, he and the dominie read together out of the little prayer book, left the window open and the lamp burning, and went to bed. Before they fell asleep, they heard the barking of a dog. "It's that poor brute, Muggins," said Coristine; "I'll go, and let him in, if that brute of a master of his won't." So, in spite of Wilkinson's remonstrances, he arose and descended the stairs to the bar-room. Nobody was there but Timotheus sleeping in a back tilted chair. He slipped quietly along in his bare feet, but Timotheus, though sleeping, was on guard. The Crew's brother awoke, soon as he tried the door, and in a moment, was on his back. "It's I, my good Timotheus," said the lawyer, and at once the grip relaxed. "I want to let that poor dog, Muggins, in." Then Timotheus unlocked the door, and Coristine whistled, and called "Hi Muggins, Muggins, Muggy, Mug, Mug, Mug, Mug!" when the mongrel came bounding in, with every expression of delight. Coristine warmly thanked The Crew's brother, pressed a dollar on his acceptance, and then retired to No. 6. Muggins followed him, and lay down upon the rag carpet outside that apartment, to keep watch and ward for the rest of the night, entirely ignoring his owner, the Grinstun man.

There was a pail of swamp water in the middle of the room, at the bottom of which lay some little black things. As this water became warm, these little fellows began to rise and become frolicksome. Like minute porpoises or dolphins, they joined in the mazy dance, and rose higher and higher. All night long, by the light of the kerosene lamp, they indulged in silent but unceasing hilarity. The [Pg 51]snores of the sleepers, the watchful dream-yaps of Muggins, did not affect them. They were bound to have a good time, and they were having it. Morning came, and the sun stole in through the window. Then, the wiggler grew tired, and came, like many tired beings, to the top. For a time he was quiescent, but soon the sun's rays gave force to the inner impulse which "rent the veil of his old husk," and transformed it into a canoe or raft, containing a draggle-tailed-looking creature with a big head and six staggery legs. Poising itself upon the raft, the outcome of the wiggler sunned its crumplety wings, till "like gauze they grew," and then all of it, a whole pailful of it, made for the sleepers, to help its more mature relations, which had come in through the open window to the light, to practice amateur phlebotomy upon them. The pedestrians awoke to feel uncomfortable, and rub and scratch their faces, heads, necks, and hands. "It's clean devoured I am, Wilks," cried Coristine. "The plagues of Egypt have visited us," replied the dominie. So, they arose and dressed themselves, and descended to the noisome bar-room. There they found Timotheus, awake and busy, while, at their heels, frisking about and looking for recognition, was their night guard Muggins. Timotheus informed them that he had already been out probing the well with a pike pole, and had brought up the long defunct bodies of a cat and a hen, with an old shoe and part of a cabbage, to say nothing of other things as savoury. They decided to take no more meals cooked with such water in that house, paid their bill to Timotheus, buckled on their knapsacks, and, with staff in hand, sallied forth into the pure outside air of the morning. Coristine ran over to the store in which the post office was kept, and posted his two letters. There was no sign of Matt, the landlord, of Mr. Rawdon, or of their assailants of the night before. Muggins, however, followed them, and no entreaties, threats, or stones availed to drive the faithful creature back to his master and the hotel where he slept.

The pedestrians passed the black, sluggish creek, out of which the wigglers had come, and struck into a country, flat but more interesting than that they had left behind them. After they had gone a couple of miles they came to a clear running stream, in which they had a splendid [Pg 52]wash, that tended to allay the irritation of the mosquito bites. Then they brought forth the remains of their biscuits and cheese, and partook of a clean meal, which Coristine called a good foundation for a smoke, Muggins sitting upon his hind legs and catching fragments of captain's biscuits and whole gingersnaps in his mouth, as if he had never done anything else. It was very pleasant to sit by the brook on that bright July morning, after the horrors of the Peskiwanchow tavern, to have clean food and abundance of pure water. As the dominie revelled in it, he expressed the opinion that Pindar was right when he said "ariston men hudor," which, said the lawyer, means that water is the best of all the elements, but how would Mr. Pindar have got along without earth to walk on, air to breathe, and fire to cook his dinner?

"I'm no philosopher, Wilks, like you, but it seems to me that perfection is found in no one thing. If it was, the interdependence of the universe would be destroyed; harmony would be gone, and love, which is just the highest harmony, be lost. That's just why I couldn't be a unitarian of any kind. As Tennyson says, 'one good custom would corrupt the world.'"

24

"Pardon me, Corry, he does not say that, but makes Arthur say:—

God fulfils himself in many ways,

Lest one good custom should corrupt the world."

"Better and better! but that's what the churches don't see, nor the politicians, nor the socialists, nor the prohibitionists, nor the scientists, nor anybody else hardly, it seems to me. When a man's got two eyes to see with, why should he shut one and keep out half the view? This 'ariston men hudor' idea—I'm not arguing against temperance, for it's temperate enough we are both—but this one thing is best notion would bring the beautiful harmonious world into dull, dead uniformity. There's a friend of mine that studies his Bible without any reference to the old systems of theology, and finds these old systems have made some big mistakes in interpreting its sayings, when a newspaper blockhead comes along and says if he won't conform let him go out of the church. There's a one-eyed man for you, an ecclesiastical Polyphemus! Our politicians are just the same, without a broad, liberal idea to [Pg 53]clothe their naked, thieving policies with. And the scientists! some of them stargazing, like Thales, so that they fall into the ditch of disrepute by failing to observe what's nearer home, and others, like Bunyan's man in Interpreter's house, so busy with the muckrake that they are ignorant of the crown held over their heads. Now, you and I are liberal and broad, we can love nature and love God too, we can admire poetry and put our hands to any kind of honest work; you can teach boys with your wonderful patience, and, with your pluck, knock a door in, and stand up, like a man, to fight for your friend. But, Wilks, my boy, I'm afraid it's narrow we are, too, about the women."

"Come, come, Corry, that subject, you know—"

"All right, not another word," interposed the lawyer, laughing and springing to his feet; "let us jog along

A village schoolmaster was he,

With hair of glittering grey;

As blithe a man as you could see

On a spring holiday.

And on that morning, through the grass,

And by the streaming rills,

We travelled merrily, to pass

A day among the hills."

"When did you take to Wordsworth, Corry?"

"Oh, many a time, but I refreshed my memory with that yesterday, when I came across the tear in the old man's eye."

"It is most appropriate, for there, on the right, are actual hills."

As the travellers approached the rising ground, which the dominie had perceived, the lawyer remarked that the hillocks had an artificial look.

"And they are undoubtedly artificial," replied Wilkinson.

"This is the township of Nottawasaga, once inhabited by the Tobacco tribe of the Hurons, who had many villages, and grew tobacco and corn, besides making beads, pipes, and other articles, for sale or barter. They made their pipes out of the Trenton sandstone. A great many village sites and ossuaries have been found in the township, the latter containing thousands of skeletons. They have all [Pg 54]been opened up by the settlers for the sake of the copper kettles and other objects buried in them. These long, narrow hillocks are earthworks, the foundation of a rude fortification or palisade round a village. The Archæological Reports of the Canadian Institute contain very full and interesting accounts of the explorations made in this very region. We are on historic ground, Corry."

"Poor old Lo!" ejaculated the lawyer, "whatever is that dog after? Hi, Muggins, Muggins!"

But Muggins would not leave the earthwork into which he was digging with rapidly moving forepaws. As Coristine remarked, it was a regular Forepaugh's circus. When the pedestrians came up to him, he had a large hole made in apparently fresh dug earth, and had uncovered a tin box, japanned above. This the pair disinterred with their walking-sticks, amid great demonstrations from the terrier. The lawyer opened it judicially, and found it to contain a lot of fragments of hard limestone, individually labelled. Looking over these, his

25

eye rested on one marked P.B. Miss Du Plessis, lot 3, concession 2, township of Flanders. Others were labelled T. Mulcahy, S. Storch, R. McIver, O. Fish, with their lots, concessions and townships, and the initials F.M. and P.

"What is the import of this?" asked the schoolmaster.

"Import or export, it's the Grinstun man, the owner of this sagacious dog, that buried this box till he had time to bring a waggon for it. These are samples of grindstone rock, and, if I am not a Dutchman, F means fair, M, middling, P, poor, and P.B., prime boss, and that is Miss Du Plessis. Gad! we've got her now, Jewplesshy, Do Please, Do Please-us, are just Du Plessis. It's a pleasant sort of name, Wilks, my boy?"

"What are you going to do with this treasure trove, might I ask?" inquired the dominie.

"Bury it," replied the lawyer.

"I trust you will make no unfair use of the information it contains, part of which was confided to me privately, and under seal of secrecy, by Mr. Rawdon?"

"Now, Wilks, howld your tongue about that. I ask you no questions, you tell me no lies nor anything else. If you think I'm going to see a girl cheated, just because [Pg 55]she is a girl, you don't know your friend. But you do, you honest old Wilks, don't you now?"

"Very well, only remember I breathed no hint of this in your ear."

"All right, old man," answered Miss Du Plessis' self-constituted advocate, as he shovelled the earth in over the tin box. "Muggins, you rascal, if you dig that up again, I'll starve you to death."

The pedestrians deserted the archæological find, and trudged away into the north west.

"Wilks, my dear, I feel like the black crow," said Coristine, as they journeyed along the pleasant highway.

"Like what?" asked the dominie, adjusting his eye-glass.

"Like the crow, don't you know?

Said one black crow unto his mate,

What shall we do for grub to ate?

Faith, it'll be an awful thing if we're going to die of starvation in the wilderness."

"I thought you were a botanist, Corry?"

"So I am, in a small way."

"Then, what bushes are those in that beaver meadow?"

In another minute, the lawyer, closely followed by Muggins, was in the meadow, exclaiming "Vaccinium Canadense! Come on, Wilks, and have a feast." Muggins was eating the berries with great satisfaction, and Coristine kept him company. The dominie also partook of them, remarking: "This is the whortleberry, or berry of the hart, vulgarly called the huckleberry, although huckle means a hump, which is most inappropriate."

"That reminds me of a man with a hump, though there wasn't much heart to him," said Coristine, his mouth full of fruit. "He undertook to write on Canada after spending a month here. He said the Canadians have no fruit but a very inferior raspberry, and that they actually sell bilberries in the shops. As a further proof of their destitution, he was told that haws and acorns are exposed for sale in the Montreal markets. Such a country, he said, is no place for a refined Englishman. I don't wonder my countrymen rise up against the English."

[Pg 56]"You forget, Corry, that I am English, and proud of my descent from the Saxon Count Witikind."

"Beg your pardon, Wilks, but you're a good Englishman, and I never dreamt your progenitor was that awful heathen:—

Save us, St. Mary, from flood and from fire,

From famine and pest, and Count Witikind's ire.

As the Englishmen said, there is no need to hask 'ow the hell got into your name."

"Corry, this is most unseemly. I wonder you are not ashamed to speak thus, with that innocent dog beside you."

"O, dad, he's heard worse things than that; haven't you now, Muggins? Trust him to live with a cad of a Grinstun man, and not to pick up bad language."

26

"Ullo, there, you dog-stealers!" fell upon the ears of the berry-pickers like a thunder clap. They looked up, and saw a neat waggonette, drawn by a team of well-kept bay horses, in which, on a back seat, sat Mr. Rawdon and a little girl with long fair hair. On the front seat were two well-dressed women, one of whom was driving; the other wore a widow's cap, and had a gentle, attractive face. The waggon stopped for them to come on to the road, which, leaving their berries, they did, taking off their hats to the ladies as they approached.

"We did all we could, Mr. Rawdon, to make your dog go back to the hotel, but he insisted on following us," said Wilkinson, apologetically.

"All very fine, my beauty, you 'ooked 'im and got 'im to shew you ware this 'ere box was. I'm hup to your larks, and you such a hinnocent too!"

Wilkinson was indignant, and denied having anything to do with the box.

"Be careful what you say, Mr. Rawdon," said Coristine, "I'm a lawyer, and may make a case, if you are not judicious in your language."

"Oh come hoff, I don't mean no 'arm; it's just my fun. 'Ave you any hobjection to give these 'ere gents a lift, Mrs. Thomas?"

"None, whatever," replied the lady who was driving.

"Then, if you don't mind, I'll get hin halongside hof your sister hin front, hand leave them to keep company [Pg 57]with little Marjorie 'ere," said the working geologist; and climbed over into the front seat outside of the attractive widow. Still, the pedestrians hesitated, till Mrs. Thomas, a by no means uncomely woman, said: "Get in, gentlemen, we shall be pleased to have your company." This decided them. They sprang into the waggon, one on each side of the little girl called Marjorie. The horses trotted along, and Muggins hovered about them, with an occasional ecstatic bark.

"I like you and your little dog," said Marjorie to Coristine, who replied: "God bless you for a little darling." After this interchange of confidence, they became great friends. Wilkinson found himself somewhat left out, but the Grinstun man threw him an odd bone, now and then, in the shape of a geological remark, keeping clear, however, of grindstones.

"What's your name, Marjorie?" asked the lawyer.

"My name is Marjorie," she replied.

"Yes, but what's your other name?"

"Marjorie Carmichael."

"Is that your father's name?"

"No, my papa's name is Captain Thomas."

"And has he got a ship on Lake Simcoe?"

"Yes, how did you know? He's got a ship, and a lumber yard, and a saw mill, and a farm, and a lot of things. Saul is on the farm, and Mr. Pratt works the mill, and Gudgeon looks after the yard, and Sylvanus is on the boat."

"Who is Saul?"

"He's the father of Sylvanus and Timotheus. Only Timotheus doesn't work for us. He wouldn't say his catechism on Sundays, so Saul said he had to go. I don't wonder he wouldn't say his catechism, do you? It speaks about God's getting awful angry and cursing. God doesn't get angry with little boys and girls and curse them, does he, Mr. What's your name?"

"My name is Coristine, but the name my little sister would have called me, if I had had a little sister like you, would be Eugene. No, I never read that God cursed any little girls and boys, nor anybody, not even the devil."

"And he's very very bad, isn't he? My cousin Marjorie Carruthers, that I'm called after, says Timotheus [Pg 58]should have learned his catechism; but she doesn't think God curses children. Then I said he oughtn't to learn what isn't true."

"O my darlint, but it's right you are. I wish I had you up on the dais at the Synod, to teach the bishops and all the clergy. Is she a nice little girl, your cousin Marjorie?"

"She's nice, but she isn't little, not a single bit. She lives away away in Toronto, and teaches school. Now, put your head down and I'll whisper something in your ear."

Coristine put his head down beside the long, fair curls, and Marjorie whispered, pointing a finger at the same time towards the widow: "That's my Aunt Marjorie, and she's Marjorie's mother."

27

"Where is cousin Marjorie now!"

"She's up at Uncle Carruthers', along with Miss Du Plessis. Do you know Miss Du Plessis? Oh, she's lovely, and, do you know?—put down your head again—that ugly little man sitting by Auntie says he's going to marry her. Isn't it too bad?"

"Infernal little beast! O, my dear Marjorie, I beg your pardon. I was thinking of that rascal of a mosquito on your hand—there, he's dead! Yes, it would be too bad, but she'll never marry such a man as that."

"Perhaps she'll have to, because she's very poor, and he says he's going to make heaps and heaps of money. People shouldn't marry for money, should they?"

"No, dear, they should marry for love, if they marry at all. Will you marry me when you grow to be a young lady?"

"No, you'll be too old then. Put your head down. You go and take away Miss Du Plessis from that naughty, bad little man, and I'll love you, O, ever so much.'

"But perhaps she won't have me."

"Oh, yes she will, because you would look very nice if you would take that black stuff that scratched me off your face."

"I will, I'll get a clean shave at Collingwood this very night."

"Then I'll get Auntie to write to Marjorie and tell her that my own Prince Charming, with a clean shave, is com[Pg 59]ing to take Cecile away from the ugly little rich man that says: 'An' 'ow is my young friend?' Won't that be nice?"

"Oh, please don't tell your aunt to write that."

"But I will, so there!"

The waggonette was now in the midst of a rather pretty village situated on a branch of the Nottawasaga River, and came to a stand still opposite the post office.

"If you gentlemen have business in the village, you can get out here," said Mrs. Thomas, "but, if not, we shall be pleased to have you dine with us."

The pedestrians thought of their last tavern experience, and felt disposed to accept the hospitable invitation, but Marjorie clinched their resolution by saying: "Eugene is coming to dinner with me, and his friend may come too," at which everybody laughed. The waggon moved on for another half mile, and then stopped in front of a pretty and commodious frame house, painted white, with red-brown doors and window frames and green shutters. Porch and verandah were covered with Virginia creeper, climbing roses and trumpet honeysuckle. Mr. Rawdon looked after himself, but Wilkinson and Coristine helped the ladies and the little girl to dismount, while an old man with a shock head, evidently Saul, took the horses round. Muggins greeted the whole party with a series of wiggles and barks, whereupon the Grinstun man gave him a savage kick that sent the dog away yelping.

"I said you were a naughty, bad, cruel man to my own self and to people I like," said Marjorie with indignation, "but now I say it right out to you, and for everybody to hear that wants to—a nasty, ugly, cruel little man!"

The working geologist was very angry and got very red in the face. Had he dared, he would probably have kicked the girl too. Policy compelled him to keep his temper outwardly, so he turned it off with a laugh, and said: "You don't know that little beast has I do, Marjorie, or you wouldn't go hand take 'is part. Of all the hungrateful, treacherous, sneakin', bad-'earted curs that ever gnawed a bone, 'e's the top-sawyer."

"I don't believe it," answered Marjorie stoutly, and with all the license allowed to a late and only child.

When the ladies took off their bonnets and rejoined their guests in the parlour, the pedestrians were much [Pg 60]struck with their appearance and demeanour, especially in the case of Mrs. Carmichael, than whom no lady could have been more gentle mannered and gracious. She had evidently had enough of Mr. Rawdon, for she turned in the most natural way to Wilkinson and engaged him in conversation on a variety of topics. The schoolmaster found her a charming talker and an interested listener. Marjorie and Coristine sat on a sofa with Muggins between them, while the working geologist banged about some photographs on a centre table. At dinner, to which Mrs. Thomas soon summoned them, Coristine had the post of honour with Marjorie to his right. Mrs. Carmichael sat at the foot of the table with Wilkinson by her side, and Rawdon was at Mrs. Thomas' left. While doing justice to an excellent repast, the lawyer informed his hostess that he was not an entire stranger to her family, and gave an account of his passage in the *Susan Thomas* from Belle Ewart to Barrie. He also referred to Sylvanus and Timotheus, and dwelt upon the excellent service rendered by the latter. The Grinstun man disliked the turn things were taking, as he felt himself out in the cold, for the widow absorbed the dominie, and Marjorie would not look at him.

When dessert came on the table, he turned to the schoolmaster and rudely interrupted his conversation, saying: "Look 'ere, Mr. Favosites Wilkinsonia, I don't see as you've hany call to keep hall the widder's talk to yourself. I move we change places," and he rose to effect the change.

"Really," said Wilkinson, with offended dignity, "I am not accustomed to anything of that description at a dinner party where there are ladies; but, if it's Mrs. Carmichael's desire that we should interchange seats, I am ready to comply."

Mrs. Carmichael evidently did not relish being called "the widder," nor the society of Mr. Rawdon, for she answered, "Certainly not, Mr. Wilkinson," and resumed her conversation with him. The baffled geologist turned to the hostess, while Marjorie engaged Coristine's attention, and in a petulant way stated his case. "You know the kind of man I ham, Mrs. Thomas, I'm a man of haction. I strike wen the hiron's 'ot. By good luck, I went back to Peskiwanchow last night, though it is a beastly [Pg 61]'ole, and got letters hat the post hoffice this mornin'. My hagent, at Toronto says, Mrs. Do Please-us is pretty badly hout for want of chink, hand that the girl's ready to jump hat hany reasonable hoffer. Now, hall I say his, give a man a chance. If she's the stunner they say she his, I'll marry her hinside of a week and make a lady of 'er, and hallow the hold 'ooman a pound a week, yes, I'll go has 'igh has thirty shillin', that's seven dollars and a 'arf. You get me a hinvite or give me a hintroduction to your brother's 'ouse in Flanders, and get the widder to back it hup with a good word to 'er daughter that's Miss Do Please-us's bosom friend, and I'll give the capting the contrack to carry hall the grinstuns shipped to Lake Simcoe ports." Then, sinking his voice to a whisper, he continued, "I'll do one better; I'll show you ware there's has fine a quarry of buildin' stun hon your farm 'ere has can be got hanyware in Canidy, wot's to 'inder your 'avin the best 'ouse twixt 'ere and Collinwood?" This last stroke of policy carried his point, and secured him the promise of an introduction, but Mrs. Thomas could not promise for her sister. All the time, Coristine, who could not help overhearing, twisted his moustache fiercely, and, under his breath, called the geologist a contemptible and unspeakable little cad.

Shortly afterwards, much to Marjorie's grief, the pedestrians put on their knapsacks and grasped their sticks for the road. They warmly thanked their hostess and her accomplished sister for their kind hospitality, and for the exceedingly pleasant hours they had spent in their company. They were cordially invited to call any time when they were near the village, and especially when the captain was at home, as he would never forgive himself for missing this treat. Marjorie kissed her Eugene, telling him to be a good boy, and remember what he had promised her about "you know who." "Ullo young 'ooman," said the Grinstun man, "you had ort to save one of them for yours haffectionately," at which the small lady was so indignant that she threatened to box his ugly big ears. "O Marjorie, how rude! whatever will these gentlemen from Toronto think!" Coristine could not bear to leave his little friend in disgrace, without a word of comfort, so he said: "Pardon me, Mrs. Thomas, for saying that the [Pg 62]rudeness did not originate with Marjorie," for which the child gave him a grateful glance. "You had better keep your dog in, Mr. Rawdon," called out Wilkinson, "or he will be after us again." The little man ran down the garden walk to get a farewell kick at his property, but Muggins, foreseeing danger, ran out of the gate, which old Saul held open for him. "You can keep the beastly cur, I don't want 'im, hungrateful, treacherous, long legged, 'airy brute," the last two adjectives being put in for Coristine's benefit, as allusions to his height and his moustache.

"Come back, Mr. Wilkinson," called Mrs. Carmichael. The dominie returned, and had a large fragrant rose pinned by fair hands to his button hole, blushing violently all the time. "You come back too, Eugene, but don't let Muggy in or he'll be kicked," cried Marjorie, who, on her favourite's return, gave him another parting salute and pinned two roses on his

29

coat. Muggins waited for them till they closed the gate finally behind them, lifted their hats three times, and began their afternoon's journey.

"That Mrs. Carmichael," remarked Wilkinson, "is one of the most intelligent and lady-like women I ever met, and she is wonderfully well read in the poets, Corry."

"I thought that subject was tabooed between us, Wilks?"

"Oh no, my dear fellow, I have no objection to the sex in a Platonic way."

"Dad, but it wasn't very platonic you looked when the pretty widow was fastening that button hole for you. Was she talking about her daughter at the schools?"

"Not a word; she did not even hint that she had a daughter. She must have been very young when the doctor married her."

"Well, that's one thing we have to thank that howling cad of a Grinstun man for. I'm real sorry I missed having a chat with Saul about the catechism."

"What is that!" So the lawyer related his conversation with Marjorie, and Wilkinson said, "Really, Corrie, as an educationist, I must say you do wrong to encourage such pertness in so young a child."

"Pertness is it? It's nature's own cleverness in the sweet little lass. Wilks, I'd give a good deal to have that little sunbeam or one like her with me all the time."

"Adopt one," suggested the schoolmaster.

[Pg 63]"Adopt one," replied the lawyer with a bitter laugh, "adopt one for Mrs. Marsh to look after? No, when I've a house of my own and a good housekeeper, and more time to spend on a child, I'll think over the hint."

The pair tramped steadily on, though the sun was hot, for there was a pleasant breeze, and the scenery became bolder and more picturesque. They came to rising ground, at the foot of which lay a fertile valley, and beyond it the Blue Mountains. Gazing across at them, the dominie exclaimed:—

Yon azure ridge,
Is it a perishable cloud—or there
Do we behold the frame of Erin's coast?

"No, Wilks, no! Erin's away on the confines of Wellington and Peel, and we are on those of Simcoe and Grey."

"Slight man, did you not perceive that I quoted poetry, and that the allusion is to your native isle?"

"Faith. I wish the real Erin was over there; it's the old lady would be in my arms as fast as I could run across. But this place deserves a song, so here goes:—

Though down in yonder valley
The mist is like a sea,
Though the sun be scarcely risen,
There's light enough for me.
For, be it early morning,
Or be it late at night,
Cheerily ring our footsteps,
Right, left, right.
We wander by the woodland
That hangs upon the hill;
Hark! the cock is tuning
His morning clarion shrill;
And hurriedly awaking
From his nest amid the spray,
Cheerily now, the blackbird,
Whistling, greets the day.
For be it early morning, etc.
We gaze upon the streamlet,
As o'er the bridge we lean;
We watch its hurried ripples
We mark its golden green.
Oh, the men of the north are stalwart,

And the norland lasses fair;
And cheerily breathes around us
The bracing norland air.
We smoke our black old meerschaums,
We smoke from morn till night,
While cheerily ring our footsteps,
Right, left, right."

[Pg 64]"Well done, Corry! I thought at first it was your own composition, but I see it is an English song."

"Yes, it came out long ago as 'The Tramp's Song' in *Sharpe's Magazine*, where I found it, and changed moor and moorland to north and norland, as better suited to our purpose. It's a good song."

"What kind of vehicle is that just in front of us?"

"It's a pole on four wheels drawn by a team of oxen, and I'm going to make a triumphant entry into Collingwood on it. The driver is a negro, as black as my boots—were." Coristine soon overtook the remarkable vehicle, and accosted the driver, telling him that he had ridden on horses, donkeys, mules, and once each on a cow, a camel and an elephant; in all sorts of carriages, carts and waggons, even to a gun carriage, but never on a pole behind an ox team. Had he any objections to letting him and his friend get aboard? The coloured gentleman showed a fine set of ivory, and said he had no dejections in the leas', and guessed the oxen didn't hab none. "The po-ul," he remarked, "is thar, not foh ridin' on, but ter keep the axles apaht, so's ter load on bodes and squab timbah. If yoh's that way inclined, the po-ul aint a gwine ter break frew, not with yoh dismenshuns. Guess the oxen doan hab ter stop fer yoh bof ter git aboahd?"

"Not a bit," said Coristine, as he jumped on the pole behind the driver. "Come on, Wilks, it's a cross between the tight rope and the tiller of the *Susan Thomas*." But the dominie refused to be charmed or inveigled into a position of peril or ridicule.

"Yoh best take this yeah feed-bag ter save yoh pants and fezz'etate the keepin' of yoh ekilibroom," said the courteous darkey, as he handed the lawyer one of the bags that formed his own cushion.

"Wilks, with a feed-bag under you, riding on a rail is just heavenly."

"If it was a rai-ul, you'd know it mighty soon, boss, fer rai-uls is angulish and shahp and hahd on the pants, but a po-ul is rounded and smoove. How are yoh comin' along?"

"In great shape, Mr.——"

"Maguffin, sah, is my applenashun. Tobias Mortimah Magrudah Maguffin. The low down folks around, [Pg 65]they teenames me Tobe and Toby, that's the shanty men and mill hans. But when I goes whar they's a meetin' of the bruddren, it's Mistah Maguffin, ebery time."

The pole cart, as Coristine called it, was going down hill, now, and the oxen began to run.

"Hole on tight, Mistah, them cattle's too lazy to stop runnin' befoh they gits to the determination ob this dercliverty," called the driver; and the lawyer held on in spite of frantic cries from his companion. "Come off, Coristine, come off, and do not make an object of yourself before the whole town." Coristine held on till the bottom of the hill was reached. Then he shook hands with his coloured brother, returned him the feed bag, and waited for Wilkinson. In friendly converse they entered the town of Collingwood, and put up at a clean and comfortable, almost fashionable, hotel. There, for the night, they may be left in safety, with this remark, that Coristine fulfilled his promise to the little girl, and got a clean shave before retiring.

CHAPTER IV.

Collingwood—Colonel Morton—Maguffin Engaged—Stepping Westward—Wild Thyme and a Bath—The Shale-works—Muggins and the Clergymen—Durham Mustard, and Marjorie—The Squire—The Grinstun Man—Lunch, Wordsworth and Original Poetry—Two Old People on the Blue Mountains.

At supper they had, for their vis-a-vis, a tall, aristocratic-looking man, attired airily in a mixture of jean and silk. His nose was aquiline, his eyes grey and piercing withal, his hair grey, but abundant, and his clean shaved mouth and chin mingled delicacy with strength of character.

"The weathah has been wahm, gentlemen," he remarked; to which statement they assented.

"I obsehved you entah the ho-tel, and pehceived that you are travelling for pleasuhe by yo-ah knapsacks. I also am travelling, partly foh pleasuhe, partly foh mattahs of family business. My ideahs, gentlemen, are old fashioned, too much so foh railyoads. The Mississippi is ouah natuhal highway from the South, but, unfohtunately, the to me unpleasant railyoad had to connect its head watahs [Pg 66]with Lake Michigan, by which route I find myself heah, on my way to a city called To-hon-to. You know it, I pehsume?"

Wilkinson's geographical lore was now unfolded. He discussed the Mississippi, although he had not been on that river, exhibited an intimate acquaintance with cities and routes which had never seen him in the flesh, and, by his quiet, gentlemanly, and, to the much older man, deferential tone, was admitted to the confidence of Colonel Morton, of Louisiana, South American trader, ship-owner and the possessor of a fine estate, which, although it had suffered greatly during the war, in which the colonel commanded a cavalry regiment, was yet productive and remunerative.

"I am a widowah, suh, and a childless old man," continued the colonel; "my only boy fell in the wah ah, and it broke his mother's heaht. Pahdon me," he said, as his voice shook a little, and the least glimmer of a tear stood in his eye, "I rahely talk of these mattahs of a puhely pehsonal kind, but, as you are kind enough to be intehested in my affaiahs, I say this much by way of explanation."

"I am sure, Colonel Morton, we deeply sympathize with you in so great a double bereavement," interposed the dominie.

"Indeed we do, sir, most sincerely," added the lawyer.

"I thank you, gentlemen," answered the courteous Southerner. "I was going to remahk that the only pehson in whom I feel a family intehest is my lamented wife's sistah, a Madame Du Plessis, who has resided foh many yeahs in yoah city of To-hon-to. May I enquiah, gentlemen, if you have, either of you, heahd the name befoah?"

Coristine replied that, incidentally, he had heard the names of both Madame Du Plessis and her daughter.

"I am awaah, suh, that my wife's sister has a daughtah. Can you tell me of my sister-in-law's suhcumstances, and what her daughtah, my niece, is like in appeahance?"

"Only from hearsay, Colonel. Madame Du Plessis is said to be in straightened circumstances, and I learn, from several quarters, that Miss Du Plessis is an attractive and amiable young lady; 'illigant' is what a countryman of mine, who served under her father, termed his young mistress."

[Pg 67]"And her baptismal name, suh?"

"Is Cecile, I think."

"Ah, to be suah, my deah wife's name, Cecilia, gallicized. She and Madame Du Plessis were Castilians of Lima. Du Plessis was theah in the ahmy, I in commehcial puhsuits, and we mahhied the sistahs, the belles of the Rimac.

Que' es la vida? Un frenesi
Que' es la vida? Una ilusion,
Una sombra, una ficcion.

You read Spanish, Mr. Wilkinson?"

"A little, sir; I think I recognize Calderon in these lines."

"Right, Mr. Wilkinson; I thank you, suh, foh yoah pleasing companionship. Good evening, gentlemen!" With a courtly bow, the colonel retired from the table.

At the coloured barber's the pedestrians met Mr. Maguffin, who greeted Coristine, saying:—

"Hopes yoh doan feel none the wuhse ob yoh ride on the po-ul," adding: "Mistah Poley, what runs this yeah stablishment, he's my nuncle's oldes' boy, and he abstracks a

32

cohnah ob the same ter my disposhul foh ohfice pupposes, supposin' I'm wahnted by folks as cahn't find me."

"That's very convenient," replied the lawyer, as he settled down in the barber's chair.

"It am, sah. I doan' tote ox teams no moah, po-ul nor no po-ul, when I kin drive and ride the fasses and sassies hawses that is made; no, sah, not much!"

"You are tired of teaming, then?"

"I am wohn out, sah, wif bein' called Toby and a po-ul-cat. I doan find no Scripcher reffunce foh Tobias, and yoh know what a po-ul-cat is; it's nuffin moah no less nor a skink."

The victims of the barber and his assistant kept the soap out of their mouths with difficulty. As his tormentor deserted him for a moment, the schoolmaster remarked that the Iroquois about the Lake of the Two Mountains called the Trappist monks there by the same savoury name, on account of some fancied resemblance between their dress and the coat of the *Mephitis Americana*.

Mr. Maguffin was listening intently, thinking the conversation was meant for his edification, and politely interposed:—

[Pg 68]"No, sah, I ain't no Mefferdis. I was bawn and raised a Baktis. Poley, now, he's a Mefferdis, and I ain't a gwine ter speak no harm of no Crishtchun bruddern what's tryin' ter do right accordin' ter they lights. But ter be called Toby and Poul-cat by low down white tresh, that trial ob the flesh and speerut is a fohgone conclusion, sah."

The shaving operation completed, the travellers returned to the hotel, and found Colonel Morton on what he called the piazza, smoking a good Havana cigar. He opened his case for his companions of the supper table, and Coristine accepted, while Wilkinson courteously declined.

"I tell you what I want to do, Mr. Cohistine. I want to puhchase two saddle hawses, a good one foh myself, and not a bad one foh my sehvant. Unfohtunately, my boy took sick on the way, and I had to send him home on the Mississippi steamah. That means, I must get me a new sehvant, able to ride well and handle hawses. I pehsume it will be hahd to find a cullahed boy, a niggro, in these pahts, so I must take whateveh can be got that will suit."

"Not at all, Colonel," replied Coristine, with effusion. "I think I can get you a negro who is out of place, is a good judge, and, I imagine, a good judge of horses. If you like, I'll go after him at once and tell him to report to you to-morrow morning."

"My deah suh, you are altogethah too kind."

"Not a bit of it; when will I tell him to call upon you?"

"Would seven o'clock be too eahly? Plantation and ahmy life have made me a light sleepah, so that I am up befoh the genehality of hotel guests."

"The very time. Excuse me for running away, I want to bag my man."

So Coristine left the colonel to parade the piazza with Wilkinson, and resought the barber shop.

The shop was closed, but a light still burned within. Coristine knocked, and Tobias opened the door. "You're the very man I want," cried the lawyer.

"Anything done gwine wrong, boss?" asked Mr. Maguffin.

The lawyer explained the circumstances to him at length, eulogized Colonel Morton, and told the negro to [Pg 69]make his best appearance at the hotel, sharp at seven next morning.

"Do yoh say the gemman'll gib me thirty dollars a munf and cloves ter boot, and me ridin' behine him all ober the roads on hawseback!" asked Tobias.

"Yes, I think I can promise those terms," replied the legal go-between.

"Then, yoh say foh me, if he's please foh ter hab me Maguffin, not Tobias, but Maguffin is his man, and I kin pick him out two lubby hawses, cheap as a po-ul-caht, and I cahn't say no cheapah. My respecs and humble expreshun ob gracious apprecherashun ter yoh, Mistah Kerosene."

The lawyer rushed back to the veranda, and found the colonel and Wilks still in conversation, and, wonder of wonder, Wilkinson was actually smoking a cigar, which he occasionally inserted between his lips, and then held away at arm's length, while he puffed out the smoke in a thin blue cloud. Wisely, he did not express astonishment at this unheard of feat of his friend, but informed the colonel that he had seen the coloured man, whose name was Tobias, but preferred to be called Maguffin, that he was willing to engage for thirty dollars a month and his clothes, and that he could put his new master in the way of getting two suitable horses. "I think, Colonel, you can reckon on his being here punctually at seven to-morrow."

"I shall nevah cease, Mr. Cohistine, to be sensible of yoah great kindness to an entiah styangah, suh. Oblige me by smoking anothah cigah, if they are to yoah liking."

So Corry lit a fresh cigar, and the three paraded the verandah till it was very late, engaging in all manner of pleasant conversation. When the stumps were thrown away, the colonel invited the comrades to visit his rooms for a moment before retiring. Entering his private sitting-room, he produced a quaintly-shaped but large glass bottle, which he flanked with three tumblers and a carafe of water. "Help yohselves, gentlemen," he said, courteously; "this old Bourbon is good foh countehacting the effects of the night aiah. Some prefer Monongahela, but good old Bourbon in modehation cahn't be suhpahssed." The pedestrians filled up, and bowed to their host as they [Pg 70]drank, and the colonel, doing the same, said, "My thanks to yoh, gentlemen, foh yoah kindness to a styangah—to yoah good health and ouah futhah pleasant acquaintance!" Then they severally retired, and the hotel closed for the night.

The next morning Coristine, whose room was just over the main entrance, was awakened by a loud discussion in the hall of the hotel. "Clare out now," cried the porter, "the bar's not opind yit, an' we don't want naygurs round whin the guests do be comin' down the stairs; clare, now, I tell yeez."

"I'se heah, Mike, on bisness wif Cunnel Morting," said a well-known voice; and continued, "yoh go and tell the cunnel that Mistah Maguffin is waitin' foh to pay his respecs."

"Go along wid yeez, Oi say, ye black scum av the airth, wid yer Cornel Mortins, the loikes av you! Faix, Oi'll tache yeez who's yer betthers wid this broom-handle."

"Gently, my good man, gently!" said the colonel, soothingly, as he laid his hand on Mike's shoulder. "This boy has business with me. Come in heah, Maguffin."

Tobias went in, with a triumphant glance at Mike, and, arrangements being completed, was soon at work, blacking his master's boots. Then he had a second breakfast at the servant's table, after which the colonel sallied forth with him, to provide him with a befitting suit of clothes, and to inspect the horses he had deemed suitable for the use of his new employer and himself. While they were gone, Wilkinson and his friend descended to a late breakfast, during which the hotel clerk handed the lawyer a telegram, signed Tylor, Woodruff, and White, and containing the words, "Look up Colonel Morton, Madame Du Plessis, 315 Bluebird Avenue, Parkdale." So the colonel had been corresponding with his firm, and he must either wait till that worthy returned, or leave a note for him. "Bawderashin, anyway, when a man's out for a holiday, can't he be left alone a bit!" Then, turning to his friend, he asked, "And, are they troubling you with letters and telegrams, too, Wilks, my darling?" The dominie replied, "I have only one letter about a poor lady teacher, who is in consumption, I fear. They want an extension of holidays for her, which is rather hard to get."

[Pg 71]"But you'll get it for her, Wilks, my dear?"

"Of course I will, if I have to do her work as well as my own."

"I knew it, Wilks, I knew it. You're as soft hearted as a girl, for all your adamant exterior. God bless you, my dear boy!"

"Corry, Corry, what allowances must be made for your exaggerated Irish language! What is there like adamant about me, I should like to know?"

"Good mawnin, gentlemen," said the soft voice of the colonel, "I am delighted to see you looking so well. I envy you Canadian gentlemen yoah fine fyesh complexions and yoah musical voices. We have sawft voices in the south, but it is a soht of niggro sawftness, gained by contact I pehsume. My sehvant and I byeakfasted some time ago."

"I trust he is to your liking, Colonel?" enquired Coristine.

"Suh, you have found me a jewel in Maguffin, and he has found me two splendid roadsters that are now being fitted with saddles. We staht for To-hon-to in an houah, gentlemen."

34

"By the bye, Colonel, I have a telegram from my firm that concerns you. It says 'Look up Colonel Morton, Madame Du Plessis, 315 Bluebird Avenue, Parkdale."

"But wheah is Pahkdale?"

"It is a suburb of Toronto. You had better keep the telegram."

"So, Mr. Cohistine, you are a lawyeh?"

"Yes; of the firm of Tylor, Woodruff, and White, but I'm not that now, I'm a gentleman out on a grand stravague."

"You may be a lawyeh, suh, but you are a gentleman as well, and I hope to meet you befoah many days are past. Good mawnin, my kind friends!"

The knapsacks were put on boldly, in the very parlour of the hotel, and their bearers strode along the lake road into the west, as coolly as if they were doing Snowden or Windermere. It was a glorious morning, and they exulted in it, rejoicing in the joy of living. The dominie had written his letter to the vulgar school-trustees, and felt good, with the approbation of a generous conscience. He recited with feeling:—

[Pg 72]

"What, you are stepping westward?" *"Yea"*—
'Twould be a wildish destiny,
If we, who thus together roam
In a strange land, and far from home,
Were in this place the guests of chance;
Yet who would stop, or fear t' advance,
Though home or shelter he had none,
With such a sky to lead him on.
The dewy ground was dark and cold;

"Faith, 'tis nothing of the kind, Wilks," interrupted Coristine; but the dominie went on unheeding.

Behind, all gloomy to behold,
And stepping westward seemed to be
A kind of heavenly destiny:
I liked the greeting; 'twas a sound
Of something without place or bound
And seemed to give me spiritual right
To travel through that region bright.
The voice was soft, and she who spake
Was walking by her native lake;
The salutation had to me
The very sound of courtesy;
Its power was felt; and while my eye
Was fix'd upon the glorious sky,
The echo of the voice enwrought
A human sweetness with the thought
Of travelling through the world that lay
Before me in my endless way.

"O Wilks, but you're the daisy. So you're going to travel through the world with the human sweetness of the soft voice of courtesy? You're a fraud, Wilks, you're as soft-hearted as a fozy turnip."

"Corry, a little while ago you called me adamant. You are inconsequential, sir."

"All right, Wilks, my darling. But isn't it a joy to have the colonel taking the bad taste of the Grinstun man out of your mouth?"

"The colonel, no doubt, is infinitely preferable. He is a gentleman, Corry, and that is saying a good deal."

"Hurroo for a specimen! look at that bank on your left, beyond that wet patch, it's thyme, it is. *Thymus serpyllum*, and Gray says it's not native, but adventitious from Europe. Maccoun says the same; I wonder what my dear friend, Spotton, says? But here it is, and no trace of a house or clearing near. It's thyme, my boy, and smells sweet as honey:—

[Pg 73]

Old father Time, as Ovid sings,
Is a great eater up of things,
And, without salt or mustard,
Will gulp you down a castle wall,
As easily as, at Guildhall,
An alderman eats custard."

"Drop your stupid Percy anecdote poems, Corry, and listen to this," cried the dominie, as he sang:—
I know a bank whereon the wild thyme grows,
I know a bank whereon the wild thyme grows,
Where oxlips and the nodding violets blow,
Where oxlips linger, nodding violets blow,
I know a bank whereon the wild thyme grow-ow-ow-ow-ows!!!

The lawyer joined in the chorus, encored the song, and trolled "ow ow ow ow ows" until the blood vessels over his brain pan demanded a rest. "Wilks," he said, "you're a thing of beauty and a joy forever."

Soon the road trended within a short distance of the lake shore. The blue waves were tumbling in gloriously, and swished up upon the shelving limestone rocks. "What is the time, Corry?" asked Wilkinson. "It's eleven by my repeater," he answered. "Then it is quite safe to bathe; what do you say to a dip?" The lawyer unstrapped his knapsack, and hastened off the road towards the beach. "Come on, Wilks," he cried, "we'll make believe that it's grampusses we are."

"What is a grampus?" enquired the dominie.

"Dad, if I know," replied his friend.

"A grampus, sir, etymologically is 'un grand poisson,' but, biologically, it is no fish at all, being a mammal, mid-way between a dolphin and a porpoise."

"So you got off that conundrum a porpoise to make a fool of me, Wilks?"

"O, Corry, you make me shudder with your villainous puns."

"That's nothing to what I heard once. There were some fellows camping, and they had two tents and some dogs for deerhunting. As it was raining, they let the hounds sleep in one of the tents, when one of the fellows goes round and says: 'Shut down your curtains.' 'Were you telling them that to keep the rain out?' asked one, when the rascal answered: 'To all in tents and purp houses.' Wasn't that awful, now?"

[Pg 74]The water was cold but pleasant on a hot day, and the swimmers enjoyed striking out some distance from shore and then being washed in by the homeward-bound waves. They sat, with their palms pressed down beside them, on smooth ledges of rock, and let the breakers lap over them. The lawyer was thinking it time to get out, when he saw Wilkinson back into the waves with a scared face. "Are you going for another swim, Wilks, my boy?" he asked. "Look behind you," whispered the schoolmaster. Coristine looked, and was aware of three girls, truly rural, sitting on the bank and apparently absorbed in contemplating the swimmers. "This is awful!" he ejaculated, as he slid down into deep water; "Wilks, it's scare the life out of them I must, or we'll never get back to our clothes. Now, listen to me." Dipping his head once more under water till it dripped, he let out a fearful sound, like "Gurrahow skrrr spat, you young gurruls, an' if yeez don't travel home as fast as yer futs'll taake yeez, it's I'll be afther yeez straight, och, garrahow skrr spat whishtubbleubbleubble!" The rural maidens took to their heels and ran, as Coristine swam into shore. In a minute the swimmers were into their clothes and packs, and resumed their march, much refreshed by the cool waters of the Georgian Bay.

"And where is it we're bound for now, Wilks?"

"For the abandoned shale-works at the foot of the Blue Mountains."

"Fwhat's that, as Jimmie Butler said about the owl?"

"The Utica formation, which crops out here, consists largely of bituminous shales, that yield mineral oil to the extent of twenty gallons to the ton. But, since the oil springs of the West have been in operation, the usefulness of these shales is gone. The Indians seem to have made large use of the shale, for a friend of mine found a hoe of that material on an island in the Muskoka lakes. Being easily split and worked, it was doubtless very acceptable to the metal wanting aborigines."

"But, if the works are closed up, what will we see?"

"We shall meet with fossils in the shale, with trilobites, such as the *Asaphus Canadensis*, a crustacean, closely allied to the wood-louse, and occasionally found rolled up, like it, into a defensive ball, together with other specimens of ancient life."

[Pg 75]"Wilks, my son, who's doing Gosse's Canadian Naturalist, now, I'd like to know? Pity we hadn't the working geologist along for a lesson."

"I am sorry if I have bored you with my talk, but I thought you were interested in science. Does this suit you better?

Many a little hand
Glanced like a touch of sunshine on the rocks,
Many a light foot shone like a jewel set
In the dark crag; and then we turn'd, we wound
About the cliffs, the copses, out and in,
Hammering and clinking, chattering stony names
Of shale and hornblende, rag and trap and tuff,
Amygdaloid and trachyte, till the sun
Grew broader towards his death and fell, and all
The rosy heights came out above the lawns."

"That's better, avic. Tennyson's got the shale there, I see. But rag and trap and tuff is the word, and tough the whole business is. Just look at that living blue bell, there, it's worth all the stony names of rock and fossil.

Let the proud Indian boast of his jessamine bowers,
His garlands of roses and moss-covered dells,
While humbly I sing of those sweet little flowers,
The blue bells of Scotland, the Scottish blue bells.
We'll shout in the chorus forever and ever,
The blue bells of Scotland, the Scottish blue bells."

"You are a nice botanist, Mr. Coristine, to confound that campanula with the Scottish blue-bell, which is a scilla, or wild hyacinth."

"Poetic license, my dear friend, poetic license! Hear this now:—

Let the Blue Mountains boast of their shale that's bituminous,
Full of trilobites, graptolites and all the rest,
It may not be so learned, or ancient, or luminous,
But the little campanula's what I love best.
So we'll shout in the chorus forever and ever,
The little campanula's worth all the rest.

Whew! What do you think of that for an impromptu song, Wilks?"

"I think that you are turning your back upon your own principle that there is no best, or no one best, and that everything is best in its place."

"Barring old Nick and the mosquitoes, Wilks, come now?"

"Well, an exception may be made in their favour, but what says the poet:—
[Pg 76]
O yet we trust that somehow good
Will be the final goal of ill.
Come, along, though, for we have much to see before sunset."

"You don't think that good is going to come out of the devil and mosquitoes?"

"Yes I do; not to themselves, perhaps, but to humanity."

"I saw a book once with the title "Why Doesn't God Kill the Devil?" and sympathized with it. Why doesn't He?"

"Because man wants the devil. As soon as the world ceases to want him, so soon is his occupation gone."

"Wilks, my dear, that's an awful responsibility lying on us men, and I fear what you say is too true. So here's for the shale works."

The pedestrians ceased their theological discussion and went towards the deserted buildings, where, in former days, a bad smelling oil had been distilled from the slaty-looking black stones, which lay about in large numbers. Wilkinson picked up fossils enough, species of trilobites chiefly, with a few graptolites, lingulas and strophomenas, to start a museum. These, as Coristine had suggested in Toronto, he actually tied up in his silk handkerchief, which he slung on the crook of his stick and carried over his shoulder. The lawyer also gathered a few, and bestowed them in the side pocket of his coat not devoted to smoking materials. The pair were leaving the works for the ascent of the mountain, when barks were heard, then a pattering of feet, and soon the breathless Muggins jumped upon them with joyous demonstrations.

"Where has he been? How came we not to miss him?" asked the dominie, and Coristine answered rather obliquely:—

"I don't remember seeing him since we entered Collingwood. Surely he didn't go back to the Grinstun man."

"It is hard to be poetical on a dog called Muggins," remarked Wilkinson; "Tray seems to be the favourite name. Cowper's dogs are different, and Wordsworth has Dart and Swallow, Prince and Music, something like Actaeon's dogs in 'Ovid.' Nevertheless, I like Muggins."

"Oh, Tray is good, Wilks:—

[Pg 77]

To my dear loving Shelah, so far, far away,
I can never return with my old dog Tray;
He's lazy and he's blind,
You'll never, never find
A bigger thief than old dog Tray."

"Corry, this is bathos of the worst description. You are like a caterpillar; you desecrate the living leaf you touch."

"Wilks, that's hard on the six feet of me, for your caterpillar has a great many more. But that dog's gone back again."

As they looked after his departing figure, the reason was obvious. Two lightly, yet clerically, attired figures were coming up the road, and on the taller and thinner of the twain the dog was leaping with every sign of genuine affection.

"I'm afraid, Wilks, that Muggins is a beastly cur, a treacherous 'ound, a hungrateful pup; look at his antics with that cadaverous curate, keeping company with his sleek, respectable vicar. O Muggy, Mug, Mug!"

The pedestrians waited for the clergy, who soon came up to them, and exchanged salutations.

"My dawg appears to know you," said the tall cassocked cleric in a somewhat lofty, professional tone.

"He ought to," replied Wilkinson, "seeing that he was given to me by a Mr. Rawdon, a working geologist, as he calls himself."

"Ow, really now, it seems to me rather an immoral transaction for your ah friend, Mr. Rawdon, to give away another man's property."

"Mr. Rawdon is no friend of mine, but his dog took a fancy to us, and followed us from Dromore to Collingwood."

"Allow me to assure you that Muggins is not this ah Mr. Rawdon's dawg at all. I trained him from a puppy at Tossorontio. The Bishop ordered me from there to Flanders, and, in the hurry of moving, the dawg was lost; but now, I should rather say stowlen. My friend, the Reverend Mr. Errol and myself, my name is Basil Perrowne, Clerk, had business in Collingwood last night, when Muggins, most opportunely, met us, and went howme with me."

"Well, Mr. Perrowne, I am very glad you have recovered your dog, which I was only too glad to rescue from a somewhat inhuman master. My name is Wilkin[Pg 78]son, of the Toronto schools, my friend is Mr. Coristine, of Osgoode Hall, barrister."

The gentlemen exchanged formal salutations, and proceeded on their way, Wilkinson with Perrowne, and Coristine with Erroll. Muggins was in the seventh heaven of delight.

38

"You belong to Tossorontio, Mr. Perrowne?" asked Wilkinson, by way of starting the conversation.

"Ow, now! I said I had trained Muggins from a pup there, but that ownly extends owver a few years. Durham is my university, which you may have heard of."

"I am familiar by name with the university and the cathedral, although the juvenile geography books say that Durham is famous for its mustard."

"Ow, now, really, they down't, do they? Ow dear, mustard! We Durham men can serve it out pretty hot, you know. You belong to the Church, of course, Mr. Wilkinson?"

"I was brought up in the Church of England, and educated in what are called Church principles; I am fond of the Prayer Book and the Service, but, to my way of thinking, the Church is far more extensive than our mere Anglican communion."

"Ow, yes, there are Christian people, who, I howpe, will get to heaven some way through the uncovenanted mercies, in spite of their horrid schism from the True Body. There is Errol, now, whom, out of mere courtesy, I call reverend, but he is no more reverend than Muggins. His orders are ridiculous, not worth a farthing candle."

"Come, come, Mr. Perrowne, his orders are as good as those of St. Timothy, which were laid on him by the hands of the Presbytery."

"That is precisely what the cheeky dissenter says himself. We have dropped that line of controversy now, for one ever so much more practical."

"I hope you don't take off your coats and fight it out? You have the advantage in height and youth, but Mr. Errol seems a strong and active man."

"Now, we down't fight. I have set a cricket club a-gowing, and he has turned a neglected field into a golf links. My club makes Churchmen, and his makes Scotch dissenters."

[Pg 79]"I thought the Presbyterian Church was established in Scotland?"

"Ow, down't you see, we are not in Scotland."

"Then, in Canada, there is no established church, unless it be the Roman Catholic in the Province of Quebec."

"Ow, well, drop that, you know; we are the Church, and all the outside people are dissenters. I down't antagonize him. He helped me to make my crease, and joined my club, and I play golf with him every fine Monday morning. But the young fellows have now true English spirit here. Errol has twenty golfers to my six cricketers. When he and I are added, that makes eight, not near enough, you know. As a mission agency, my club has not succeeded yet, but every time I make a cricketer, I make a Churchman."

"I have known some very good cricketers that were not Anglicans."

"Now you haven't, my dear sir; you thought you have, but you haven't; that's the trouble with those who reject Church authority. The Methodist plays rounder, what you call base-ball; the Independents and Baptists played croquet and lawn tennis after other people stopped playing them; the Presbyterian plays golf; and the Churchman plays cricket."

"To argue with one who sweeps all experience aside with a wave of his hand," said the schoolmaster, indignantly, "is not to argue at all. It is a case of *Roma locuta*."

"Ow, yes, just sow, you know, we down't argue, we simply assert the truth."

"How d'ye like the Durham mustard, Wilks, my boy?" put in Coristine from the rear, where he and Mr. Errol were laughing amusedly; "it's hot, isn't it, not much solid food, but lots of flavour? It reminds me of The Crew, when he said what was, is, and ever shall be, Amen. Mr. Perrowne is the owner of a splendid dog, and he is a splendid dogmatist. What he doesn't know isn't worth knowing."

"Ow, thanks awfully, Mr. Coristine, you are really too flattering!" gravely and gratefully replied the parson. Wilkinson was afraid that his friend's banter might become too apparent, as the simple egotism of the graduate of [Pg 80]Durham led him on, so, he changed the subject, and soon had the cleric quoting Virgil and Mrs. Hemans.

Meanwhile Coristine and Mr. Errol were taking one another's measure. The lawyer recited to his companion the conversation between Marjorie and himself relative to Timotheus. He found that Errol knew Marjorie, who had often been in his church and Sunday school in Flanders. "She's a comical little piece," he said; "her Sunday school teacher asked her who killed Goliath? and what do you think was her reply!"

"Give it up."

"It was 'Jack,' no less than Jack the Giant-Killer."

"The darlin'!" cried the lawyer, with admiration, and straightway won the minister's heart.

"Marjorie has a cousin stopping at the house of Mr. Carruthers, one of my elders, since last Tuesday night, as blithe and bonnie a young leddy as man could wish to see. While she's here, she's just the light of the whole country side."

Mr. Coristine did not care for this turn in the conversation.

"Tell me some more about little Marjorie," he said.

"Ah," replied the minister, "then you know that her cousin is called Marjorie, too! Little Marjorie went to church once with Miss Du Plessis, whom Perrowne had got to sing in the choir, that was last summer, if I mind right, and, when the two rideeclus candles on the altar were lighted, and the priest, as he calls himself, came in with his surplice on, she put her face down in Miss Cecile's lap. 'What's the trouble, Marjorie?' asked Miss Du Plessis, bending over her. 'He's going to kiss us all good-night,' sobbed the wee thing. 'No he is not, Marjorie; he's on his knees, praying,' replied the young leddy, soothingly. 'That's what papa always does, when he's dressed like that, before he kisses me good-night, but he takes off his boots and things first,' and she sobbed again, for fear Perrowne was coming to kiss them all, put out the candles, and go to bed. If Miss Du Plessis had not been a sober-minded lass, she would have laughed out in the middle of the choir. As it was, she had to hand Marjorie over to a neighbour in a back seat, before the bit lassie would be comforted."

[Pg 81]"Ah! did you ever now? the little innocent!"

"It's not that improbable that there'll be a marriage in the church before long. Perrowne's just clean daft and infatuated with his occasional soprano. He's sent her the 'Mirror of Devotion' and the 'Soul's Questioner,' and a lot of nicely bound trash, and walks home with her whenever he has the chance, to the scandal and rage of all his farmers' daughters. It's very injudeecious o' Perrowne, and has dreeven two of his best families to the Kirk. Not that she's no a braw looking lass, stately and deegnified, but she has na the winsomeness of Miss Marjorie."

"Is that your quarter, Mr. Errol?"

"Hech, sirs, I'm an old bachelor that'll never see five and forty again; but, as we say in Scotch or the vernacular Doric, 'an auld carle micht dae waur.' There's not a more sensible, modest, blithesome, bonnie lassie in all the land. It's a thousand peeties some young, handsome, well-to-do steady, God-fearing man has na asked at her to be 'the light o' his ain fireside.' Gin I were as young as you, Mr. Coristine, I would na think twice about it."

"Avaunt, tempter!" cried the lawyer, "such a subject as matrimony is strictly tabooed between me and my friend."

"I'll be your friend, I hope, but I cannot afford to taboo marriages. Not to speak of the fees, they're the life of a well-ordered, healthy congregation."

A neat turn-out, similar to that of Mrs. Thomas, came rattling along the road. "That's John Carruthers' team," remarked the minister, and such it turned out to be.

"Maister Errol," said its only occupant, a strong and honest-faced man with a full brown beard, "yon's a fine hanky panky trick to play wi' your ain elder an' session clerk."

"Deed John," returned the minister, relapsing into the vernacular; "I didna ken ye were i' the toon ava, but 'oor bit dander has gien us the opportunity o' becomin' acquent wi' twa rale dacent lads." Then, turning to the lawyer, "excuse our familiar talk, Mr. Coristine, and let me introduce Squire Carruthers, of Flanders." The two men exchanged salutations, and Perrowne, having turned back with Wilkinson, the same ceremony was gone through with the latter. They were then all courteously[Pg 82]invited to get into the waggon. Errol and Perrowne sprang in with an air of old proprietorship, but the two pedestrians respectfully declined, as they were especially anxious to explore the mountain beauties of this part of the country on foot and at their leisure.

"Aweel, gentlemen," cried the squire, "gin ye'll no come the noo, we'll just expect to see ye before the Sawbath. The Church and the Kirk'll be looking for the wayfarers, and my house, thank Providence, is big eneuch to gie ye a kindly welcome."

The parsons ably seconded Mr. Carruthers' peculiar mixture of English and Lowland Scotch, on the latter of which he prided himself, but only when in the company of someone who could appreciate it. Wilkinson looked at Coristine, and the lawyer looked at the dominie, for here they were invited to go straight into the jaws of the lion. Just then, they descried, climbing painfully up the hill, but some distance behind them, the Grinstun man; there was no mistaking him. "Hurry, and drive away," cried Coristine, in an under tone; "that cad there, the same that stole Muggins, is going to your house, Squire. For any sake, don't facilitate his journey."

"I'll no stir a hoof till ye promise to come to us, Mr. Coristine, and you, Mr. Wilkins, tae."

"All right, many thanks, we promise," they cried together, and the waggon rattled away.

"Now, Wilks, over this ditch, sharp, and into the brush, till this thief of the world goes by. We've deprived him of a ride, and that's one good thing done."

Together they jumped the ditch, and squatted among the bushes, waiting for the Grinstun man. They heard him puffing up the rising ground, saw his red, perspiring face in full view, and heard him, as he mopped himself with a bandanna, exclaim: "Blowed if I haint bin and lost the chance of a lift. Teetotally blawst that hold hass of a driver, and them two soft-'eaded Tomfools of hamateur scientists ridin' beside 'im. I knew it was Muggins, the cur I stole, and guv a present of to that there guy of a Favosites Wilkinsonia. I don't trust 'im, the scaly beggar, for hall 'is fine 'eroic speeches. 'E'll be goin' and splittin' on me to that gal, sure as heggs. And that Currystone, six feet of 'ipocrisy and hinsolence, drat the long-[Pg 83]legged, 'airy brute. O crikey, but it's 'ot; 'owever, I must 'urry on, for grinstuns is grinstuns, and a gal, with a rich hold huncle, ridin' a fine 'orse, with a nigger behind 'im carryin' his portmantle, haint to be sneezed hat. Stre'ch your pegs, Mr. Rawdon, workin' geologist hand minerologist!"

"By Jove!" cried Coristine, when the Grinstun man was out of sight; "that cad has met the colonel, and has been talking to him."

"A fine nephew-in-law he will get in him!" growled Wilkinson; "I have half a mind—excuse me Corry."

"I thought you were very much taken with the old Southerner."

"Yes, that is it," and the dominie relapsed into silence.

"It's about lunch time, Wilks, and, as there's sure to be no water on the top of the hill, I'll fill my rubber bag at the spring down there, and carry it up, so that we can enjoy the view while taking our prandial."

Wilkinson vouchsafed no reply. He was in deep and earnest thought about something. Taking silence for consent, Coristine tripped down the hill a few yards, with a square india rubber article in his hand. It had a brass mouthpiece that partly screwed off, when it was desirable to inflate it with air, as a cushion, pillow, or life-preserver, or to fill it with hot water to take the place of a warming-pan. Now, at the spring by the roadside, he rinsed it well out, and then filled it with clear cold water, which he brought back to the place where the schoolmaster was leaning on his stick and pondering. Replacing the knapsack, out of which the india rubber bag had come, the lawyer prepared to continue the ascent. In order to rouse his reflective friend, he said, "Wilks, my boy, you've dropped your fossils."

"I fear, Corry, that I have lost all interest in fossils."

"Sure, that Grinstun man's enough to give a man a scunner at fossils for the rest of his life."

"It is not exactly that, Corry," replied the truthful dominie; "but I need my staff and my handkerchief, and I think I will leave the specimens on the road, all except these two Asaphoi, the perplexing, bewildering relics of antiquity. This world is full of perplexities still, Corry." [Pg 84]So saying, the dominie sighed, emptied his bandanna of all but the two fossils, which he transferred to his pocket, and, with staff in hand, recommenced the upward journey. In ten minutes they were on the summit, and beheld the far-off figure of the working geologist on the further slope. In both directions the view was magnificent. They sat by the roadside on a leafy bank overshaded with cool branches, and, producing the reduplication of the Barrie stores procured the night before at Collingwood, proceeded to

41

lunch *al fresco*. The contents of the india rubber bag, qualified with the spirit in their flasks, cheered the hearts of the pedestrians and made them more inclined to look on the bright side of life. Justice having been done to the biscuits and cheese, Coristine lit his pipe, while the dominie took a turn at Wordsworth.

With musical intonation, Wilkinson read aloud:—

Some thought he was a lover, and did woo:
Some thought far worse of him, and judged him wrong:
But verse was what he had been wedded to;
And his own mind did like a tempest strong
Come to him thus, and drove the weary wight along.
With him there often walked in friendly guise,
Or lay upon the moss by brook or tree,
A noticeable man with large grey eyes,
And a pale face that seemed undoubtedly
As if a blooming face it ought to be;
Heavy his low-hung lip did oft appear,
Depress'd by weight of musing phantasy;
Profound his forehead was, though not severe;
Yet some did think that he had little business here.
He would entice that other man to hear
His music, and to view his imagery.
And, sooth, these two did love each other dear,
As far as love in such a place could be;
There did they dwell—from earthly labour free,
As happy spirits as were ever seen:
If but a bird, to keep them company,
Or butterfly sate down, they were, I ween,
As pleased as if the same had been a maiden queen.

"That's the true stuff, Wilks, and has the right ring in it, for we love each other dear, and are as happy spirits as were ever seen, but not a large grey eye, pale face, or low-hung lip between us. Just hear my music now, and view my imagery with your mind's eye:—

[Pg 85]

Far down the ridge, I see the Grinstun man,
Full short in stature and rotund is he,
Pale grey his watery orbs, that dare not scan
His interlocutor, and his goatee,
With hair and whiskers like a furnace be:
Concave the mouth from which his nose-tip flies
In vain attempt to shun vulgarity.
O haste, ye gods, to snatch from him the prize,
And send him hence to weep—and to geologize!"

"The rhythm is all right, Corry, and the rhyme, but I hope you do not call that poetry?"

"If that isn't superior to a good many of Wordsworth's verses, Wilks, I'll eat my hat, and that would be a pity this hot weather. Confess now, you haythen, you," cried the lawyer, making a lunge at his companion with his stick, which the latter warded off with his book.

"There are some pretty poor ones," the schoolmaster granted grudgingly, "but the work of a great poet should not be judged by fragments."

"Wilks, apply the rule; I have only given you one stanza of the unfinished epic, which unborn generations will peruse with admiration and awe, 'The Grinstun Quarry Restored':—

I have striven hard for my high reward
Through many a changing year
Now, the goal I reach; it is mine to teach.
Stand still, O man, and hear!
I shall wreathe my name, with the brightness of fame,
To shine upon history's pages;

42

It shall be a gem in the diadem
Of the past to future ages!
Oh, Wilks for immortality!" cried the light-hearted lawyer, rising with a laugh.

Looking back towards the ascent, he perceived two bowed figures struggling up the hill under largish, and, apparently, not very light burdens.

"Wilks, my dear, we're young and vigorous, and down there are two poor old grannies laden like pack mules in this broiling sun. Let us leave our knapsacks here, and give them a hoist."

The schoolmaster willingly assented, and followed his friend, who flew down the hill at breakneck speed, in a rapid but more sober manner. The old couple looked up with some astonishment at a well-dressed city man tearing [Pg 86]down the hill towards them like a schoolboy, but their astonishment turned to warmest gratitude, that found vent in many thankful expressions, as the lawyer shouldered the old lady's big bundle, and, as, a minute later, the dominie relieved her partner of his. They naturally fell into pairs, the husband and Wilkinson leading, Coristine and the wife following after. In different ways the elderly pair told their twin burden-bearers the same story of their farm some distance below the western slope of the mountain, of their son at home and their two daughters out at service, and mentioned the fact that they had both been schoolteachers, but, as they said with apologetic humility, only on third-class county certificates. Old Mr. Hill insisted on getting his load back when the top of the mountain was reached, and the pedestrians resumed their knapsacks and staves, but the lawyer utterly refused to surrender his bundle to the old lady's entreaties. The sometime schoolteachers were intelligent, very well read in Cowper, Pollock, and Sir Walter Scott, as well as in the Bible, and withal possessed of a fair sense of humour. The old lady and Coristine were a perpetual feast to one another. "Sure!" said he, "it's bagmen the ignorant creatures have taken us for more than once, and it's a genuine one I am now, Mrs. Hill," at which the good woman laughed, and recited the Scotch ballad of the "Wee Wifukie coming frae the fair," who fell asleep, when "by came a packman wi' a little pack," and relieved her of her purse and placks, and "clippit a' her gowden locks sae bonnie and sae lang." This she did in excellent taste, leaving out any objectionable expressions in the original. When she repeated the words of the Wifukie at the end of each verse, "This is nae me," consequent on her discovery that curls and money were gone, the lawyer laughed heartily, causing the pair in front, who were discussing educational matters, to look round for the cause of the merriment. "I'm the man," shouted Coristine to them, "the packman wi' a little pack." Then Mr. Hill knew what it was.

[Pg 87]

CHAPTER V.

Conversation with the Hills—Tobacco—Rural Hospitality—The Deipnosophist and Gastronomic Dilemma—Mr. Hill's Courtship—William Rufus rouses the Dominie's Ire—Sleep—The Real Rufus—Acts as Guide—Rawdon Discussed—The Sluggard Farmer—The Teamsters—The Wasps—A Difference of Opinion.

It was very pleasant for all four, the walk down the mountain road; and the pedestrians enjoyed the scenery all the more with intelligent guides to point out places of interest. The old schoolteacher, having questioned Wilkinson as to his avocation, looked upon him as a superior being, and gratified the little corner of good-natured vanity that lies in most teachers' hearts. Coristine told the wife that he trusted her daughters had good places, where they would receive the respect due to young women of such upbringing; and she replied:—

"O yes, sir, they are both in one family, the family of Squire Carruthers in Flanders. Tryphena is the eldest; she's twenty-five, and is cook and milker and helps with the washing. Tryphosa is only twenty, and attends to the other duties of the house. Mrs. Carruthers is not above helping in all the work herself, so that she knows how to treat her maids properly. Still, I am anxious about them."

"Nothing wrong with their health, I hope?" asked the lawyer.

"No, sir; in a bodily way they enjoy excellent health."

43

"Pardon me, Mrs. Hill," interrupted Coristine, "for saying that your perfectly correct expression calls up that of a friend of mine. Meeting an old college professor, very stiff and precise in manner and language, he had occasion to tell him that, as a student, he had enjoyed very poor health. 'I do not know about the enjoying of it, sir,' he answered, 'but I know your health was very poor.' Ha, ha! but I interrupted you."

"I was going to say, sir, that I have never been ambitious, save to keep a good name and live a humbly useful life, with food convenient for me, as Agur, the son of[Pg 88]Jakeh, says in the Book of Proverbs, in which, I suppose, he included clothing and shelter, but I did hope my girls would look higher than the Pilgrims."

"You don't mean John Bunyan's Christian and Christiana, and Great Heart, and the rest of them?"

"Oh, no!" replied the old lady, laughing, "mine are living characters, quite unknown to the readers of books, Sylvanus and Timotheus, the sons of old Saul Pilgrim."

"Oh, that's their name, is it? The Crew never told me his surname, nor did Captain Thomas."

"You know Sylvanus' captain, then? But, has he many sailors besides Pilgrim?"

"No; that's why I call him The Crew. It's like a Scotch song, 'The Kitty of Loch Goil,' that goes:—

For a' oor haill ship's companie,
Was twa laddy and a poy, prave poys

Sylvanus is The Crew, who goes on a cruise, like Crusoe. O, do forgive me, Mrs. Hill, for so forgetting myself; we have been so long away from ladies' society," which, considering the circumstances of the preceding day, was hardly an ingenuous statement.

"I am not so troubled about the elder Pilgrim and Tryphena," continued the old lady, "because Tryphena is getting up a little in years for the country; I believe they marry later in the city, Mr. Coristine?"

"O yes, always, very much, I'm sure," answered the lawyer, confusedly.

"Tryphena is getting up, and—well, she takes after her father in looks, but will make any man a good wife. Then the elder Pilgrim has good morals, and is affectionate, soft I should be disposed to call him; and he has regular employment all the year round, though often away from home. He has money saved and in the bank, and has a hundred-acre farm in the back country somewhere. He says, if Tryphena refuses him, he will continue to risk his life among the perils of the deep, by which the silly fellow means Lake Simcoe." Here the quondam schoolmistress broke into a pleasant laugh that had once been musical.

"And Miss Tryphosa, did I understand you to say you apprehend anything in her quarter from the Pilgrims?" enquired Coristine.

[Pg 89]"Please say Tryphosa, sir; I do not think that young girls in service should be miss'd."

"But they are very much missed when they go away and get married; don't grudge me my little joke, Mrs. Hill."

"I would not grudge you anything so poor," she replied, shaking a forefinger at the blushing lawyer. "You are right in supposing I apprehend danger to Tryphosa from the younger Pilgrim. She is—well, something like what I was when I was young, and she is only a child yet, though well grown. Then, this younger Pilgrim has neither money nor farm; besides, I am told, that he has imbibed infidel notions, and has lately become the inmate of a disreputable country tavern. If you had a daughter, sir, would you not tremble to think of her linking her lot with so worthless a character?" Before the lawyer could reply, the old man called back: "Mother, I think you had better give the gentleman a rest; he must be tired of hearing your tongue go like a cow-bell in fly time." Coristine protested, but his companion declined to continue the conversation.

"The mistress is as proud of wagging that old tongue of hers," remarked the dominie's companion, "as if she had half the larnin' of the country, and she no more nor a third class county certificut."

"Many excellent teachers have begun on them," remarked Wilkinson.

"But she begun and ended there; the next certificut she got was a marriage one, and, in a few years, she had a class in her own house to tache and slipper."

44

"Your wife seems to be a very superior woman, Mr. Hill."

"That's where the shoe pinches me. Shuparior! it's that she thinks herself, and looks down on my book larnin' that's as good as her own. But, I'll tell ye, sir, I've read Shakespeare and she hasn't, not a word."

"How is that?"

"Her folks were a sort of Lutherian Dutch they call Brethren. They're powerful strict, and think it a mortal sin to touch a card or read a play. My own folks were what they called black-mouthed Prosbytarians, from the north of Ireland, but aijewcation made me liberal-minded. It never had that effect on the mistress, although her [Pg 90]own taycher was an old Scotch wife that spent her time tayching the childer Scott, and Pollok's 'Course of Time,' and old Scotch ballads like that Packman one she was reciting to your friend. Now, I larnt my boys and gyurls, when I was school tayching, some pieces of Shakespeare, and got them to declaim at the school exhibitions before the holidays. I minded some of them after I was married, and, one day when it was raining hard, I declaimed a lovely piece before Persis, that's the mistress' name, when the woman began to cry, and fell on her knees by the old settle, and prayed like a born praycher. She thought I had gone out of my mind; so, after that, I had to keep Shakespeare to myself. Sometimes I've seen Tryphosa take up the book and read a bit, but Rufus, that's the baby, is just like his mother—he'll neither play a card, nor read a play, nor smoke, nor tell lies. I dunno what to do with the boy at all, at all."

"But it is rather a good thing, or a series of good things, not to play cards, nor smoke, nor tell lies," remarked Wilkinson. "Perhaps the baby is too young to smoke or read Shakespeare."

"He's eighteen and a strapping big fellow at that, our baby Rufus. He can do two men's work in a day all the week through, and go to meetin' and Sunday school on Sundays; but he's far behind in general larnin' and in spirit, not a bit like his father. Do I understand you object to smoking, sir?"

"Not a bit," replied his companion, "but my friend Coristine smokes a pipe, and, as smokers love congenial company, I had better get him to join you, and relieve him of his load." So saying, Wilkinson retired to the silent pair in the rear, took the old lady's bundle from the lawyer and sent him forward to smoke with the ancient schoolmaster. The latter waxed eloquent on the subject of tobackka, after the pipes were filled and fairly set agoing.

"There was a fanatic of a praycher came to our meetin' one Sunday morning last winter, and discoorsed on that which goeth out of a man. He threeped down our throats that it was tobackka, and that it was the root of bitterness, and the tares among the wheat, which was not rightly translated in our English Bible. He said using tobackka was the foundation of all sin, and that, if you [Pg 91]counted up the letters in the Greek tobakko, because Greek has no c, the number would be 483, and, if you add 183 to that, it would make 666, the mark of the Beast; and, says he, any man that uses tobackka is a beast! It was a powerful sarmon, and everybody was looking at everybody else. When the meetin' was over, I met Andrew Hislop, a Sesayder, and I said to him, 'Annerew!' says I, 'what do you think of that blast? Must we give up the pipe or be Christians no more?' Says Andrew, 'Come along wi' me,' and I went to his house and he took down a book off a shelf in his settin' room. 'Look at this, Mr. Hill,' says he, 'you that have the book larnin', 'tis written by these godly Sesayders, Ralph and Ebenezer Erskine, and is poetry.' I took the book and read the piece, and what do you think it was?"

"Charles Lamb's farewell to tobacco," said Coristine wildly:—

Brother of Bacchus, later born,

The Old World were sure forlorn,

Wanting thee.

'No, sir; it was a 'Gospel Sonnet on Tobackka and Pipes'; pipes, mind you, as well—all about this Indian weed, and the pipe which is so lily white. Oh, sir, it was most improvin'. And that fanatic of a praycher, not fit to blacken the Erskines' shoes, even if they were Sesayders! I went home and I says, 'Rufus, my son,' and he says, 'Yes, fayther!' Says I, 'Rufus, am I a Christian man, though frail and human, am I a Christian man or am I not?' Rufus says, 'You are a Christian, fayther.' Then says I, 'What is the praycher, Rufus, my boy?' and

Rufus, that uses tobackka in no shape nor form, says, 'He's a consayted, ignerant, bigitted bladderskite of a Pharisee!' Sir, I was proud of that boy!'

"That was very fine of your son to stand up for his father like that. You can't say that your foes were those of your own household. In such cases, young people must do one of two things, despise their parents or despise the preacher; and, when the parents go to church, the children, unless they are young hypocrites, uniformly despise such preachers."

"Yes, and to think I had never told Rufus a word about the 'Gospel Sonnets of the Sesayders!' It's a great [Pg 92]pleasure, sir, to an old man like me to smoke a pipe with a gentleman like yourself."

Coristine replied that it afforded him equal satisfaction, and they puffed away with occasional remarks on the surrounding scenery.

Meanwhile, Wilkinson was striving to draw out the somewhat offended mistress.

"Your husband tells me, Mrs. Hill, that you are of German parentage," he remarked blandly.

"Yes," she replied; "my people were what they call Pennsylvania Dutch. Do you know German, sir?"

"I have a book acquaintance with it," remarked the dominie.

"Do you recognize this?

Yo een fayter in der ayvig-eye,
Yo een fayter in der ayvig-eye,
Meen fayter rue mee, Ee moos gay
Tsoo lowwen in der ayvig-eye."

"No; I distinctly do not, although it has a Swabian sound."

"That is the Pennsylvania Dutch for 'I have a Father in the Promised Land,' a Sunday School hymn."

"Were you brought up on hymns like that?"

"Oh, no; I can still remember some good German ones sung at our assemblies, like:—

Christi Blut und Gerechtigkeit,
das ist mein Schmuck und Ehrenkleid,
damit will ich vor Gott besteh'n,
wenn ich in Himmel werd 'eingeh'n.

Do you know that?" asked the old lady, proud of her correct recitation.

"Yes; that is Count Zinzendorff's hymn, which Wesley translated:—

Jesus, thy blood and righteousness
My beauty are, my glorious dress;
Midst flaming worlds, in these arrayed,
With joy shall I lift up my head.

The translation is wonderfully free, and takes unpardonable liberties with the original."

"Graf Zinzendorff revived our Brethren when persecution had almost destroyed them. He was in America, too, and had his life saved by a rattlesnake. The Indians were [Pg 93]going to kill him, when they saw him sleeping with the snake by his side, and thought it was his Manitou."

"I hope that is not a snake-story, Mrs. Hill. I had a boy once in my school who came from Illinois, and who said that his mother had seen a snake, which had stiffened itself into a hoop, and taken its thorny tail in its mouth, trundling along over the prairie after a man. The man got behind a tree just in the nick of time, for the hoop unbent, and sent the thorny tail into the tree instead of into the man. Then the man came out and killed it. That was a snake story."

"I give the story as I heard it from our people; you know, I suppose, that there is a Moravian Indian Mission on the borders of the counties of Kent and Middlesex. I once thought of going there as a missionary, before I fell in with Mr. Hill."

"I knew a lady who married a clergyman, with the express understanding that he was to become a foreign missionary. His church missionary societies refused to accept him, because of some physical defect, so he had to settle down to a home charge. But his wife

46

never went to hear him conduct service. She said she could not listen to a fraud who had married her under false pretences."

"It is a great pity he married such a woman. If a wife has not the missionary spirit in her own house, how can she expect to acquire it by going abroad? Besides, there is so much mission work to be done in a new country like this. A few years ago, this place was almost as bad as Peskiwanchow, but now it has greatly improved."

"There was a young man we met there, Mrs. Hill, in whom my friend and I were much interested," said the dominie, and proceeded to give an account of the exploit of Timotheus. He also narrated what Coristine had told him of his hero's attitude towards the catechism, as accounting for his present position. The old lady relented in her judgment of the younger Pilgrim, thought that Saul, perhaps, was too severe, and that the catechism could stand revision. Wilkinson agreed, and, the ice being completely broken between them, they also proceeded to view the scenery in a poetic light, or rather in two, the dame's a Cowperish, and the dominie's a Wordsworthian reflection. Suddenly, the latter saw the father of Try[Pg 94]phena and Tryphosa open a gate, and turn into a side road, along which the lawyer seemed not quite disposed to accompany him. The elder smoker, therefore, came back to the gate, and waited for Wilkinson and the old lady to come forward.

"Mother!" said the old man, as the pair came up to the halting place, "you've got a soft blarneying Lutheran tongue in your head—"

"Henry Cooke," she replied sharply, "how often must I tell you that Lutheran is wrong, and that I am not a Lutheran, and have ceased even to be a United Brother since I cast in my lot with you; moreover, it is not pleasant for an old woman like me to be accused of blarneying, as if I were a rough Irishman with a grin on his broad face."

"Well, well, mother, I don't care a snuff if you were a Sesayder or even a Tommykite—"

"A Tommykite?" cried Coristine, anxious to extend his knowledge and increase his vocabulary.

"It's a man called Thomas," answered the interrupted husband, "that made a new sect out our way, and they call his following Tommykites; I dunno if he's a relation of the captain or not. Give a dog a bad name, they say, and you might as well hang him; but the Tommykites are living, in spite of their name."

"Henry Cooke, your remarks are very unnecessary and irrevelant," said his wife, falling into bad English over a long adjective.

"I was just going to say, mother, that I wanted you to try and keep these gentlemen from going beyond our house to-night, because you can put it so much better than I can."

The old lady, thereupon, so judiciously blended coaxing with the apology of disparagement, that the only alternative left the pedestrians was that of remaining; for to go on would have been to treat the disparagement as real, and a sufficient cause for their seeking other shelter. The house they entered was small but neat. It consisted almost altogether of one room, called a living room, which answered all the purposes of eating, sleeping and sitting. Outside were a summer kitchen and a dairy or milk-house, and, a short distance off, were the barn and the stable, the [Pg 95]sole occupant of the latter at the time being a cow that spent most of its leisure out of doors. Supper did not take long preparing, and the travellers did ample justice to a very enjoyable meal. The dominie engaged the hostess in conversation about German cookery, Sauer Kraut, Nudeln and various kinds of Eierkuchen, which she described with evident satisfaction.

"Mrs. Hill and Wilkinson are regular Deipnosophists," remarked Coristine to the host.

"That's too deep for me," he whispered back. "But tell it to the mistress now; she's that fond of jawbreakers she'll never forget it."

"We were remarking, Mrs. Hill, that you and Wilkinson are a pair of Deipnosophists."

The old man looked quizically at his wife, and she glanced in a questioning way at the dominie.

"My friend is trying to show off his learning at our expense," the latter remarked. "One Athenæus, who lived in the second century, wrote a book with that name, containing conversations, like those in 'Wilson's Noctes Ambrosianæ,' but upon gastronomy."

"I was not aware," said the hostess, "that they had gas so far back as that."

Wilkinson bit his lip, but dared not explain, and the lawyer looked sheepish at the turn affairs were taking.

"It's aisy remembered, mother," put in the quondam schoolmaster.

"Think of astronomy, and that'll give you gastronomy; and a gastronomer is a deipnosophist. That's two new words in one day and both meaning the same thing."

The hostess turned to the dominie, with a little shrug of impatience at her husband, and remarked: "The life of a deipnosophist in gastromical works must be a very trying one, from the impure air and the soft coal dust; do you not think so, Mr. Wilkinson?"

That gentleman thought it must, and the lawyer first chewed his moustache, and then blew his nose severely and long. Fortunately, the meal was over, the host returned thanks, and the party left the table. The old man took a pail and went to water the stock, which seemed to consist of the cow, while the wife put away the supper things, and prepared for the evening's milking.

[Pg 96]The pedestrians, being told there was nothing they could do, strolled out into the neighbouring pasture, and pretended to look among the weeds and stones, at the end of the fence farthest away from the stock-waterer for botanical and geological specimens; but, in reality, they were having a battle royal.

"Corry, you ass, whatever put it into your stupid head to make a fool of that kind little woman?"

"Sauer Kraut and Speck Noodle, what did you begin with your abominable Dutch dishes for?"

"I had a perfect right to talk German and of German things with Mrs. Hill. I did not insult her, like an ungrateful cur, I know."

"I never insulted her, you blackguard, wouldn't do such a thing for my life. I had a perfect right, too, to talk Greek to the old man, and it was you put your ugly foot in it with your diabolical gastronomy. I wonder you don't pray the ground to open up and swallow you."

"I consider, sir, an apology from you to our host and hostess absolutely necessary, and to be made without any delay."

"I'll apologize, Wilks, for the deipnosophist part of it, but I'll be jiggered if I'll be responsible for your nasty gastronomy."

"That means that you are going to put all the onus of this hideous and cruel misunderstanding on my shoulders, when I explained your expression in charity to all parties, and to help you out."

"Help me out, is it? I think it was helping me into the ditch and yourself, too."

"Will you or will you not accept the responsibility of this whole unfortunate business? Here is my ultimatum: Decline to accept it, and I return to Collingwood this very night."

"Wilks, my boy, that would never do. It's dead tired you'd be, and I'd hear of you laid up with fever and chills from the night air, or perhaps murdered by tramps for the sake of your watch and purse."

"It matters nothing. Right must be done. *Fiat justitia, ruat coelum.* Every law of gratitude for hospitality cries aloud: 'Make restitution ere the sun goes down.' I understand, sir, that you refuse." So saying, the offended [Pg 97]dominie moved rapidly towards the house to resume his knapsack and staff.

"Wilks, if you don't stop I'll stone you to death with fossils," cried the repentant lawyer, throwing a series of trilobites from his tobacco-less pocket at his retreating friend. The friend stopped and said curtly: "What is it to be?"

"Wilks, you remind me of an old darkey woman that had a mistress who was troubled with sneezing fits. The mistress said: 'Chloe, whenever I sneeze in public, you, as a faithful servant, should take out your handkerchief, and pretend that it was you; you should take it upon yourself, Chloe.' So, one day in church, the old lady made a big tis-haw, when Chloe jumped up and cried out: 'I'll take dat sneeze my ole missus snoze on mysef,' waving her handkerchief all around."

"I did not delay my journey to listen to negro stories, Mr. Coristine."

48

"It has a moral," answered the lawyer; "it means that I am going to take all this trouble on myself, and hinder you making a bigger ass of yours. I'll apologize to the pair of them for me and you."

"That being the case, in spite of the objectionable words, 'bigger ass,' which you will live to repent, I shall stay."

Mrs. Hill was proceeding to milk the cow, and her husband was busy at the wood-pile. Coristine sauntered up to the old lady, and carried the milking pail and stool for her, the latter being of the Swiss description, with one leg sharp enough to stick into the ground. The lawyer adroitly remarked:—

"Turning to the subject of language, Mrs. Hill, one who has had your experience in education must have observed fashion in words as in other things, how liable speech is to change at different times and in different places."

Yes; Mrs. Hill had noticed that.

"You will, I trust, not think me guilty of too great a liberty, if I say, in reference to my friend's remark at the supper table, that gastronomy, instead of meaning the art of extracting gas from coal, has now come to denote the science of cookery or good living, and that the old mean[Pg 98]ing is now quite out of date. I thought you would like to know of the change, which, I imagine, has hardly found its way into the country yet."

"Certainly, sir, I am much obliged to you for setting me right so kindly. Doubtless the change has come about through the use of gas stoves for cooking, which I have seen advertised in our Toronto religious paper."

"I never thought of that," said the perfidious lawyer. "The very uncommon word deipnosophist, hardly an English word at all, when employed at the present day, always means a supper philosopher, one who talks learnedly at supper, either about cookery or about other things."

"I see it very clearly now. In town, of course, supper is taken by gas light, so that the talker at supper is a talker by gas-light?"

"Yes, but the word gas, even the idea of it, has gone out of fashion, through its figurative use to designate empty, vapouring talk; therefore, when deipnosophist and gastronomer are spoken, the former is employed to denote learned talkers at supper, such as we were half an hour ago, and the latter, to signify one who enjoys the culinary pleasures of the table."

"I am sure I am very much indebted to you, sir, for taking the trouble to correct an old woman far behind the age, and to save her the mortification of making mistakes in conversation with those who might know better."

"Do not mention it, I beg. Should I, do you think, say anything of this to Mr. Hill?"

"Oh, no," replied the old lady, laughingly; "he has forgotten all about these new words already; and, even if he had not, he would never dare to make use of them, unless they were in Shakespeare or the Bible or the School Readers."

By this time the milking was over, and the lawyer, relieved in part, yet with not unclouded conscience, carried pail and stool to the milkhouse.

The old man and Coristine sat down on a bench outside the house and smoked their pipes. Mrs. Hill occupied a rocking-chair just inside the doorway, and the dominie sat on the doorsill at her feet.

"Mother," called Mr. Hill to his spouse, "whatever has become of Rufus?"

[Pg 99]"You know very well, Henry Cooke, that Rufus is helping Andrew Hislop with his bee, and will not be back before morning. The young people are to have a dance after the bee, and then a late supper, at which the deipnosophists will do justice to Abigail's gastronomy." This was said with an approving side glance at the lawyer. When Wilkinson looked up, his friend perceived at once that his offence was forgiven. The husband, without removing the pipe from between his teeth, mumbled, "Just so, to be sure."

"Is your son's name William Rufus, Mrs. Hill?" enquired the dominie.

"No; it is simply Rufus. William, you know, is not a Scripture name. We thought of baptizing him Narcissus, which comes just before Tryphena, but my husband said, as he was the youngest, he should come lower down in the chapter, and after Persis, which is my name."

"I was tayching school, and a bachelor," put in the said husband, "when there was a county meeting—they call them conventions now—that Persis was at. They called her Miss Persis Prophayt, but it was spelled like the English Prophet. She was that pretty and nice-spoken then I couldn't kape my eyes off her. She's gone off her nice looks and ways a dale since that time. Then I went back to the childer and the Scripture readins, with a big dictionary at my elbow for the long names. 'The beloved Persis' was forever coming up, till the gyurls would giggle and make my face as red as a turkey cock. So I had this farrum and some money saved, and I sent to ask the beloved Persis to put me out of my misery and confusion of countenance."

"Indeed he did," said the old lady, with a merry laugh, "and what do you think was his way of popping the question?"

"Oh, let us hear, Mrs. Hill," cried Coristine.

"Mother, if you do," interposed the old man, "I'll put my foot down on your convention of retired taychers at Owen Sound." But mother paid no attention to the threat.

"He asked if I knew the story of Mahomet and the mountain, and how Mahomet said, if the mountain will not come to the prophet, the prophet must go to the moun[Pg 100]tain. So, said he, you are the prophet and must come to my house under the mountain, and be a Hill yourself. It was so funny and clever that I came; besides I was glad to change the name Prophet. People were never tired making the most ridiculous plays upon it. The old Scotch schoolmistress, who taught me partly, was named Miss Lawson, so they called us Profit and Loss; and they pronounced my Christian name as if it was Purses, and nicknamed me Property, and took terrible liberties with my nomenclature." At this the whole company laughed heartily, after which the dominie said: "I see your pipe is out, Corry; you might favour our kind friends with a song." The lawyer did not know what to sing, but took his inspiration, finally, from Wilkinson's last question, and sang the ballad of William Rufus, as far as:—

Men called him William Rufus because of his red beard,
A proud and naughty king he was, and greatly to be feared;
But an arrow from a cross-bow, sirs, hit him in the middell,
And, instead of a royal stag that day, a king of England fell.

Then the correct ear and literary sense of the dominie were offended, and he opened out on his friend.

"I think, Corry, that you might at least have saved our generous hosts the infliction of your wretched travesties. The third line, Mrs Hill, is really:—

But an arrow from a cross-bow, sirs, the fiercest pride can quell.

There is nothing so vulgar as hitting in the verse, and your ear for poetry must tell you that *middle* cannot rhyme with *fell*, even if it were not a piece of the most Gothic barbarity. Thus a fine English song, such as I love to hear, is murdered."

"My opinion," said the host, "my opinion is that you could'nt quell a man's pride better than by hitting him fair in the middle. It might be against the laws of war, but it would double him up, and take all the consayt out of him sudden. I mind when Rufus was out seeing his sisters, there was a parson got him to play cricket, and aggravated the boy by bowling him out, and catching his ball, and sneering at him for a good misser and a butter-fingers; so, when he went to the bat again, he looked carefully at the ball and got it on the tip of his bat, and, the next thing he knowed, the parson was doubled up like a [Pg 101]jack knife. He had been hit fair in the middle, where the bad boy meant to do it. There was no sarvice next Sunday, no, nor for two weeks."

"That was very wrong of Rufus," said the old lady with a sigh, "however, he did offer to remunerate Mr. Perrowne for his medical expenses, but the gentleman refused to accept any equivalent, and said it was the fortune of war, which made Rufus feel humiliated and sorry."

Night had fallen, and the coal oil lamp was lit. The old lady deposited a large Bible on the table, to which her husband drew in a chair, after asking each of his guests unsuccessfully to conduct family worship. He read with emphasis and feeling the 91st Psalm, and thereafter, falling on his knees, offered a short but comprehensive prayer, in which the absent children were included, and the two wayfarers were not forgotten. While the good wife went out to

50

the dairy to see that the milk was covered up from an invisible cat, the men undressed, and the pedestrians turned into a double bed, the property of the missing Rufus. The head of the household also turned in upon his couch, and coughed, the latter being a signal to his wife. She came in, blew out the lamp, and retired in the darkness. Then four voices said "good-night"; and rest succeeded the labours of the day. "No nightmares or fits to-night, Corry, an' you love me," whispered the dominie; but the lawyer was asleep soon after his head touched the pillow. They knew nothing till morning, when they were awakened by the old man's suppressed laughter. When they opened their eyes, the wife was already up and away to her outdoor tasks; and a well-built, good-looking young fellow of the farmer type was staring in astonishment at the two strangers in his bed. The more he stared, the more the father laughed. "There's not a home nor a place for you, Rufus, with you kapin' such onsaysonable hours. It's a sesayder you'll be becoming yourself, running after Annerew Hislop's pretty daughter, and dancing the toes out of your stockings till broad daylight. So, if you're going to sesayde, your mother and me, we're going to take in lodgers."

"What are they selling?" asked the Baby.

"Whisht! Rufus, whisht! come here now; it's not that they are at all, but gentlemen from the city on a pedestrian tower," the father replied in an audible whisper.

[Pg 102]"What do they want testering the beds for! Is that some new crank got into the guvment?"

"Rufus, Rufus, you'll be the death of your poor old father yet with your ignorance. Who said anything about testing the beds? It's a pedestrian tower, a holiday walking journey for the good of their healths, the gentlemen are taking. Whisht, now, they're waking up. Good morning to you, sirs; did I wake you up laughing at the Baby?"

The roused sleepers returned the salutation, and greeted the new comer, apologizing for depriving him of his comfortable bed. Rufus replied civilly, with a frank, open manner that won their respect, and, when they had hastily dressed, led them to the pump, where he placed a tin basin, soap and towels, at their disposal. After ablutions, they questioned him as to the events of last evening, and were soon in nominal acquaintance with all the country side. He was indignant at the free and easy conduct of a self-invited guest called Rodden, who wanted to dance with all the prettiest girls and to play cards. "But when he said cards, Annerew, that's a sesayder, told him to clare, although it was only four in the morning, and he had to clare, and is on his way to Flanders now."

"I suppose you did not hear him make any enquiries regarding us?" asked the dominie.

"But I did, and it was only when he hard that you hadn't been past the meetin'-house, that he stopped and said 'ee'd 'ave a lark. Do you know him?"

"Yes," said Coristine, "he is the Grinstun man," whereat they all laughed; and the old lady, coming in with her milking, expressed her pleasure at seeing them such good friends.

After prayers and breakfast, the pedestrians prepared to leave, much to the regret of the household.

"Where are you bound for now?" asked Mr. Hill, to which Wilkinson replied, with the air of a guide-book, "for the Beaver River." The Baby, nothing the worse of last night's wakefulness, volunteered to show them the way by a shorter and pleasanter route than the main road, and they gladly availed themselves of his services. As the party walked on, the guide said to Coristine, "I hard fayther say that you were a lawyer, is that true?" Coristine answered that he was.

[Pg 103]"Then, sir, you ought to know something about that man Rodden; he's a bad lot."

"What makes you think so?"

"He knows all the doubtfullest and shadiest settlers about, and has long whispers with them, and gets a lot of money from them. His pocketbook is just bulging out with bank bills."

"Perhaps it is the payment of his grindstones, Rufus."

"You don't tell me that a lawyer, a clever man like you, believe in his grindstones?"

"Why not? Doesn't he make and sell them?"

51

"Yes; he makes them and sells them in bundles of half-a-dozen, but the buyer of a bundle only has two to show, and they're no good, haven't grit enough to sharpen a wooden spoon."

"How do you know all this?"

"Mostly out of big Ben Toner. He used to be a good sort of fellow, but is going all to ruination with the drink. I saw his grindstones and what came between 'em. It's more like a barl than anything else, but Ben kept me off looking at it close."

"Where does Toner live?"

"Down at the river where you're going. There's a nice, quiet tavern there, where you'll likely put up, and he'll be round it, likely, and pretty well on by noon. He don't drink there, though, nor the tavern-keeper don't buy no grindstones like he does. Well, here you are on the track, and I must get back to help dad. Keep right on till you come to the first clearing, and then ask your way. Good-bye, wishing you a good time, and don't forget that man Rodden." They shook the Baby warmly by the hand, and reciprocated his good wishes, Coristine promising to keep his eyes and ears open for news of the Grinstun man.

"Did you overhear our talk, Wilks, my boy?" he asked his friend.

"No; I thought it was private, and kept in the background. I do not consider it honourable to listen to a conversation to which one is not invited, and doubtless it was of no interest to me."

"But it is, Wilks; listen to this now," and volubly the lawyer poured forth the information and his suspi[Pg 104]cions concerning Mr. Rawdon. That gentleman's ears would have tingled could he have heard the pleasant and complimentary things that Coristine said about him.

The first clearing the pedestrians reached, after an hour's walk since parting with Rufus, was a desolate looking spot. Some fallow fields were covered with thistles, docks, fire-weed and stately mulleins, with, here and there, an evening primrose, one or two of which the lawyer inserted in his flower-press. There was hardly any ground under cultivation, and the orchard bore signs of neglect. They saw a man in a barn painfully rolling along a heavy cylindrical bundle which had just come off a waggon. As they advanced to ask him the way, he left his work and came to meet them, a being as unkempt as his farm, and with an unpleasant light in his bloodshot eye.

"What are you two spyin' around fer at this time o' day, stead o' tendin' to your work like the rest o' folks? Ef you want anything, speak out, 'cause I've no time to be foolin' round."

"We were directed to ask you, sir, the way to the Beaver River," said the dominie, politely. The man sulkily led them away out of view of the barn, and then pointed out a footpath through his farm, which he said would lead them to the highroad. As they were separating, Wilkinson thanked the man, and Coristine asked him casually:—

"Do you happen to know if a Mr. Rawdon, who makes and sells grindstones, has passed this way lately?"

"No," cried the sluggard farmer; "who says he has?" Then, in a quieter tone, he continued: "I heern tell as he passed along the meetin'-house way yesday. What do you want of Rawdon?"

"My friend, here, is a geologist, and so is that gentleman."

"Rawdon a geologist!" he cried again, with a coarse laugh. "Of course he is; allers arter trap rock, galeny, quartz and beryl. O yes, he's a geologist! Go right along that track there. Good day." Then he rapidly retraced his steps towards the barn, as if fearful lest some new visitor should interrupt him before his task was completed.

"It may be smuggling," said the lawyer, "but it's liquid of some kind, for that dilapidated granger has given [Pg 105]his friend away. What do hayseeds know about galena, quartz and beryl? These are Grinstun's little mineralogical jokes for gallon, quart and barrel, and trap rock is another little mystery of his. What do you think of the farmer that doesn't follow the plough, Wilks?"

"I think he drinks," sententiously responded the schoolmaster.

"Then he and Ben Toner are in the same box, and both are friends or customers of the workin' geologist. I believe it's whiskey goes between the grindstones, and that it's smuggled in from the States, somewhere up on the Georgian Bay between Collingwood and Owen Sound. The plot is thickening."

When the pedestrians emerged from the path on a very pretty country road the first objects that met their view were three stout waggons, drawn by strong horses and driven by bleary eyed men, noisy and profane of speech. Their waggon loads were covered with buffalo robes and tarpaulins, which, however, did not effectually conceal the grindstones beneath. The drivers eyed the pedestrians with suspicion, and consigned them to the lower regions and eternal perdition.

"Wilks, my dear," said the lawyer, in a sort of cool fever heat, "there's a revolver and a box of cartridges in my pack that I'd like to have in my right hand pocket for that kind of cattle."

"I have one, too," said the dominie, quietly, "but we had better pass on and not heed them. See, they are armed as well."

Just as he spoke there was a report; a pistol in the hand of the first teamster smoked, and a poor little squirrel, that had been whirring on the limb of a basswood, dropped to the ground dead.

"I'd as lief as not put a hole into the back of them d——d packs," said the second teamster, whereupon the others swore at him to shut up and save his cartridges.

"Wilks, I could once hit a silver dollar at twenty yards. Dad, I'll get the thing out anyway." The lawyer sat down, undid his knapsack and primed his revolver, which he then placed with the box of cartridges in the pocket out of which he had thrown the fossils. The dominie did the same, all the time saying: "No violence! my [Pg 106]dear friend; in this world we must pretend not to see a great many things that we cannot help seeing." The teamsters went by, and no further use for the revolver appeared. Wilkinson would not allow his companion to shoot at birds or chipmunks, and, on being expostulated with, the kindly lawyer confessed that it would have been a shame to take their innocent young lives. At last they saw a gray paper-like structure of large size on the limb of an oak pretty high up. "I'll bet you can't hit that, Wilks," said the lawyer. "I shall try," replied the dominie. They fired simultaneously and both struck the grey mass, and then the warriors ran, ran as they had hardly done since they were boys, for a hundred wasps were after them, eager to take vengeance on the piercers of their communal home. After two hundred yards had been done in quick time, they stopped and faced each other.

"I've killed three that got down my back, but the beggar that stung me on the lip escaped," said Coristine.

"I have one sting on the left hand and another on the right temple," replied Wilkinson.

"Is it safe to stop yet, Wilks?"

"Yes; they have given up the pursuit."

"Then, my poor boy, let us go into hospital." So he produced his flask and bathed the dominie's temple and hand with the cooling spirit, after which Wilkinson loosened his friend's flannel shirt and applied the same remedy to his afflicted back, down which the three dead wasps slid to the ground. The lawyer healed his own lip by allowing a little of the cratur, as he termed it, to trickle over into his mouth. "It seems to me, Wilks, that, when a man is looking for war, he's bound to get it."

"Yes; I suppose that that is what is meant by 'they that take the sword shall perish with the sword.'"

"Bad luck to these wasps; they revolved on us."

As the travellers continued their journey, Coristine turned to his friend and asked him for counsel.

"You've studied casuistry, Wilks, and I want you, as a judge of what a loyal citizen should do, to say what is our duty in regard to the Grinstun man."

"What are you, Corry, a lawyer in general practice or a revenue detective?"

[Pg 107]"A lawyer, of course, but a citizen too."

"Have you, as lawyer or as citizen, a case against Mr. Rawdon?"

"As a contributor to the revenue of the country, I think I have."

"How?"

"Well, he is making money by cheating the Government."

"Where is your proof?"

"Look at what Rufus said, at the doings of that bogus farmer, at these three teams on the road."

"Mere inferences based on circumstantial evidence."

"They're things that should be looked into, though."

"Perhaps so, but is it your business to do so? Are you a whiskey informer?"

"Come now, Wilks, that's a pretty bad name to call a man."

"That may be, but it seems to denote the rôle you have set before yourself."

"I'd like to run that brute into the ground."

"Worse and worse; you are going to prosecute, not from principle, but from malice."

"I'm going to show up a scoundrel."

"If that is your work you will never lack employment. But, seriously, Corry, *cui bono?*"

"To keep him off Miss Du Plessis' land, to prevent him marrying her, to hinder him corrupting the farmers and causing their farms to go to waste with smuggled liquor."

"As you like, but Wordsworth says:—

Whatever be the cause, 'tis sure that they who pry and pore
Seem to meet with little gain, seem less happy than before."

"A fig for Wordsworth, and his tear in the old man's eye! I'll not be happy till I bring that murdering thief of the world to justice."

Further conversation was checked by the view of the river from the top of the hill, challenging the admiration of the two lovers of scenery, and they began their descent towards the hamlet that lay on either side of the bridge which crossed the swiftly-flowing stream. Then the lawyer commenced the recitation of a poem in one of the old Irish readers:—

River, river, rapid river,

[Pg 108]in which the dominie sharply interrupted him, recommending his tall, mustachioed friend to put a stick of candy in his mouth and go back to petticoats and pinafores.

"Wilks, you remind me of a picture I saw once, in *Punch* or somewhere else, of a nigger sandwich man advertising baths, and a sweep looking at him, and saying: 'It's enough to tempt one, he looks so jolly clean hisself.' That's the way with you, always firing out Wordsworth's silly twaddle, and objecting to a piece of genuine poetry because it's in a reader. The pig-headed impudence of you birchers beats all."

CHAPTER VI.

The Maple Inn—Mr. Bigglethorpe's Store—Dinner—Worms—Ben Toner—The Dugout—Fishing in the Beaver River—The Upset Suckers—The Indignant Dominie Propitiated and Clothed—Anecdotes of Mr. Bulky—A Doctor Wanted.

A very clean and attractive hostelry received the travellers, and compelled the dominie to remark cheerfully, "Now shall I take mine ease in mine inn," which led to his lately indignant friend's response:—

Who'er has travell'd life's dull round,
Where'er his stages may have been,
May sigh to think he still has found
The warmest welcome at an inn.

P. Lajeunesse was the name on the sign, which displayed a vegetable wonder of the painter's art meant for a maple tree, for Madame Lajeunesse kept the Maple Inn. That lady, a portly brunette, with a pleasant smile and a merry twinkle in her eye, received the distinguished guests in person. Wilkinson replied to her bow and curtsey with a dignified salutation, but the lawyer shook hands with her, saying: "I hope you're very well, Madame; it's a lovely place you have here." Madame replied that it was lofely when the moustique was not, and summoned Pierre to help the dominie off with his knapsack, saying "permittit me," as she unfastened the straps of Coristine's, and removed that burden, which she deposited upon a table in the sitting-room adjoining the hall. Pierre, a bald-[Pg 109]headed French-Canadian, hiding his lack of hair under a red tuque, and sporting a white moustache of large

54

dimensions, arrived too late to help the schoolmaster, but he elevated his eyebrows, grimaced, rubbed his hands, and slid his feet apart, in pleased welcome.

"Ze chentlemans ave come to feesh lika many in ze springa monses? Feeshing not so coot as zen, bot in ze cool place vare is oles onder ze trees feesh lorrik. Is zat spoken correct, zat vord lorrik? I ave learn it from Meestare Bulky. O, a ver great feesherman."

Wilkinson replied that lurk was an excellent word, and very expressive of the conduct of fish in warm weather, explaining that he was no fisherman himself, but that his friend was attached to that kind of sport.

"Dinnare, Messieu, in one hour," remarked Madame, as she returned to her duties.

"Where can I get fishing tackle, landlord?" asked the lawyer.

"At ze store, zare is onelly one. You vill not lose yourself long in zisa city," replied mine host with an attempt at wit.

Wilkinson remained in the cool parlour, inspecting the plates on the walls and a few books on a side table. The latter were chiefly poor novels in English, left by former guests as not worth taking home, but among them was a thoroughly French paper-bound copy of Alphonse Karr's Voyage autour de mon Jardin. Falling into an easy chair, the schoolmaster surrendered himself to the charming style and subtle humour of this new found treasure.

The lawyer went straight to Mr. Bigglethorpe's store, and found himself, at the time, its sole customer. The proprietor was an Englishman of some five and thirty years, tall and thin, wearing a long full beard and overhanging moustache. He sold fishing tackle and was himself a fisherman, the latter being the reason why he had come to the Beaver River and set up store. It occupied him when fishing was poor, and helped to check the consumption of his capital. Before he married, he locked the door, when the fishing was good, and put the key in his pocket, but now Mrs. Bigglethorpe minded the shop in his absence. Having supplied Coristine with hooks and lines, and recommended him what kind of a rod to cut out of [Pg 110]the bush for ordinary still fishing, he offered to lend him one of his own fly rods, and opened his fly book for his inspection. Soon the pair were deep in all kinds of artificial flies and their manufacture, Black and Red and White Hackles, Peacock Fly, Mackerel, Green Grasshopper, Black Ant, Governor, Partridge, and a host more. The lawyer declined the rod, as the storekeeper informed him that, so late in the season and in the day, it was utterly useless to look for trout. He had better get old Batiste at the Inn to dig him up some earthworms, and go fishing with them like the boys. He would find a canoe moored near the bridge which he could use. Who it belonged to Mr. Bigglethorpe didn't know, but it was of no consequence, for everybody took it that wanted it for a morning or afternoon. If Mr. Coristine heard of any new kind of fly, perhaps he'd be good enough to remember him and let him know, something killing for autumn use, or, as people say here, for fall fishing. Mr. Coristine promised to remember him, and departed with his purchases, just as a voice, feminine but decided, called to Mr. Bigglethorpe by name to come and hold the baby, while its owner dished the dinner. "Talk about Hackles," said the lawyer to himself on the way Inn-wards, "I imagine he has somebody in there that can hackle him, long beard and all."

The dinner bell at the Maple was ringing vigorously. Monsieur Lajeunesse had taken off his coat to ring it, and stood in the doorway in a flaming red waistcoat, the companion of his tuque, over a spotlessly white shirt, to let all who dwelt on the Beaver River know that the hour of noon had arrived. The dinner, over which Madame presided, was excellent. With the soup and the fish there was white wine, and good sound beer with the entrées and solids. The schoolmaster spoke French to the hostess, chiefly about the book he had been reading, and the lawyer discussed fishing with Pierre, who constantly referred to his great authority, Meestare Bulky. Madame, charmed that her guest could converse with her in her mother tongue, generously filled his glasses, and provided his plates with the most seductive morsels. Monsieur Veelkeenson was the white-haired boy at that table, and he felt it, yielded to the full satisfaction of it. He had dined [Pg 111]royally, and was fit for anything. When his friend asked him if he would go fishing, he replied jauntily, and in a way quite unlike himself: "Why, suttenly, which would you rather do or go fishin'?"

"O Wilks," cried the lawyer, "you're a patent pressed brick! I feel like old Isaac Walton's Coridon, that said, d'ye mind, 'Come, hostess, give us more ale, and let's drink to him,' which is natural, seeing I'm called Corry."

The companions had a glass of ale after dinner, which was quite indefensible, for they had had a sufficiency at that bounteous repast. Evidently, the dominie was in for a good time. A wizened old fellow, named Batiste, with a permanent crick in his back, dug the worms, and presented them to the lawyer in an empty lobster tin, the outside of which was covered with texts of Scripture. "It seems almost profane," remarked the recipient, "to carry worms inside so much Bible language." But the merry schoolmaster remarked that it was turn about, for he had heard a Scotch preacher, who seemed to know the whole Bible by heart, say in prayer, on behalf of himself and his people, "we are all poor wurrums of the airth." "Probably, however," he continued, "he would have objected to be treated as a worm."

"They say even a worm will turn, which, if your parson was a large man, might be serious enough," replied the lawyer. "I remember, when I was a small boy, thinking that the Kings of Israel kept large men for crushing their enemies, because they used to say, 'Go and fall upon him, and he fell upon him and he died.' That might be the way with the human wurrum. It's not always safe to trust these humble men."

"Corry, you're a profane man; your treatment of sacred things is scandalously irreverent," said the dominie.

"Who began it?" retorted the victim.

"You did, sir, with your textual lobster can," replied the reprover.

"The ancient Hebrews, in the height of their pride and glory, knew not the luxury of lobster salad," Coristine remarked, gravely, as if reciting a piece.

"How do you know that?"

"Because, if I offer a prize of a Trip to the Dark Continent to the first person buying a copy of our published [Pg 112]travels, who finds the word lobster in the Bible, I shall never have occasion to purchase the ticket."

As they moved in the direction of the river, Pierre came after them and asked:—

"You make your feeshing off ze bord or in ze vatars!"

"I prefer the board," replied Coristine, "if it's as good of its kind as that you gave us at dinner."

"Keep quiet, you do not understand him," interposed the schoolmaster; "he means the shore, the bank of the river by the bord. N'est ce pas, Monsieur?"

"Oui, oui, M'syae, le bord, le rivauge de la rivière."

"Non, Monsieur Pierre, nous allons prendre le bateau," answered Wilkinson, with a dignity that his companion envied.

The red-nightcapped host called Baptiste.

"Vau t-en donc, Bawtiste, dépêche twa, trouve deux petits bouts de plaunche pour le canot."

Batiste soon returned with two boards.

"Canot 'ave no seat, you placea zem over two ends for seet down," said Pierre, relapsing into English.

Wilkinson assumed the responsibility of the boards and the fishermen proceeded to the river bank near the bridge to find the canoe. It was long, and, for a dug-out, fairly wide, but ancient and black, and moist at the bottom, owing to an insufficiently caulked crack. Its paddles had seen much service, and presented but little breadth of blade.

"I should like to place these boards," said Wilkinson, as he surveyed first them and then the dug-out; "I should like to place these boards, one across the bow and the other across the stern, but I really cannot decide which is the bow and which is the stern."

"She's a sort of a fore and after, Wilks, like the slip-ferry steamboats. I think, if you could find a bit of chalk or charcoal, and write bow on one plank and stern on the other, it would make her ship-shape and settle the business."

"I have no sympathy, Corry, with makeshifts and factitious devices. I wish to arrive at the true inwardness of this boat. At what end of a boat is the anchor let down?"

"In the *Susan Thomas* it was pretty near the bow, and I think I've seen yachts riding at anchor that way in Toronto harbour."

[Pg 113]"In the time of St. Paul, however, there were four anchors, if I remember aright, cast out of the stern."

"I don't see how the anchor is going to help us. This long Tom Coffin has nothing of the kind."

"You are sadly deficient in observation, Corry, or you would have observed a rope, very much abraded indeed, but still a rope, by which the vessel may be said, even though figuratively, to be anchored to this stake."

"It's you're the clever man, Wilks; education has done wonders for you. Now, I remember that rope is the painter; that's what The Crew called it on the dingy, and of course it was fastened to the bow."

"But to the stern of the larger vessel."

"Yes, but here there is no larger vessel. If you want one, for argument sake, you'll have to imagine the post to be it. The coffin is bow on to the shore."

"Corry, I insist, if I am to trust myself to this craft, that you call it by some other name."

"Were you ever in anything of the kind before, Wilks?"

"Never."

"Nor I." These simple words had in them a depth of meaning.

A young man came on to the bridge and leaned over the rail, looking at the fishermen. He was respectably clad in a farmer's holiday suit, was tall, strongly built, and with good features that bore unmistakable marks of dissipation. "I'll bet you that's Ben Toner," whispered the lawyer, who was examining the new-found bow prior to depositing his boards.

"Goin' fishin'?" asked the new comer, in a not unpleasant voice.

"Yes," replied Coristine; "we're going in this—what do you call it?"

"Dug-out, and mighty poor at that. Fishin's no good here now. River was a pardise for Trontah folks wunst, but it's clean fished out. I seen fellers go to a ho-ul up thayer," said the supposed Ben, pointing in the opposite direction, "and take out a hull barl-ful afore sundown. 'Taint to be did, not now, wuss luck! Wait to I come down, and I'll haylp you off with that kinew."

The speaker descended, untied the frayed painter, and [Pg 114]hauled the dug-out to a point where, the bank being higher, embarkation was more easy. He dissuaded the navigators from sitting on the boards placed over the gunwales, as likely to be, what he called, parlous, and recommended that the boards be placed on the floor of the craft to keep the water off their "paants." The fishermen consented, and sat down safely at each end facing one another, with his assistance to hold the dug-out steady, the dominie in the bow and the lawyer in the stern. They thanked their ally, bade him good afternoon, and proceeded to paddle. Ben Toner laughed, and cried to Coristine: "I'll lay two to one on you, Mister, for you've got the curnt to haylp you." The dugout, in spite of the schoolmaster's fierce paddling, was moving corkscrew-like in the opposite direction, owing largely to the current, but partly to the superior height of the lawyer, which gave his paddle a longer sweep. Still, he found progress slow, till a happy thought struck him.

"Wilks, my boy, it's paddling our own canoe we are, but too much that way. We're a house divided against itself, Wilks. Either you must turn round or I must, and, if I do, then you'll be the stern and I the bow."

"I thought there was something wrong, Corry, but the excitement incident on a new sensation absorbed my attention. Of course, I shall move, as it would be very confusing, not to say ridiculous, to invert the relative positions of the boat."

"Then, Wilks dear, wait till I paddle her near the bank, for fear of accidents."

When the bank was reached, the dominie landed, picked up his board and placed it farther back, then sat down gingerly, with his legs spread out before him, and began paddling on the same side as his companion, which zigzagged the frail craft more than ever, and finally brought it to the shore. Ben Toner, who had been laughing at the city innocents, ran down to a point opposite the dug-out, and told them to paddle on opposite sides, giving directions how to steer with one of the emaciated propellers. After that, the course of the vessel was a source of continual self-commendatory remark by the voyageurs.

After a while, they came to a wooden bridge, built upon piles resting in the stream. "This," said the school[Pg 115]master, "is the *Pons sublicius*, like that which Ancus Martius built over the Tiber. Shall we shoot it, Corry, or shall we call a halt and proceed to fish?"

The dug-out bumped on the piles, and the navigators trembled, but Wilkinson, bravely gathering his legs under him and rising to his knees on the board, threw his arms round a pile, when, in spite of Coristine's efforts, the craft slewed round and the stern got under the bridge ahead of the bow.

"Hold on, Wilks," the lawyer cried; "another bump like that and the old thing'll split in two. Now, then, we'll drop the paddles and slip her along the bridge to the bank. There's a hole under that birch tree there, and some fine young birches that will do for rods back of it. Doesn't the birch make you feel like England, home and duty, Wilks?"

"The quotation, sir, is incorrect, as usual; it is England, home and beauty."

"Well, that's a beauty of a birch, anyway."

They got ashore, and fastened the painter to a sapling on the bank, because it was not long enough to go round a pile. Then they produced their knives, and, proceeding to the place where the young birches grew, cut down two famous rods, to which they attached lines with white and green floats and small hooks with gut attachments. The lobster can was produced, and wriggling worms fixed on the hooks. "A worm at one end and a fool at the other," said the lawyer. "Speak for yourself, sir," replied the dominie. The next thing was to get into the canoe, which was safely effected. Then, the question arose, how was she to be moored in the current? Wilkinson suggested a stake driven into the bottom for the deep-sea mooring, and an attachment to the exposed root of the lovely overhanging birch for that to landward. So Coristine sprang ashore, cut a heavier birch, and trimmed one end to a point. Bringing this on board, he handed it to his companion, and, paddling up stream, brought him opposite the overarching tree. The dominie drove the stake deep into the river mud and pressed it down. The stake was all that could be desired for a deep-sea mooring, and to it the painter was attached.

"What are you going to do about your end of the vessel, Corry?" he asked.

[Pg 116]"That's all right," replied the lawyer, who, forthwith, took off coat and waistcoat.

"You are not going to undress, I hope," remarked his friend; "there is a bare possibility that people, even ladies, might be walking this way, sir, and I do not wish to be disgraced."

"Never fear, Wilks, my boy, it's my braces I am after." With this, Coristine took off these articles, and, fastening a button hole over a rusty nail in the stern, tied the other end about a root of the birch. The dug-out was securely fastened, so that the current only rocked it a little, causing the lawyer to sing "Rocked in the Cradle of the Deep." Then they sat down on their boards and began fishing.

They had a very pleasant hour hooking shiners and chub, and an occasional perch that looked at a distance like a trout. The dominie, *apropos* of his friend's braces, told Alphonse Karr's story of the *bretellier* in the Jardin des Plantes, and the credulous sceptic who did not believe that a suspender tree existed. He knew that cotton grew on a shrub, and that caoutchouc exuded from a tree, and admitted the possibility of their natural combination, but thought his deceivers had reference to braces with metal attachments.

"That reminds me," said the lawyer, "of a man from Lanark that came into our office asking where he'd find a mining geologist. He had some grey-looking cork and leather wrapped up in a newspaper, and said he had dug them out of the ground where there was lots more of both of them. I told him he had likely come on the remains of an old picnic, and that the leather was the skin of the ham they had taken out to make sandwiches of; but the impudent creature laughed in my face, as if any child doesn't know that leather is the skin of beasts, and cork, of a tree!"

"Nevertheless, Corry, he was no doubt right, and you were wrong in your scepticism. What are called mountain cork and mountain leather are forms of asbestos. They are of no use, unless it be for the lining of safes. The fibrous asbestos can be made into fire-proof clothes."

58

"So, old Leather Corks had the laugh on me there! Dad, I'll apologize for sending him to the marines next [Pg 117]time he comes in. What a thing it is to have the larnin' like you, Wilks!"

"A mere mineralogical trifle, my dear Corry, nothing more."

"Wilks, do you mind the 'Fisher's Song,' composed by the late Mr. William Bass, that's in the 'Complete Angler'? I don't suppose it would scare the fish much. It goes to the tune of 'The Pope, he leads a happy life,' like this:—

Of recreation there is none
So free as fishing is alone;
All other pastimes do no less
Than mind and body both possess;
My hand alone my work can do,
So I can fish and study too.
I care not, I, to fish in seas—
Fresh rivers best my mind do please,
Whose sweet calm course I contemplate,
And seek in life to imitate:
In civil bounds I fain would keep,
And for my past offences weep.
And when the timorous trout I wait
To take, and he devours my bait.
How poor a thing, sometimes I find,
Will captivate a greedy mind;
And when none bite, I praise the wise,
Whom vain allurements ne'er surprise.
But yet, though while I fish I fast,
I make good fortune my repast;
And thereunto my friend invite,
In whom I more than that delight:
Who is more welcome to my dish
Than to my angle was my fish."

"Well done, Corry—a very good song and very well sung,

Jolly companions every one.

Why will these wretched rhymsters couple such words as sung and one? It is like near and tears in the American war-song, 'The Old Camp-Ground.' Some people are like these fish; they have no ear at all. A practical joker, like you, Corry, once corrected a young lady who was singing:—

Golden years ago,
In a mill beside the sea,
There dwelt a little maiden,
Who plighted her troth to me.

[Pg 118]He suggested Floss for sea, because of George Eliot's Mill on the Floss, and, you would hardly believe it, did I not vouch for its truth, she actually rhymed Floss and me. It was excruciating."

"I can beat that, Wilks. I was out in the country on business, and stopped at our client's house, a farmer he was. The man that led the music in his church, an old Yank, who drawled out his words in singing, like sweeowtest for sweetest, was teaching the farmer's daughter to play the organ. He offered to sing for my benefit, in an informal way, one of my national melodies; and he did. It was 'The harp that once through Tara's halls,' and—O Wilks—he sang it to a tune called Ortonville, an awful whining, jog-trot, Methodistical thing with a repeat. My client asked me privately what I thought of it, and I told him that, if Mr. Sprague had said he was going to sing it in an infernal way, he would have been nearer the truth."

"Your language is strong, my friend. The late Mr. William Basse, as you designate him, would not have condescended to the use of such terms."

"Faith, the language isn't made that's too bad for Ortonville. You've got a big one this time, Wilks, my boy—play him!"

The dominie succeeded in bringing in his fish, a big fellow, between a pound and a-half and two pounds in weight, on which he gazed with delight, as the lawyer unhooked it, and deposited it, with a smart rap on the head, at the bottom of the canoe.

"Is that a trout, Corry?" the Dominie asked with eager pride.

"No; it's not a brook or speckled trout, for it has no speckles, and it's not a relative of the late William Basse, for it isn't deep enough in the body, nor a perch, for it's too big and has no stripes. It's either a salmon trout or a pickerel, Wilks."

"Is there not some fable about the latter fish?"

"Yes; old Isaac says that it's produced from the pickerel weed, the Pontederia, that should be coming into flower about now. I haven't seen any yet. There's another, for me this time—ugh, it's only a perch."

The schoolmaster, emboldened by success, declared that he was too cramped, and, gathering his legs together, while [Pg 119]he held on to the sides of the dug-out, succeeded in grasping the top of the deep-sea mooring. Then, with the other hand, he raised the board, and transferred it to the gunwale. Sitting upon the improvised seat with his back to the bow, he expressed satisfaction at facing his companion, for one thing, and at being out of the way of the fish in the canoe, for another. Coristine followed suit, and, when his plank was in position, said he felt something like old Woodruff in a small way.

"How is that?" asked the inquisitive dominie.

"He's a director in ever so many institutions, and is always out, sitting on boards. I have only one so far; as Shakespeare says, it's a poor one, but mine own."

"Tut, tut," replied his disgusted friend; "more desecration."

Nevertheless he smiled, as a thought came into his mind, and he remarked that the vessel was rather a small concern to have two boards of direction; to which the lawyer answered that it was no worse off in that respect than the Province of Quebec, or the Church, or the universities, which could not trust one governing body to do their work.

"I have another, a large fish," shouted the schoolmaster, wildly excited and rising to his feet. The fish pulled hard up stream till the whole extent of line and rod combined was out at arm's length. Eager to secure the prey, and thinking nothing of the precarious foundation on which he stood, he placed a foot upon the gunwale in order to reach still farther out.

"Look out, Wilks!" cried Coristine, as he also rose and grasped an overhanging branch of the birch; but it was too late. The dug-out tipped, the boards slid into the water, and with them went the dominie, rod, fish, and all. When the canoe recovered its equilibrium, Wilkinson, minus his wide awake, which was floating down the stream, was seen apparently climbing the deep-sea mooring post, like a bear on a pole, his clothes dripping where they were out of the water, his hair plastered over his eyes, and his face flushed with anger. The lawyer could not restrain his mirth, although he knew the vengeance it would excite in the dominie's breast.

"O Wilks, Wilks, my poor drowned rat of a friend, ha! ha! ha! O Moses! but it's too comical you are; [Pg 120]the nuns couldn't help it, Wilks, no, nor the undertaker's drum-major, nor a hired butler, even. Howld on, just one second more, till I'm fit to steady this divil of a dug-out for you to get in. If I only had a kodak, Wilks, you would be immortal, and the expenses of our trip would be paid. Oh, garrahow, ha! ha!"

The dominie climbed on to the bow of the dug-out, while Coristine balanced it, and made his silent way to the shore end, from which he gained the bank. There he shook himself like a Newfoundland dog, and brushed the wet hair out of his eyes. He muttered a great deal, but said nothing loud enough to be intelligible; his tone, however, was far from reassuring to his companion. The lawyer unmoored the dug-out at both ends, and set forth to recover the missing articles. He found the hat and the two boards on the shore, a short way down the river, and, in the middle of the stream, recaptured the fishing-rod. To his great delight, the fish was still on the hook, and he imparted the joyful news to his shivering friend, but got no single word in reply. It was another salmon trout, or pickerel, or some such fish, and he deposited it gleefully in the bottom of the canoe with the others, which had not escaped in the tip-over. Returning, he handed Wilkinson his hat, and hoped he was none the worse of his ducking. The schoolmaster took the wide-awake, but gave no answer. Then the lawyer invited him to take his place in the boat, when the storm burst.

"Am I a fool, Mr. Coristine, an abject, unthinking, infatuated fool, to entrust my comfort, my safety, my life, to a man without the soul of a man, to a childish, feeble-minded, giggling and guffawing player of senseless, practical jokes, to a creature utterly wanting in heart, selfish and brutal to a degree?"

"Oh, Wilks, my dear boy, this is too bad. I had nothing in the mortal world to do with your tumbling out of the old dug-out, 'pon my honour I hadn't."

"Kindly keep your silence, sir, and do not outrage my sufficiently harrowed feelings by adding worse to bad. I shall go to the inn on *terra firma*, and leave you in charge of what you seem so able to manage in your own clownish, pantomimic way. Be good enough to bring my fish, and do not distinguish yourself by upsetting them [Pg 121]into their native element." With these words, and in great apparent scorn, the draggled dominie took his course along the bank and soon disappeared from view. The lawyer followed in the canoe, but more slowly, as the current was against him, and often turned the boat round. By dint of strenuous efforts he gained the bridge, and found the supposed Ben leaning over it.

"I see you've drownded your man," he remarked with a laugh.

"Yes," replied Coristine; "we had a spill."

"Had any luck?"

"Pretty fair," the lawyer answered, exhibiting his treasures.

"Perch, and chub, and shiners, and them good-for-nawthun tag ends of all creation, suckers."

"Is that what they are?" asked the disappointed fisherman, holding up the spoil of Wilkinson's rod.

"That's jest what they are, flabby, bony, white-livered, or'nary suckers. Niggers and Injuns won't touch 'em, ony in the spring; they'd liefer eat mudcats."

The lawyer tied his dug-out to the stake, while Ben, who informed him that his name was Toner, got a willow twig with a crotch at the thick end, and strung his fish on it through the gills.

"I guess you'd better fire them suckers into the drink," he said, but Coristine interposed to save them from such a fate.

"They are my friend's catch," he said, "and I'll let him do what he likes with them."

Then, attended by Mr. Toner, carrying the string of fish, suckers included, he bent his steps towards the Maple Inn.

When they arrived, they found Madame standing in the doorway. She admired the fish, and complimented Coristine on his success. He, however, disclaimed most of them in favour of his friend, for whose health and whereabouts he enquired with much earnestness.

"Ze pauvre Meestare Veelkeensen retires himselfa in ze chomber to shongje his vet habillement vit datta o' Pierre. I 'opes he catcha no cold."

"Better mix him a hot drink, Madame," said Mr. Toner.

[Pg 122]"I 'ave fear, Ben, you lofe too moch hot dreenks," replied Madame.

"That's jest where you're out, Missus; I take my little tods cold."

"Hot or cold, you take nossing in our salon."

"Naw, not so long as I can get better stuff, real white wheat that ain't seen the water barl."

The lawyer noticed this unguarded saying of Toner's, but this did not hinder his asking if Madame had hot water, and could mix some real Irish punch for his afflicted friend. Madame had no Irish, but she had some good Scotcha veesky, which Coristine said would do, only, instead of Irish punch, the mixture would be Scotch toddy. The toddy procured, he sprang up-stairs, two steps at a time, meeting Monsieur Lajeunesse, descending with an armful of wet clothes. Bursting into the room to which the dominie had been led, he found him on a chair drying himself by detachments. Already his upper man had been rubbed by Pierre, and clothed with a shirt, vest and velveteen coat from his wardrobe. Now he was polishing his nether extremities with a towel, preparatory to adding a pair of gaudy striped trousers to his borrowed gear. Striding up to him with a ferocious air, the lawyer presented the smoking glass, exclaiming: "Drink this down, Wilks, or I'll kill you where you sit."

"What is it?" feebly asked the schoolmaster, feeling the weakness of his kilted position.

"It's toddy, whiskey toddy, Scotch whiskey toddy, the only thing that'll save your life," cried Coristine, with firmness amounting to intimidation. The dominie sipped the glass, stirred it with the spoon, and gradually finished the mixture. Then, laying the tumbler on the table beside his watch and pocketbook, he finished his rubbing-down, and encased his legs in Pierre's Sunday trousers. As he turned up the latter, and pulled on a pair of his own socks, he remarked to his friend that he felt better already, and was much obliged to him for the toddy.

"Don't mention it, my boy, I'm so glad it's done you good."

"I fear, Corry, that I was hasty and unjust to you when I came out of the water."

"Oh well, Wilks darlin', let us say no more about it, [Pg 123]or, like the late Mr. William Basse, I'll for my past offences weep. I don't know what it is exactly you're like now. If you had the faytures, you would do for one of the Peoplesh. You and the grinstun man could hunt in couples. With a billy cock-hat on the side of your head, you'd make a sporting gent. Are you feeling pretty well, Wilks, as far as the clothes will let you?"

"Yes; I am all right again, I think."

"Then I must damp the ardour of ingenuous youth,
And dash the cup of joy to earth
Ere it be running o'er.
Wilks, prepare yourself for a blow."

"Quick, Corry, make no delay—has the colonel fallen from his horse? Has his niece accepted Mr. Rawdon?"

"No; my dear friend, but those big fish, one of which you risked your precious life after, are—suckers. Ben Toner wanted to fire them into the drink, but I restrained his sucker-cidal hand. You seem to bear the news with resignation."

The lawyer accompanied his resuscitated friend down stairs. The velveteen waistcoat exhibited an ample shirt-front, and had pockets with flaps like the coat. The dominie's own blue and yellow silk handkerchief was tied in a sailor's knot round a rakish collar, that compromised between a turn-down and a stand-up; and his nether garments began with the dark and light blue broad-striped trousers and ended in a large pair of felt slippers, admirable footgear, no doubt, for seasons of extreme cold. Thus attired, Wilkinson occupied the sitting-room, and returned to the study of Alphonse Karr. Mr. Toner had left the string of fish by the door, where it was quite safe. There seemed to be no boys, no dogs, no cats, about the quiet Beaver River. Once in a long while, a solitary figure might be perceived going to or returning from the store. The only possible thief of the fish would have been a stray mink or otter prospecting for a new home, unless, indeed, Madame's fowls had escaped from the poultry yard. Coristine brought the string to his disguised companion, just as the hostess arrived to enquire after his health and renew the French conversation. Having replied politely to her questions, the schoolmaster expressed his regret that the [Pg 124]fish were so poor and especially that he had been deceived in the "suceurs." Madame did not comprehend, and said "Plait il?" whereupon he called his friend near and pointed out the offending fish. "Aw oui, M'syae, ce sont des mulets de l'eau douce, un petit peu trop tawrd dons la saison, autrement un morceau friaund." Then she proceeded to say that the smaller fish could be cooked for supper, "comme les éperlans de law baw," pointing with her finger eastward, to designate, by the latter words, the Gulf of St. Lawrence. She would boil the mullets, if Monsieur did not object, and give them to the fowls; did Monsieur take an interest in fowls? Generously the dominie handed over all the fish, through Coristine, for Madame to do what she liked with, and expressed an interest in various descriptions of poultry, the names of which he was entirely ignorant of. The interview over, he returned to his book, and the lawyer went to look for his civil acquaintance, Mr. Toner. Him he found on the bridge, and in a somewhat sulky humour, apparently by no means pleased at being sought out. Not wishing to intrude, Coristine made an excuse for his appearance in the bits of board, which he professed to have forgotten to take out of the dug-out. "That sort of lumber don't count for much in these parts," remarked Ben, suspiciously, and his intending companion retired, feeling that, though a limb of the law, he was a miserable sham.

While in the chamber which witnessed the dominie's transformation, the lawyer had perceived that its window commanded the bridge and the adjoining parts of the river. Leaving his friend in the enjoyment of his book, he ascended to the room, and watched like a detective. Soon he saw a waggon roll up to the bridge, and, almost simultaneously, a large punt in which was Ben Toner, come from nowhere. Three bundles of apparent grindstones were laboriously conveyed from the waggon to the punt, after which the waggon went back and the punt went forward, both becoming lost to sight in the foliage of road and river. Once more the bell of the Maple Inn sounded loudly, to inform the general public that the hour of six had arrived, and to summon guests to the early supper. Descending to the sitting-room, the amateur detective found his friend there, and escorted him, with much unnecessary[Pg 125]formality, to the tea table. The fish were there, betrayed, even afar off, by their not unpleasant odour, and there also was an attractive looking ham, flanked by plates of hot cakes and other evidences of culinary skill on Madame's part. She poured out a good cup of tea for the table quartette, while Pierre aided in distributing the solids. The conversation turned on fish, and, as before, the dominie spoke French to the hostess, while M. Lajeunesse made the lawyer acquainted with some piscatorial exploits of Mr. Bulky. Mr. Bulky had once been upset from the canoe, but, unlike Mr. Wilkinson, he could not swim. The case might have been a very serious one, destructive to the reputation of L'Erable ("zatta ees maybole in ze Fraynsh langwitch," the host explained) and of city visits to the Beaver River.

"How was he saved?" enquired the lawyer.

"He vas save by potting 'is foot to ze bottom," replied the host.

"I've heard of a man putting a stone on his head and walking through a river under water, but haven't believed it yet," continued Coristine.

"He had not necessity of a stone; 'is head vas op; ze rivare vas not so 'igh zan ze jouldares of Meestare Bulky," answered Pierre quite seriously.

"Then he saved himself?"

"No, sare, 'is foot save 'im; Meestare Bulky 'ave a veray 'eavy foot. Eef 'is foot hadda been also leetle as ze foot of M'syae, Meestare Bulky vould 'ave drown."

Madame's sharp ears overheard this conversation while carrying on that with Wilkinson, and broke in upon her erring spouse:—

"Teh twa, Pierre! c'n'est paw trop poli d'se moquer des pieds d'un bon pawtron."

"Mez, Angélique, mwa, me moquer, mwa? et de M'syae Bulky? Aw, ma bonne Angélique, fi donc!" and M. Lajeunesse withdrew from the table, overwhelmed with the mere suspicion of such foul treachery and base ingratitude.

Batiste had put out three wooden arm chairs, and a rocker for Madame, on the verandah, whither the party of the tea table retired. Coristine asked her permission to smoke, when it appeared that Pierre had been waiting for [Pg 126]a sign that either of his guests indulged in the weed. As he also filled his pipe, he remarked to his fellow smoker that "Meestare Bulky vare good shentleman, and rest 'ere longatimes, bot ze perfume of ze 'bonne pipe,' same of ze cigawr makea 'im seek."

"Does that interfere with your liberty to smoke?" Wilkinson asked.

"Aw, preciselly; zen most I go to ze stebble and tekka ze younga guestes zat smoke not in chombres *bouchees*, vat you call zat?"

"Literally, it means corked," replied the dominie; "but I presume you mean, with door and window closed, as it were, hermetically sealed."

"Preciselly; ve 'ave ze vord in ze Fraynsh langwitch, *érémitique*, zat ees as a religious oo leeves all alone, vis person zere bot 'imselluf. I tekka ze guestes zat lofe not ze eremitique life to ze stebble, vare ve smale ze stingy tawbawc of Bawtiste. M'syae parle Francea, meh peutehtre ne conneh le tawbawc puant, en Anglah*stingy*, de Bawtiste. C'n'est paws awgréable, M'syae. Aw, non, paw de tout, je vous asshere!"

"That is very considerate of you," remarked the schoolmaster, approvingly. "I wish all users of the narcotic were as mindful of the comfort and health of their neighbours. Regard for the feelings of others is perhaps the chief distinguishing mark of a gentleman."

"Meestare Bulky ees a shentleman, bot he 'ave no sharitay for smokinga men," replied Pierre, ruefully.

"That's where the shoe pinches, not your feet, Wilks," said the lawyer, with a laugh. "You could touch bottom, like Mr. Bulky, with these gunboats, but on all your privileged classes. Why should Bulky bulk so large in any place of entertainment as to send everybody else to a stable? Catch me smoking with that old garlic-perfumed Batiste! How about the garlic, and peppermint, and musk, and sauer-kraut, and all the other smells. Any smells about Mr. Bulky, Pierre?"

"Aw yehs; 'ees feeshing goat smale, aw, eet smale an' smale of som stoff he call ass-afeetiter, ze feesh liike ze smale, bot I am not a feesh."

"See that now, Wilks. This selfish pig of a Bulky, as Monsieur says, has no charity. He drives clean, whole[Pg 127]some smoke out of the hotel, and stinks the place up with as nasty a chemical mixture as disgusting science ever invented. He reminds me of a Toronto professor of anatomy who wouldn't allow the poor squeamish medicals to smoke in the dissecting room, because, he said, one bad smell was better than two. If I had my way with Bulky I'd smoke him blue in the face, if for nothing but to drown his abominable assafoetida, the pig!"

"Aw, non, M'syae," interrupted Pierre, to protect the idol of the Maple Inn; "Meestare Bulky ees not a peeg, but assafeetiter is vorse zan a peeg-stye. N'est ce paw, Angélique?"

"I 'ave no vord to say of M'syae Bulky," replied Madame, taking up her mending and entering the house. She was at once recalled to the verandah by a juvenile voice that called "Mrs. Latchness!" The speaker soon appeared in the person of a small boy, about twelve years old, who, hatless, coatless, and shoeless, ran up from the river bank. "Vat you vant vis me, Tommee?" asked Madame. "I come from Widder Toner's—Ben's dyin', she says, and can't move a stir. She wants to know if they's anybody here as knows anything about doctorin', and, she says, hurry awful quick!" cried the breathless youngster.

"I 'ear you spick of medical, M'syae Coristine; do you know it? Can you 'elp ze pauvre vidow?" asked Madam.

"It's mighty little I know, Madame, but I'll go. Wait till I get my flask," said the lawyer, going after his knapsack in the sitting room. Returning, he handed it to the hostess with the request that she would fill it with the best, and add any remedy she had in the house. Soon she came out of the railed-off bar with a filled flask and a bottle of St. Jacob's Oil. Pocketing them both, the lawyer said, "Come on, Tommy," and, with his guide, set out for Widow Toner's.

[Pg 128]

CHAPTER VII.

Ben's Sudden Sickness—The Spurious Priest—Coristine as Doctor—Saved by the Detective—Anxiety at the Maple—A Pleasant Evening—Sunday Morning and Ben—The Lawyer Rides—Nash and the Dominie Talk Theology on the Road—At the Talfourds—Miss Du Plessis the Real—The False Meets Mr. Rawdon—Mr. Terry and Wilkinson at the Kirk.

"What is the matter with Ben?" asked Coristine, as they single-filed along the narrow path by the river.

"He's tumbled down over some grindstones, and hurt himself, and fainted right away," replied the youthful Tommy, pulling up handfuls of tall grass and breaking an occasional twig from a bush as he stumbled along.

"What are you to the Toners?"

"I ain't nuthun' to the Toners."

"How did you come to be their messenger, then?"

"I was runnin' to the farm to tell the widder that the priest was comin', when she come out cryin' and sent me off. Guess the priest's there by now."

"What priest is it you saw?"

"I didn't see no priest. Old Mum Sullivan, she saw him, and sent and told mother to tell widder Toner, 'cos she's a Roman, too. She said it was a new priest, not Father

64

McNaughton, the old one, and she guessed he was all right, but she didn't like his looks as well as t'other's."

"Then you are not a Roman."

"Naw, what are you givin' us? I play a fife on the Twelfth."

"Oh, you are an Orangeman?"

"Yum, Young Briton, same thing."

"So, you Orangemen run to help the Roman Catholics when they are sick or want to know if the priest is coming, and then, on the Twelfth, you feel like cutting each other's throats."

"I don't want to cut nobody's throat, but we've got to sass 'em on the Twelfth to keep up the glorious, pious and immortal memory, and to whistle 'em down 'The[Pg 129]Protestant Boys.' We've got three fifes and three drums in our lodge."

After more of this edifying conversation, the pair arrived at a clearing on the river, containing a house and some out buildings, not far from its bank. These communicated by a private road with the public one, which crossed the stream about an eighth of a mile farther on. Turning the corner of the barn, Coristine saw a gray-haired woman, and a clean shaven man in clerical garb, leaning over the prostrate figure of Ben.

"Are you a doctor, sir?" asked the tearful woman, rising and coming towards him.

"Not exactly, Ma'am," replied the lawyer; "but perhaps I may be of use."

He then leaned over the sick man, and saw that he not only breathed, but had his eyes open upon the world in quite a sensible way. "What is the matter?" he asked the reverend gentleman, who was also contemplating the recumbent Toner.

"He says his back is sore, paralyzed, and that he can't move a limb," replied the priest in an unprofessional tone.

"How did it happen, Mr. Toner?" enquired the lawyer; and Ben, in a feebly and husky voice, replied:—

"I was rollin' quite a loaud on the slaant, when I got ketched with a back sprain, and the loaud slipped and knocked me down, and rolled over my stummick. That's all."

"Quite enough for one time," said Coristine; "is there such a thing as a loose door, or some boards we can make into a stretcher, anywhere about?" Ben called to his mother to show the doctor where the door was that he was going to put on the hen-yard. This was soon found, and, a blanket or two being laid upon it, the clergyman and the improvised doctor transferred the groaning patient to it, and so carried him into the house, where they undressed him and put him to bed on his face. "Say, doctor, I'll choke like this," came from the bed in the sick man's muffled voice, to the lawyer, who was ordering the widow to get some hot water and provide herself with towels or cotton cloths. "No you won't, Toner; turn your head to one side," he called. "That's better," remarked the patient, as he took advantage of the per[Pg 130]mission, and then continued: "I'd like ef you'd call me Ben, doctor, not Toner; seems as ef I'd git sooner that way." Coristine answered, "All right, Ben," and withdrew to a corner with the priest for consultation. "What's the matter?" asked the priest, in a businesslike, unsympathetic tone.

"So, you give me back my question. Well, as the water will be some time getting ready, and it will do our man no harm to feel serious for a few minutes more, I'll go into it with your reverence homeopathically. The root of his trouble is a whiskey back. That accidentally led to a muscular strain, involving something a little more paralyzing than lumbago. He has no bones broken in that strong frame of his, but the grindstones have bruised him abdominally. I hope my treatment for the root of the disease will be more successful than that of the oriental physician, who prescribed for a man that had a pain in his stomach, caused by eating burnt bread. The physician anointed him with eye salve, because he said the root of the disease lay in his eyes; had they been all right, he would not have eaten the burnt bread, and consequently would not have had the pains."

The priest chuckled beneath his breath over the story; then, with earnestness, asked, or rather whispered: "Will he get well soon?"

"Well enough, I think, to sit up in half-an-hour," replied the doctor of the moment.

"My dear sir, may I ask you to delay your treatment until I perform a religious office with your patient? This is a favourable time for making an impression," said the hitherto callous priest.

"Certainly, Father, only be short, for he is suffering physically, and worse from apprehension."

"I shall require all persons, but the one to whom I give the comforts of religion, to leave the room," called the priest aloud.

"It isn't the unction, Father?" cried Ben, piteously.

"Oh, doctor, the boy's not going to die?" besought the mother, at the boiler on the stove.

"I can answer for his reverence and myself," replied the lawyer; "he will not administer the last rites of the Church to the living, nor will I let my patient die."

[Pg 131]Then he and the widow retired, as the priest took out a book, knelt by the bedside, and opened it. The reverend gentleman, however, was in too great a hurry to begin, and too little sensible how far his penetrating voice would carry, for, at the first words of the prayer, Coristine made an indignant start and frowned terribly. The words he heard were, "Oratio pro sickibus, in articulo mortis, repentant shoulderе omnes transgressores et confessionem makere——"

He felt inclined to rush in and turn the impudent impostor and profaner of the sacred office out of the house neck and crop, especially as the poor mother took him by the arm, and, with broken voice through her tears, said: "O, doctor, doctor, it's the last words he's taking!" But his legal training acted as a check on his impetuosity, and, standing where he was, he answered the grief-stricken woman: "Never fear, Mrs. Toner, you and I will pull him through," which greatly comforted the widow's heart.

Five minutes passed by Coristine's watch, and then he determined to stand the nonsense no longer. He coughed, stamped his feet, and finally walked in at the door, followed by the widow. The pseudo priest was sitting on a chair now, listening to the penitent's confidences. "Time is up," said the lawyer fiercely, and the impostor arose, resumed his three-cornered black wideawake, pocketed his book, which really was a large pocket book full of notes in pencil, and expressed his regret at leaving, as he had another family, a very sad case, to visit that night. As he passed Coristine, the latter refused his proffered hand and hissed in his ear: "You are the most damnable scoundrel I ever met, and I'll serve you out for this with the penitentiary." The masquerader grinned unclerically, his back being to the other occupants of the house, and whispered back, "Not much you won't, no nor the halfpenny tentiary either; bye-bye!"

"How are you feeling, Ben?" the lawyer asked the sick man, as he approached his bedside.

"Powerful weak and so-er," replied the patient.

Coristine called the mother, poured some St. Jacob's Oil into the palm of her hand, and bade her rub down her son's back at the small. "Rub hard!" he said; and she rubbed it in. Three or four more doses followed, till the back was a fine healthy colour.

[Pg 132]"How does that work, Ben?"

"It smarts some, but I can wriggle my back a bit."

Then the doctor poured some whiskey out of his flask in the same way and it was applied.

"Do you think you can turn round now?" he asked; and, at once, the patient revolved, lying in a more convenient and seemly position.

"Bring the hot clothes, Mrs. Toner, and lay them on the bruised part, as hot as he can stand it. The patient growled a little when the clothes were abdominally applied, one after the other, but they warmed him up, and even, as he said, 'haylped his back.'"

"Now, Ben, when did you take whiskey last?"

"I ain't had nary a drop the hull of this blessed day."

"Is that true?"

"Gawspel truth, doctor, so haylp me."

"If you don't promise me to quit drinking, I can do nothing for you."

"But he will promise, doctor; won't you now, Benny dear?" eagerly asked the mother.

66

"Yaas!" groaned the sufferer, with a new hot cloth on him; "yaas; I guess I'll have to."

Then, the perfidious doctor emptied his flask into a glass, and poured in enough oil to disguise its taste. Adding a little water, he gave the dose as medicine to the unconscious victim, who took it off manfully, and naturally felt almost himself again.

"Have you plenty coal-oil in the house, Mrs. Toner?" enquired the family physician; and the widow replied that she had. "Rub the afflicted parts with it, till they will absorb no more; then let him sleep till morning, when he can get up and go about light work. But, mind, there's to be no lifting of heavy weights for three days, and no whiskey at all."

With these words, Coristine received the woman's warm expressions of gratitude, and departed.

Tommy had gone, so the lawyer had to go back to the Inn alone, and in the dark. He turned the barn, before which one bundle of grindstones still lay, the one, apparently, that had floored Ben. Then he made his way along a path bordered with dewy grass, that did not seem quite familiar, so that he rejoiced when he arrived at the road [Pg 133]and the bridge. But, both road and bridge were new to him, and there was no Maple Inn. He now saw that he had taken the wrong turning at the barn, and was preparing to retrace his steps, when a sound of approaching wheels and loud voices arrested him. On came the waggons, three in number, the horses urged to their utmost by drunken drivers, in whom he recognized the men that he and Wilkinson had met before they took the road to the Inn. Coristine was standing on the road close by the bridge as they drove up, but, as the man with the first team aimed a blow at him with his whip, he drew back towards the fence. "Shoot the d——d spy, boys," the ruffian cried to the fellows behind him, and, as they slacked their speed, the lawyer jumped the fence to put some solid obstacle between himself and their revolvers, which, he knew, they were only too ready to use. At that moment a horseman rode towards the party from the other side of the bridge, and, while aiming a blow with a stout stick at the first scoundrel, a blow that was effectual, called to the others, in a voice of authority, to put up their pistols "O Lord, boys, it's Nash; drive on," called one, and they whipped up their patient animals and rattled away in a desperate hurry. "You can come out now, Mr. Coristine," said the horseman; "the coast is clear."

"You have the advantage of me, sir," remarked the lawyer, as he vaulted back again into the road.

"No I have not," replied the other; "you called me a damnable scoundrel, and threatened me with the penitentiary, a little while ago. How's Toner?"

"I am obliged for your interference just now on my behalf, but must decline any intercourse with one who has been guilty of what I regard as most dishonourable conduct, profaning the sacred name of religion in order to compass some imfamous private end."

"My ends, Mr. Coristine, are public, not private, nor are they infamous, but for the good of the community and the individuals composing it. I know your firm, Tylor, Woodruff and White, and your firm knows me, Internal Revenue Detective Nash."

"What! are you the celebrated Mr. Nash of the Penetang Bush Raid?" asked the lawyer, curiosity, and admiration of the man's skill and courage, overcoming his aversion to the latest detective trick.

[Pg 134]"The same at your service, and, as the best thing I can do for you is to take you to your Inn, a dry way out of the dew, you can get on my beast, and I'll walk for a rest," replied the detective, alighting.

Coristine was tired, so, after a little pressing, he accepted the mount, and, of course, found it impossible to refuse his confidence to the man whose horse he was riding.

"What did you do with your clerical garb?" he asked.

"Have it on," replied Nash; "it's a great make up. This coat of black cord has a lot of turned up and turned down tag ends, the same with the vest, and the soft hat can be knocked into any shape with a dift of the fist. With these, and three collars, and moustache, beard, and whiskers, that I carry in my pocket, I can assume half-a-dozen characters and more."

"How do you justify your assumption of the priestly character?"

"I want information, and assume any character to get it, in every case being guilty of deception. You think my last rôle unjustifiable because of the confessional. Had I simulated

67

a Methodist parson, or a Presbyterian minister, or a Church of England divine, you would have thought much less of it; and yet, if there is any bad in the thing, the one is as bad as the other. Personally, I regard the confessional as a piece of superstitious ecclesiastical machinery, and am ready to utilize it, like any other superstition, for the purpose of obtaining information. Talk about personating the clergy; I have even been bold enough to appear as a lawyer, a quaker, a college professor, a sailor, and an actress."

"You have certainly led me to modify my opinion of your last performance."

"Which nearly gave me away. So you won't send me to the penitentiary; thanks! And now, as I said at first, how's Toner?"

"Oh, Toner's all right, with the fieriest skin on him that ever lay between two sheets. He has promised to give up drinking."

"It's very likely he'll have to."

"Why so?"

[Pg 135]"They don't allow refreshments so strong in gaol."

"Be as easy as you can with the poor fellow, Mr. Nash."

"All depends on his future behaviour, and, in some other capacity, I shall let him know his danger."

As the two figures came down the road toward the Inn, a voice hailed them, the voice of the dominie. "Is Mr. Coristine there?" it shouted.

"Yes; here am I," came from the back of the horse.

"What bones are broken or wounds received?" was the pitiful but correct question.

"Not a bone nor a wound. Mr. Nash has treated me to a ride."

"Aw ça!" ejaculated Pierre, "M'syae Nasha homme treh subtil, treh rusé, conneh tout le monde, fait pear aux mauveh sujah."

"What is he?" asked the schoolmaster, speaking English, in his eagerness; and the landlord replied in the same.

"Ee is vat you call detecteur, police offisare vis no close on 'im. Anysing vas to go in ze custom house and goes not, he find it out. O, a veray clevaire mann!"

Coristine dismounted for the purpose of introducing his companion. Personally, he would as readily have performed this office on horseback, but he knew that the schoolmaster was a stickler for ceremony. While the introduction was going on, Pierre took Mr. Nash's horse by the bridle, and led the procession home. There, Madame stood in the porch eagerly waiting for news of "ce jeune homme si courageux, si benveillont," and was delighted to hear that he was safe, and that Mr. Nash, an old acquaintance, was with him. When the party entered the house, Wilkinson looked at the detective, and then, with a start, said: "Why, you are Dowling, the Dowling who came to the Sacheverell Street School, with a peremptory letter from the trustees, to take the lower division boys, and disappeared in ten days."

"The same, Mr. Wilkinson; I knew you as soon as I heard your voice."

"You disarranged our work pretty well for us, Mr. Dow—Nash. What were you after there, if it is a fair question?"

[Pg 136]"I was after the confidence of some innocent youngsters, who could give me pointers on grindstones and their relation to the family income. As I know you both, and our friends of the hotel are not listening, I may say that I am so interested in this problem as to have made up my mind to go into grindstones myself."

These remarks led to an animated triangular conversation over the Grinstun man, in which the two pedestrians gave the detective all the information they possessed regarding that personage. They urged that an immediate effort should be made to hinder his acquiring the hand and property of Miss Du Plessis, and, thereafter, that united action should be taken to break up his injurious commerce. Mr. Nash prepared to accompany them on their walk to church in Flanders, and asked the lawyer if he had any objection to ride his horse part of the way, with a bundle behind him, if he, the detective, would carry his knapsack. Coristine consented, on condition that his new friend would also lend him his riding gaiters. Madame produced the wherewithal to spend a social half-hour before retiring, and, in answer to the detective, said: "Ze sack ees in ze commode in ze chombre of M'syae." Mr. Nash laughed, and over his glass and clay pipe, confided to his fellow-conspirators that he had a few little properties in that bag, and was much afraid that some of them would compel him to desecrate the Sabbath. "You are used to my religious performances, Mr Coristine; I hope your friend, and my old principal, Mr. Wilkinson, will not be as hard on me as you were."

Then the dominie was informed of the events of the evening, and the parties separated for the night.

Sunday morning dawned clear and cloudless, giving promise of a glorious day. Everybody in the inn was up before six o'clock; for at seven it was the intention of the three guests to take the road for a place of worship in Flanders. Ben Toner was waiting on the verandah for the appearance of Coristine; and, when that gentleman came out to taste the morning air, greeted him with clumsy effusion, endeavouring, at the same time, to press a two-dollar bill upon his acceptance. The lawyer declined the money, saying that he had no license to practise, and would, consequently, be liable to a heavy fine [Pg 137]should he receive remuneration for his services. He enquired after Ben's health, and was pleased to learn that, while his heroic remedies had left the patient "as rayd as a biled lobister," externally, he was otherwise all right, except for a little stiffness. Mr. Nash came down-stairs, dressed in a well-fitting suit of tweed, and sporting a moustache and full beard that had grown up as rapidly as Jonah's gourd. Going up to the man whom he had confessed the night before, he asked him: "Do you know me again, Toner?" to which Ben replied: "You bet your life I do; you're the curous coon as come smellin' round my place with a sayrch warnt two weeks ago Friday." Satisfied that his identity in Ben's eye was safe, the detective led him away on to the bridge, and engaged in earnest conversation with him, which made Mr. Toner start, and wriggle, and back down, and impart information confirmatory of that extorted the night before, and give large promises for the future. The two returned to the verandah, and, before the lawyer went in to breakfast, his patient bade him an affectionate farewell, adding, "s'haylp me, Mr. Corstine, ef I don't be true to my word to you and the old woman about that blamed liquor. What I had I turned out o' doors this mornin', fust thing, and I shaant take in no more. That there bailiff's done me a good turn, and I won't ferget him, nor you nuther, Doctor, ef so be it's in my power to haylp you any." Coristine took his leave of the simple-hearted fellow, and went to join the company at the breakfast table. Mr. Nash was there, but, for convenience of eating and not to astonish the host and hostess, he had placed his beard and moustache in his pocket. It was handy, however, and could be replaced at a moment's warning.

Batiste brought round the detective's horse, and the lawyer, in borrowed riding gaiters, bestrode him, hooking on to the back of the saddle a bundle somewhat larger than a cavalry man's rolled-up cloak. The bundle contained Mr. Nash's selected properties. That gentleman allowed Madame to fasten the straps of Coristine's knapsack on his shoulders, while Pierre did the same for Wilkinson. The dominie had paid the bill the night before, as he objected to commercial transactions on Sunday, so there was nothing to do but to say good bye, bestow a trifle on[Pg 138]Batiste and take to the road. The detective, after they had done half a mile's pleasant walking, took command of the expedition, and ordered The Cavalry, as Coristine called himself, to trot forward and make a reconnoisance. His instructions were to get to the Carruthers' house in advance of the pedestrians, to find out exactly who were there, and to return with speed and report at headquarters, which would be somewhere on the road. Saluting his friend and his superior officer, the lawyer trotted off, his steed as well pleased as himself to travel more speedily through the balmy atmosphere of the morning. The dominie and his quondam assistant were thus left to pursue their journey in company.

"Do you enjoy Wordsworth, Mr. Nash?" asked Wilkinson.

"Oh yes," replied the detective, "the poet, you mean, We are seven, and the primrose by the river's brim. Queer old file in the stamp business he must have been. Wish I could make $2,500 a year like him, doing next to nothing."

"There is a passage that seems to my mind appropriate. It is:—

Us humbler ceremonies now await;
But in the bosom with devout respect,
The banner of our joy we will erect,
And strength of love our souls shall elevate;

69

For, to a few collected in His name.
The heavenly Father will incline His ear.
Hallowing Himself the service which they frame.
Awake! the majesty of God revere!
Go—and with foreheads meekly bow'd,
Present your prayer: go—and rejoice aloud—
The Holy One will hear!"

"You should have been a parson, Mr. Wilkinson; you do that well. I'd like to take lessons from you; it would help me tremendously in my profession. But I find it mighty hard to do the solemn. That time in your school was almost too much for me, and your friend twigged my make-up last night."

"I find it hard," said the schoolmaster, "not to be solemn in such scenery as this on such a morning. All nature seems to worship, giving forth in scent and song its tribute of adoration to the Creator, to whose habitation made with hands we are on our way as worshippers."

[Pg 139]"'Fraid I shan't do much worshipping, church or no church. You see, Mr. Wilkinson, my business is a very absorbing one. I'll be looking for notes, and spotting my men, and working up my clues all the time the parson's bumming away."

"Ah, you have read Tennyson's 'Northern Farmer'?"

"Never heard tell of it; but I've got my eyes on some northern farmers, and they'll have my attention soon."

"Your expression, 'bumming away,' occurs in it, so I thought you had found it there. It is rather a severe way in which to characterize the modern preacher, who, take him on the whole, deserves credit for what I regard as a difficult task, the presentation of some fresh subject of religious thought every Sunday all the year round."

"My mind works too fast for most of them. I can see where the conclusion is before they have half got started. There's no fun in that, you know."

"Do you not sometimes meet with clergymen that interest you?"

"Now and then. The learned bloke who cuts his text into three, and expounds them in detail, I can't stand; nor the wooden logical machine that makes a proposition and proceeds to prove it; nor the unctuous fellow that rambles about, and says, 'dear friends,' and makes you wish he had studied his sermon. But, now and then, I fall in with a man who won't let me do any private thinking till he's done. You hear his text and his introduction, and wonder, how the dickens he is going to reconcile the two. He carries you on and on and on, till he does it in a grand whirl at the end, that lifts you up and away joyful with it, like the culminating arguments of the counsel for the prosecution, or the peeler's joyful run in of a long-sought gaol-bird. I like that sort of a parson; the rest are jackdaws."

"Perhaps they suit the average mind?"

"If they did, we ought to have graded churches as well as graded schools. But they don't, except, in this way, that people have got accustomed to the bumming. The preachers I like would keep up the interest of a child. There was one I heard on the text, 'I form the light and create darkness.' His introduction was, 'God is light and in Him is no darkness at all.' He jerked us [Pg 140]up into the light and banged us down into the darkness, almost laughing one minute and crying the next. Then he went to hunt up his man, and found him in the devil and the devil's own, all fallen creations of God. Any schoolboy could follow that sermon and take its lessons home with him. There was a logical bloke, at least he thought himself logical, who took for his text Joseph's coat of many colours, a sort of plaid kilt I should think; and said, 'I shall now proceed to prove that this was a sacerdotal or priestly garment. First, it occupies a prominent position in the narrative; second, it excited the enmity of Joseph's brethren; and third, they dipped it in blood when they sold their younger brother.' I could have proved it as logically to be Stuart tartan, and, at the same time, the original of the song 'Not for Joe,' because he lost it before he became steward to Pharaoh. Bah! that's what makes people sick of going to church. I've pretty nigh quit it."

The pedestrians trudged on for a time silently, the detective, doubtless, revolving schemes in his brain, the dominie inwardly sighing over his companion's captious criticism, to which he could not well reply, and over the absence of his legal friend, whose warm Irish heart would have responded sympathetically to the inspiration of the Sabbath morning walk. At last, Mr. Nash resumed the conversation, saying:—

"I'm afraid, Mr. Wilkinson, that you think me a pretty hard-hearted, worldly man, and, perhaps, that my calling makes me so."

"I have no right to judge you, Mr. Nash," answered the schoolmaster; "but I should think that the work of hunting down law-breakers would have the effect of deadening one's sensibilities."

"It shouldn't, any more than the work of a clergyman, a doctor, a teacher, or a lawyer. We all, if we are honest, want to benefit society by correcting evils. I see a lot of the dark side of human nature, but a little of the bright too, for, thank Heaven, there is no man so bad as not to have some little good in him. There's that Toner, once a fine young fellow; I hate to see him going to the dogs, wasting his property, breaking his old mother's heart. I'd rather save that man any day than gaol him."

[Pg 141]"Give me your hand, sir," said the dominie, heartily, transferring his staff to his left, and offering the right; "I honour you for the saying, and wish there were more officers of the law like you."

"Oh, as for that matter," replied the detective, "I and my colleagues have tried to save many a young fellow, but then—"

"What is the obstacle?"

"The obstacle is that there are men who simply won't be saved."

"Oh, I suppose that is true theologically as well as legally."

"Of course; if the law don't want to have a lot of criminals to hunt out and shut up and punish, it stands to reason that the Source of all law doesn't. But, for the good of society and the world, these criminals have to be separated from them, and their bad work stopped. To say that the law hates them, and takes vengeance on them like a Corsican, is utterly to misunderstand the nature of law. Yet, that is what nine-tenths of the parsons teach."

"That is very unfortunate."

"Unfortunate? it's diabolical. If I were to go into a good man's house, and present his children with a hideous caricature of their father, so as to terrify some and drive others clean away from him, wouldn't I deserve to be kicked out? I should think so! Now, I say every good thing in man must be found a million times better in man's Maker. If the foundation principle of human law is benevolence to society, the foundation principle of divine law must be something higher and better, not revenge. But you know these things better than I do."

"Not at all; I could not express myself better. What you have found out is stated by Dr. Whewell, the famous Master of Trinity, in the Platonic form, that every good thing in man and in the world has its archetype in the Divine Mind. Every bad thing, such as revenge and anger, has no such archetype, but is a falling away, a deflection, from the good."

"How do you explain the imputation of bad things to God, such as hate, revenge, terrorism, disease, death, beasts of prey, and all the rest?"

"In two ways; first, as a heathen survival in Chris[Pg 142]tianity, borrowed partly from pagan national religions, partly from the misunderstood phraseology of the Old Testament; and, second, as the necessary result of a well-meant attempt to escape from Persian and Manichaean dualism."

"But there is a dualism in law, in morals, in nature, and in human nature, everywhere in this world; there's no getting over it."

"Of course there is, but the difference between the dualism of fact and that of the Persian system is, that the evil is not equal, but inferior and subordinate, to the good."

"It gets the upper hand pretty often, as far as this world is concerned."

"And why? Just for the same reason that bad governments and corrupt parties often get the upper hand, namely, by the vote of the majority, through which the minority has to suffer. Talk about vicarious suffering! Every good man suffers vicariously."

"These are deep things, Mr. Wilkinson, too deep for the average parson, who doesn't trouble himself much with facts unless he find them confirmed by his antiquated articles."

"Yet my attention has been drawn to them by thoughtful clergymen of different denominations."

"Well, I don't think I'll trouble the clergymen to-day, thoughtful or not thoughtful. I've had my sermon in the open air, a sort of walking camp meeting. What did they call these fellows who studied on the move?"

"Peripatetics."

"That's it; we're a peripatetic church."

"But, without praise or prayer or scripture lessons, which are more important than the sermon."

"Oh, you can do the praise and prayer part in a quiet way, as a piece of poetry says that I learnt when I was a boy. It ends something like this:—

So we lift our trusting eyes
To the hills our fathers trod,
To the quiet of the skies,
And the Sabbath of our God.

That's pretty, now! Hallo! here's the doctor!"

Coristine came up at the gallop, and reported that all the people he expected to find at the Carruthers' were [Pg 143]there, Grinstun man, Mrs. Carmichael, and Marjorie, included, all except Miss Du Plessis, who was staying at a house three miles this side of the farm, helping to nurse a sick neighbour.

"Has Rawdon seen her?" asked the detective. The lawyer did not know, but suggested that they could find out by calling at the house of Mrs. Talfourd, the sick woman, on the way.

"How far are we from it?" enquired Mr. Nash.

"About a mile or a mile and a-half," replied Coristine.

"Then, Mr. Wilkinson, let us stir our stumps a bit. Can you sing or whistle? There's nothing like a good tune to help a quick march."

"Yes; sing up, Wilks," cried The Cavalry; and the dominie started "Onward, Christian Soldiers," in which the others joined, the detective in a soft falsetto, indistinguishable from a half-cultivated woman's voice. He was combining business with pleasure, dissimulation with outward praise.

"Pretty good that for a blooming young lady of five foot ten," remarked Mr. Nash, at the end of the hymn.

"Blooming young ladies with a tonsure," replied Coristine, gazing on the detective's momentarily uncovered head, "are open to suspicion."

"Wait till you see my hair." chuckled the ex-priest.

The mile and a-half was soon covered, and the trio stood before a roomy farm-house. A boy, not unlike Tommy, but better dressed, was swinging on the gate, and him the detective asked if he could see Miss Du Plessis on important business. The boy ran into the house to enquire, and came back to the gate, accompanied by the lady in question. She changed colour as her eye took in The Cavalry, immovable as a life guardsman on sentry. The detective handed her his professional card, and explained that he and his two friends had been entrusted with the duty of protecting her property and herself. "You need have no doubts, Miss Du Plessis, for the Squire, as a J.P., knows me perfectly," he continued.

"I have no fear, Mr. Nash," answered the lady, in a pleasant voice, with just a suspicion of a foreign accent; "your name is known to me, and you are in good company."

[Pg 144]Wilkinson, standing by his friend's stirrup, heard this last statement, and blushed, while The Cavalry thought he had heard a voice like that before.

"Has Mr. Rawdon seen you, or have you seen him?" asked the detective.

"Neither; but the two Marjories have been here, and have told me about him. They do not seem to admire Mr. Rawdon."

"The darlins!" ejaculated the lawyer; whereupon Wilkinson pinched his leg, and made him cry "Owch!"

The rest of the conversation between the plotters at the gate was inaudible. At its conclusion, the lady's face was beaming with amusement.

"Give me that bundle for Miss Du Plessis," said Nash to Coristine, who lifted his hat to her, and handed the parcel over.

72

"Now, for instructions," continued the commander-in-chief. "The Cavalry will go to Bridesdale, that's Squire Carruthers' place, and keep Mr. Rawdon from going to church, or bring him back if he has started, which isn't likely. This branch of the Service will also make sure that all children are out of the way somewhere, and inform older people, who may be about, that Miss Du Plessis is coming to the house during church time, and is very much altered by night-watching and sick-nursing, so that they need not express astonishment before Mr. Rawdon. Fasten these knapsacks about you somehow, Horse-Doctor; put the beast up where he'll get a drink and a feed; and go to church like a good Christian. The Infantry will halt for the present, and afterwards act as Miss Du Plessis' escort. Infantry, attention! Cavalry, form threes, trot!"

Coristine took the knapsacks, made another bow, and trotted away, while the dominie walked up to the gate, and was introduced to the fair conspirator.

After showing the detective and his bundle into an unoccupied apartment, Miss Du Plessis returned to the sitting-room where she left the dominie. In the few minutes at their disposal, he informed his new acquaintance of his chance-meeting with her uncle, of whose arrival in Canada she was in complete ignorance. The imparting and receiving this news established such a bond between the two as the schoolmaster had hitherto thought impos[Pg 145]sible should exist between himself and one of the weaker sex. Yet, in her brief absence, he had taken pains to dust himself, and shake up his hair and whiskers. His companion was preparing to tell how she had heard of him from Miss Carmichael, when another young lady, almost her counterpart in general appearance, entered the room.

"Now," said the newcomer, in a deep but feminine voice, "now the false Miss Du Plessis will go on with her nursing, while the real one takes Mr. Wilkinson's arm and keeps her appointment at the Squire's."

Miss Du Plessis clapped her hands together and laughed heartily. Wilkinson, thinking, all the time, what a pretty, musical laugh it was, could not help joining in the amusement, for Nash was complete from his wig down to his boots. The colonel's niece threw a light, woolly shawl over the detective's shoulders, and accompanied the pair to the gate, where, before dismissing them, she warned her double not to compromise her to Mr. Rawdon.

"I hope soon to have the pleasure of meeting you, Mr. Wilkinson, under more favourable circumstances," she called after that gentleman, as they moved off, and then ran into the house to hide her laughter.

The dominie felt his face getting red, with a pretty young lady hoping to meet him again, on the one hand, and a not by any means ill-looking personation of one hanging on to his arm, on the other. After a minute, the detective withdrew his hand from his companion's arm, but continued to practise his assumed voice upon him, in every imaginable enquiry as to what he knew of Miss Du Plessis, of her friend Miss Carmichael, and of the working geologist's intentions. He was thus pretty well primed, and all promised well, till, within a quarter of a mile of the house, a vision appeared that filled him and the disguised Nash, to whom he communicated his fears, with grave apprehensions as to the success of the plot. It was no less a person than the veteran, Mr. Michael Terry, out for a Sunday walk with the Grinston man. Their dread increased as the old man came running forward, crying: "An' it's comin' back yez are, my darlin' Mish Ceshile. It's a throifle pale yer lookin', an' no wonder." Saying this, Michael shook hands with Nash, and whispered: "Niver fare, sorr, Mishter Coristine towld me all about it."

[Pg 146]The made-up lady introduced her father's old servant to Wilkinson, whose apprehensions were dispelled in a similar way, so that all were prepared to give Mr. Rawdon the reception intended.

"Ullo, hold Favosites Wilkinsonia," cried the working geologist, swaggering up with a cigar in his mouth, "'ow's yer bloomin' 'ealth? That hold bloke of a Hirish haint in a 'urry to do the hamiable between 'is hold guvner's gal an' yours truly. My name, Miss, is Rawdon, Haltamont Rawdon, workin' geologist and minerologist and, between you and me and the bedpost, a pretty warm man."

"Yes; Mr. Rawdon," replied the pseudo Miss Du Plessis, "you look—well, not pretty—but warm."

"O, dash it hall, that haint wot I meant, Miss Do Please-us; I mean hi'm a man that's got the dibs, the rhino, the blunt, you know, wot makes the mare go. I don't go geologizin' round for nothin'."

"You pick up stones, I suppose?"

"Yes; grinstuns, limestun grit, that's the stuff to make you jolly."

"I have heard of drawing blood out of a stone, Mr. Rawdon, but never of extracting merriment or exhilaration from a grindstone."

"Then you don't know my grinstuns, Miss; they're full o' fun."

"Are they indeed? How amusing! In what way does the fun display itself?"

"A bundle of my grinstuns, distributed at a loggin' bee, a raisin' bee, or a campaign caucus, ware there's a lot of haxes to grind, can make more fun than the Scott Act'll spile in a month. But silence is silence 'twixt partners, which I opes you and me is to be."

The fictitious Miss Du Plessis, with much simpering and affectation, quite unworthy of the original, drew the working geologist out, and inspired him with hopes of securing her hand and property. Mr. Rawdon spoke very freely of the wealth he had in the hand and in the bush, of his readiness to make allowance for Madame Du Plessis, if that "haffable hold gent," her brother in law, was not prepared to provide for her. When they reached the house, they found that no one was at home but Tryphena, who was confined to the kitchen by culinary duties. They, [Pg 147]therefore, occupied the parlour, the Grinstun man seeing no impropriety in being there alone with a young lady whom he had met for the first time. Indeed, he was much gratified to find that the lady was not at all stiff and offish, as he had feared, but as "haffable as her huncle and more." The lady laughed, and blushed at loud compliments, as loud as the check of Mr. Rawdon's clothes, and asked flattering questions, which he answered with a jolliky and recklessness that almost astonished himself. Was there no romance, no spice of daring in his occupation? she had asked, and he, remembering that he was talking to a soldier's daughter, who would, doubtless, appreciate courage, replied enigmatically that the grinstun business was about the riskiest business on earth, and required 'eroism of no hordinary kind.

While this conversation was going on, the dominie and the veteran were walking churchward, for, as the former had signified his intention of going to a place of worship, the old man insisted on accompanying him.

"Oi was born a Catholic, sorr, and a Catholic Oi'll doie, though my darter is a Pratestant, and what's more, a Prosbytarian. She rades her Boible an' Oi rade moine, an' there's sorra a bit av differance betwane thim. If the church is good enough for her, it's good enough for the loikes av me."

"That is what I call being a Catholic in the truest sense of the term. We will not deprive people of the kingdom of Heaven because they refuse to go our way."

"Till me now, sorr, what's that that's pertindin' to be my dear young misthress, Miss Ceshile?"

"An old soldier knows how to keep a secret, I am sure. It is the famous detective, Mr. Nash."

"Sure I hope, by my sowl, that he'll make the crathur gnash his tayth. It was all I could do to kape my hands aff him, as we were walkin' along to mate yez. Him to make up to the cornel's darter, the misherable, insignifikint, bad shpokin, thavin' scrap av impidence!"

The church bell had ceased ringing, the horses and waggons were in the driving shed without any attendant, and, as the pair approached, they could hear the sound of hearty singing coming through the open windows. They entered together, the old man crossing himself as he did [Pg 148]so, and sat down in a pew near the door. The schoolmaster saw that the church was that of Mr. Errol, who occupied the pulpit. He looked round, but could not see his friend Coristine; nor was little Marjorie anywhere visible. They must have strolled on farther to Mr. Perrowne's consecrated edifice for the sake of the walk. Then, with reverent mind, the dominie joined in the simple worship of the Kirk.

CHAPTER VIII.

The Services—Nash Routs Rawdon—The Dinner Talk—The Pedestrians with the Ladies—Singing out of One Hymn-book—Grinstuns Again—The Female Vagrant and the

74

Idiot Boy—Little Marjorie—Nash's Thoughts—The Captain and the Plot—Arrival of Rufus and Ben—To Arms!

Mr. Errol's sermon was on the text, "Lord, I knew thee, that thou art an hard man." He elaborated the unfaithful servant's harsh opinion of God, and, before he sat down, completely exonerated the Father in Heaven from the blasphemous judgment of those who call themselves His children. There is a thief in the world who comes to steal and kill and destroy; he is not God, but the enemy of God's children. The dominie's heart warmed to the man who, though of a different communion, fulfilled St. Paul's ideal of a clergyman, in that he arrogated no dominion over the people's faith, but was a helper of their joy. The sermon lifted the schoolmaster up, and brought God very near; and the hearty hymns and reverent prayers helped him greatly. When the service was over, he waited, and soon Carruthers presented his comely, matronly wife, while Mrs. Carmichael recalled herself to his remembrance; and, finally, the minister, having divested himself of gown and bands in the vestry, came down the aisle with cheery step and voice to bid him welcome to Flanders. Wilkinson was happy—happier than he had been for many a long year. He seemed to have so many friends, and they were all so cordial, so glad to see him—not a hard man or woman among them; and, therefore, God could not be hard. He walked with the minister, [Pg 149]who was going to dine at Bridesdale and then ride five miles to preach at another station. He thanked him for his sermon, and talked over it with him, and, of course, quoted "The Excursion":—

If the heart
Could be inspected to its inmost folds,
By sight undazzled with the glare of praise,
Who shall be named—in the resplendent line
Of sages, martyrs, confessors—the man
Whom the best might of conscience, truth and hope,
For one day's little compass, has preserved
From painful and discreditable shocks
Of contradiction from some vague desire
Culpably cherished, or corrupt relapse
To some unsanctioned fear.

"That's just all the trouble, Mr. Wilkinson," said the delighted minister. "People think to honour and glorify God by being afraid of Him, forgetting that perfect love casts out the fear that hath torment, and he that feareth is not made perfect in love."

With such conversation they beguiled the way till they stood at the gate of Bridesdale, and entered the hospitable mansion, there to be received by the odious Grinstun man.

"What in aa' the warld, Marjorie, did Susan mean, sending us yon godless, low-lived chairact o' a Rawdon?" asked the Squire of his sister, Mrs. Carmichael.

"I cannot understand it, John," she answered; "for her own Marjorie fairly detests the little man. Perhaps it is some business affair with the Captain."

"Aweel, aweel, we maun keep the peace, sin' I'm a judge o't; but I do not like thee, Dr. Fell."

Then they all entered the house together. Wilkinson found the spurious Miss Du Plessis gone.

The dominie saw that the working geologist was boring Mrs. Carmichael, after her return to the drawing-room from laying aside her walking attire, and valorously interposed to save her. He enquired for her niece, Marjorie, and learned that that young lady had annexed Coristine as her lawful prey, and, introducing him to her grown-up cousin, had arranged the triangular journey to Mr. Perrowne's church. The service there was longer than in the kirk, so that half an hour would probably elapse before the two Anglican perverts appeared with their captive, the lawyer. Before the absentees made their appearance, a [Pg 150]man—dressed in Mr. Nash's clothes, but with the beard and moustache recognized by Ben Toner as those of the bailiff—was ushered in and greeted by the Squire as Mr. Chisholm. The rest of the company seemed to know the transformed detective, including the Grinstun man, whom he rallied on his attentions to a young lady.

75

"You're a nice man, Rawdon, when every decent person has gone to church, gallivanting with young ladies. I saw you at the Talfourds."

"Don't care a 'ang if you did," replied Rawdon, "if Miss Do Pleas us takes a shine to a warm man, and gives you 'and-to-mouth beggars the go-by, that honly shows 'er common sense."

"What has Miss Du Plessis got to do with it?"

"She's got this to do with it, that she's promised to be my missus before the week's hout."

"When?"

"Wy, this mornin'; 'ere in this blessed room."

"Oh, come, Rawdon, you are joking. Miss Du Plessis hasn't been out of Mrs. Talfourd's to-day."

"Don't you try none of your larks hon me, Mr. Chisholm. You can't take a rise hout of this kid, hinnercent has he looks."

"But, I tell you she has not. Who do you think that girl was you brought home Talfourd's place?"

"Wy, Miss Do Please us, of course; 'oo else could it be?"

Mr. Chisholm laughed loud and long, and at last ejaculated: "Miss Du Plessis! Oh, but you're a green hand, Rawdon, to take Martha Baggs for her; the daughter of old Baggs, in the revenue service. Hope you didn't give your friends away, Rawdon?"

"You think you're pretty clever, Mr. Chisholm, comin' hover me with your Marther Baggses. Hold Hirish knows Miss Do Please-us, I should say, and wouldn't go takin' no Marther Baggs for 'er."

"Mr. Rawdon," interposed the Squire, "I'll thank you to speak more respectfully of my father-in-law; as good a man, I judge, as yourself."

"No hoffence, Squire; but I wish you'd hask the hold gent to come 'ere and shut up this 'ere bailiff's mouth with 'is Marther Baggs."

[Pg 151]Mr. Terry, who preferred the society of the kitchen to that of the parlour, was produced, and, on being asked if the lady with Mr. Rawdon was Miss Du Plessis, answered that his "sight was gettin' bad, an' the sinse av hairin' too, an' if it wor Miss Jewplesshy, she had changed her vice intoirely, an' got to be cruel rough an' common in her ways. Av coorse, it moight have been the young misthress; but Talfer's was nigh to han', an' it was aisy axin'."

A horrible suspicion came over the Grinstun man, and paled his rubicund visage. He darted up to his room, and speedily re-appeared with knapsack on back and staff in hand, ready for the road. Mr. Carruthers pressed him to stay at least for dinner, but he was resolved to solve the mystery by a visit to the Talfourds, and said that, if Mr. Chisholm was right, he would not be back for a while. His retreating figure was watched with positive pleasure by most of the company, and with still greater satisfaction by the small party returning from the Anglican service.

"What garred ye fricht Rawdon awa, Mr. Chisholm?" asked the Squire.

"I wanted to eat my dinner comfortably," replied the detective, putting beard and moustache in his pocket, when all the company, except the dominie who knew, cried out, "it's Mr. Nash."

"To think of you deceiving me," exclaimed Mr. Carruthers, "and me a justice of the peace. I've a thocht to bring you up for conspiracy."

"There can be no conspiracy without at least two persons," answered the detective.

"But, man, you are two persons, that I've known off and on as Chisholm and Nash."

"When he was one of my masters," put in the dominie, "his name was Dowling."

"And this morning," remarked the man of aliases, with a smile, "I was Miss Du Plessis or Martha Baggs, so Rawdon will have hard work to find the lady of his affections."

At this juncture Coristine and his fair companions entered, and, while the young Marjorie renewed her acquaintance, Wilkinson was gravely introduced to one of his own teachers, to the no little amusement of the lady [Pg 152]herself, of the lawyer, and of the company generally who were in the secret. Miss Carmichael explained that Mr. Perrowne had declined to come to dinner, but would look in later in the day when Cecile came home; whereat many smiled, and the dominie frowned heavily. Mrs. Carruthers now announced dinner, when the Squire took in his sister, Wilkinson, her daughter, Coristine, Marjorie, and Mr. Errol, the hostess. All the pairs agreed in congratulating themselves on the absence of the Grinstun man, and looked with approbation on Mr. Nash, who, all alone but cheerful, brought up the rear. There was no room at the table for the five youthful Carruthers, who rejoiced in the fact and held high carnival in the kitchen with Tryphena and Tryphosa and their maternal grandfather. Mr. Errol had said grace, and dinner was in progress, when the hall door was heard to open, and, immediately, on went the detective's facial disguise. But the lightness of the step that followed it reassured him, so that his smooth features once more appeared. Shortly afterwards Miss Du Plessis entered, apologizing for her lateness, and taking the vacant chair between the host and the dominie.

"I was really frightened," she said to the former, "by a dreadful little man, with an Indian hat and a knapsack, who stopped and asked me if I was Miss Do Please-us. When I told him that my name was Du Plessis, he became much agitated, and cried 'Then I'm done, sold again and the money paid,' after which he used such very bad language that I actually ran away from him. I looked round, however, and saw him hurrying away towards the Talfourds'." Wilkinson looked very fierce and warlike, and attacked his food as if it were the obnoxious Rawdon.

"Cecile," said Miss Carmichael across the indignant dominie, "I told a fib about you this morning, but quite innocently. I said you would not be home to dinner."

"Neither I would, were it not that Mrs. Talfourd's sister came in after church, and offered to stay with her the rest of the day. Whom did you tell?"

"Your devoted friend, Mr. Perrowne."

Miss Du Plessis blushed a little, and the schoolmaster cut the clergyman up several times and stuck his fork into him savagely. Then he commenced a conversation with the Squire, into which the lady between them was almost [Pg 153]necessarily drawn. Mr. Nash edified Mrs. Carmichael; her daughter conversed with the minister, to the latter's delight; while Coristine divided his attentions between the hostess and Marjorie.

"What was Mr. Perrowne preaching on, Marjorie?" asked Mrs. Carruthers.

"Pillows on the ground," replied that young person.

Her cousin laughed, and came to the rescue, saying: "It was the Church, the pillar and ground of the truth; Marjorie seems to associate all English Church services with bedtime."

"There wasn't much bedtime about the service this morning," interposed the lawyer; "the parson rattled along in grand style, and gave Miss Carmichael, and all other broken reeds of dissenters, some piping hot Durham mustard. Did it sting, Miss Carmichael?"

"Is that the effect mustard has on broken reeds, Mr. Coristine?"

"It is rather a mixing of metaphors, but you must make allowance for an Irishman."

Mrs. Carruthers at once conversed with her countryman, or rather her father's countryman, on Ireland, its woes and prospects, during which Marjorie informed Mr. Errol that she had not known what made her cousin's cheeks so red when looking on Eugene's prayer-book. Now she knew; it was Durham mustard that stings. There must have been some in the book. The victim of these remarks looked severely at the culprit, but all in vain; she was not to be suppressed with a frown. She remarked that Saul had a hymn-book that made you sneeze, and she asked him why, and he said it was the snuff.

"What did Eugene put mustard in his prayer-book for?"

"Mr. Coristine didna say he put mustard in his bookie, Marjorie," said the minister; "he said that Mr. Perrowne put mustard in his sermon, because it was so fiery."

"I don't like mustard sermons; I like stories."

"Aye, we all like them, when they're good stories and well told, but it's no easy work getting good stories. That was the way our Saviour taught the people, and you couldna get a higher example."

"Why have we hardly any of that kind of teaching now?" asked Miss Carmichael.

[Pg 154]"Because the preachers are afraid for one thing, and lazy, for another. They're afraid of the most ignorant folk in their congregation, who will be sure to charge them with childishness and a contempt for the intellect of their people. Then, it takes very wide and varied reading to discover suitable stories that will point a Scripture moral."

77

"You seem to be on gude solid releegious groond doon there, meenister," interrupted the master of the house; "but Miss Du Plessis and Mrs. Carmichael here are just corruptin' the minds o' Maister Wilkinson and Maister Nash wi' the maist un-Sawbath like havers I ever hard at an elder's table. We had better rise, gudewife!"

Shortly after the company returned to the parlour, Mr. Errol signified that he must take his departure for the Lake Settlement, where his second congregation was. At this Mr. Nash pricked up his ears, and said he would saddle his horse and ride over with him. "Na, na!" cried the Squire, "he'll no ride the day; I'll just get the waggon oot, and drive ye baith there and back." Orders were given through Tryphosa, a comely, red-cheeked damsel, who appeared in a few minutes to say that Timotheus was at the gate. All went out to see the trio off, and there, sure enough, was Timotheus of Peskiwanchow holding the restive horses. It transpired that Carruthers, having lost his house servant through the latter's misconduct, had commissioned his sister to find him a substitute, and Marjorie's interest in Timotheus had resulted in his being chosen to fill the vacant situation. He grinned his pleased recognition of the two pedestrians, who bravely withstood all the temptations to get into the waggon and visit the Lake Settlement. When the waggon departed, Mrs. Carruthers went to her children, taking Marjorie with her, and Mrs. Carmichael went upstairs for a read of a religious paper and a nap. The young ladies and the tourists were the sole occupants of the sitting-room. The lawyer went over to Miss Du Plessis, and left his friend perforce to talk to Miss Carmichael.

"I hear, Miss Du Plessis, that you own a farm and valuable mineral land," said Coristine.

"Did Messrs. Tylor, Woodruff and White give you that information?" she asked in return.

"No, indeed; do you know my firm?"

[Pg 155]"Very well, seeing I have been two years in Mr. Tylor's office."

"Two years in Tylor's office, and me not know it?"

"You do not seem to take much interest in feminine stenographers and typewriters."

"No, I don't, that's a fact; but if I had known that it was you who were one, it would have been a different thing."

"Now, Mr. Coristine, please make no compliments of doubtful sincerity."

"I never was more sincere in my life. But you haven't answered me about the land."

"Well, I will answer you; I have no farm or valuable minerals, but my father left me two hundred acres of water and wild land near what's called the Lake Settlement, which he bought when Honoria married Mr. Carruthers and took up her residence here."

"Do you know if the taxes are paid on your land?"

"No, I was not aware that wild land and water could be taxed."

"Taxed is it? You don't know these municipalities. If you had a little island in your name, no bigger than this room, they'd tax you for it, and make you pay school rate, and do statute labour beside, though there wasn't a school or a road within ten miles of it. For downright jewing and most unjustifiable extortion on non-residents, commend me to a township council. You'll be sold out by the sheriff of the county, sure as eggs, and the Grinstun man'll buy your property for the arrears of taxes."

"Whatever shall I do, Mr. Coristine?" asked the alarmed young lady; "I do not wish to lose my father's gift through negligence."

"You should have taken advice from the junior member of Tylor, Woodruff and White," replied the lawyer, with a peculiar smile; "but the Grinstun man has bagged your estate."

"Oh, do not say that, Mr Coristine. Tell me, what shall I do? And who is the man you mean?"

"The man I mean is the one that met you when you came here to dinner. He is going to quarry in your farm for grindstones, and make his fortune. But, as he wants yourself into the bargain, I imagine he can't get the land without you, so that somebody must have paid the taxes."

[Pg 156]"Then it is the little wretch Marjorie told me of, the cruel creature who kicked a poor dog?"

78

"The very same; he is the Grinstun man. I've got a poem on him I'll read you some day."

"That will be delightful; I am very fond of good poetry."

"Wilks says it isn't good poetry; but any man that grovels over Wordsworth, with a tear in the old man's eye, is a poor judge."

"I admire Wordsworth, Mr. Coristine, and am afraid that you are not in earnest about poetry. To me it is like life, a very serious thing. But, tell me, do you think the land is safe?"

"Oh yes; I wrote to one of the salaried juniors, giving him instructions to look after it, just as soon as I heard what Grinstuns had his eye on."

"Mr. Coristine! How shall I ever thank you for your kindness, you, of all men, who profess to treat us workers for our living as positive nonentities?"

"By forgetting the past, Miss Du Plessis, and allowing me the honour of your acquaintance in future. By the-bye, as you admire Wordsworth, and good poetry, and airnest, serious men, I'll just go and send Wilks to you. I have a word for Miss Carmichael. Is she constructed on the same poetic principles as yourself?"

"Go away then, *farceur*! No; Marjorie is inclined to frivolity."

With a wave of her fan, she dismissed the lawyer, who began to think lady stenographers and typewriters a class worthy of platonic attention. "Short hand!" he muttered to himself; "hers is rather a long one and pretty, and she is a favourable type of her kind, but I'm afraid a pun would make her faint, when Wilks would certainly call me out and shoot me dead with his revolver."

"Wilks, my boy," said Coristine aloud, when he reached the stiff chair in which the dominie sat erect, facing Miss Carmichael on a lounge at safe distance; "Miss Du Plessis would like to hear you discuss Wordsworth and other Sunday poets. She doesn't seem to care about hearing my composition on the Grinstun man."

The dominie eagerly but properly arose, answering: "Miss Du Plessis does too much honour to my humble [Pg 157]poetic judgment, and, in regard to your doggrel, shows her rare good sense." He then walked across the room to the object of his laudation, and, taking Coristine's vacated chair, remarked that few poets preach a sermon so simply and beautifully as the author of "The Excursion." Would Miss Du Plessis allow him to bring down his pocket volume of the Rydal bard? Miss Du Plessis would be charmed; so the schoolmaster withdrew, and soon reappeared with the book all unconsciously open at "She was a phantom of delight." With guilty eyes, he closed it, and, turning over the pages, stopped at the fifth book of "The Excursion," announcing its subject, "The Pastor." It was now the lady's turn to be uncomfortable, with the suggestion of Mr. Perrowne. The lawyer, whose back had been turned to the poetic pair, looked unutterable things at Miss Carmichael, who, not knowing to what extreme of the ludicrous her companion might lead her, suggested a visit to the garden, if Mr. Coristine did not think it too warm. "It's the very thing for me," answered the lawyer, as they arose together and proceeded to the French windows opening upon the verandah; "it's like 'Come into the garden, Maud.'" They were outside by this time, and Miss Carmichael, lifting a warning finger, said: "Mr. Coristine, I am a school teacher, and am going to take you in hand as a naughty boy; you know that is not for Sunday, don't you now?"

"If it was only another name that begins with the same letter," replied the incorrigible Irishman, "I'd say the line would be good for any day of the week in fine weather; but I'm more than willing to go to school again."

"Sometimes," said the schoolteacher quietly, "sometimes the word 'garden' makes me sad. Papa had a great deal of trouble. He lost all his children but me, and almost all his property, and he had quarrelled with his relations in Scotland, or they had quarrelled with him; so that he was, in spite of his public life, a lonely, afflicted man. When he was dying, he repeated part of a hymn, and the refrain was 'The Garden of Gethsemane.'"

"Ah, Miss Carmichael, dear, forgive me, the stupid, blundering idiot that I am, to go and vex your tender heart with my silly nonsense. I'm ashamed, and could cry to think of it."

[Pg 158]"I will forgive you, Mr. Coristine," she replied, recovering from her serious fit, and looking at the victim in a way that blended amusement with imperiousness: "I will forgive you this once, if you promise future good behaviour."

An impulse came over the lawyer to shake Miss Carmichael's hand, but she made him no shadow of an excuse for so doing. It was plain that the mutual confidences of the girls, which embraced, using the word in a mere logical sense, their year long distant acquaintance with the transformed pedestrians had given maturity to the closer and more pleasant acquaintance of the day. Little Marjorie's appropriation of the lawyer as her Eugene added another ripening element to its growth; so that the two garden explorers felt none of the stiffness and uncertainty of a first introduction. What Miss Carmichael's thoughts were she only could tell, but she knew that the impetuous and affectionate Coristine required the merest trifle of encouragement to change the steady decorous tide of advancing knowledge and respect into an abruptly awkward cataract, threatening the rupture of pleasant relations or the loss of self-respect. She would have preferred talking with Wilkinson, as a check upon the fervour of his friend, but, although she laughed at the dominie's culpable ignorance of her city existence, in her secret soul it piqued her not a little. No; she would rather take refuge with the clergy, Mr. Errol or Mr. Perrowne.

Many roses were still in bloom, but, spite of many hints, Coristine's button hole remained empty. He admired the pinks, the carnations, the large-eyed pansies, "like Shakespeare's winking Mary-buds," he said, but all in vain, save a civil answer. The Day-lilies and the sweet-scented pure white and Japan lilies, the early Phloxes, the Honeysuckles against the arbours, and many other floral beauties he stopped to inspect, and wondered if Mrs. Carruthers would mind his gathering a few, although the house was full of flowers. His companion did not satisfy his wonder, only answering that she thought flowers looked so much better growing. Then he pulled himself together, and answered naturally, joking on the tall Scarlet Lychnis, now almost a garden flower of the past, which boys call scarlet likeness and scarlet lightning, and ran on [Pg 159]into accounts of botanical rambles, descriptions of curious plants, with here a little bit of reverent natural theology, and there an appropriate scrap from some flower loving poet, or a query as to where the worshippers of Wordsworth had got, if they had left "The Excursion" for the smaller pieces on the Daisy, and the Celandine, the Broom, the Thorn and the Yew. In thus talking he gained his end without knowing it, for, instead of a mere routine lawyer and impulsive Irishman, Miss Carmichael found in her companion an intelligent, thoughtful, and cultured acquaintance, whose society she thoroughly enjoyed. Occasionally an unconscious and half-timid lifting of her long eye-lashes towards his animated, handsome face thrilled the botanist with a new, if fleeting, sensation of delight. As they passed through a gate into a hillside meadow, at the foot of which ran a silvery brook, they were made aware of voices in song. The voices were two, one a sweet but somewhat drawly female soprano, the other, a raucous, loud, overmastering shout, that almost drowned the utterance of its companion. The masculine one furnished the words to the promenaders, and these were:—

Shayll we gaythurr at thee rivverr
Whayerr bright angel feet have traw-odd?

"Do you know who these are?" asked Miss Carmichael.

"If I thought he knew as much tune," replied Coristine, "I should say he was The Crew."

"Oh, tell me, please, who is The Crew?" Thereupon the lawyer launched out into a description of his travels, so comical a one that his fair companion laughed until the tears stood in her eyes, and she accused him of making her break the Sabbath. "No," she said at last; "that is not Sylvanus, but it is his brother Timotheus with Tryphosa. They are sitting in a ferny hollow under these birches down the hill, with a hymn-book between them, and as grave as if they were in church. Do you not think, Mr. Coristine, that that is a very nice and proper way for young people to improve their acquaintance?"

"Very much so, Miss Carmichael. May I go in and get a hymn book? I can run like a deer, and won't take a minute over it. One will be enough, won't it?"

[Pg 160]The lady laughed a little pleasant laugh, and replied: "I think not, sir. We are not servants, at least in the same sense, and the piano and organ are at our disposal when we wish to exercise our musical powers."

"Snubbed again," muttered Coristine to himself; then aloud: "I wish I were Timotheus."

80

"If you prefer Tryphosa's company to mine, sir, you are at liberty to go; but I think your champion of Peskiwanchow would object to such rivalry."

"Oh, I didn't mean with Tryphosa."

"You do not know what you mean, nor anybody else. Let us return to the house."

As they sauntered back, the lawyer suddenly cried out: "What a forgetful blockhead I am. I have had ever so many business questions to put to you, and have forgotten all about them."

"Had you not better leave business till to-morrow, Mr. Coristine?" asked the lady, gravely, almost severely.

"Your father's name was James Douglas Carmichael, was it not?" asked Coristine, ignoring this quietus.

"Yes," she answered.

"He came to Canada in 1848, and was, for a time, in military service at Kingston, before he completed his medical studies. Am I right?"

"How do you happen to know these things? My father was singularly reticent about his past life; but you are right."

The lawyer opened his pocket-book and took out a newspaper cutting, which he handed to his companion. "I found that at Barrie," he said, "and trust I have not taken too great a liberty in constituting myself your solicitor, and opening correspondence with Mr. MacSmaill, W.S., regarding your interests."

"It was very kind of you," she answered; "do you think it will bring us any money, Mr. Coristine?"

"Yes; it must bring some, as it is directed to heirs. How much, depends upon the wealth of your father's family."

"They were very wealthy. Papa told mamma to write home to them, but she would not. She is too independent for that."

"Will you sanction my action, and allow me to work [Pg 161]this case up? Your mother cannot be an heir, you know, save in a roundabout way; so that you, being of age, are sole authority in the matter."

"How do you know I am of age?"

"I don't; but thought that, perhaps, you might be, seeing you are so mature and circumspect in your ways."

"Thank you for the doubtful compliment. I am of age, however."

"Then will you authorize me to proceed?"

"With all my heart."

"Do you know it makes me very sorry to become your solicitor?"

"Why?"

"Because henceforth ours are mere business relations, and I, a struggling junior partner, must be circumspect too, and stand in proper awe and distant respect for a prospective heiress."

"Do not allow your reverence to carry you too far to an opposite extreme. You have been very good during most of our walk, and I have enjoyed it very much."

As she tripped in at the French window, Coristine could not reply. It is probable that he ejaculated inwardly, "the darlin'!" but, outwardly, he took out his pipe and sought consolation in the bowl of the Turk's head. While patrolling the long path down towards the meadow, he heard a low whistle, and, proceeding to the point in the fence whence it came, found Mr. Rawdon, as pale as he well could be, and much agitated. "Look 'ere, Mr. Currystone," he said, "I've bin down to Talfourds and a good bit further, and I find a fellow called Nash 'as bin about, plottin' to 'urt my business along of that brute of a Chisholm. They can't 'urt it much, but I can 'urt them, and, wot's more, I will. 'Ow I found out wot they're about is my haffair. I hain't got no time to lose, so you tell the genniwin Simon Pure Miss Do Please-us as I'll hoffer 'er a thousan' dollars cash for that there farm of 'ers till to-morrow mornin'. 'Er hacceptance must be hat the Post-hoffice hup the road hany time before ten o'clock, and the deed can be drawn hup between you and me and the Squire just has soon therehafter as she pleases. Ha, ha! pretty good, eh? Miss Do Please-us, she pleases! Bye, bye! Mr. Currystone, don't you forget, for it's business."

The Grinstun man stole along the meadow fence and travelled over the fields, back way, towards the Lake Settlement. Emptying his pipe, the lawyer found Miss Du Plessis and at once announced Mr. Rawdon's proposal, which he urged her not to accept. She said the land was certainly not worth any more, if it were worth that amount, and that a thousand dollars would be of much immediate use to her mother. But Coristine reminded her that Colonel Morton was, in all probability, with her mother now, and begged her at least to wait until their joint opinion could be procured. To this she agreed, and further conversation was checked by the arrival of Marjorie, the five young Carruthers and Mr. Michael Terry.

The whole party sallied out of the windows on to the verandah, the lawn, and thence out of the front gate, where they found the dominie in a state of radiant abstraction, strutting up and down the road, and quoting pages of his favourite poet. He had just completed the lines:—

And yet a spirit still, and bright

With something of an angel light.

The lawyer went up to him before he came near and hissed at his friend, "What about our compact?" to which the dominie, with a fierce cheerfulness, replied, "It is broken, sir; shivered to atoms; buried in oblivion. When a so-called honourable man takes a young lady walking in garden and meadow alone, and breathes soft trifles in her ear, the letter, the spirit, the whole periphery of the compact is gone. Your conduct, sir, leaves me free to act as I please towards the world's chief soul and radiancy. I shall do as I please, sir; I shall read Louisa and Ruth and Laodamia and the Female Vagrant, none daring to make me afraid. A single tress of ebon hair, a single beam of a dove-like eye, shall be enough to fortify my heart against all your legal lore, your scorn, your innuendos, your coward threats."

"Wilks, you're intoxicated."

"Such intoxication as mine is that of the soul—a thing to glory in."

"Well, go and glory, and read what you please; only add the Idiot Boy to the Female Vagrant and you'll be a lovely pair. I'm going to do as I please, too, so we're both happy at last."

Thus saying, the lawyer returned to Marjorie, while the dominie stood stock still in the road, like a man thunderstruck, repeating: "The Idiot Boy, the Female Vagrant, a pair?—and he was once my friend! A pair, a pair—the Female Vagrant, the Idiot Boy!—and that slimy, crawling, sickening caterpillar of a garden slug was once known to me! Truly, a strange awaking!"

It was now six o'clock, the time under ordinary circumstances for tea; but the circumstances were extraordinary, as the Squire, Mr. Nash and the minister had to be waited for. The party was in the road waiting for them. "Look, Eugene!" cried Marjorie; "there's Muggins. Here Muggy, Muggy, good doggie!" Muggins came on at full speed, and, striding at a very respectable pace, his master followed.

"Ow, Mr. Coristine, sow glad to see you again, I'm shore. I was delighted to see you bringing two straye sheep into the true fowld this morning. I howpe Miss Marjorie will turn out a good churchwoman; woun't you now, Marjorie?"

"I'm not a woman, and I won't be one. A woman wears dirty clothes and a check apron and a sun-bonnet. We've had a charwoman like that in our house, and a washerwoman; and in Collingwood there's a fish-woman and an apple-woman. I've seen them with my very own eyes. I don't think it a bit nice of you, Mr. Brown, to call me a charwoman."

"I said churchwoman, my dear, not charwoman."

"It's the same thing; they scrub out churches. I've seen them do it. And they're as old and ugly—worse than Tryphena!"

"Hush, hush, Marjorie!" interposed Miss Du Plessis; "you must not speak like that of good Tryphena. Besides, Mr. Perrowne means by a churchwoman one who is like me, and goes to the Church of England."

"If it's to be like you, and you will marry Eugene and go to the Church of England, I will be a churchwoman and go with you."

Mr. Perrowne glowered at the lawyer, whom, a moment before, he had greeted in so friendly a way. Coristine laughed, as he could afford to, and said: "I'm sorry, Marjorie, that it cannot be as you wish. I am not serious [Pg 164]enough for Miss Du Plessis, nor a sufficient judge of good poetry. Your friend wouldn't have me at any price; would you now, Miss Du Plessis?"

"Certainly not with that mode of asking. How unpleasantly personal children make things."

Muggins and the young Carruthers were having lots of fun. He sat up and begged for bread, he ran after sticks and stones thrown by feeble hands, he shook paws with the children, had his ears stroked and his tail pulled with the greatest good-nature. Right under the eyes of the still dumbfoundered dominie, his owner accompanied Miss Du Plessis into the house, while Coristine prevailed on Marjorie to sing a hymn with a pretty plaintive tune, commencing:—

Once in royal David's city
Stood a lowly cattle shed,
Where a mother laid her infant
In a manger for his bed;
Mary was that mother mild,
Jesus Christ her little child.

The old soldier left his grandchildren with Muggins and came to hear the hymn. "The Howly Vargin bliss the little pet," he ejaculated, and then crooned a few notes at the end of each verse.

"Fwat is it the Howly Scripchers says, sorr, about little childher an' the good place?" he asked Coristine.

The lawyer took off his hat, and reverently replied: "Of such is the Kingdom of Heaven."

The veteran crossed himself, and said: "There niver was a thruer word shpoke or in wroitin', an' fwat does the childher, the innicents, know about Pratishtants an' Cathlics, till me that now?"

As Coristine could not, the pair refilled their pipes and smoked in company, an ideal Evangelical Alliance.

Soon the waggonette came rattling along the road, and Marjorie ran to meet her Uncle John and the minister, with both of whom she was a great favourite. Mr. Nash also had a word to say to her: "You remember scolding me for not going to church when I was Mr. Chisholm? Well, I've been there this afternoon, and Mr. Errol told us we are all getting ready here for what we are to do in Heaven. Now, you're a wise little girl, and I want you to tell me what I will be able to do when I get there. It [Pg 165]can't be to hunt up bad people, because there are no bad people in Heaven. What do you think about it?"

"I know," answered Marjorie, gravely; "play chess with dead uncles and ministers, and teach tricks to the little children that never growed up."

"Out of the mouths of babes!" ejaculated Mr. Errol, who overheard the conversation; then continued: "Could anything be truer? The training in observation and rapid mental combinations, which has made you successful in your profession, is the foundation of your prowess on the chess board. Your skill in every sort of make-up enables you to manipulate handkerchiefs and oranges for children's amusement. The same training and skill our Father can turn to good account in the upper sanctuary."

"Thank you, Mr. Errol, thank you, Marjorie, my dear. Perhaps the good God will be kinder than we think, and find some use for a poor, lonely, careless detective." Mr. Nash was unusually thoughtful, yet still had an eye to business. He made diligent enquiries about Rawdon, and, at last, getting on the scent through Miss Du Plessis, found out all that Coristine and Timotheus had to tell of him. The latter had watched the working geologist slinking off in the Lake Settlement direction across the fields and by bush tracks. Mr. Terry and the children, having partaken of tea, remained out in the front with Muggins, and sang some more hymns, Marjorie leading their choir. The rest of the household, reinforced by Mr. Perrowne, who, much to Wilkinson's disgust, monopolized Miss Du Plessis, sat round the ample tea-table. In a shamefaced way, as if engaged in an illegal ecclesiastical transaction, the

English clergyman mumbled: "For what we are about to receive," and the evening meal proceeded. The Squire had ceded his end of the table to his sister, and had taken his post at her left, where he talked to the dominie, his next neighbour, and across the table to Mr. Errol. Perrowne flanked the hostess on the right, and Nash on the left. Miss Du Plessis sat between Perrowne and Wilkinson, a stately and elegant bone of contention; while the lawyer had the detective on one side and Miss Carmichael on the other. As that young lady had something to do with the arrangement of the table by Tryphosa, in the matter of napkin rings, it was, if Coristine only knew it, a [Pg 166]mark of her confidence in him that she permitted his presence on her right. Nevertheless he profited little by it, as she gave all her conversation to the minister, save when the attention of that elderly admirer was taken up by her uncle. As Perrowne was compelled to be civil to Mrs. Carruthers, while Mr. Nash entertained the lawyer, an opportunity was afforded the schoolmaster of improving his acquaintance with Miss Du Plessis, of which he took joyful advantage, feeling that in so doing with all brilliancy he was planting thorns in the breasts of two innocent beings, whom he inwardly characterized as a clerical puppy and an ungrateful, perfidious, slanderous worm. Neither the puppy nor the worm were happy, as he joyfully perceived.

The meal was over, and they were preparing to have early evening prayers for the sake of the children, when a vehicle drove up, and a burly form, clad in navy blue broadcloth with a plentiful trimming of gilt buttons, descending from it, came along the path towards the house, accompanied by Marjorie.

"It's papa!" she cried to Carruthers and his wife, who had gone to the door to see who their visitor was, and call the children in. It was the Captain, and in the buggy, holding the reins, sat The Crew. "Don't sit grinning there, you blockhead!" shouted the ancient mariner to Sylvanus; "hev ye been so long aboard ship ye can't tell a stable when you see it? Drive on, you slabsided swab!" The Captain's combination of lumbering with nautical pursuits gave a peculiar and not always congruous flavour to his pet phrases; but Sylvanus did not mind; he drove round the lane and met Timotheus.

"We have just finished tea, Captain," said Mrs. Carruthers with her pretty touch of a cultivated Irish accent; "but Marjorie will tell Tryphosa to set yours on the table at once."

"All right, Honoria!" growled Mr. Thomas; "I'm in port here for the night, and I'm a goin' to make fast; so be I hev to belay on to the lee side of a stack of shingle bolts. Now, Marjorie, my pet, give daddy another kiss, and run away for a bit. John, I want you right away."

With the latter words, the Captain took the Squire off to the far end of the verandah, and sat down with his legs dangling over among the flowers, causing his brother-[Pg 167]in-law to do the same. "John," said he, taking off his naval cap, and mopping his forehead, "you're all goin' to be murdered to-night in your bunks, else I wouldn't ha' quit dock o' Sunday."

"Whatever do you mean, Thomas?"

"I mean what I say, and well to you and yourn. Sylvanus was down at Peskiwanchow, gettin' some things his brother left there, when he shipped for you. There's a bad crew in that whiskey mill, and, fool as he is, he was sharp enough to hear them unbeknown. Says one of 'em, 'Better get out the fire-engines from town,' and he laughed. Says another, 'Guess the boys'll hev a nice bonefire waitin' for us, time we get to Flanders.' Then the low-down slab-pilers got their mutinous heads together, and says, 'The J.P. and the bailiff's got to be roasted anyway, wisht we could heave Nash in atop.' I've left the cursing and swearin' out, because it's useless ballast, and don't count in the deal any more'n sawdust. Now, John, what do you think of that?"

"It looks serious, Thomas, if your man is to be depended on."

"My man depended on? Sylvanus Pilgrim to be depended on? There's no more dependable able-bodied seaman and master mill-hand afloat nor ashore. He's true as the needle to the pole and the gang-saw to the plank. Don't you go saying wrong of Sylvanus."

"I must take Nash into confidence with us, and call up your informant," said the Squire, leading the Captain into the house and setting him carefully down at the tea table, where Mrs. Carruthers waited upon him. Then he looked up Sylvanus in the kitchen, and told him to report as soon as he had taken his supper. "We have no time to lose, Pilgrim," he added, "so let Tryphena alone till our talk is over. She'll keep."

"I ain't agoin' ter persume ter tech Trypheeny, Square, an' I'll be along in a half tack," replied The Crew.

Next, Nash was found smoking a cigar, and talking very earnestly with Mr. Errol about presentiments, and sudden remembrances of childhood's days. He dropped the conversation at once when business was mentioned, and, in a few minutes, the Squire's official room contained five men, with very serious faces, seeking to come to a full understanding of what seemed a diabolical plot on the [Pg 168]part of some spiteful malefactors. Four of these have already been indicated; the fifth was the lawyer, who proved a useful addition for pumping Sylvanus dry and taking careful notes.

While the consultation was in progress, a gentle tap came to the door, and, following it, a voice that thrilled the lawyer, saying, "May I come in, uncle; I have some news for you?" Carruthers opened the door, when Miss Carmichael told him that young Hill, the girls' brother, had arrived with another man, and wanted to see him immediately on special business that would not wait, and that they seemed to have been out shooting. The Squire went out and returned with Rufus and Ben Toner. The former related how Ben had gone to afternoon meetin' to tell what he knew of the conspiracy to clean out all the scabs in Flanders, and have trade run smooth. Coristine examined his old patient, who readily responded, and Nash, who was now Chisholm in beard and moustache, helped the interrogation. Toner's information, like that of Sylvanus, came from accidentally overhearing the talk of four men in a waggon, driving Flanders way during church time, while he was fishing in the river.

"I heerd 'em say as they'd be a big blayuz afore mornin', and as Squier Cruthers, and the bailiff, and Nash, and a raivenue gaal, had got to go to kingdom come. One on 'em says he seen Mr. Nash and got a hit off his stick. He's a goin' to lay for him straight and for them two walkin' spies likeways."

"What made you look up Rufus?" asked the lawyer.

"I thort the raivenue gaal might a been one of his sisters that's here. Besides, he's got a gun, and so have I, and I'm a goin' to be true to my word, Doctor, to you and the bailiff too, ef I have to shoot aivery mother's son of them vilyins."

The Captain and Sylvanus, with Rufus and Ben, all testified to the moving of several teams, with rough-looking characters on board, along the roads that led towards Flanders, and the Lake Settlement in particular. The Squire and Mr. Nash had noticed the same.

"Ben," said the latter, taking off his disguise, "I think I can trust you. I am the detective Nash."

Toner started, but quickly recovered himself, and, rising, gave his hand to the man of aliases, saying, "You [Pg 169]kin, Mr. Nash, s'haylp me. Old man Newcome swears he's a goin' to hev your life, but he won't ef I'm any good."

The detective shook hands warmly, and, taking Ben aside, found that he had no personal knowledge of Rawdon, the Newcome of whom he spoke being apparently the go between. The intimacy between them, which was near ruining the young man, had come about through Toner's attention to Newcome's daughter, Sarah Eliza. "But," continued the unhappy lover, "the old man's been and had Serlizer off for more'n a year, and puts me off and off and better off, till I just up and wouldn't stand it no more. I ain't a goin' to sell his stuff, nor drink his stuff, nor hev nawthun more to do along of his gang, but I'd like to know where Serlizer's put to, and I'm here and my gun, with a lot of powder and shot and slugs, for the stummik of any gallihoot as lays a finger on you, Mr. Nash, or the doctor or the gals."

Returning to the group, the detective urged immediate defensive action, leaving the offensive till the morrow. The Squire at once looked up his armoury, consisting of a rifle, a fowling piece (double-barrelled) and a pair of heavy horse-pistols, with abundant ammunition. The Captain reported that Sylvanus had a shotgun (single-barrelled), and that he had brought the blunderbuss with which he fired salutes off the *Susan Thomas*. Coristine answered for the revolvers carried by himself and the dominie. The clergy were called in and the situation explained, when both volunteered for service. Mr. Perrowne had a very good gun at his lodgings; and his landlady, whose father had been in the army, possessed a relic of him in the shape of an ancient carbine, which he was sure she would lend to Mr. Errol, with bayonet complete. He went for them, under escort of Rufus and Ben. When Mr. Terry was told, he begged for his son in law's "swate-lukin' roifle," and was as cheerful as if a wedding was in progress. Finally, Timotheus got the fowling piece and the Squire looked to the priming of his pistols. Mr. Nash, of course, had both revolver and dirk knife concealed somewhere about his person. Then Mr. Errol conducted family prayers, the children were sent to bed, the ladies briefly informed of the situation, and the garrison bidden a more than usually affectionate good-night.

[Pg 170]

CHAPTER IX.

The Squire Posts Sentries—Sylvanus Arrests Tryphosa—Change of Watchword—Nash Leads an Advance—The Cheek of Grinstuns—The Hound—Guard-room Conversation—Incipient Fires Extinguished—The Idiot Boy—Grinstun's Awful Cheek—The Lawyer and the Parson Theologize—Coristine's Hands—Doctor and Miss Halbert.

The full strength of the garrison was twelve able-bodied men, of whom five carried fowling pieces, one a blunderbuss, another a carbine, another a rifle, and four were armed with pistols. The Squire was in supreme command, and Mr. Nash was adjutant. They decided that the garrison as a whole should go on guard for the night, that is, from ten o'clock till six in the morning, a period of eight hours, making, as the Captain put it, four watches of two hours each. Thus the remaining ten were divided into two guards of five, and, as the morning guard, from four to six, would probably not be required, it was determined to put those who had most need of rest on the companion one from twelve to two. These were Captain Thomas, the veteran Terry, the two parsons, with Wilkinson, who was thrown in simply as a pistol man, the only other of the kind being the lawyer. With ammunition in their pockets, or slung round their shoulders, the first guard sallied forth under the Squire's guidance. Coristine was left to watch the front of the house behind the shrubbery bordering the fence, and keep up communication with Nash, who patrolled the road on horseback. Ben Toner's station was the path running parallel with the palings on the left of the garden, beyond which was an open field, not altogether destitute of stumps. Silvanus was posted on the edge of the meadow, at the back of the garden and out-houses; and Timotheus, on the right of the stables and connected buildings. Just where the beats of the brothers met, there was a little clump of timber, the only point affording cover to an advancing enemy, and to that post of honour and danger Rufus was appointed. [Pg 171]Having placed his men, the Squire returned to the guard-room, his office, and ordered Tryphosa to bring refreshments for the guard, to which he added a box of cigars. The guard discussed the cold ham, the cheese and biscuits, and, in addition, Mr. Errol indulged in some diluted sherry, Perrowne and Wilkinson in a glass of beer, and the Captain and the veteran in a drop of whiskey and water. The Squire took a cigar with those who smoked, but maintained his wakefulness on cold tea. Every half hour he was out inspecting the sentries. Coristine had suggested that the friendly answer to a challenge should be Bridesdale, but, lest the enemy should hear this and take advantage of it, all suspicious persons should be required also to give the countersign, Grinstuns. The dominie sneered at him for the latter; but, when he saw his friend sally forth with loaded pistol to the post of danger, his enmity died, and, rising, he silently shook hands with him at the door. Returning to the guard-room, he breathed a silent prayer for his friend's safety, and then fortified his inner man with the fare provided. Conversation accompanied the impromptu supper, and the subsequent cigar or pipe, at first led by the divines, but afterwards taken clean out of their mouths by the Captain and the veteran, who furnished exciting accounts of their experience in critical situations.

The Squire had gone out for the second time to inspect the sentries. It was eleven o'clock. Coristine, who was first visited, reported a sound of voices at the back of the house, and Toner confirmed the report. The commander-in-chief hastened to the gate leading into the hill meadow, and perceived a figure struggling in the strong grasp of Sylvanus. The sentinel's left arm was round the prisoner, and the gun was in his right hand. As they came towards the gate, the Squire heard piteous entreaties in a feminine voice to be let go, and the answer: "'Tain't no kind o' use, Tryphosy, even ef ye was arter Timotheus an' not me; that ain't it, at all. It's this: yer didn't say Bridesdale when I charlinged yer, nor yer couldn't bar-sign Grinstuns. All suspicious carriters has got to be took up, and, ef that ain't bein' a suspicious carriter, this mate on the starn watch don't know what is. I'm rale sorry for yer, and I'm sorry for Timotheus, but juty is juty and orders is [Pg 172]strict. Come on, now, and let us hope the Square'll be marciful."

"What is the meaning of this nonsense, Pilgrim?" asked the commander, angrily.

"It's a suspicious carriter as can't give no account of itself, Square. She might ha' been shot as like as not, ef I hadn't gone and took her pris'ner."

"Let the girl alone, and don't make a laughing stock of yourself. You've already said the passwords loud enough for any lurker to hear, so that we'll hae to change them aa because o' your stupeedity. Be serious and keep your eyes and gun for strange folk, men or women."

Tryphosa fled into the house, whither Tryphena—who, falling into the same error, had crossed the beat of Timotheus—had already betaken herself, being driven off the field by the more sensible and merciful younger Pilgrim. When the Squire had completed his rounds, he returned to the guard-room, and, telling the story of Sylvanus' folly, which roused the Captain's ire, showed the necessity for new watchwords and better instruction of sentries.

"It maun be something the lads and all the rest o' us ken weel, Squire. What think ye o' Cricket and Golf?" asked Mr. Errol.

"I am afraid that Ben Toner might not know these words," put in the dominie.

"What?" cried Mr. Perrowne, "do you really mean to say that this—ah—Towner needs to be towld what cricket is?"

"I fear so," Wilkinson answered; with the effect that no heathen could have fallen lower in the parson's estimation than did Ben.

"I say good, ship-shape words are Starbud and Port," growled the Captain.

"In Sout Ameriky it was Constituthion and Libertad," suggested Mr. Terry.

"Pork and Beans 'll no' do; nor Burdock and Blood Bitters; nor Powder and Shot," said the Squire, ruminating; "for the one ca's up the tither ower nayteral like. What say ye, Maister Wilkinson?"

Wilkinson was taken aback by the suddenness of the question, and blurted out what had been only too much in his thoughts; "Idiot and Boy."

[Pg 173]"Capital!" "Well said!" "The very thing!" "Jest suits Sylvanus!" the various voices responded; and the Squire went out to the sentries to make the desired change. The lawyer chuckled when he received the new words, and all the other sentinels repeated to themselves the poetic terms "Eejut and Boy."

It was just on the stroke of midnight, time to relieve the guards, when the distant sound of pistol shots in rapid succession fell simultaneously on the ears of Coristine, Ben and Sylvanus. The lawyer, stepping hastily to the house, called out the armed inmates, and in another minute or so Nash came galloping up. "Stay where you are, Squire, with your sentries; and, you other men, look to your loading and come on with me. I've been fired at by a waggon load of them." The five unposted men hastened out into the road and away after the detective to the left. After going a short distance, the adjutant called a halt, and told the veteran to advance in military order. "Now, min," said Mr. Terry quietly, "extind about tin paces from aich another to the lift, an' Oi'll be the lifthand man. Thin kape wan eye on me an' the other before yeez, and advance whin Oi advance undher cover av the stumps and finces and things. Riddy now—extind!" The movement was well executed, and, as the veteran was eager for the fray, he led them more rapidly than it could be thought the old man had the power to run, until they reached the spot where the waggon had halted. It was gone, without a sign; so the gallant skirmishers re-formed in the road and marched back to quarters. When they arrived at the gate, Coristine could not resist the temptation of a challenge, unnecessary as it was. The dominie was leading, and him he hailed: "Who goes there?" With momentary hesitation, Wilkinson answered in the same undertone:—

"Friends."

"The word, friends?"

87

"Idiot."

"The countersign, Idiot?"

"Boy."

"Pass, Idiot Boy, and all's well!"

The schoolmaster could have boxed that sentry's ears, have slapped his face, have caned him within an inch of [Pg 174]his life; for there was a light in an upper window, and he knew that bright eyes were looking down through the slats of the closed green shutters, and that sharp ears had caught the sound of the obnoxious words. He could detect the accents of a voice, which he knew so well, pleading the cause of silence with another that trembled with suppressed laughter as it made ineffectual promises to be quiet. The two clergymen also heard the friendly altercation at the window, so still was everything else, and chuckled as they filed past the legal sentry, now on the broad grin. The Captain and Mr. Terry were above taking notice of such trifles, for they were eagerly persuading each other to take just the least drop before going out into the heavy night dews. No sooner had the five entered the guard-room than the Squire re-formed them and marched them off to relieve the old sentries. The lawyer's place was taken by the dominie, Toner's by the Captain, that of Sylvanus by Perrowne, that of Timotheus by Errol, and Rufus' post of honour by the veteran, who would accept no other. There was a sixth guard in the person of Muggins, who kept his master company and behaved with the greatest propriety and silence. Sylvanus and Timotheus, Rufus and Ben had a separate guard-house of their own in the kitchen, where Mrs. Carmichael, who could not sleep because of her apprehensions of evil to some unknown defender, furnished them with bread and cheese and innocuous hot elderberry wine and cold cider. After partaking plentifully of the refreshments, Sylvanus and Ben lit their pipes, and the latter communicated to the company the story of his woes in the case of Serlizer. Sylvanus related his adventure in capturing Tryphosa, which caused Timotheus to move into a corner with Rufus and declare solemnly and in a low tone, that "Ef Sylvanus warn't my brother and older'n me, and the next thing t' engaged to Trypheeny, I'd be shaved an' shampooed ef I wouldn't bust his old cocoanut open." Rufus, however, replied that girls had no business to be about in war times, unless it was to nurse the sick and wounded, which was only done in hospitals, thus justifying Sylvanus' action as a pure matter of military duty, and reconciling Timotheus to the slight put upon his lady love.

The Squire and Coristine were alone in the guard-room, save when Mrs. Carmichael put her head in to ask [Pg 175]after the welfare of the party, especially of the older members.

"Grandfather knows campaigning and can take care of himself," the Squire answered; "and the Captain's used to out-door life; but there's the minister now, puir man! Weel, weel, Marjorie, when I gang the roonds, I'll see if he needs onything."

Then the pair chatted away, chiefly about the Grinstun man, whom Carruthers came to regard in the light of a spy. Though surrounded on every side by suspicious circumstances, there was nothing definite against him, the nearest evidence to a conviction being the geological or mineralogical expressions which the unguarded dilapidated farmer on the way to the Beaver River had coupled with his name, and his own admissions to the spurious Miss Du Plessis.

"Maister Coristine," said the Squire, "gin I thocht yon deevil, seein' it's Monday mornin' the noo, was at the foondation o' this ploy, I'd think naething o' spendin' five thoosand to pit an end til's tricks."

"All right, Squire; I think I'll go into criminal law, and work it up for you."

"What's yon? I maun gang out, for I hear Mr. Wilkinson calling me."

The lawyer accompanied him to the door. Nash was at the gate to report that he had seen small parties and single individuals, some distance off the road on both sides of the house, whose actions were more than suspicious. Had they carried firearms larger than pistols he would have been sure to detect the gleam of steel. He was sorry now he had drawn the fire of the waggon on himself, and thus given the miscreants to understand that their plot was known. Still, they were at it, and meant mischief. As he could do no further good patrolling the road, he would put up his horse, and help the Squire to guard the house and outbuildings. Hardly was his horse in the stable, and himself in the guard-room, than Mr. Errol's voice, and then the dominie's, were heard challenging loudly. The Squire flew to the minister, and Nash to Wilkinson. A stout but elastic figure, so far as the step went, was coming along the road from the right, whistling "The Girl I left behind Me." As it came near, the [Pg 176]whistling stopped, and Rawdon, with knapsack on back and staff in hand, appeared before the astonished eyes of the sentinels. He started at the sight of the minister's carbine. "Wy, Mr. Herl," he said, "wot the dooce are you a doin' of at this time o' night? Are you lookin' for night 'awks or howls hafter the chickins, or did you think I was a wistlin' bear. And you too, Squire! I thought the Hinjins was all killed bout. Blowed if there haint hold Favosites Wilkinsonia, and a man as looks like Chisholm! Are you campin' out, 'avin' summer midnight manoovers for the fun o' the thing?"

Nash went back to the house. "If it's a fair question, Mr. Rawdon," said the Squire, "where are you going at this time of night?"

"Fair enough, Squire; I'm bound for Collinwood to ketch the mornin' train. Bye, bye! no time to lose." Off trudged the Grinstun man, once more whistling, but this time his tune was "It's no use a knockin' at the door."

The Squire, the detective, and the lawyer held a council of war.

"Pity we hadn't arrested that chap," remarked Mr. Nash.

"Couldn't do it," said Coristine; "there is no warrant for his arrest, no definite charge against him. A justice of the peace can't issue one on mere suspicion, nor can he institute martial law, which would of course cover the case."

"If what Maister Nash has seen be as he thinks," added the Squire, "it's as weel we laid nae han' on him, for it would just hae preceepitated metters, and hae brocht the haill o' thae Lake Settlement deevils doon upon us. D'ye think Rawdon's gaun to Collingwood, Nash?"

"Not a bit of it. I believe he came past here, openly and dressed as he was, for three reasons. First, he wants to prove an alibi for himself, whatever happens. Second, he wanted to see how we are guarded, and by that loud whistling has informed his confederates not far off that it is useless to try the house from the front. Thirdly, he has circled round to take command of the villains that fired on me out of the waggon we couldn't find."

"What's to be done then?" asked the Squire and the lawyer in a breath.

[Pg 177]"We must watch the means of access from the left to the right. You see, there are bushes, young willows and alders, all along the bank of the creek, behind which they can steal towards that ferny hollow under the birches, and, from thence, either make for the bit of bush Mr. Terry is guarding, or creep behind the scattered boulders towards the fence. Your shrubberies about the house and live hedges and little meadow copses are very pretty and picturesque, Squire, but a bare house on the top of a treeless hill would be infinitely better to stand a siege."

"Aye, aye, Nash; but I'm no gaun tae cut doon my bonnie trees an' busses for a wheen murderin' vagabones."

"Well, I'll get a gun from one of the men in the kitchen, and explore the hillside below the Captain."

Having secured Ben Toner's gun, the best of the lot, the detective walked down the garden to the gate, where he found Perrowne vainly endeavouring to comfort Muggins. The poor dog did not even whine, but shivered as he stood, otherwise paralyzed with abject terror.

"Crouch down by the fence," whispered the detective in the parson's ear, and at once crouched down beside him.

"Do you see that moving object coming up the hill from the birches? By Jove! there's another crawling behind it. What is it?"

"It's an animal of some sawrt," answered Perrowne.

"That accounts for your dog's fear. It isn't a bear, is it? There may be some about after early berries."

"Now, it's not a bear, though I've been towld dawgs are very much afraid of bears."

Just then the animal keeled over, and immediately there followed the report of a rifle. The crawler behind the beast slid back into the hollow and disappeared. Then, from the left of the house came a volley that woke the echoes all round; it was the explosion of the Captain's blunderbuss. The detective ran along the fence to Mr. Terry's beat, and found the veteran reloading his rifle from the muzzle. "Keep your post, Mr. Terry," he cried, "while I run and see what it is you have bagged. I imagine your son-in-law will look after the Captain." Mr. Nash ran down the hill, closely followed by the lawyer, who had come out to see the fun. All the bedroom windows were lit up, and eager eyes strained to learn the [Pg 178]cause of the firing, while the remaining sentinels prepared for action. The animal shot was a large bloodhound, in life a dangerous brute with horrid, cruel-looking fangs, but now in the agonies of death. The detective drew his long dagger-like knife, and drove it into the creature's heart. Then, while Coristine lifted it by the two hind legs, he took a grasp of its collar, and they carried the trophy of the veteran's rifle on to the lawn in front of the house. There they learned that the Captain, being half asleep with no chance of an enemy in sight, dreamt his ship had been saluted coming into port on a holiday, and, as in duty bound, returned the salute. The blunderbuss had not exploded; it always made that grand, booming, rattling, diffusive sort of a report. The dead hound's collar was examined, and was discovered to bear the initials A.R. "Who is A.R.?" asked the Squire; and Mr. Nash replied: "He is no doubt my affianced bridegroom, Haltamont Rawdon."

It was two o'clock in the morning; so the guard was relieved, and the former sentries returned to their posts; but the Squire noticed, with a frown, that just as the relief arrived at Mr. Errol's beat, a female form clothed in black darted round the stables towards the kitchen door. Also, he saw that the minister had a most unmilitary muffler, in the shape of a lady's cloud, round his neck, which he certainly had not when he went on duty. His high respect for the reverend gentleman hindered any outward expression of his combined amusement and annoyance. Muggins came back with Mr. Perrowne, but obstinately refused to go near the dead hound.

"Do you think he has ever seen it before?" asked the detective.

"I shouldn't be at all surprised," replied the clergyman.

"I lawst Muggins, you know, at Tossorontio, and there was a man there at the time, a short man in a pea-jacket or cowt, down't you know, who had a big dawg. When Muggins disappeared, I thought the big dawg might have killed him. But now I think the man with the pea-cowt saved him from the big dawg, and that's how Muggins came to gow after him. What do you imagine that beast was after, coming up the hill towards Muggins?"

[Pg 179]"I think he was coming to overpower you, Mr. Perrowne, and bring all our forces to your aid, while the fellow behind him slipped in and fired the house or did some similar mischief."

"I tell you, Mr. Nash, he'd have had my two barrels first, and I'm a pretty fair shot, down't you know? But, look here, it's dry work mounting guard, sow I'll have another pull at the tankard."

The Squire came in from guard mounting, somewhat fatigued. He had been on the stretch mentally and physically ever since the Captain's arrival. "You had better go to bed, grandfather, and take Thomas with you," he said to the veteran.

"Not a wink this blissid noight, Squoire," replied Mr. Terry, "the smill av the powther has put new loife into my owld carcash. The Captin can go iv he plazes."

"Avast, there! I say, messmate," growled Captain Thomas, "I don't run this mill, but my youngster's here under hatches, and I'm a goin' to keep watch on, watch off along of any other man. I don't think that o' yours is half up to the mark, Mr. Terry."

"Oi was thinkin' I was a bit wake mysilf," replied the old soldier, filling up his glass, and handing the decanter to his neighbour, who likewise improved the occasion.

"Oi'm suppawsin now, sorr," continued the veteran, addressing the dominie, "that this is yer first apparance on shintry."

"You are right, Mr. Terry, in your supposition."

"An', sorr, it's a cridit to yeez to be shtandin' an' facin' the inimy wid divel a thing in yer hand but a pishtil. Oi moind a big sthrappin' liftinant av ours was called Breasel, an' sid he was discinded from the great Breasel Breck av Oirish hishtry. Wan noight he was slapin', whin four nagurs av Injuns kim into his tint, an' picked the sword an' pishtils and the unifarm aff the bid he was on. Thin he woke up, an' him havin' sorra a thing to difind himself wid but a good Oirish tongue in his hid. But it's Tipperary the liftinant foired at the haythens, an' it moight ha' been grape an' canister, for they dhropped the plundher and run

90

for loife, all but wan that got howlt av an anhevis drawin' plashter the liftinant had for a bile [Pg 180]an the back av his neck, an' wasn't usin' at the toime. Someways the plashter got on to his nakid chist an' gripped him, an' he was that wake wid froight, the other nagurs had to carry him away. Afther that the Injuns called Breasel by the name of Shupay, a worrud that in their spache manes the divil—savin' yer prisence, Mishter Wilkinson."

"One time the *Susan Thomas* was at Belle Ewart loadin' on lumber," growled the Captain. "Sylvanus heerd as how the Mushrats, that's the folks acrost on t'other side of the bay, was a comin' over to fasten him and me down in the hold and paint the schooner. They was a goin' to paint her The Spotted Dog, than which there's no meaner kind o' fish. So, I bid Sylvanus pile a great heap of useless, green, heavy, barky slabs on top o' the good lumber; then we took the occasion of a little wind, and stood her out to anchor a little ways from the dock. Sure enough, when night come, the Mushrats came a hollerin' aand yellin'. Unfortnitly I'd left the salutin' blunderbuss here at home, and hadn't but one pike-pole aboard. 'How many boat loads of 'em is there, Sylvanus?' I says. 'Two,' says he. 'All right,' says I, 'that's one apiece. Take off your coat, and roll up your shirt sleeves, Sylvanus,' says I, 'for you're a goin' to have heavy work slab heavin'!' On they come to board us, one on each side. 'Fire out them or'nary useless slabs, Sylvanus,' says I. 'But there's a boat with a lot of men in it,' says he, a-chucklin' like an ijut. Hope I haven't given the pass word away, John? Well, I said: 'Fire out the slabs, and let the men get out o' the way.' And he began firing, and I kept my side a-goin', and the slabs fell flat and heavy and fast, knockin' six at a shot, till they cussed and swore, and hollered and yelled murder, and that was the last we two saw of the Mushrats and the paintin' of the *Susan Thomas*."

Subdued but hearty laughter followed these stories, and, when the Captain ended, the veteran pushed the decanter towards him, remarking: "A good shtory is a foine thing, Captin, dear, but it makes ye just a throifle dhroy." The Captain responded, and told Mr. Terry that he was neglecting himself, an omission which that gentleman proceeded to rectify. Mr. Errol, with his muffling [Pg 181]cloud still round his neck, was asleep in an easy chair. In his sleep he dreamt, the dream ending in an audible smack of his lips, and the exclamation "Very many thanks, ma'am; the toddy's warm and comforting." When his own voice aroused him, he was astonished to witness the extreme mirth of all parties, and was hardly convinced when it was attributed to the stories of the veteran and the Captain. The Squire, though amused, was resolved to have a word with his widowed sister.

The lawyer paced up and down in the cool night, trying to combine two things which do not necessarily go together, warmth and wakefulness. Everything was so quiet, that he seemed to hear Timotheus and Sylvanus pacing about rapidly like himself, when suddenly a little spark of fire appeared at the far end of the verandah towards the stables. Cautiously, under cover of bushes he approached the spot, but saw nothing, although he smelt fire. Then he knelt down and peered under the flower laden structure. The light was there, growing. In a moment it became a flame, and, as he rushed to the spot, a lad fell into his arms. Clutching his collar with his left hand in spite of kicks and scratches, he hauled his prisoner back to the verandah, and, thrusting in his right arm beneath the floor, drew out the blazing rags and threw them on the gravel walk or on the grass until he was sure that not one remained. Some watcher at the front window had alarmed the guard-room, for out tumbled its occupants, and the lad was secured by Nash, and handed over to the Captain and Mr. Errol. Calling to Toner to keep an eye on the whole front, the detective, taking in the situation, hastened to the stables along with the lawyer, while the Squire and Mr. Perrowne went round the back way on the same errand. No guard was visible, and there was fire in two places, both happily outside sheds, one abutting on the garden fence, the other farther to the right. The Squire went for water-pails, while Nash and the veteran followed the course of the incendiaries towards the bush guarded by Rufus. But the lawyer and the parson, seizing stout poles, which were apparently Tryphena's clothes props, knocked the blazing sheds to pieces with them, and scattered the burning boards over the ground. Before the water came, the report of a rifle, a fowling piece, and of [Pg 182]several pistol shots, rang through the air. No more signs of fire were discovered, so the water was poured upon the still burning boards, and the firemen waited for the report of the pursuers. While thus waiting, they heard a groan, and, going to the place whence it proceeded, discovered

Timotheus, with a gag plaster on his mouth and an ugly wound on the back of his head, lying close to the garden fence below the fired shed. Some water on his face revived him, and at the same time moistened the plaster, but as it would not come off, Coristine cut it open with his penknife between the lips of the sufferer. Even then he could hardly articulate, yet managed to ask if all was safe and to thank his deliverers. He was helped into the house, and delivered over to the awakened and dressed Tryphena and Tryphosa, the latter behaving very badly and laughing in a most unfeeling way at the comical appearance cut by her humble swain. When Tryphena removed the plaster, and Tryphosa, returning to duty with an effort, bathed his head, the wounded sentry felt almost himself again, and guaised he must ha' looked a purty queer pictur. Soon after, Rufus staggered into the kitchen in a similar condition, and his affectionate sisters had to turn their attention to the Baby. These were all the casualties on the part of the garrison, and, overpowered though the two sentries had been, their arms had not been taken by the enemy.

The Squire went forward to see after the welfare of his father-in-law, and found Mr. Terry carrying his own rifle and the gun of Sylvanus, while the said Pilgrim helped the detective to carry a groaning mass of humanity towards the kitchen hospital.

"Oi tuk my man this toime, Squire," said Mr. Terry, gleefully; "Oi wuz marciful wid the crathur and aimed for the legs av' im. It's a foine nate little howl this swate roifle has dhrilled in his shkin, an' niver a bone shplit nor a big blood vissel tapped, glory be, say Oi!"

It appeared, on examination of the parties, that Ben Toner and Sylvanus had indulged in a prolonged talk at the point where their beats met, during which a party of six, including the two prisoners, creeping up silently through the bush, prostrated Rufus with the blow of a bludgeon on the back of the head. Then, they advanced[Pg 183]and repeated the operation on Timotheus, after which three of them, with cotton cloths soaked in oil, fired the sheds and the verandah. But for the lawyer's discovery of the spark under the latter, the fire might have been beyond control in a few minutes, and the end of the murderous gang accomplished. The whole household was roused; indeed, save in the case of the children, it can hardly be said to have been asleep. Mrs. Carruthers descended, and, sending Tryphosa to look after her young family, helped her father to bind up the wound of the grizzled incendiary, who refused to give any account of himself. "I know him," said the detective to the Squire; "his name is Newcome and he's a bad lot." Soon the Captain and Mr. Errol brought their prisoner in. The hospital and guard-room was the winter kitchen of the house, a spacious apartment almost unused during the summer months. When the lad was brought into it, he seemed to recognize the place with his dull big grey eyes, and spoke the first words he had uttered since his capture. "Bread and meat for Monty." "Why," said Tryphena, "it's the ijut boy." "So it is," ejaculated Mrs. Carruthers, "What is your name, Monty?" With an idiotic smile on his face, but no light in those poor eyes, he answered: "Monty Rawn, and mother's in the water place." Mrs. Carruthers explained that the lad had been often in the kitchen in winter, and that she had told Tryphena to feed him well and be kind to him, so that it is no wonder he recognized the scene of his former enjoyment. "Puir laddie," said the Squire, "he's no' responsible, but the born deevil that set him on should be hanged, drawn, and quartered."

"Squire," answered Mr. Errol, "I'm aye on the side o' maircy, but to yon I say Amen."

"Come, come!" Carruthers cried hastily, regaining his natural speech; "we must take off these haverals, Sylvanus and Toner, and bring them in to guard the prisoners. They are not fit for sentry duty." Leaving the Captain and the veteran as temporary guards, he sallied forth, followed by the lawyer and the two parsons.

To the Squire's great delight, he found the dominie walking up and down the front of the house, humming "A charge to keep I have." "Mr. Wilkinson," he said,[Pg 184]"you're a pairfec' treasure," and that so loud that the schoolmaster was sure it was heard by the occupants of the window over the porch. He marched along with redoubled pride and devotion. Mr. Perrowne took Toner's place, and the lawyer that of Sylvanus. Carruthers marched the two haverals to the kitchen, and placed the prisoners in their charge, after roundly abusing them for talking on guard. This set free the Captain and Mr. Terry, who were posted together by the outbuildings, although the veteran was very anxious to go down to the bush for the purpose of potting the Lake Settlement haythens. There being no post for the minister, he was appointed hospital chaplain and commander of the prisoners' guard. Mr. Nash, carrying Ben's gun, was investigating the strip of bush and the clump of birches down the hill for traces of the enemy. While so doing, two pistol bullets flew past his head and compelled him to seek the cover of a tree trunk. Finding he could do nothing in the imperfect light, he retired gradually towards the sentries, and aided them in their weary watch. At length, as daylight was coming in, and affording a pretext for the fair occupants of the front room, whose windows hailed the beams of the rising sun, to leave their seclusion and mingle with the wakeful ones below, the sound of wheels was heard coming along the road to the left. Hurriedly, the detective became Mr. Chisholm, and joined the dominie at the gate. There were three men in the waggon, and one of them was the Grinstun man, as cheerful as ever. What was in the waggon could not be seen, as it was covered over with buffalo robes and tarpaulin, but the detective could have sworn he saw it move, and give forth a sound not unlike a groan. Mr. Rawdon jumped down, telling a certain Jones of truculent countenance to drive on, as he guessed he'd walk the rest of the way this fine morning. The waggon drove off accordingly and at a rapid rate, while the working geologist accosted the sentinels.

"Wy, wot's hup 'ere, gents? 'Ere you hare on guard yet, and Jones there terls me 'ee 'eard shots fired has 'ee was comin' along slowly. I 'ope there hain't no gang o' city burglars bin tryin' hany o' their larks on the Squire. We don't want none o' that sort hout in rural parts."

[Pg 185]The dominie and the detective declined to satisfy him, but the former said:—

"I thought you had pressing business at Collingwood, Mr. Rawdon?"

"So I 'ad, and stand to lose two or three 'undred dollars by missin' the mornin' train. But, wen I got quite a step on the road, all of a suddin' I remembers my hoffer to Miss Do Please-us, and 'er hanswer as was to be hat the Post Hoffice before ten. So I turned back, hand, lucky for me, fell in with Jones and 'is man takin' 'ome some things from town. But, come! tell a man can't you? 'As there bin any burglary or hanythink, any haccident, anybody 'urt? I've got an hour and more to spare, if I can be of any 'elp."

"I don't think we need trouble you, Rawdon," said the false Chisholm. "Your suspicions are correct so far, that an attempt has been made to fire the Squire's house, but by whom is a mystery, for there is no man more respected in the neighbourhood."

"Respected! I should say 'ee is. Fire 'is 'ouse! O Lor'! wot a bloomin' shame! Really, I must go him, if it's honly for a hinstant to hexpress my feelins of hindignation to the Carrutherses."

The Grinstun man entered the gate, which was just what the detective did not want. However, he held it open for him, saying: "You'll find the Squire in his office talking to Nash, but I don't suppose he'll mind being interrupted for a minute. Mrs. Carruthers is in the kitchen, and you'll likely meet an old acquaintance of yours there, Mr. Perrowne of Tossorontio."

Rawdon drew back. Nash he knew: Mr. Perrowne, of Tossorontio, he did not; but the unknown to men of his stamp is often more dreaded than the known. He wouldn't intrude upon his friends just now, while everything must be upset. Playfully, he asked Favosites Wilkinsonia to remind Miss Do Please-us of that hoffer and the hanswer before ten, and straightway resumed his journey in the direction of the Lake Settlement.

"Of all the impudent blackguards that I have met in the course of my experience, that fellow takes the cake," said the detective, removing his disguise.

"What about Jones and the waggon?" asked the dominie.

[Pg 186]"The waggon is the one I saw when patrolling. Jones and his man are two of the ruffians who were in it. Old Newcome, here, is a third. The boy—by-the-bye, what a wonderful inspiration that was of yours to give us Idiot and Boy for passwords—well, the boy must have come from some other quarter. But there's either one or two wounded men under these buffaloes and bits of canvas, for I hit one in the waggon and sent the contents of Ben's gun after another down the hill. They both squealed. Men of that kind almost always squeal when they're hit. The impudence of that fellow Rawdon! Pon't forget Miss Du Plessis' letter; that's our card now. Never in all my life have I met with such colossal cheek!"

The Squire came out and dismissed the guard. The parson and the lawyer strolled in together after Wilkinson and Nash. Coristine remarked "The sunshine is a glorious birth, as my friend Wilkinson would say."

"Yes," answered Perrowne; "it brings to memory one verse of Holy Writ: 'Truly the light is sweet, and a pleasant thing it is for the eyes to behold the sun.' The words are very simple, but beautiful in their simplicity. People are apt to say there's no dogma in them, and that's why they are so acceptable to all. But that's a mistake. They contain a double dogma; for they make a dogmatic statement about light, and another about the relation of the sun to the human eye. In the Church we down't get much training in dogma, outside of the dogma of the Church, and a little in the Articles and the Catechism. Sow Mr. Enrol often flores me with his texts. But I down't bear him any malice, you know, nor any malice to dogma, so long as it's the dogma of the Holy Scriptures; because that is just like the verse I quoted, it says what is true of a thing in itself, or in its relation to man. To reject that sort of dogma is to reject the truth."

"Still," replied the lawyer, "a man in a burning desert, or who had been sunstruck, might curse the sun."

"Very true; but you know how wrong is the motto *ex uno disce omnes*. Believe that, and we are all scoundrels, because your Grinstun man was once under this roof."

"There are, however, many ecclesiastical dogmas pro[Pg 187]fessedly taken from the Bible, against which good men, and earnest seekers after truth, rebel."

"Of course! Mr. Errol says—I do wish he were a Churchman, he is such a thoughtful, clever fellow—he says prejudice, imperfect induction, a wrong application of deductive logic, and one-sided interpretation, down't you know, literal, figurative, and all that sort of thing, are causes of false dogmatic assertions."

"My friend Wilkinson, who is a long way past me in these matters, thinks the dogmatists forget that Revelation was a gradual thing, that the ages it came to were like classes in a graded school, and each class got only as much as it could understand, both mentally and morally; and as, of course, it was able to express."

"Yes; Errol says the same, but with exceptions; because the prophets said a whowle lot of things they didn't understand. But, my dear fellow, whatever is the matter with your hands and face? You're burnt, you pore sowl, and never said a word about it. Come on here, I saye; come on!"

Mr. Perrowne laid hold on the lawyer's arm, and dragged him into the hall. "Miss Marjorie!" he called; "hi! Miss Carmichael, come along here, quick, I beg of you, please." The lady invoked came running out of the breakfast room, looking very pretty in her fright. "Look here, Miss Marjorie, at our pore friend's hands and face, all got by saving you ladies from being burnt alive."

Miss Carmichael exhibited great concern, and took the patient, who insisted his wounds were nothing to make a fuss over, into the work room, setting him down, with the pressure of her two hands on his broad shoulders, in a comfortable chair between a sewing machine and a small table. Then she brought warm water, and sponged the hands, anointed the wounds with some home-made preparation, and clothed them in a pair of her uncle's kid gloves, which were so large and baggy that she had to sit down and laugh at her victim, who felt very happy and very foolish. Finally she found that Mr. Errol, whose hands were more shapely, had an old pair of gloves in his pocket. So the Squire's were taken off, and the discovery made that the hands needed more washing, soaping, and anointing. Coristine said his ring, a very handsome one, hurt [Pg 188]him; would Miss Carmichael please take it off and keep it for him? Miss Carmichael removed the obnoxious ring, and did not know where to put it, but, in the meantime, to prevent its being lost, slipped it on to one of her own fingers, which almost paralyzed the lawyer with joy. He could have sat there forever; but the gong sounded for prayers, and he accompanied his nurse into the dining-room. There the whole household was assembled, even to the idiot Monty, with the exception of Tryphena, engaged in culinary duties, and Sylvanus, who mounted guard over the wounded Newcome. Ben Toner also was absent, having ridden off to summon Dr. Halbert. Mr. Perrowne, at the Squire's request, read the chapter for the day, and the minister offered a prayer, brief but fervent, returning thanks for the deliverance of the past night, and imploring help in every

94

time of need, after which the entire company, Mr. Terry included, joined in the Lord's Prayer. Adjourning to the breakfast room, the events of the night were discussed over the porridge, the hot rolls and coffee and the other good things provided. Mr. Terry had been induced to desert the kitchen for once, and he and Coristine were the heroes of the hour. The lawyer put in a good word for the parson, and the Squire for Wilkinson, so that Miss Du Plessis and the other ladies were compelled to smile on both gentlemen. While the dominie blushed, the Captain settled his eye on him. "I told him when he was aboard the *Susan Thomas* that, with all his innercent sort of looks, he was a sly dog, with his questions about an old man's pretty niece. I knowed I'd see him in Flanders makin' up to the gals, the sly dog! Got set down right beam on to their weather ports every time, even when he wasn't told to go on watch at all, the sly dog. Wilkison is his name; it'll be Will-kiss-em some day, ha! ha! ha! the sly dog!"

The schoolmaster was dreadfully uncomfortable, and his lady teacher hardly less so. It was a blessed relief when a buggy drove up to the gate, and Mrs. Carruthers, having left her sister-in-law in charge while she went out to meet its occupants, returned shortly with the doctor and his blooming daughter, who, as a friend of the family, insisted on accompanying him to offer her services if she could be of help.

[Pg 189]"Come, Doctor!" said the Squire, rising with the rest of the party to greet him and his companion; "the patients are in no immediate danger, so you and Miss Fanny must sit down and help us with breakfast."

Miss Fanny was nothing loath to do so, after an invigorating drive, and in the company of such a number of eligible bachelors as was rarely seen in Flanders. She had a word for Mr. Errol, for the detective, for the lawyer and the dominie, but to Wilkinson's great relief she finally pitched upon Mr. Perrowne and held him captive. Then Wilkinson improved the time with Miss Du Plessis, using as his excuse the letter or note she was to send to Rawdon declining his offer for the present, which the schoolmaster expressed his desire personally to take to the office. Breakfast over, the doctor inspected his patients, Newcome, Rufus, and Timotheus. The two latter he dismissed as all the better of a little blood letting, recommending lots of cold water applied externally. The case of the incendiary was more serious, but not likely to be fatal.

CHAPTER X.

Doctor Summoned to the Select Encampment—Newcome Interviewed—Nash's Discovery—His Venture—Drop the Handkerchief—The Dominie's Indignation—The Pedestrians Detained—The Doctor Stays—A Trip to the Lakes—Conversation on the Way—The Richards—Fishing—Songs—The Barrier in the Channel—Nash's Dead Body Found—His Crazed Sister Comes to Bridesdale.

It was only eight o'clock when the elders finished their breakfast, and the children prepared to succeed them. All the party, except Mrs. Carruthers and Mrs. Carmichael, who had domestic duties before them, and Miss Du Plessis, who had her note to write, strolled out into the garden in groups. Shortly, a buckboard drove up to the gate, and its occupant, a washed out looking youth, enquired if the doctor was there, Dr. Halbert. The subject of the enquiry went forward, and found that he was wanted at the Select Encampment, for a man who had shot himself.

[Pg 190]"I tell you frankly, my man," said the doctor, "I don't care to go to your Select Encampment; there is too much mystery about it."

"I guess the pay's all O.K.," answered the youth.

"Why do you not get Dr. Smallpiece to look after your man?"

"'Cos we don't know nuthun about him, and he's too small a piece for our boss. You best hurry up yer cakes and come on, doctor."

Re-entering the house for his instruments, the doctor confided to Carruthers his distaste for the work before him, on account of the mystery surrounding it, but said he supposed it was his duty to relieve human suffering.

"Where is it?" asked the Squire.

"All I can tell you is that it is out on the lakes beyond the Lake Settlement."

"I thocht as muckle," remarked the Squire to the detective, after the doctor was carried away on the buckboard.

"Let as go and see Newcome," said the detective; and the pair went round to the kitchen, where the wounded man lay on an improvised couch, and was waited upon by big Ben Toner, anxious for news of Serlizer. Mr. Nash began:—

"The doctor says that talking won't hurt you, Newcome."

"Dawn't spause 'twull," answered the surly fellow.

"Setting fire to buildings with intent to take life is a hanging matter, Newcome."

"Oo said t'warnt?"

"You seem prepared for your fate."

"Ma vate was aw raight to I got t'bahl i'my laig."

"I mean, you don't seem to care if you are going to be hanged."

"Oo's a gaun to hahng us an' vor wat?"

"You'll be hanged for arson with intent to kill. There are witnesses to prove you threatened to kill me at least."

Newcome started, and so did Ben.

"Yaw cahn't prove nowt."

"Yes I can. I've got your pocket book and the odd papers out of your coat pocket."

[Pg 191]"Aw'll hae yaw oop vor stalun as well as shootun, zee iv I dawn't, yaw bloody thafe!"

"Keep a civil tongue in your head, man, or I'll send you to the lockup at once," interposed the Squire.

"Leave him to me Squire; I'll manage him," whispered Nash.

Then, turning to the injurious Newcome, he continued:

"Your daughter, Sarah Eliza, is at Rawdon's Select Encampment, where the stuff you sell is turned out. She can give some fine evidence. The Peskiwanchow crowd, the man that pretends to be called Jones, and the rest of them, were picked up by you in a waggon, I know, last night. The coal oil and fire marks are on your hands still, and this pretty rag came out of your side pocket. What is more, I don't need to ask the Squire here to commit you. I've got a warrant already, on the evidence of Henry and Stokes and Steadman. I'll serve that warrant on you now, and have you off to the county gaol, where Dr. Stapfer is bound to cut off your leg, if you don't own up quick, for I have no time to lose."

"Daw yaw thenk as Stapper ull ambitate ma laig?"

"I'm sure of it. He always does; he has a perfect mania for amputation. You know Driver?"

"Yaas."

"Who cut off his leg for a little bruise?"

"T'wer Stapper."

"And who cut of Sear's arm at the shoulder for a trifle of a rusty nail?"

"Stapper taw. O, aw zay, Mezder Nahsh, dawn't zend us ta naw Stappers."

"But I will, I must, if you don't confess immediately all that the Squire and I want to know. Turn Queen's evidence, and make a clean breast of it. You can't save Rawdon and his gang; we have them tight. But confess, and I'll get you out on bail, and send you home to your wife to be nursed; and, when the trials come, I'll get you off your liquor charge with a fine. Refuse to, and you go straight to Stapfer's to lose your leg, and then to the gallows."

"Aw dawn't moind chancin' t'gallas, but ma laig! Wat daw yaw wahn't ta knaw?"

At once all the people, Ben included, were ordered out of the hospital, and Coristine, much to his disgust, sent [Pg 192]for. His hands were useless for writing, but, as he had a good memory, he could help in the examination. So Mr. Errol was called in to act as clerk, Mr. Perrowne refusing to do so, on the ground that all confessions made in the presence of a clergyman are sacred. Little by little the hardened old sinner revealed Rawdon's business, its centre and methods, his accomplices and victims. Then the whole story of the plot which culminated in the night attack was drawn from him, appearing blacker and more diabolical at every new revelation of villainy. It appeared that the Grinstun man had with him in the attack, which he conducted personally, his own six men from the so called Encampment, together with the idiot boy, and two lots of teamsters or distributors, the five from

96

Peskiwanchow brought by Newcombe, and four from another quarter. He had thus sixteen ruffians in his force, besides himself and the boy.

"Whose boy is that?" asked the detective, eagerly. He had been looking closely at the lad more than once and listening to his voice.

"Ah beeslong ta Rowdon."

"Who is his mother?" asked Nash, with a strange light in his eye.

"Her's cawd Tilder."

"Is she Rawdon's wife? Speak, man!"

"Naw, nawt az aw niver heerd."

"What was her name before he—brought her there?"

"Aw donno, but t'lahd's cawd Mawnta Nehgull."

"O my God!" cried the detective, as he fell back in his chair, and seemed to lose all power of speech.

"Come away, Nash," said the Squire, taking one arm of the stricken man, while Mr. Errol, handing his notes to the lawyer, took the other. They led him tenderly to the office, where Carruthers forced a glass of wine upon him. Nash revived, and begged that the door might be closed and locked.

"I may never have a chance to tell this again, so I want to tell it to you two, and to you alone. My real name is Nagle, not Nash. I was born in Hamilton, where my father was a wheelwright. I got a good schooling, and went into a lawyer's office, for father wanted me to become a lawyer. But I got reading detective books, and did a [Pg 193]few sharp things for the firm that got me into notice and brought me private detective business. So I got on till I rose to be what I am, such as it is. When my parents died they left my sister Matilda in my care. I was only twenty then, and she, eighteen, a bright, pretty girl. She kept my rooms for me, but I was away most of the time, so she became tired of it, as we had no relations and hardly any friends we cared to associate with. She insisted on leaving me and learning the millinery in Toronto; so I had to let her go. I saw her often, and frequently sent her money. She got good wages at last and dressed well, and seemed to have respectable people about her. Suddenly her letters stopped. I went to her place of business, and heard that she had left to be married to a rich man in the country; but nobody, not even her closest acquaintances among the girls, knew where, or who the man was. I advertised, neglected business to hunt up every clue, travelled all over the country looking for my lost sister, promised my dead parents never to marry till I found her. And at last, at last, O God! I have found Matilda, and you know where, a woman without name or character, the victim of the greatest scoundrel unhung, the associate of brutal criminals, the unlawful mother of an idiot boy! No! no more wine, Squire, not a drop. I want a steady head and a strong hand this morning more than any day of my life. Open the door and the windows now, please; and give me a little air."

Nash, for so he may still be called, sent Coristine away to Talfourd's for his bundle, and Miss Du Plessis, having handed the note for Rawdon to the dominie, accompanied the hero of the gloves in the Squire's buggy, so as to lose no time. Wilkinson was warned not to post the letter before his comrade's return. While waiting in the office, Mr. Errol, whose heart was deeply touched, locked the door again, saying: "John, let us kneel down and pray our Heavenly Father to comfort our friend in his great sorrow, and bless him in his present work." The Squire knelt with the minister, and the detective fell on his knees beside him, their hearts joining in the quiet but earnest supplications of the good man of religion. When they rose from their knees, Nash, almost tearfully, pressed their hands and bade God bless them.

[Pg 194]Coristine enjoyed the society of Miss Du Plessis; nevertheless he drove fast, for the business demanded haste. The buggy returned in little over half an hour, and the bundle was handed to the detective, who took it up stairs, and, soon after, descended as a countryman, in flannel shirt, light soiled coat, and overalls. The rim of his wideawake was drawn down all round, half hiding his face disguised with a ragged beard. It could not conceal his refined, almost aristocratic, features, but such a country type is not uncommon in many parts of Canada, even accompanied with perfect boorishness. His boots were small, which also was quite Canadian, but he had rubbed the blacking off, and trusted to the dust still further to disguise them. Smiling and courteous, he bade everybody whom he could trust

97

good-bye, and slipped a large pocket-book full of money and memoranda into the hands of the Squire. "You can keep it till I come back," he said; "if I don't, get Mr. Errol and this lawyer chap, who seems a good fellow, to help you to make it out." Then, the dominie expressed his readiness to take the note to the post office, and Miss Du Plessis, a little piqued at Coristine's apparent want of attention to her, said that, if Mr. Wilkinson had no objections, she should, above all things, like a short walk after a cramping drive. The schoolmaster was only too delighted, in spite of Mr. Perrowne's glance of jealousy, which Miss Halbert saw and noted with a tap of her dainty foot on the verandah. So, Wilkinson and his inamorata tripped along the road, and, some distance behind them, shambled Simon Larkin, the hawbuck from away back, alias Mr. Nash. The children came out to play, led by Marjorie. Perrowne was still talking to Miss Halbert, Mr. Errol was closeted with the Squire, and the Captain and the veteran, on a garden bench, were telling yarns. "Cousin Marjorie," said her juvenile namesake, "we are going to play drop the handkerchief, because we've got such a lot of nice people to play it" Miss Carmichael answered: "Oh no, Marjorie, try some other game." But Marjorie insisted. So, a ring was formed, with Marjorie as handkerchief holder, outside. The ring consisted of the Captain and little Susan Carruthers, Mr. Perrowne and Marjorie of the same family, Coristine and Miss Halbert, Mr. Terry, pipe and all, and Honoria junior, John Carru[Pg 195]thers junior and Miss Carmichael, and baby Michael, but with whom? Marjorie suggested the two aunties and Tryphosa, but finally concluded that there had to be an odd one any way, so baby Michael took the Captain's hand and Miss Carmichael's, and the game began. Of course Marjorie dropped the handkerchief on her Eugene, and Eugene caught her and kissed her with great gusto. Then he had to drop it, and Honoria saluted him with effusion. Mr. Perrowne was her choice, and the parson, tell it not in Gath, the perfidious parson gave himself away on Miss Halbert, who captured him, blushed, and submitted. The Captain and Mr. Terry were becoming indignant and shocked. Miss Halbert had mercy on John Carruthers junior, who went wild with delight, and brought out Miss Carmichael. She, pitying the Captain, gave him the handkerchief and a long chase, but Mr. Thomas finally triumphed, and chose Susan Carruthers as his victim. Susan took grandpa, who pocketed his pipe, and, after a sounding smack, passed the handkerchief on to his grandchild Marjorie. She, true to her name, chose the lawyer, and that gentleman, emboldened by the parson's precedent, dropped the terrible symbol on the shoulder of the girl who was all the world to him. She pursued him, and he ran as he well could do, but at last he got weak and tired, and she overtook him against her will and his, and Coristine was in the seventh heaven of delight. They could take him and trample on him, and flaunt his recreancy before Wilkinson even; he didn't want to kiss any more, even the fresh young lips of the children. He wanted that one impression to stay forever.

Miss Du Plessis and the dominie were not in a hurry to get back to Bridesdale. She had received a letter from her mother, saying that Uncle Morton was coming to see her, and that she would try to induce him to accompany her to the country, as she did not wish to shorten her daughter's brief holiday by calling her home. Imparting the news to Wilkinson, a long and interesting conversation began which branched off into a variety of topics, treated seriously, at times poetically, by the kindred minds. Miss Da Plessis was quite unreserved, yet dignified, and without a trace of coquetry; nevertheless, the dominie assured himself that Mr. Perrowne had not a ghost of a chance in [Pg 196]that quarter. She was pleased with the generous way in which he referred to his companion pedestrian, in spite of the provocation which she knew the lawyer had given his friend. The adventures of the past night, the fresh air of the morning, the rural scenery and his delightful companionship, made the schoolmaster eloquent; yet his sense of propriety and natural politeness kept him from monopolizing the conversation, so that his silent attention was even more flattering than his appeals to the lady's intelligence and culture. Outside of the English classics and current literature, her reading lay chiefly among French and Spanish authors, most of which were not unknown to the studious dominie. A few ripples of well-bred amusement were raised by his recital of his experience at the Beaver River, where he found the Voyage autour de mon Jardin, especially by his specimens of Lajeunesse French and the story of the dug-out. Of course, he did not offend a lady's ear with a word so vulgar; it was always the canoe. Too soon the pleasant morning walk was over, and they stood before the garden gate at

Bridesdale, just at the moment when Coristine accidentally stumbled and was captured by the fair possessor of the handkerchief. "How good of your friend to please the children by taking part in their games," remarked Miss Du Plessis in all sincerity. "I cannot express the depth of my humiliation," replied the dominie; "it is scandalous—a violation of the rights of hospitality."

"But, see! Mr. Wilkinson, Mr. Perrowne is there; and Fanny also."

"I have nothing to do, Miss Du Plessis, judging them that are without; Mr. Coristine pertains to my inner circle, and shall know my opinion of his shameful conduct before the sun rises much higher in the heavens."

"Hi! there, shipmate," bawled the Captain, "come on and add a link to this here endless chain. I told you your real name, you sly dog! Ha, ha! Will-kiss-em, eh Marjorie? Not you, you little puss; but your cousin there, colourin' up like a piney rose."

"I relinquished such sports with my pinafores," answered the dominie, grandly.

It was very unjustifiable of Mr. Perrowne, but two things annoyed him; one being the fact that he was [Pg 197]equally guilty with the lawyer, the other that Miss Du Plessis had deserted him for this prig of a schoolmaster. Loud enough to be heard by all, he remarked:—

"A very learned and distinguished man was once playing with some children, when he suddenly cried, 'Children, we must stop, for I see a fool coming.' What do you think of that, Captain!"

"Never said a truer word in your life," growled Mr. Thomas, and continued, "anything as calls itself a man and can't romp with the youngsters, nor give a joke and take it, had ought to be set in a high chair with a bib, let alone petticuts."

"He said pinnies, papa," Marjorie corrected.

"Pinnies or petticuts, it's all the same thing. Me and Terry here, old enough to be his fathers!"

"An' it 'ud be a grate 'anner for me, anyway, to be father to a foine, praper, illigant gintleman loike Mishter Wilkerson," put in the veteran, anxious to keep the peace. The embers, however, were smoking on both sides when little Marjorie ran up to the dominie and, taking his hand, said beseechingly: "Please don't scold the poor boys and girls, Wilks, because it was my fault—all my fault. I made them play. Now, put down your head and kiss me, and say, 'I forgive you this once, but don't you go to do it again'; just like papa says."

There was no help for it, though everybody laughed to hear the terror of the Sacheverell Street school called Wilks, and the grown-up people, girls and boys. The dominie had to repeat the formula and seal it with a kiss, when the perfidious child turned upon him very gravely, saying: "Now, sir, you can't speak, for you've done it your very own self." Thus it was that a storm was averted, and "drop the handkerchief" broke up in good nature.

"Corry," said his friend, "I'm going upstairs for my knapsack. You had better get yours, and prepare to follow our route. Colonel Morton and Miss Du Plessis are coming here, so that we, as entire strangers, ought no longer to intrude upon the hospitality of Mrs. Carruthers."

"All right, Wilks, my boy!" replied the tender-hearted lawyer, who felt as if his heart was breaking. In a few minutes the pedestrians descended ready for the road, when [Pg 198]the Squire opened his office door and threw up his arms in amazement.

"What in aa conscience is the meanin' o' this?"

Wilkinson explained, and expressed a desire to find Mrs. Carruthers, that he might thank her for her kind hospitality.

"Here, gudewife, and as ye four Marjories, and Miss Cecile," cried Carruthers, lustily, "come ye as here, and garr thae twa wanderin' Jews bide."

Then there was a commotion, as the ladies flocked with the children into the hall, with many exclamations of astonishment and reproach, surrounding the recreant young men. Mr. Errol, the Captain, the veteran, and even Mr. Perrowne, came to learn what was the matter. When they heard the intentions of the pair, Mr. Thomas and the parson were prepared to make the most abject apologies to the dominie, who insisted that there was no necessity; on the contrary, he alone was to blame, but all that was past. Mrs. Carruthers would not hear of their going just as they were becoming so pleasantly acquainted, assured them that Bridesdale had ample accommodation, and commanded the veteran to form a company of his grandchildren and arrest the would-be deserters. Marjorie clung to her Eugene's right leg. Mr. Errol accused him of stealing away with his gloves, and finally the lawyer confided to Mrs. and Miss Carmichael that he didn't want to go a bit, was never happier in his life. Miss Du Plessis put a hand on the dominie's arm, a hand that tingled away in to his very heart, and said her uncle would be so disappointed when he arrived to find that his friends of Collingwood had not deemed him worth waiting for. Finally, the Squire took them both aside, and, speaking seriously, said he had no right selfishly to detain them, but the time was critical, poor Nash was away on a dangerous errand, and their services, already great and highly appreciated, might yet be of the greatest importance. Besides, after the fatigue and excitement of the past night, they were not fit to travel. The dominie confessed that, with all the excitement and possible danger, he had enjoyed himself amazingly, that his only motive for leaving was the fear of trespassing upon the kindness of Mrs. Carruthers, and that, if his humble services were of any value, he trusted the Squire would [Pg 199]draw upon them to the utmost. The lawyer, hearing his companion's decision, wanted to give a wild Irish hurroo, but, checking himself, ground the Squire's right hand with his own kid-gloved afflicted member, as if he had been a long lost brother. When they next reached the hall, Miss Halbert was there taking in the situation with the other young ladies. She had already seen enough to know that neither of her fair companions was capable of properly addressing the culprits, so she made up for their deficiency, saying: "Go upstairs at once, you naughty boys, and take off these pads." The naughty boys ascended, with a strangely combined feeling of joy and smallness, and, when the knapsacks were removed, Coristine sank into a chair laughing. "O Lord, Wilks," he said, "she called them pads!"

The doctor arrived in time for dinner, and reported three wounded men instead of one. Two had pistol wounds that had evidently been attended to from the first, the other had a gunshot in the back, and must have dragged himself a long way after it, for he was almost gone with loss of blood. "That'll be the chiel' puir Nash fired at wi' Ben's gun," said Carruthers.

"Can your wife put me and Fanny up for the night, John?" asked the doctor, looking serious.

"Just delighted to do so," replied the Squire; "we have more space than we know how to fill."

"I must tell you why. These rough fellows at the Encampment are furious, and one of them, in his gratitude, warned me, on no account, to be in or near your house to-night."

"Doctor, that's another thing. I have no right to let you risk yourself and Miss Fanny in time of danger in my house."

"But we will, John. Come here, Fanny!" Telling his daughter the circumstances, the doctor asked her decision, and she at once answered: "Of course, Mr. Carruthers, we shall stay. Papa has two pistols in his gig, and, if necessary, will lend me one. I am a good shot, am I not, papa?"

"Yes, John, she has a fine eye and nerve for a mark."

At the dinner table Doctor Halbert conversed with the pedestrians about the scenery they had passed through, [Pg 200]and recommended them, by all means, not to fail in visiting the Flanders' lakes. He informed them that they constitued a long and perplexing chain, being more like a long continuous sheet of water, narrowing every here and there into straits, affording little more than room enough for two boats to pass through, than an actual succession of lakes. To penetrate far in would be dangerous, but his guide had informed him that no visitors to the first three ran any risk of interference.

"By the bye, Miss Cecile," interrupted the Squire, "some of these lakes are your property, are they not?"

"Yes, Mr. Carruthers," the lady replied; "but they would be so no longer if a very kind friend had not paid the taxes for them."

"Hoot toot, lassie, what's the taxes on a bittock o' wild land and useless water?"

"I should like above all things to see these lakes," remarked the dominie.

"Do you know," said Mr. Perrowne, "for sow long a time as I have been in Flanders, I have never seen the lakes. One down't like to gow alowne, you know."

100

"I say we go this afternoon," proposed the lawyer.

"I'm with you, sir," responded the minister. "We'll drop cricket and golf, the day, Perrowne." Then in a whisper to Carruthers, "I'm anxious about poor Nash."

"Then, meenister, see that ye aa tak' your revolvers and cartridges. I can supply you and Perrowne."

Coristine proposed to botanize, but did not care to detain the expedition by continually opening his knapsack, nor to incommode himself with the burden of the strap press. He regretted that he had not brought his vasculum, when Miss Carmichael spoke up, and said that she would furnish him with one when the party was ready to start. After dinner the company lounged for half an hour on the verandah and in the garden. There the Captain made up his mind to go with the exploring party, and take charge of Richards' scow on the first lake, that being the only craft available. Ben Toner came round from the kitchen and asked the Squire if he had anything for him to do, as Sylvanus wanted to stay with old man Newcome and read the Bible to him.

"Do you know the lakes, Toner?" asked Mr. Carruthers.

[Pg 201]"If you don't mind Squier, I'd sooner you'd call me Ben."

"Well, Ben, then?"

"Yaas, leastways I've ben at the laiuk as is nighes to han.'"

"Do you mind taking your gun, and looking out for sport with these gentlemen?"

"They isn't nawthin I'd laike bettr'en that."

So, Ben got his gun and ammunition, and the Captain was furnished with a stout walking-cane loaded in the head. The two parsons, the dominie, and the lawyer had pistols in their pockets. When ready to start, Miss Carmichael came up to Coristine carrying some mysterious object behind her back. Rapidly bringing it forward, she threw a thick green cord over the lawyer's shoulders, from which depended a browny black japanned tin candle-box. Of course, it was an accident that the cord was short, and that Coristine bent his head just as the fair damsel stood on tiptoe to adjust the improvised vasculum.

"I hope I didn't hurt you with my awkwardness, Miss Carmichael," pleaded the penitent knight of the order of the candle-box.

"Not at all, Mr. Coristine, it was my fault. I am afraid your nose suffered."

"Ha! ha!" chuckled the Captain, "young fellows can stand a lot o' that sort o' punishment. Reefs o' that kind don't do human vessels no harm."

Wilkinson was getting sick of the Captain and his aggressive vulgarity. Coristine didn't mind him; anybody belonging to Miss Carmichael was, for the present, delightful. Nevertheless, for marching purposes, he fell in with Toner, while the Captain accompanied Mr. Errol, and Wilkinson, Mr. Perrowne. They had six miles to tramp, which took them a good hour and a-half. The Captain discussed navigation in Scripture times with the minister, and decided that the Jews might have been good at punting round, but were a poor seafaring lot. The dominie and the parson were deep in the philosophy of the affections, in the course of which excursus the former quoted the words:—

Like Dian's kiss, unasked, unsought,
Love gives itself, it is not bought
Nor voice nor sound betrays
Its deep, impassionated gaze.
It comes, the beautiful, the free,[Pg 202]
The crown of all humanity,
In silence and alone.
To seek the elected one.

Mr. Perrowne was struck with these verses, and, taking out his note book, begged that his companion would repeat them, as he recorded their sublime sentiment for future use. They then proceeded to eulogize Miss Du Plessis, of whom the parson formed a very high estimate, which he qualified by the statement that, were he not in holy orders, he would say Miss Fanny Halbert was more fun and ever so much jollier. Mr. Wilkinson really could not say, speaking conscientiously and without reserve, that he regarded jollity as an essential element in true womanhood. In his estimation it sank the peculiar grace and sacred dignity of the sex too nearly to a level with ordinary prosaic humanity. Mr. Perrowne concurred in a measure, but thought it was awfully nice for men of serious occupations, like the dominie and himself, to have somebody to liven them up a little; not too much, down't you know, but just enough to dispel the blues. The lawyer interrogated Toner. "Well, Ben, have you got any news of your young lady?"

"Yaas, Doctor."

"Never mind calling me doctor, Ben, because I'm not one yet. My name is Coristine."

"Then, Mr. Corsten, I heern from old man Newcome as Serlizer's out in that there Slec Camp in the laiuks. She's cookin' for twainty dollars a month, and that's tarble good wages for gals, ef so be she gets her money all right."

"Not a very nice place for a good girl to be, Ben."

"No, it ain't; log roll and timber slide the hull consarn."

"These are queer expressions you've got."

"Yaas, Mr. Corsten, I waynt and promised that there priest as looked like Mr. Nash, guaiss it must ha' bin his brother, as I wouldn't sweaur no moer. And now, it keeps my mind workin' mornin' and night, so'st to know what to spit out when I'm raiul mad and hoppen."

"It must be quite an anxiety to you, Ben."

"Anxiety? It's wearin' my life away. I've got a bit of a rest jest now on loggin' and lumberin', but them words 'll soon be used up."

[Pg 203]"What's to hinder you repeating them, or leaving them out altogether? I hardly ever feel the need of them."

"It's the way you're broughten up, like your food. What 'ud do you for dinner, wouldn't be nigh enough for me. Same ways in speakin', they must be something to fill your talk out."

"Swearing is a poor business, Ben. Our Saviour, when He was on earth, said, Swear not at all."

"Is that in the Bible, Mr. Corsten?"

"Yes."

"Wall, it may be in some, but t'aint in the one Sylvanus was readin' to old man Newcome, fer that says in black and white as Jesus cussed the barrn fig tree, and I'd laike to know what's odds between cussin' and swearin'. It stands to reason and natur that He wouldn't go and tell folks not to do things He did Himself; don't it?"

"If you had read the chapters, there are two of them, that tell the story of the fig tree, you would have found that the disciples called it cursing when it was only a quiet saying: 'Let no fruit grow on thee henceforth.' You wouldn't call that cursing, would you?"

"O my, no, that ain't wuth callin' a cuss; they ain't no cuss about it. Now, fer whole souled, brimstun heeled cuss words, they's——"

"Never mind telling me any. They wouldn't do me any good, and the clergyman forward there might hear them."

"Do these clergy belong to the Church?"

"They both think they do in different ways, but, strange to say, neither of them belongs to your Church."

"Wall, I ain't got no quarrl at 'em. I guaiss all the good folks 'll get to Heaven somehow."

"Amen!" answered the lawyer, and the conversation ended.

There was no visible cart track to the lakes. If Rawdon's whiskey mill, as Ben called it, was really somewhere among them, there must of necessity have been a road tapping their shores at some point, for an extensive business employing so many men could hardly exist without a means of easy transportation. To the neighbourhood of the Lakes Settlement, however, this road was a mystery. The party halted at a log house by the side of [Pg 204]the road proper, and Mr. Perrowne, who claimed Richards as a parishioner, asked his wife if he and his friends could have the use of her boat. Mrs. Richards gave the required permission very graciously, and the excursionists struck into the bush path which led to Lake No. 1, or Richards' Lake. The bush had once been underbrushed, perhaps a long time back by the Indians who generally made for water; but the underbrush was now replaced by a dense growth of Canadian yew, commonly called Ground Hemlock, the crimson berry of which is one of the prettiest objects in the vegetable world. It, and other shrubs and small saplings, encroached on the narrow path, and, in places, almost obliterated it. The land rose into a ridge a short distance from the water, so that it was invisible until the crest was reached. Then, a dark circular lake, seemingly altogether shut in by the elsewhere dense forest, made its appearance. There were remains of a log shelter near the shore on the left, and, between it and the somewhat muddy beach, Toner lit a fire of drift wood to drive away the flies which followed the party out of the bush. The punt was soon discovered moored to a stake, a punt with three seats flush with the gunwales, one each fore and aft, and one in the centre.

"O, I saye," cried Mr. Perrowne, "look at that lovely little island out there! See, you can hardly see it because of the black shadows. What a place to fish! and here we are without a single rod."

"Ain't no need to trouble about rods," remarked Ben; "I kin cut you half-a-dozen in two shakes of a dead lamb's taiul."

"And I've got three hooked lines," added the lawyer, producing part of his Beaver River purchase from his breast pocket. The dominie did not wish to trust himself in a doubtful craft with Coristine again, and he distrusted the Captain, save on the *Susan Thomas.* His former success in fishing, and his present pleasant relations with Perrowne, prompted him to join that gentleman in practising the gentle art. But what about bait? The question having been put to Toner, who returned with three springy saplings, and worms having been suggested, that veteran fisherman told Mr. Perrowne that he might as well look for a gold mine as for worms in new land.[Pg 205]When, however, some envelopes were produced from various pockets, he proceeded to fill them with grasshoppers and locusts. He also excavated a little pond near the shore, and gathered a collection of caddice worms from the shallow border of the lake, after which he found an old bait tin in the log shelter, that he filled with water, into which he transferred the pond's inhabitants for transportation. "Ef them baiuts don't suit, they's a heap o' little frawgs in the grass of that there island," he finally remarked, before unmooring the scow. Then the dominie and Mr. Perrowne got on board with their rods, lines, and bait, and were poled and paddled by Ben over to their isle of beauty. Their lines were in the water, and a bass was on each hook, before the scow returned to the shore.

Now the Captain took command of the craft, occupying the entire stern thwart; while Ben, with his gun resting on the floor and pointing its muzzles out over the bow, held that end of the vessel. The commander would not allow the passengers who sat amidships to do any work, but said they might talk or sing if they had a mind to. Then the lawyer sang:—

The floatin' scow ob ole Virginny
I've toiled for many a day,
Workin' among de oyster beds,
To me it was but play.

When he ended, Mr. Errol gave the company "Flow gently, Sweet Afton, amang thy green braes," and Coristine wondered much if "My Mary" that occurs in the song had any reference to a Marjorie, one who, as he said inwardly,

Shall never be thine,
But mine, but mine, so I fondly swear,
For ever and ever mine!

After Mr. Errol's effort, which won applause from the Captain, the lawyer waved his handkerchief as a farewell sign to the busy fishermen, for, just at that moment, the apparently land-locked shore opened, and a narrow channel between cliffs came into view. The second lake, into which they soon glided, was more beautiful than the first. A few jays and woodpeckers were flying about, and Toner was anxious to have a shot at a golden woodpecker, which he called a Highholder, and which sat unconcernedly on a [Pg 206]limb within splendid range. Mr. Errol dissuaded him, saying he had heard that the report of a gun was carried through all the channels to the very end by the echoes, and reverberated there like the noise of thunder; after last night, they had better be as quiet as possible. To take his mind off the disappointment, Coristine asked Ben if he could sing and paddle too. He guessed he could, as paddling wasn't taking his breath away any. So Ben was pressed to sing, and at once assumed a lugubrious air, that reminded the lawyer of The Crew. The song was about a dying youth, who is asked what he will give in legacy to his mother, his sister, and various other relatives. He is liberal to all, till his lady-love's name is mentioned, and, for some unknown reason, excites his indignation. The tune was not the same as The Crew's copyright.

"What will you give your sweetheart, my comfort and my joy?
What will you give your sweetheart, my darling boy?"
"Oh! a gallows to hang on!
Mother, make my bed soft;
I've a pain in my chest;
I want to lay down."

The last line was sung in a very solemn and affecting monotone. Coristine had to pretend to be deeply moved, to turn round facing the Captain, and chew first his moustache and then half of his pocket handkerchief. "Eh, Ben," said the graver minister, "I'm afraid that was no' a very Christian spirit to die in."

"No, your raiverence," replied the singer, "but ef I hadn't a knowed it was old man Newcome as took Serlizer away, I'd be cant-hooked and pike-poled ef I wouldn't ha' sung jest them words, that's ef I had a paiun in my chaist and wanted to lay down." When they reached the third lake, through a channel similar to the last, the Captain said sternly: "I'm in command of this vessel, and expect orders to be obeyed. No more singin' nor laughin' out nor loud talkin'. Doctor says it's as much as life's worth to go beyond it. You've heerd orders; now mind 'em." Everything was silent, save the soft dip of the paddles in the water; the quiet was painfully oppressive. Ugly thoughts of bad men mingled with a sense of the natural beauty of the scene. Toner in the bow silently pointed to a square artificial-looking white object at the entrance to the next channel, which was the limit of the voyage. At [Pg 207]last the punt came up to it, and its occupants found the channel barred by a heavy grating, that passed down into the water. Above it was a notice in the usual form, indicating the prosecution of trespassers, and signed by order of the proprietor, Miss Du Plessis, with the name of John Carruthers, J.P. "The villain!" ejaculated Mr. Errol. "John has neither been here nor sent here. It's a forgery, an impudent forgery."

"Let us take it down and carry it back with us," said the lawyer.
"Na, na, my lad; we maun just wait till we come in force."
"Time to 'bout ship," growled the Captain.
"Hush!" whispered the minister, "I hear a voice, a woman's voice."
"Come on!" said the lawyer, jumping ashore; "will you come, Ben?"
"Don't ask me that, Doctor, I dassent," replied Toner, shivering with superstitious fear.

"Let me go with him," said the minister to the Captain; "we'll not be a minute away."
"Look sharp, then!" growled Mr. Thomas. "Are you loaded?"

The two explorers looked to their revolvers, and then climbed the bank, which was no easy task, as it was a mass of felled timber and dead brush; but the notes of a woman's voice led them on, and, at last, they found themselves on the shore of the fourth lake. They saw nothing, so they crouched down listening for the voice.

"Steve, Stevy dear, wake up and let us go away. Oh, why are you sleeping when every moment is precious? He will come, Stevy, I know he will, and kill you, dear!" The voice was very near. Simultaneously the intruders looked up the bank, and, at the foot of a standing hemlock, saw a woman, with gray hair hanging loose over her shoulders, who knelt by a recumbent figure. "Steve, dear brother," she continued, "do wake up! You used to be so good and sensible." Coristine crept nearer behind some bushes till he was within a very short distance of the pair. With a white, sad face, trembling in every limb, he came back as silently to the minister, and whispered: "It's poor Nash, and she calls him brother; Mr. Errol, he's [Pg 208]murdered, he's dead." The warm-hearted Errol, who had come out to look after the detective's safety, at once became a hero.

"Bide you there, Coristine," he said, "bide there till I call you." Then he arose and went to the spot, but the woman, though he was in full view, took no notice of him. He stooped and touched her. For a moment she shrank, then looked up and saw it was not the person she dreaded. "Matilda Nagle," whispered the minister, "we must get poor Steevie away from here." Then he saw that her intellect was gone; no wonder that she was the mother of an idiot boy. "Oh, I am so glad you have come, Mr. Inglis," she cried, softly; "won't you try and wake Stevy, perhaps he will mind you better than me." The minister brushed the tears from his eyes, and strove to keep the sobs out of his voice. "I have a friend here and will call him," he said, "and we will carry Steevie away to the boat, and all go home together." So he called Coristine, and they picked the dead man up, the dead man from whose smooth, girl-like face the disguise had been torn away, and bore him painfully but tenderly over the rough fallen timber safely to the other side, the woman following. Ben shivered, as he saw the strange procession come down the hill, but, like the Captain, he uttered neither word nor cry. The bearers propped the dead man up against the middle thwart with the face towards the bow, and then set the woman down beside the Captain, who said: "Come along, my dear, and we'll see you both safely home." The old man's honest face won the poor sister's confidence, as she took her seat beside him and left her Stevy to the care of the minister and Coristine. With all their might and main paddled the Captain and Ben. Joyfully, all the company saw stretch after stretch of the lake behind them, until, at last, they passed the fishermen and landed on the shore. The minister and the lawyer laid their coats upon the boards of the log shelter, and placed their burden upon them. "Let him sleep a bit," said Mr. Errol to the mad woman; "let him sleep, and you help my friend to get a few flowers to take home with him." So Coristine took his candle-box from the floor of the punt, and, with his strange companion, gathered the skullcaps and loose-strifes and sundews that grew by the shore. She knew the flow[Pg 209]ers and where to find them, and filled the lawyer's improvised vasculum almost to overflowing with many a new specimen. He only took them to humour her, for what cared he for all the flowers that bloom when death, and such a death, was but a few yards away.

Ben Toner brought the fishers back with two good strings of fish; but, when they heard the story, they threw them into the lake. Ben was a handy man. He cut down two stout poles, and with leather wood bark constructed a litter, light but strong. On this the sleeping detective was laid, and while Mr. Errol and the Captain stumbled through the ground hemlock on either side of the now cheerful mad woman, the other four carried their ghastly load, with scalding tears streaming from every eye. "S'haylp me," said Ben to the lawyer, "ef I don't hunt the man as killed him till he dies or me." After a painful journey they reached the Richards' house, and Richards was at home. Mr. Perrowne told him all about it, and the brave fellow answered:—

"Bring it in here, passon; we've a place to put it in where it'll be safe till they send for it. I ain't scared, not I. You know my four boys in your club; they've all got guns and can use 'em, and I've got mine to boot." So, they left the body there, and persuaded the sister to come with them on their six mile walk home. It was seven o'clock before they had accomplished half the journey, and had been met by the representatives of an anxious household, the Squire and his father-in-law, the latter with rifle in hand, prepared for action. The first joy at beholding them safe and sound was damped by the news they brought. As soon as Carruthers could recover himself he spoke to the weird woman and invited her to come and rest at Bridesdale. Then he hastened on ahead to warn his wife and sister, and make arrangements for the reception of the strange visitor. When the party arrived at the house they found a large company, young and old, assembled to meet them, for, in addition to the doctor and his daughter, there was Mrs. Du Plessis with her daughter on one side, and, in all its soldierly dignity, the tall form of Colonel Morton on the other. The lawyer also noticed the ebon countenance of Mr. Maguffin peering over the palings in the direction of the stables. Matilda Nagle was hurried away to [Pg 210]the back of the house by Mrs. Carruthers and her sister-in-law, there to find her idiot boy, to partake of necessary food provided by the compassionate Tryphena, and, for a time, altogether to forget the sad tragedy of the day. Tryphosa prepared tea for the truants in the breakfast room, and, after the formalities of introduction and reacquaintance had been gone through, Miss Carmichael poured out tea for the five, while Tryphosa did the same for Ben in the kitchen. The Captain told how Mr. Errol and the lawyer braved the terrors of the barred-in lakes, which appalled the stout heart of big Ben Toner. The two heroes hastened to put all the credit on one another's shoulders, in which, so far as one person's estimation was concerned, the minister triumphed, for, through the tears that shimmered in her eyes, Coristine could see that the presiding goddess was proud of him, and, with all his simple-heartedness, he knew that such pride has its origin in possession.

CHAPTER XI.

Old Man Newcome's Escape, Arrest and Conveyance Home—The Colonel's Plan of Campaign—He Takes Command—Maguffin's Capture by Messrs. Hill and Hislop—The Richards' Aid Enlisted—Squire as Colonel, and Mr. Terry, Sergeant-Major—The Skirmish— Harding Murdered—Wilkinson and Errol Improving the Time—The Young Incendiary— Mr. Hill Crushes Maguffin.

Everybody grieved for the offtaking of the detective. In the front of the house, the Squire and the minister, who knew his history, were most affected; in the back, Ben Toner was the corypheus of grief. An old man on a couch in an adjoining room heard the news, and, little thinking that his deposition and confession were safe in the Squire's possession along with many other documents, rejoiced thereat, and conceived a heroic project. At first, he thought of enlisting the idiot boy, but had to give up the idea; for the boy was happy with those whom he knew, and obstinately refused to go near the old reprobate. Sylvanus no longer watched him; he was basking in the smiles of Tryphena, and, at the same time, amusing Monty. There was a passage from the room he was in to the back of the main hallway, which led into the open air, [Pg 211]independently of the summer kitchen. His coat was gone and his hat, both his boots were removed, and his wounded leg was bandaged, but he was a tough old criminal, and a bare back rider from a boy. He slipped off the couch, and helped himself along by the wall, thankful that his boots were off and he could move quietly. Still, simple Sylvanus, taken in by the good old man who loved to have the Bible read to him, neglected his duty. Newcome gained the hall, the porch, the open air, and, at last, could hardly believe his good luck to find himself in the stable unperceived. What a lot of horses were there with nobody to look after them! He saw one that suited him, a handsome beast he had seen in Collingwood, the travelling powers of which he knew. To that stall he went, and braced himself against the partition for a spring, after he had loosed the halter, and slipped on a bit and bridle. He backed his steed out, turned in the passage way and made for the door. Another moment and he would be free. No horse in the stable, even if saddled and bridled, would be able to overtake him, once he was on the road. But, at the door he met an obstacle in the shape of a mountain of straw, that caused the horse to back. The desperate man dug his knees into the flanks of the beast, and urged it on. Down went the straw mountain, and the luckless Timotheus beneath it, and Newcome rained a few exultant curses on him, as he forced his steed; when a well-dressed negro sprang up from nowhere, and, seizing the rein nearest him, spoke to the intelligent animal, and backed it to one side. In a moment Timotheus wriggled himself unhurt out of the litter, and, by main force, pulled the escaped prisoner down; while Mr. Maguffin remarked that "hoss thieves ain't pumculiah ter no paht of the habitatable yeth."

Newcome squirmed and fought as well as he was able, but to no avail. Timotheus was simple and he was clumsy, but he was no weakling. Maguffin led the horse back into the stable, spread his litter, and replaced the bridle on the wall. Then he came out quite unruffled, and asked Timotheus if he would like him to use his new boots on the prisoner, to which that worthy replied with a grin: "I guess I've pooty nigh parlyzed his laigs to stop his wrastlin' tricks aready." Sylvanus, in a lucid moment, [Pg 212]remembered his charge, and found the bird had flown. He came out to look for his Bible-loving friend, dreading the Captain's wrath, and great was his relief when he found him a victim in the strong arms of his brother. "Here, Sylvanus, you hold him, so's the Square'll think t'was you as cotched him," said the unselfish Timotheus. So Sylvanus, nothing loath, seized the hypocrite, and Timotheus went for the Squire, while Maguffin looked calmly on, occasionally glancing at his heavy-soled new boots, as if regretting that there was no immediate call for their services. The Squire was angry, for he had been kind to the old sinner; but he saw that the prisoner was an element of weakness in the house. What was to hinder him escaping again, committing murder, setting the place on fire? He called up Toner. "Ben," he said, "how long would it take you to convey Newcome to his home in a farm waggon with a good team?" "Ef the teeum's smart, I guaiss an houer 'ud do," answered the prospective son-in-law of the victim. Accordingly a springless waggon was produced, some straw thrown in, and Newcome securely bound with ropes, lying flat on his back, with his own coat and a sack or two put under his head for a pillow. "Timotheus," continued Mr Carruthers, "you had better go with Ben. Take your guns, both of you, and bring them back as quick as you can." Off started the ambulance, at first gently and humanely. When out of sight of the house, Toner grinned at Timotheus, and Timotheus grinned back at Ben. "It can't be haylped, Timotheus," remarked the latter in a low tone, "we're bound to git back airly, ef they's moer guyard mountin' to be did. So here goes, Serlizer or no Serlizer." The horses were pretty fresh, and they tore along, enjoying the fun, and answering with their heels to every playful flick of the whip. The road was rough and hilly; the jolting almost threw the occupants of the box seat off the waggon that had no springs. Old man Newcome groaned, and implored Ben, for the sake of Serlizer, to go easy or leave him on the roadside to die. "Ef you don't laike my teamin'," said Toner, in a simulated huff, "I'll quit. Here, Timotheus, you had ought to know them hosses better'n me." Timotheus took the reins, and cried: "Gerlang, we ain't no time ter lose; rattle the brimstun an' [Pg 213]merlasses old malufacture over the stones, he's ony a firebug as nobody owns." The delight of The Crew's brother in getting off this new and improved version of an ancient couplet made him reckless. He and Ben jumped into the air like shuttlecocks, and seemed to like it. "I heern say," remarked Toner, while moving momentarily skywards, "I heern tayll as this here joltin' beats all the piulls and pads as ever was made for the livyer."

"Yaas," cheerfully responded Timotheus, coming down with a sounding bump; "myuns is like what the doctor out our way said to fayther wunst. Says he, 'Saul, your livyer's tawpidd.' So's myun, Ben; it's most tarble tawpidd. Gerlang, yer lazy, good fer nawthun brutes; poor old man Newcome won't get home this blessed night, the way yer a-goin'."

The waggon reached the Newcome shanty. The old man was unbound and lifted out into his own bed. Strong as he was, he had fainted, which his charioteers were not sorry to see. "He's had an accident, Miss Newcome," said Ben to the man's wife; "but he'll soon be all right." Fortunately, the doctor had done his duty well, and the shaking had failed to loosen the bandages over the wound. The drivers got into the waggon again and drove home more gently, exchanging a few words with each other; one being: "Guaiss old man Newcome's out o' mischief fer one night."

While Bridesdale was being delivered from the presence of one unwelcome guest, the welcome ones of the front were discussing with the Squire the programme for the night. He had made out a warrant for the arrest of Rawdon, should he again have the hardihood to turn up, and otherwise proposed to repeat the guards of the night before. While the excursionists were at tea, the colonel and Mr. Terry had been walking about with an object in view; and the latter gentleman informed his son-in-law that "the cornel has a shplindid oiday in his moind." Colonel Morton was requested to favour the company with it, and proceeded to do so. "From what infohmation I have had fuhnished me by my fellow-soldieh, Mr. Tehhy, I pehsume you have pehmitted the attacking fohce to select its own basis of opehations, and have yohselves stood almost entihely on the defensive. With a small [Pg 214]fohce, this is vehy often the only couhse to puhsue. But, as I now undehstand from reeliable infohmation brought in, the enemy's fohce of seventeen is reduced by four, while that of the gahhison is augmented by three—the doctor, myself and my sehvant. Ah, no; I fohgot you have had one sad casualty, as my niece infohms me, in the fall of Mr. Nash; which leaves the strength of the gahhison fohteen, as against thihteen of the assailants. My friend, Mr. Wilkinson, infohms me that a small detachment of five men, well ahmed, holds a foht some six miles in the dihection of the enemy. Now, gentlemen of the council of wah, can we not obtain that this friendly outpost make a divehsion in conceht with the offensive paht of our ahmy? Send a scout with instyuctions foh them to occupy the wood neah their foht, and, eitheh with blank or ball cahtyidge—as you, Genehal Cahhathers, may dihect— meet the enemy as ouah troops dyive them back, and thus pehvent them seeking the coveh of the trees against us. This being done, send a scout, mounted if possible, to guahd against attack from the left; post pistol sentinels round the buildings, and fohm the rest of the available fohce into an attacking pahty occupying the strategic point examined by Mr. Tehhy and me: I allude to the plantation to the reah of the right wing. Just as soon as the enemy comes up to occupy that position, chahge them like bulldogs and drive them as fah as possible towahds the road, and at last bring them undeh the guns of our friendly foht. That, I think, is bettah than losing heaht by watching all night long and endangehing the safety of the ladies. Such, gentlemen, is my humble counsel."

"Hark till him, now, jantlemen; pay attintion till him, all av yeez," exclaimed Mr. Terry; "fer 'tis the wurrud av a sowldjer and an offisher."

"Assume command, Colonel, if you please. We are all ready to obey orders," said the Squire. "Is that not the case, friends?"

To this the whole company answered "Yes," and Colonel Morton at once gave his commands.

The garrison was paraded on the lawn, its armament strengthened by two rifles borrowed in the neighbourhood, of which the Squire carried one and the lawyer the other. The post office had been cleared out of its complete stock [Pg 215]of powder and shot by Carruthers, early in the morning, to the no little disgust of the Grinstun man when he went for his mail. "Volunteehs foh the foht, foh mounted patyol, foh plantation picket—three!" called out the colonel. Perrowne volunteered for the first, as likely to have most influence with the Richards. "Blank cartridge," said the Squire, as he rode away amid much waving of handkerchiefs. "Oi'm yer picket, cornel," said Mr. Terry, stepping out of the ranks with his rifle at the shoulder in true military fashion. "Ef it's a gennelman wot knows riden, sah, and kin fiah a pistol or revolvah, I respectuously dedercates my feeble servishes," volunteered Mr. Maguffin, who mounted and patrolled poor Nash's beat, with a revolver handy; while the veteran ran at a regular double to the far end of the strip of bush. "The Squiah had bettah take the field, as he knows the ground and I do not," said the colonel; "I will command the gahhison. I shall want the captain, the doctah, Mr. Wilkinson and Mr. Ehhol—four. My deah sistah-in-law can shoot; and so, I believe, can Miss Halbeht, so we are seven."

"There's Wordsworth for you, Wilks, my boy," Coristine remarked, nudging his right hand man.

"Corry, my dear fellow, whatever induced you to take that gun?" answered the dominie, apprehensive for his friend's safety in the field.

"It's no gun, Wilks; it's a rifle. If I only get a sight at Grinstuns, I'll commit justifiable homicide. Then I wish the Squire would punish me by sending me down here for thirty days."

"The gahhison will take three paces to the fyont; quick, mahch!" commanded the colonel.

The four came out in pretty straggling order, and the two ladies named fell in beside them.

"Now, Squiah, I leave yoah command of five men, which Mr. Pehhowne will soon augment to six, and Mr. Tehhy to seven, in yoah hands. If I have no fuhtheh need of a mounted patyol, my sehvant will join the gahhison."

The colonel then left to post his sentries, which he did so judiciously that three were enough, namely, the doctor, the minister and the dominie. The ladies kept watch by turns on the front of the house. Soon a voice was heard [Pg 216]at the gate calling for Colonel Morton. The colonel answered the summons in person. It was Maguffin dismounted, and behind him came two men, honest farmers apparently, one of whom led the coloured man's horse, while the other held his fowling piece at the port, ready for action in Maguffin's rear.

"Maguffin," said the colonel, sternly, "consideh youhself undeh ahhest, suh."

"I doan need ter hab ter, sah; that's jess wot I is this bressid minit."

"Good evening!" said the two farmers, amiably, and the colonel returned the salutation. "Good evening, gentlemen! but I feah you have made a mistake in ahhesting my sehvant."

"When a naygur on a fine beast gallops down on two quiet folk, and orders them to go back, disperse, and surrender, and them coming to see after the safety of their children and friends, the only one thing to do, if you have your guns along, is to arrest the naygur."

"Do I undehstand, Maguffin, that you ordehed these wohthy people to go back, dispehse, and suhhendah without any wahhant?"

"And presinted his pistil, too," continued the tall man, who had already spoken, and who was the coloured man's guard.

"Have you no answwah, Maguffin?"

"I fought, Cunnell, I was ter patterole this heah road and repawt all the folkses I see on or off'n it."

"Yes, repoht to me, as youh officeh, suh."

"Oh, I fought yoh meant to repawt em wif a revolvah, sah."

"I suppose, gentlemen, you will let my sehvant go, when I say I deplohe his foolish mistake, and apologize foh his insolence?

"To be shure, sir," replied the guard; "give the man his horse, Annerew."

Maguffin remounted, and, receiving more minute instructions from his master, returned to his patrol duty.

"We're just coming in to help the Squire, and me to look after my childer, Tryphena and Tryphosa and Baby Rufus. When the Baby didn't come back this mornin', I said to his mother, 'Persis' says I, 'I must go and see the [Pg 217]boy.' So here I am. My name is Hill, sir, Henry Cooke Hill, and this is my neighbour, and some day, perhaps, Rufus's father-in law, Annerew Hislop"—then in an undertone—"a very dacent man, sir, though a Sesayder."

"Is that the case?" asked the colonel with eagerness, advancing towards Andrew. "Were you on ouah side, suh, in the wahah?"

"Naw, naw, surr, I'm no sodjer, but a humble maimber o' the pure gospel Secession kirk. As the fufty-fufth parryphrase says:—

With heevenly wappons I have focht
The baittles o' the Lord."

"Ah yes, pahdon me my mistake. Come in, gentlemen; the Squiah will be happy to see you."

Maguffin's captors entered, were warmly greeted by their friends in hall and kitchen, partook of a hasty supper, and were ready for the engagement of the night.

Perrowne, who was a good rider, soon made his appearance, reporting that the Richards were only too glad to make the desired repulse of the evil crew from their neighbourhood, and, as members formerly of a volunteer company, understood something of military tactics. The parson also reported that he had nearly fallen in with the advancing attacking force of, he should say, twenty men; but, sighting them ahead, he advanced slowly until he saw them move solidly to his left into the fields, with the evident intention of coming at the house through the strip of bush. The villains could not be far off. "Now, Squiah," said the colonel, "hasten, suh, to join Mr. Tehhy; a few minutes make all the diffehence in case of an attack."

The Squire had now nine men under his command, including his father-in-law, for Ben and Timotheus were safely back, having passed the formidable Maguffin. The other six were Sylvanus and Rufus, Messrs. Hill, Hislop, Perrowne, and Coristine. All were armed with loaded guns and rifles; the carbine and the blunderbuss remained to guard the house. Rapidly they reached the bush which hid them from view, and rejoiced the veteran's heart with their array.

"Now, grandfather," said Carruthers, "you must get us all into shape."

[Pg 218]"Well now, we'll make belave this is a bittillion, an' you're cornel, an' Oi'm sargint-major. It's ten shtrong we are, an' there's three roifles an' two double barrels anyhow. You git in the rare, Cornel an' Mishter Coristine an' Mishter Parrowne an' Ben Toner; the rist av yeez shtay where yeez are, till I say 'Extind!' thin, tin paces apart for the front rank, an' tin for the rare rank; but the rare alternatin' wid the front. Whin Oi say, 'Front rank!' that rank'll diliver it's foire, an' go on wid its loadin' behind a three, moind! an' so on wid the rare. By the powers, here the varmints come. Shtiddy min, lishten till me an' be quoiet—Extind!"

There were some loudly beating hearts at that moment, for the enemy was in force, and partly armed with guns of some sort. Instead of advancing across the fields, as the defenders had hoped, they descended to the creek, in order to find cover from the bushes on its bank, until they reached the piece of wood. The veteran, telling his command to preserve its formation, wheeled it to the right, and ordered perfect silence. Leaving his rifle at his post, he slipped from tree to tree like a cat, having thrown off his shoes for the purpose. When he returned, the enemy, moving almost as silently, had entered the bush, but, anticipating no sentry at that point, had sought no cover. "Shtiddy, now min," whispered the sarjint-major; "take good aim, Front Rank, Riddy!" Five guns rolled out a challenge to the invaders, and, before they had time to seek cover, came, "Rare Rank, Riddy," and his own rifle led the other four weapons of the second line. "Are yeez loaded, front an' rare?" asked the ancient warrior; and, satisfied that all were, he put himself in the front and ordered a charge to outflank the enemy and hinder them getting away among the bushes. All perceived his intentions, except, perhaps, the two Pilgrims and Perrowne, who, however, were borne along by the rest. Dashing through the creek, part of the force volleyed the miscreants from there, and drove them into the open, while the remaining part kept them from seeking refuge in the bush. The Squire's men had the shelter of the brook alders and willows, now, and, led by Mr. Terry, in single file, at a rate almost as rapid as that of Rawdon's retreat, faced now and again to the left to fire, and loaded as they ran. At last [Pg 219]the shelter ceased, and all were in the open, both pursued and pursuers. "Kape it up," cried the indomitable veteran; "don't give the murtherin' blagyards a minit's resht!" Up, up the hill, they chased the said blackguards, until they reached the road. Within the skirting rail fences the Squire kept his men, faint but pursuing, and firing an occasional shot to lend the speed of terror to the miscreants' heels. In an hour from the beginning of the pursuit, the hunted Rawdonites were at the wild lands on the lakes, and prepared to enter the forest and make a stand or hide; when Carruthers cried: "Down flat on your faces every man," and five reports from in front rang through the air. The Richards were on guard, but either Perrowne had forgotten to tell them about blank cartridge, or they did not think proper to obey the order. "Come on a bit farther, lads, till we find where these villains turn in," cried the Squire. In another minute the victors combined with the Richards' party, and chased the thoroughly demoralized Rawdonites, whose guns and pouches strewed the ground, to a desolate rocky spot beside a swamp, where felled trees lay in indescribable confusion, over which the fugitives scrambled in desperate haste for home. The lawyer caught sight of a figure that he knew, far up the rocky slope, preparing to leap down from a prostrate trunk resting on three or four others, and aimed his rifle at it. The Squire threw up the weapon just in the nick of time. "It's ower gude a death for the likes o' him, Coristine. Gie him time to repent, an' let the law tak' its coarse. The cunning scoundrel! Even at the risk o' 's life he wadna let us ken whaur his waggon road is, but I've a thocht, man, that it's yonner whaur the rock rises oot o' the swamp." Then the good Squire took off his hat, and thanked God for the defeat of the evil doers.

Light though the night was, to continue the pursuit would have been the height of folly. The force was mustered and inspected by the so-called Colonel Carruthers, and the Sergeant-Major Terry. Including themselves, it was found to consist of no fewer than seventeen persons, one of whom was a woman, and the other a lad of about fifteen years of age, Matilda Nagle and her boy Monty. "I will show you where the road is," she said to the Squire; "it is hard to find, but I know it. When Stevy tried to [Pg 220]find it, Harding and he put him to sleep, so that I couldn't wake him up. Harding is asleep now too; I put him, and Monty helped, didn't you, Monty?"

Carruthers looked, and saw that the woman's right hand and that of the idiot boy were alike stained with blood. All his own men were safe and sound, not a scratch on any one of them. The veteran's rapid tactics had given the enemy hardly an opportunity to return the fire, and had destroyed their aim from the very beginning. All honour to the sergeant-major! All had behaved well. Father Hill and his friend Hislop felt like boys; and while the Sesayder took a fatherly interest in Rufus, the parent of Tryphena and Tryphosa was pleased with the bearing of the Pilgrims. Ben Toner's conscience was a little troubled about his treatment of old man Newcome, but he also had a feeling that he was getting nearer to Serlizer. The veteran and Mr. Perrowne were filled with mutual admiration; and Coristine felt that that night's work had brought to his suit, as an ordinary year's acquaintance could not have done, the vote and influence of the Squire. The victors gathered up the spoils of the vanquished, and, by a unanimous vote, handed them over to the grateful Richards, whom Carruthers and Perrowne warmly thanked for their timely aid. "It's about time, Squire,

110

we crushed them fellows out," said father Richards, to which the Squire replied: "If you and your sons are ready, we'll do it to-morrow as soon as the inquest is over."

"Boys," asked Richards, "are you fit for a man hunt to-morrer?"

"Fitter'n a fiddle," answered the boys; "then we can go fishin' where we durn please."

They bade their allies good bye, carrying their spoil with them, and twelve persons set out for a six-mile tramp home.

"Yeez can march at aise, march aisy, boys," ordered the veteran; and the party broke up into groups. The woman clung to the Squire, and the boy to Sylvanus, who had made whittled trifles to amuse him. Mr. Hill cultivated Timotheus, and formed a high opinion of him. Rufus, of course, addicted himself to his future father-in-law, the Sesayder. Mr. Terry thought it his duty to hold out high hopes to Ben in regard to the rescue of Serlizer; [Pg 221]and Perrowne and the lawyer journeyed along like brothers. There was a light in the post office, and the post-mistress at the door asked if the doctor had gone home yet, for two wounded men had sought shelter with her, and told her that one named Harding was lying down the hill near by. The Squire promised to bring the doctor to the wounded, and asked his father-in-law and Coristine, as if they were his nearest friends, to go down and see if they could find the wounded Harding. They went down and found him, but he was dead, with two of the Bridesdale kitchen-knives planted in his heart. In part, at least, the murder of Nash was avenged. They picked the slain assassin up and carried him to the road, where the post office stood, and deposited the body in an outbuilding to await the verdict of the morning.

Meanwhile, the dominie was happy; his rival, the parson, his tormentor, the lawyer, were away, and even that well-meaning Goth, the tired Captain, was asleep in the guard-room, opposite a half-empty glass of the beverage in which he indulged so rarely, but which he must have good. The doctor's lively daughter had left Mrs. Du Plessis to guard the front of the house, and was talking to her father on his beat, and he had a suspicion that Mrs. Carmichael was wrapping that cloud again round the minister's neck. When the battle commenced below, the colonel was everywhere, directing Maguffin, inspecting the posts, guarding on all sides against the possibility of the enemy's attack being a mere feint. All unknown to the rest of the company, Miss Carmichael was up in the glass-enclosed observatory at the top of the house, without a light, watching the movements of the hostile ranks beyond the bush, and inwardly praying for the success of the righteous cause and for the safety of those she loved. Of course her uncle John was among them, and the simple-hearted old grandfather of her young cousins, and even, in a way, Mr. Perrowne, who had behaved bravely, but there was a tall, unclerical form, which Mr. Terry and the Squire had difficulty in keeping up with, that her eye followed more closely. Every report of the lawyer's rifle seemed to press a warm spot on her maiden cheek, and then make the quick blood suffuse her face, as she thought of the morning and Mr. Wilkinson. That gentleman was [Pg 222]happy on guard at the top of the hill meadow, for a tall female figure, muffled up slightly as a preventive to chill from the night dews, came down the path towards his post, eager for news from the seat of war.

"Be careful, Miss Du Plessis, I beg of you!" implored the dominie; "heavy firing is going on not far off, and a stray bullet might easily find its way hither. Permit me to conduct you to a place of safety." So he led her with grave courtesy within the gate, and placed her on a garden seat in front of two trees large of bole, and interceptive of possible missiles. Of course, his own safety was a matter of no moment; he went out of the gate and to the utmost limit of his watch to gain, by eye and ear, tidings of the progress of the skirmish, which he returned every minute or two to report to the anxious young lady. Thus it was that, when the colonel came to inspect the posts, he found two sentinels at each, pertaining to different sexes. Returning to his sister-in-law on the verandah, he explained to that lady the peculiar difficulty of his position.

"You see, my deah sistah, that this is altogetheh contyahy to militahy discipline, and I ought to ordeh all undeh ahhest, but, were I to do so, madam, where would my sentinels come from?" Miss Du Plessis perceived the difficulty, as she handled the colonel's silver-mounted revolver, with an air of old practice; and proceeded to ask what her brother-in-law knew of the young gentleman who was furnishing Cecile with information of the fight.

Thereupon the colonel launched out into a panegyric of the dominie's noble qualities, imputing to him all that Coristine had done on his behalf, and a chivalrous Southern exaggeration of the school-master's learning and expressions of sympathy. "Marjorie appears to think more highly of the other pedestrian," remarked Mrs. Du Plessis, to which Colonel Morton replied that Mr. Coristine was indeed a handsome and excellent young man, but lacked the correct bearing and dignified courtesy of his friend, and, he should judge, was much his inferior in point of education. When the tide of battle rolled away to the right, altogether out of sight and almost out of hearing, the double sentries were still at their posts, no doubt con[Pg 223]versing with all propriety, but of what, they only individually knew. Even Miss Halbert did not confide to others the substance of a favourable criticism on Mr. Perrowne to which she treated her worthy father.

It was between one and two in the morning when the victorious army returned, and was received with open arms, literally in the case of the Squire and the veteran, and of Mr. Hill and Rufus in the kitchen, metaphorically in that of the remaining combatants. Mr. Carruthers released the doctor, and took him to visit the wounded at the post office. The minister and the dominie were also relieved, and Mr. Hill and the Sesayder, at their own request, put in their vacant places; while Maguffin dismounted, and, being armed with a gun and set in the doctor's post, constituted a guardian trio with his late captors. Of course, the warriors and past sentries had to eat and drink in guard room and kitchen, the latter apartment being more hilarious than it would have been had the seniors on duty formed part of its company. There was no old Bourbon for the colonel, but he managed to find a fair substitute for it, and informed Coristine, in answer to that gentleman's enquiry, how he happened to arrive so speedily at Bridesdale.

"It was Satuhday, suh, when my sehvant and I ahhived in Tohonto, and I met my deah sisteh in-law. At once, I sent Maguffin back by rail with the hohses to Collingwood, giving them Sunday to recoveh from the effects of the jouhney, tyavel by rail being vehy hahd on hohses. This mohning, or,ratheh I should say yestehday mohning, Madame Du Plessis and I went to Collingwood by rail, where my sehvant had secuhed her two places in the mail caht, and I had the honouh of escohting her to this pleasant place, and of beholding my chahming niece for the fihst time. I was indeed vehy fohtunate in ahhiving when I did, to be able to contribute a little to the secuhity of Bridesdale."

"You are doubtless aware, Colonel, that our enemies of to-night are in unlawful possession of Miss Du Plessis' property?"

"Suh, you astonish me. As her natuhal guahdian, I cannot, though in a foheign land, allow that foh a day, suh."

[Pg 224]"We think, at least Squire Carruthers thinks, of attacking them in force, after the double inquest to-morrow."

"Then, Mr. Cohistine, I shall claim the privilege of joining yoah fohce as a volunteeh. I wish the ground were fit foh cavalhy manoeuvehs, suh."

"We may need a few mounted men, as we hope to discover a masked road."

"That is vehy intehesting, suh. Will you kindly explain to me the chahacteh of the ground?"

The lawyer told all that he knew of the region, from hearsay and from personal experience. The supposed masked road, the actual rocky ascent covered with felled timber, an abatis, as the colonel called it, the access by water, and the portcullis at the narrows, were objects of great interest to the old soldier. He enquired as to the extent of the means of transportation, the probable numbers of the available force, and other particulars; and, when the weary Squire returned and bade all good people go to rest, if they could not sleep, in view of past wakefulness and the morrow's work, he begged, as a perfectly fresh man, to be excused and left in command of the guard, adding: "I shall study out a thyeefold convehging attack on the enemy's position, by wateh and by land, with cavalhy, infantry and mahines." The guard-room company joined in a laugh at the military joke, after which they dispersed, with the exception of the Captain, whom it was a pity to disturb, and Carruthers, who lay down upon a sofa, while the colonel went out to inspect his posts.

The pedestrians occupied a large, double-bedded room at the right corner of the house, above the verandah. The dominie was sleeping peacefully, but the lawyer had not even removed his clothes, with the exception of his boots, if they may be so called, as he lay down upon his bed to rest, with a window half open in front of him. Precisely at the moment when, the night before, he had discovered the incipient conflagration, there came to his nostrils the smell of unctuous fire. Pocketing his loaded revolver, he stepped out of the window on to the sloping verandah roof, off which, in spite of his efforts, he slid heavily to the ground. At once he was seized with no gentle hands by [Pg 225]at least three persons, who turned out to be Mr. Hill, the colonel, and Maguffin. "Catch that boy," he cried, as soon as they perceived their mistake, referring to a juvenile figure that he had seen slipping back towards the meadow. Sentry Hislop would probably have caught him, but there was no necessity. The idiot boy was in the arms of his wakeful mother, who, thinking he was going to Rawdon's quarters, as he probably was, intercepted him, saying: "Not back there, Monty, no, no, never again!" So deeply had his unnatural father, with brutal threats, impressed the lesson of incendiarism upon the lad that, all mechanically, he had repeated the attempt of the previous night. Fortunately for Coristine's hands, there was a garden rake at hand to draw out from under the verandah two kitchen towels, well steeped in coal oil, the fierce flame from which had already charred three or four planks of the floor. Two pails of water relieved all apprehensions; but the Squire awoke Sylvanus and ordered him to take Monty into his room, and, with his companions, be responsible for his safe keeping. Then, turning to the lawyer, and laying a friendly hand on his shoulder, he said: "If ye canna sleep, ye had better come in and tak' the Captain's chair; he's awa til 's bed, puir man." So Coristine entered the porch, and, as he did so, heard a voice above say: "No, Cecile, it is not your hero; it is mine again." "What are thae lassies gabbin' aboot at this time o' nicht?" said the Squire, harder of hearing. "Gang awa to the land o' Nod, and dinna spoil your beauty sleep, young leddies." The apostrophized damsels laughed lightly, whispered a few more confidences, and then relapsed into silence. John Carruthers had a high opinion of his niece, and said some very nice things about her, but, so far short did they fall of the lawyer's standard of appreciation, that he regarded them almost as desecrations. Still, it was very pleasant to be on such friendly terms with the Squire of the neighbourhood, the master of hospitable Bridesdale; and Miss Carmichael's uncle. "A splendid honest fellow," he said to himself, "as good every bit as Wilks' foreign aristocracy!" From time to time the colonel looked in upon the pair, and remarked that the contents of the Squire's decanter pleased him as well as Bourbon or Monongahela.

[Pg 226]When daylight came, the weary sentries were dismissed to the kitchen, where, under Tryphena's direction, the insane woman took much pleasure in providing for their creature comforts. The restraints upon Mr. Maguffin's eloquence being removed, it flowed in a grandiloquent stream. "Lave the cratur to me, Annerew," whispered Mr. Hill; "lave the nagur to me, and if I don't flummix and flabbergast his consayted voccabuelary, I was never a taycher." Then, turning to the coloured gentleman, he remarked in an incidental sort of way: "Were you ever in the company of deipnosophists before, Mr. Magoffin, deipnosophists mind! enjoyin' a gastromical repast?"

Mr. Maguffin's eyes expanded, and his jaw dropped.

"Yoh's got the devantidge ob yoh 'umble sarvant, Mistah Hill."

"It's not possible that a gentleman of your larnin' is ignorant of such simple, aisy polysyllables as them?"

"I'se afeard yoh's got me this time, sah."

"It stands to raison that there's limits to everybody's voccabuelary, unless it's a great scholard like Mr. Wilkinson; but I thought, perhaps, it was for a school taycher you would be settin' up?"

"Oh my! no, Mistah Hill, my eduracation was passimoniously insurficient. Most all my bettah class language I'se acquied fom clugymen ob de Baktis pussuasion."

"And they never tayched ye deipnosophist nor gastromical?"

"No, sah, they didn't, I'se humblerated ter confess."

The old schoolmaster looked at Mr. Hislop with a serious expression of mingled incredulity and commiseration, saying: "Such ignorance, Annerew, such ignorance!"; and somehow Mr. Maguffin did not see his way to gathering up the broken threads of conversation.

Timotheus was despatched by the Squire to summon a brother J.P., and the township constable, in order that immediate action against known criminal parties might be taken, as well as to notify the farmers adjacent that they were expected to sit in a coroner's jury. Having made all necessary legal arrangements, the Squire returned to the colonel, who, from a memorandum before him, sketched the plan of campaign. He proposed to put the five Richards as marines under the command of the Captain [Pg 227]to break down the grating between the third and fourth lakes, and push on to attack the enemy from that side. He wanted four mounted men armed with revolvers, and with stout sticks in lieu of swords, fearless horsemen whom he could lead through swamp or over obstacles to hold the masked road. The remaining body under the Squire, he thought, might follow the track of the fugitives of the night, and constitute the main besieging force. As to those who should perform the respective duties, apart from the persons named, the Squire suggested waiting till the inquests—which would bring some additions to the local population—were over. He hoped much from his fellow justice of the peace, Mr. Walker. Tom Rigby, an old pensioner, and the township constable, would probably have his hands full looking after the prisoners. Fortunately, the post office store of ammunition was not yet exhausted, to say nothing of that contained in various flasks and shot belts, and in the shape of cartridges. The colonel, apropos of warlike weapons, bemoaned the absence of bayonets, and warmly advocated a proposition of the lawyer's, that each combatant should carry, slung over the shoulder or in such way as not to interfere with the handling of his gun, a strong stick like those proposed by the commander-in-chief for his cavalry. Toner and Rufus were immediately roused from their slumbers, and sent to cut the requisite bludgeons, and drill them with holes to pass a cord through. Shortly after they had departed on their errand, the household awoke to life and activity, and, through casually opened doors, there came the gratifying odours of breakfast in preparation.

[Pg 228]

CHAPTER XII.

Mr. Bangs Accredits Himself—Silences Squire Walker—Constable Rigby in the Kitchen—The Inquests—Arrests, and Mr. Newberry—The Beaver River Contingent—Mr. Bangs and the Squire Consult—The Army Prepares—Wilkinson's Heroics—Mr. Bigglethorpe on Fishing.

When Timotheus returned, he was not alone; a slightly built man of medium stature, and rather flashily attired, rode beside him. The Squire strode to the gate, to learn that the younger Pilgrim had accomplished his various missions successfully, and to be presented by him, in his usual clumsy way, to Mr. Bengs, a friend of Mr. Nash as was. "Yore men is right, Squire; my neme is Bengs, Hickey Bengs, end pore Nesh sent for me to kem end help ferret out a geng of dem excise slopers, end here I find my pore friend merdered. I tell you, Squire, it's too dem bed, O, too dem bed!"

The Squire felt he must be cautious these times, but that did not hinder him being hospitable. "Come in, Mr. Bengs, and breakfast with us. My man will put your horse up. I have Nash's papers in my possession from his own hand, and, if I find they confirm your story, we will all be glad to take you into our confidence. You, of all men, understand the necessity for caution, and will, I hope, not take my precaution amiss."

"O Lud, no, Squire; yo're pretty shore to find letters frem me ameng pore Nesh's papers, or some memorenda about me. H.B., you know, Hickey Bengs."

Timotheus led the new detective's horse away, and the gentleman himself entered the house and office with the Squire. "Coristine," said the latter, familiarly addressing the lawyer, "would you mind looking up Errol quietly and sending him here?"

Of course he didn't mind, and soon returned with the minister. Both noticed that the Squire had two loaded pistols on the table before him, the stranger being on the other side. "You can remain, Coristine. I must introduce you, and the Reverend Mr. Errol, my fellow trustee [Pg 229]in the matter of these papers, to Mr. Bengs. Mr. Coristine is in the law, Mr. Bengs."

The dapper gentleman with the red tie and large scarf pin bowed amiably to the two witnesses of the interview, and Mr. Carruthers, with the minister by his side, proceeded to examine the papers. "Here it is," he said, after a few minutes of painful silence, "but what in aa the warld's the meanin' o't? B.R.—B.T.—R.C.P. The date is Saturday night."

"I think I know," interrupted the lawyer. "How will this do: Beaver River, Ben Toner, Roman Catholic Priest?"

"The very thing! Well, here's Sabbath. Prom. cum S.W.L.C. sup. eq."

Coristine had written the words down to study them. At last he said: "It's a mixture of French, Latin, and English abbreviations; Promenade or walk with Schoolmaster Wilkinson, Lawyer Coristine on the horse."

"Eh, man!" ejaculated the pleased Squire; "I'll hae to turn lawyer mysel'. Now, here's later doon, the same day—B.D.—S.C.—P.O. scripsi H.B. ven. inst. Come, my prophetic friend."

Triumphantly, the lawyer rolled out: "Bride's Dale, Squire Carruthers, Post Office. I have written H.B. to come instanter."

"Have you his letter, Mr. Bengs?" the Squire asked, and at once it was produced with the Flanders post mark on it, written on the Bridesdale paper, and in Nash's peculiar way. Still Mr. Carruthers doubted. How could he be sure that the letter had fallen into the right hands, or that this smooth-spoken swell was not a cunning agent of Rawdon's?

"John," said the minister, stooping, and lifting something off the carpet, "here's a bit of paper you've dropped out of the pocket-book, or perhaps out of that bookie you're reading from."

The Squire eyed the paper, and then, stretching his arm over the table, shook the detective warmly by the hand. "It was very foolish of me, Mr. Bangs, not to have seen that at first. It gives notice of your arrival, and describes you perfectly. There's a bit of Latin, Mr. Errol, you might ask our friend. It seems to be a sort of watchword with a countersign."

[Pg 230]The minister took the paper and read, "quod quaeris?" whereupon the detective smiled, and answered promptly, "molares ebrii."

"What in aa the warld's yon, Coristine?" enquired the Squire.

"Mr. Errol asked Mr. Bangs, 'What are you looking for?' and he answered, 'For full grindstones.'"

"When a man is *ebrius*, John," continued the minister, "he's no' just sober. Weel, weel, the catechis is over, and ye can tak' puir Nash's frien' into our plans. Thank Providence, there's the breakfast gong."

The ladies were astonished to see the new arrival enter the dining-room, the breakfast-room table being too small, with his three inquisitors. He was quite polite, however, though a little stiltedly so, as if not to the manner born. Mr. Terry insisted on vacating his seat in Mr. Bangs favour. He said: "There's a foine Oirishman from the narth by the name av Hill Oi wud be plazed to have some conversation wid, so yeez 'll jist koindly ekshcuse me all," and left for the kitchen. There were sixteen people at the table, so when Squire Walker turned up, Marjorie, who had been brought in to equalize the sides, had to yield her place to him, and follow the veteran to the lower sphere, in one apartment of which the children, under Tryphosa's rule, had a separate table. To this Mr. Terry invited his countryman, the old schoolmaster, who, in spite of his recent deipnosophistic repast with Mr. Maguffin, was ready for something warm. He confidentially whispered to Mr. Terry that no doubt nagurs had sowls and were human, but he wasn't pudden' fond of their society. In the dining-room, Mr. Bangs and Squire Walker, in the centre of the table, were in exile, for Wilkinson and the Captain flanked the former, and Coristine and Mr. Perrowne the latter. Mrs. Du Plessis sat between Carruthers and Mr. Thomas; Miss Halbert between the minister and Mr. Perrowne; Miss Du Plessis between the dominie and the doctor; and Miss Carmichael between Coristine and the colonel. Mrs. Carruthers, who occupied one end of the table, had the colonel on her right, and her sister-in-law, who took the other end, was supported in the same way by the host. Squire Walker, a portly man, but not too heavy for exercise, with a baldish head and large red[Pg 231]dish whiskers, sporting a velveteen shooting coat, high shirt collar, and large blue silk scarf with white spots, was a man of much intelligence and a good talker. His conversation compelled attention, and, like the glittering eye of the ancient mariner, held, now Mr. Perrowne and now the lawyer from much pleasanter ones with their respective ladies. He seemed to take a fiendish pleasure in capturing Wilkinson from Miss Du Plessis, and the Captain from her mother, and even sent his conversational shafts far off to the Squire and the doctor, and to the presiding matrons. Mr. Errol and the colonel were happily sheltered from him. Perhaps the new detective perceived the state of unrest and terrible suspense in which many of the company were on account of Squire Walker's vagaries, and chivalrously sought to deliver them. Eyeing keenly the autocrat of the breakfast table, he remarked, "I'm afraid you heve fergotten me, Squire?"

"Don't think I ever had the pleasure of your acquaintance, sir."

"Oh, perdon me, you hed though. Two years ago, a large, stout, heavy bearded men kem to yore ohffice, with a yeng Cuban who could herdly speak a word of Inglish, asking you to commit him fer smeggling cigars—"

"Haw! haw! haw!" laughed Mr. Walker, "and you were the bearded man were you, eh?"

"Do please favour us with the whole story, Mr. Bangs," asked the hostess.

"Go on, Bangs," added its victim, "I don't mind, haw! haw!"

"The Squire asked the big revenue detective how he knew the cigars were smeggled, and he said that nobody could pay the duty and sell these cigars for seven dollars a hendred. The Squire asked to see the cigars, and while the pore yeng Cuban with the bleck mousteche stood twirling his sombrero and looking guilty, he took one, smilt it, and then smouked it. He said to the big detective, 'I won't let you hev a warrent for that pore foreigner on any sech evidence, for I ken bey the very same cigar at Beamish's for five dollars.' The detective said, 'Are you shore the cigar is the same?' when the Squire pulled a drawer open end brought out a box of the identical erticles. Then, the big men thenked him, [Pg 232]hended him a revenue card, end took the pore Cuban away. Next day Beamish's was raided, end Nesh and I kem in for quite a reword."

"Then the detective was Nash?" asked Mr Walker.

"Yes, Nesh, with a big men's clowthes on, padded out."

"And what were you in the matter?"

"Oh, I wes the pore yeng Cuban thet could herdly speak Inglish."

"I don't think he can yet," whispered Miss Carmichael to Coristine, who thought it an immense joke.

"So you made Squire Walker an informer against his will, Mr. Bangs," said Carruthers.

"Yes; but it was complimentary, too. We knew if there were any good cigars in the village, the Squire's wes the best place to look for them."

"You should have had me up for having smuggled goods in my possession," said the complimented talker.

"No, no, Squire; you see you were the next thing to Queen's evidence, and they always go scotfree."

"A receiver and Queen's evidence! and the miserable little Cuban! Haw! haw! haw!"

That is the story of how Squire Walker was silenced.

After breakfast there were prayers, as usual, conducted by the two clergymen, and when they were over, the three J.P.'s, Doctor Halbert being one, assembled for consultation in the office. Tom Rigby, the constable, reported himself to the magistrate's court, and thereafter adjourned to the kitchen, there to hold converse with his brother veteran, Mr. Terry. Tom was tall, and as straight as if he had swallowed a ramrod. He gave the military salute with great precision and regularity. He was a widower, and a frequent visitor in the Bridesdale servants' quarters, whence it was commonly reported that he had an eye on Tryphena. Sylvanus had heard of this, with the effect that he lost no opportunity of running down the trade of a soldier, and comparing it most unfavourably with the free, rollicking life of the heaving sea. To hear Sylvanus speak, one would imagine that the *Susan Thomas* was annually in the habit of circumnavigating the globe. The children's breakfast was over, and they were all out in the garden picking certain permitted flowers, and presenting them to their favourites among the guests; but Mr. Terry had still[Pg 233]remained, conversing with Mr. Hill, whose book-larnin' was so voluminous that he made slow progress with his breakfast, having had his cold tea thrice removed by his eldest daughter and replaced with hot. When Rigby entered and saluted, the veteran rose and returned the salute. "Good morning, Sergeant Terry! was it company colour sergeant or on the staff you were, sir?"

"Lasht noight, Carporal Rigby, Oi was sargint-major for the firsht toime in my loife. I wuz promawted loike."

"That would be in the volunteer service, Sergeant-major."

"Yiss; but we had a rale cornel in command that's been through the Amerikin war, they till me."

"Sergeant-major, there are no American soldiers."

"Shure, an' Oi'm thinkin', corporal," said the veteran, feeling a metaphorical thrid on the tail av his coat. "Oi'm thinkin' there's some pretty foine foightin's been done in Ameriky; Oi've sane it, corporal, wid my own two eyes."

"A dog can fight, Sergeant-major, and cats are tantamount to the same thing; but where, I say, is the soldierly bearing, the discipline, the spree-doo-cor, as they say in France? Sergeant-major, you know and I know that a man cannot be a tailor today and a soldier tomorrow, and an agent for pictorial family bibles the day after."

"I dunno, for you see you're a conshtable an' Oi'm a hid missenger in a governmint ahffice in the city."

"A soldier, Sergeant-major, can always serve the country, is, even as a soldier, a government officer; that is a very different thing, Sergeant-major."

"The cornel here was tillin' me there was min in his rigiment that was merchints an' lawyers an' clerks, an' shtudints, as good sowldjers as iver foired a carrboine or drawed a shabre on the inimy."

"That was a case, Sergeant-major, of mob meeting mob. Did these men ever charge as our cavalry charged at Balaclava; did they ever stand, Sergeant-major, as we, myself included, stood at Inkerman? Never, Sergeant-major, never! They might have made soldiers, if taken young; but, as they were, they were no more soldiers than Sylvanus Pilgrim here."

"You shet up yer tater-trap, Consterble Rigby, an' don't go fer to abuse better men nor you aint," angrily inter[Pg 234]rupted the subject of the corporal's unflattering comparison. Then, seeing the veteran, hopeless of convincing his opponent, retire to the garden to join the children, Sylvanus waxed bold. "A soldier, Trypheeny, a common soldier! Ef I owned a dawg, a yaller dawg, I wouldn't go and make the pore beast a soldier. Old pipeclay and parade, tattoo and barricks and punishment drill, likes ter come around here braggin' up his lazy, slavish life. Why don't he git a dawg collar and a chain at wonst and git tied up ter his kennel. Ef you want a man, Trypheeny, get one as knows

A life on the ocean wave
And a home on the rollin' deep,

none o' your stiff starched, nigger driven, cat o' nine tails, ornery common soldiers."

Tryphena snickered a little, but the constable went on with his breakfast, not deigning to waste a syllable on such unmilitary trash as Sylvanus, with whom it was impossible to reason, and to come to blows with whom might imperil his dignity. Some day, perhaps, Pilgrim might be his prisoner; then, the majesty of the law would be vindicated.

A messenger came and summoned the constable to accompany the coroner, Dr. Halbert, to Richards, and bring the body of the murdered detective to the post office. On such an occasion, the pensioner's dignity would not allow him to drive the waggon, so Rufus had to be pressed into the service. Squire Walker, as the presiding magistrate, in view of Carruthers personal connection with the death of the subject of the jury's verdict, appointed the detective temporary clerk of the court that should sit after the inquests were over. Fearing that few of the settlers warned would turn out as jurors, through fear of the Select Encampment people, the master of Bridesdale chose a sufficient number of men for the purpose from the present sojourners at his house. These, some time after the doctor's departure, sauntered leisurely towards the most public place in the neighbourhood. Arrived at the post office, they found a large unfinished room in an adjoining building prepared for the court. This building had been begun as a boarding house, but, [Pg 235]when almost completed, the conviction suddenly came to the post office people that there were no boarders to be had, all the transients of any financial value being given free quarters in the hospitable mansion of the Squire. Hence the house was never finished. The roof, however, was on, and the main room floored, so that it had been utilized for church and Sunday school purposes, for an Orange Lodge, for temperance and magic lantern itinerant lectures, and for local hops. Now, with the dead body of Harding laid out upon an improvised table of rough boards on trestles, it assumed the most solemn aspect it had ever exhibited. Three oldish men were there, whom people called Johnson, Newberry, and Pawkins; they were all the summoned jurors who had responded. Soon, from the other side, the waggon came in sight, and when it came forward, the remains of Nagle, alias Nash, were lifted reverently out and into the hall, where they were placed beside those of one of his murderers. The elder Richards accompanied the doctor, in order to give his testimony. The mad woman and her son were also there, in charge of Sylvanus and Ben Toner. Just as the party prepared to constitute the coroner's court, a stumpy figure on a high stepping horse came riding along. He was well disguised, but several persons recognized him. "Seize him," cried Squire Carruthers. "It's Grinstuns," said the lawyer. "Stop him!" shouted Bangs. But, Rawdon, having seen what he wanted, wheeled his horse and galloped away. There was neither saddled horse to pursue him, nor rifle to bring him down. "All the better," remarked Mr. Walker to his brother J.P.'s; "had he seen mounted men and fire-arms among us, he'd have smelt a rat. As it is, he thinks we are on the defensive and moving slowly." It was evident, from what people heard of the presiding magistrate's conversation, that the court had decided in favour of measures offensive.

It was easy to get twelve good men and true for the first inquest. In addition to Johnson, Newberry, and Pawkins, there were the constable and Mr. Terry, Messrs. Hill and Hislop, Sylvanus, Timotheus, and Rufus, with Mr. Bangs and Maguffin. The colonel was an alien, and Carruthers did not care to sit on the jury. Dr. Halbert presided, flanked by his fellow justices, and Wilkinson, [Pg 236]though a minor witness, was made clerk. Several persons identified the slain Nagle or Nash, and gave evidence as to his relations with Rawdon's gang. Ben Toner's information and Newcome's attested confession were noted. Mr. Errol and Coristine, backed by the Captain and Ben, told how the body was found. Wilkinson and Perrowne related their share in conveying the corpse to Richards' house, and Richards confirmed their story. The coroner himself, having examined the body, affirmed that the deceased came to his death by a fracture of the skull, inflicted by a heavy blow from some blunt instrument from behind, followed by a pistol shot in front through the temple. Two persons, evidently, were concerned in the murder. Who were they? Matilda Nagle was sworn. She repudiated the name of Rawdon. She testified that a man called Harding brought her a note from her long lost brother Steven, asking her to meet him at the barred gate in the narrows at a certain hour late on Monday morning. She went, but Rawdon would not let her go beyond the barred gate, so she called Stevy over. He came to the foot of a tree, where Rawdon told her she must stay; and then she saw Harding run up behind him and hit him over the head with an iron bar, and he fell down and went to sleep. Did Rawdon shoot him? She shivered, and didn't know, nor could any cross examination extract this evidence from her. Harding knocked him down with the iron bar, and he went to sleep, and she couldn't wake him. Then she went to the corpse and cried: "Oh, Stevy, Stevy, wake up, do wake up quick, for he'll come again." The court and jury were deeply affected. Old Mr. Newberry, the foreman of the jury, brought in the verdict to the effect that the deceased was murdered by a blow from an iron bar administered by one Harding, producing fracture of the skull, and by a pistol shot in the left temple by some unknown person. Thus the first inquest came to an end. The second inquest would have been a matter of difficulty, on account of the large number of people supposed to be implicated in Harding's death, had not Ben Toner, who had been called out of court, returned with three good men and true, namely Mr. Bigglethorpe, M. Lajeunesse, and a certain Barney Sullivan. These three parties, moved by the [Pg 237]entreaties of Widow Toner, had set out early in the morning to look up the missing Ben; and were so delighted with their success, and so tired with their walk, that they were willing to sit on anything, even a coroner's jury. Accordingly, a new jury was empanelled, consisting of Messrs. Johnson, Newberry, and Pawkins, Bigglethorpe, Lajeunesse and Sullivan, Errol, Wilkinson and Richards, with the Captain, Mr. Bangs, and Squire Walker. The latter was chosen foreman. The coroner himself acted as clerk. Ben Toner had seen the deceased in company with one Newcome, and had heard him addressed as Harding. The coroner testified to having examined the body, which exhibited no shot wound of any kind, but the forehead was badly bruised, evidently by a stone, as gritty particles were to be seen adhering to it, and two table knives were still resting in the neighbourhood of the heart. The jury examined the corpse, and, led by the foreman under guard of the constable, went out across the road and over the fence into the field where Mr. Terry and Coristine found the dead Harding lying. The place was well marked by the beaten down grass, blood stains on a large boulder and on the ground, and by the finding of a loaded revolver. Carefully examining the spot, the detective pointed out, at last, the very root, not more than three quarters of an inch thick, which formed a loop on the surface of the ground, in which the unfortunate man's foot had caught, precipitating him upon the stone. Every member of the jury having examined it, Mr. Bangs took out his knife and cut it away in order to prevent similar accidents in future. The coroner did not think the blow sufficient to kill the man, though it must have rendered him insensible. The killing was done by means of the knives. These were identified by the Squire and Timotheus as belonging to the Bridesdale kitchen. There was neither time nor necessity for prolonging the examination. Matilda Nagle and her son Monty, with much satisfaction, confessed that they had followed the Bridesdale force and had seen the man fall, that she had turned him over on his back and struck him to the heart with the knife she carried, which she left there, because she had no further need for it. Her son had followed her example. The jury retired, or rather the court retired from the [Pg 238]jury, and, when Squire Walker called the coroner in again, he read the second verdict, to the effect that the deceased Harding, while in a state of insensibility owing to a fall, had been murdered by one Matilda Nagle with a table knife, and that her son, commonly known as Monty, was accessory to the deed. The double inquest was over, and the bodies were transferred to coarse wooden shells, that of Nagle being claimed by his fellow detective, and Harding's being left for a time unburied in case some claimant should appear.

The magistrates, and Mr. Bangs as clerk, now sat in close session for a little over half an hour, inasmuch as they had already come to certain conclusions in the office at Bridesdale. One result of their conference was the arrest of the madwoman and her son, much to the regret of the Squire, Mr. Errol, and many more. Rigby was ordered to treat them kindly, and convey them, with a written order signed by the three justices, to the nearest town, there to hand them over to the police authorities to be forwarded to their appropriate lunatic asylum. Old Mr. Newberry, whom the case had very much affected, volunteered to accompany the criminals, as he had to go to town at any rate, and offered to drive them and the constable there, and take his wife as company for the insane Matilda. Accordingly, he brought round the waggon in which he had driven up, and took the constable and his prisoners away towards his own house, which was on the road to their destination. The Squire and his battalion were much relieved to find that they were not responsible for Harding's death, although the fact reflected on their aim as sharpshooters. The two wounded men were informed that a magistrates' court was sitting, but evinced no anxiety to lodge a complaint against any person or persons in connection with their injuries. The coroner paid Messrs. Johnson and Pawkins their fee as jurymen, and, with the Squire's permission, invited them to dine at Bridesdale; but they declined the invitation with thanks, and returned, in company, to the bosom of their families. The lawyer, filled with military zeal as a recruiting officer, seeing that the new Beaver River contingent was armed, asked Carruthers if he had room for them.

"The mair the merrier," answered the Squire, and bade [Pg 239]him invite them. So Coristine invited the three to dinner, and to help in the support of the justices in the afternoon. Barney Sullivan said he wasn't going to leave Ben. Mr. Bigglethorpe, as a fisherman, had always wanted to see these lakes, and, if it would help the cause of good fishing, he was ready to lend a hand to drive out poachers and pot-hunters. Pierre doubted how Madame would take his absence; of course there was Bawtiste, but, well yes, for the sake of the poor dead M'syae Nash and Meestare Veelkeenson, he would stay. Que dommage, Meestare Bulky was not there, a man so intelligent, so clever, so subtle of mind! Mr. Bigglethorpe was introduced to the drawing-room, but Pierre, though invited, would not enter its sacred precincts. He accompanied Barney to the kitchen, and was introduced by Ben to the assembled company. His politeness carried the servants' quarters by storm, and wreathed the faces of Tryphena and Tryphosa in perpetual smiles. Mr. Hill and the Sesayder

119

succumbed to his genial influence, and even the disheartened Maguffin, though deploring his poor English and lack of standing colour, confessed to Rufus that "his ways was kind o' takin'."

"Squire Carruthers," said the detective, as they re-entered the office, "there is wen thing you failed to have den at the inquest."

"What is that, Mr. Bangs?"

"To search the bedy of the men, Herding; bet I attended to thet, and found pore Nesh's letter to his sister. Pore Nesh mest hev lost his head for wence, since he trested thet dem villain. I seppowse there's no such thing as a kemera ebout here?"

"No; what did you want a camera for?"

"To phowtogreph this Herding; there's a mystery about him. Nesh trested him, and he terned out a dem traitor. Nesh mest hev known him before; he would never trest a stranger so. Is there no wey of taking his likeness?"

"There's a young lady staying here, you saw her at breakfast, Miss Du Plessis, who's very clever with brush and pencil, but it's no' a very pleasant task for a woman."

"No, but in the interests of jestice it might be well to risk offending her. If you will reintroduce me more formally, I will esk the lady myself."

[Pg 240]Mr. Bangs was escorted to the garden, where the lady in question was actually sketching Marjory and the young Carruthers in a variety of attitudes. To the Squire's great astonishment, she professed her readiness to comply with the detective's desire in the afternoon, if somebody could be left to accompany her to the post office adjunct.

"How long will it take, Miss Du Plessis?" he asked. "A few minutes," she answered, "a quarter of an hour at most."

"Then, if you will allow me, I shell be heppy to be your escort, and indicate the features that should be emphasized for purposes of recognition. As I ride, I ken easily overtake the perty." This being agreed to, Mr. Bangs asked Carruthers to let him look over Nash's last memoranda, as they might be useful, and any recently acquired papers. Among the latter, taken from Newcome, was a paper of inestimable value in the form of a chart, indicating, undoubtedly, the way to the abode of Serlizer and the Select Encampment generally. In the memoranda of Nash's note-book the detective found a late entry F. al. H. inf. sub pot. prom, monst. via R., and drew the Squire's attention to it. "Look here, Squire, et our dog Letin again; F. perhaps Foster alias H, Herding, informer, under my power (that's through some crime entered in this book), premises to show the way to Rawdon's. This premise was made last Tuesday, at Derham, a whole week ago."

"Why is Harding called an informer?"

"Because he belengs to an infamous cless raised up by our iniquitous kestoms administration. These informers get no selery, bet are rewerded with a share of the spoil they bring to the depertment. Semtimes they accuse honest men, and ectually hev been known to get them convicted falsely. Semtimes they take bribes from the greatest scoundrels, and protect them in their villainy. Nesh thought he hed this fellew safe by the law of fear; bet fear and envy and the dread of losing Rawdon's bribes, combined in his treacherous heart to make a merderer of him."

"But Nash couldn't have written that letter last week. He knew nothing of his sister's whereabouts till yesterday morning."

[Pg 241]"Exectly; see here is the nowte, a sheet out of this very book fowlded ep. End it says: 'Meet me at wence, not later than noon, outside the barred chennel. You say he followed Rawdon from the powst office; then, at sem point behind Rawdon, this Herding must hev terned ep, end, O dem the brute if he is dead! hev cheated the cleverest fellow in the service."

"But why should he have killed him? Why not leave that to Rawdon?"

"Rawdon's kenning and deep. When he knew it wes Nesh, he got a fright himself end then frightened Herding into doing it. I'll bet you whet you like, thet revolver found with his body is the kelibre of the bellet wound in pore Nash's head. I'll look when I go ep this efternoon. His trick was to lay it all on Herding; I shouldn't wender if he towld thet med woman to kill him. It's jest like him, dem the brute!"

120

In order that due preparations, in the shape of accoutrements, might be made, and after dinner delay avoided, the Squire and the colonel assembled the forces. Including the absent Richards family, the upholders and vindicators of the law numbered twenty-six. The Captain had already signified to Richards senior his willingness to take command of the scow and its complement of five men, armed with guns, and with axes for cutting away the barrier at the narrows. There was much romance about this side of the campaign, so that volunteers could have been got for marine service to any extent; but the means of transportation were limited, and even that able-bodied seaman Sylvanus had to be enrolled among the landsmen. Happily Tom Rigby was not there to see him descend once more to the level of military life. The colonel, rejoicing in Newcome's chart of the marked road, called for cavalry volunteers. Squire Walker, Mr. Bangs and Maguffin, having their horses with them, naturally responded. It then came to a toss-up between Mr. Perrowne and Coristine; the parson won, and the disappointed lawyer was relegated to the flat feet. As the doctor had been major in a volunteer regiment, the Squire ceded the command of the infantry to him. It was proposed to have at least one man behind as a home guard, but nobody was prepared to volunteer for this service, Messrs. Errol, Wilkinson, [Pg 242]and Lajeunesse, who were severally proposed, expressing their sense of the honour, their high regard for the ladies, and anxiety for their well-being, but emphatically declining to be absent from the common post of duty and danger. Miss Halbert voiced the opinion of the fair sex that, being eight in number, including the maids, they were quite able to defend themselves. Nevertheless, the Squire inwardly determined to send old Styles, the post office factotum, back with Miss Du Plessis. The main attacking force of infantry consisted of Doctor Halbert, in command, sergeants Carruthers and Terry and their two squads, the first comprising privates Errol, Wilkinson, Coristine, Bigglethorpe, Lajeunesse, and Hill; the second, privates Hislop, Toner, Sullivan, Hill junior, and the two Pilgrims. Then, arms were inspected, and the twenty bludgeons dealt out, five for the cavalry, and fifteen for the infantry. Most of these had attachments of stout common string, but those of the three commanders, the Squire, the two clergymen, and the two pedestrians, were secured with red window cord, a mark of preference which rejoiced the hearts of three of them, namely, the younger men. With doubtful hands the dominie received his gun, and the minister more boldly grasped a similar weapon. At the request of the colonel the cavalry were served with a hasty luncheon, and thereafter set forward, with the exception of the detective, Miss Du Plessis' escort, to patrol the road and open communication with the Richards for the purpose of intercepting the enemy's possible scouts. Two waggons were ordered to take the infantry to the lake settlement, so that they might be fresh for the work before them.

In his martial accoutrements, the dominie's soul was stirred within him. He repeated to his bosom friend pieces from Körner's Leyer und Schwert, but as the lawyer's acquaintance with the Teutonic tongues was limited, including *sauer kraut, lager bier, nix kum araus, donner-wetter*, and similar choice expressions, he failed to make an impression. Nobody in the house knew German, unless it were Tryphena and Tryphosa, who had picked up a little from their mother, and, of course, he could hardly lie in wait to get off his warlike quotations on them. Ha! he remembered Wordsworth, and rolled forth:—

"Vanguard of liberty, ye men of Kent!
They from their fields can see the countenance
Of your fierce war, may ken the glittering lance,
And hear you shouting forth your brave intent."

Still failing to awake a responsive echo in the heart that once beat in poetic unison with his own, he turned to Mrs. Du Plessis, and, alluding to the departed colonel, recited in her native tongue:—

"Honor al Caudillo,
Honor al primero,
Que el patriota acero
Oso fulminar.
La Patria afligida
Oyo' sus acentos,
Y vio' sus tormentos,

En gozo tornar."

"That is very pretty, Mr. Wilkinson, and I thank you much for recalling the pleasant memories of my early speech. Is there not an English translation of these words?"

"There is, Mrs. Du Plessis, by Sir John Bowring, It is:—
Hail, hail to the Chieftain,
All honour to him
Who first in the gleam
Of that light bared the sword!
The drooping land heard him,
Forgetting her fears;
And smiled through her tears,
As she hung on his word."

The dominie had thought only to give expression to the poetic fervour called forth by the circumstances, but accomplished a good deal more, the establishment of a common ground between himself and the nearest relative of a very charming and cultivated young lady. The said young lady came up to join in the conversation, and request Mr. Wilkinson to repeat all that he knew of the battle hymn. The lawyer was secretly of the opinion that his friend was making an ass of himself, and that, if he were to try that poetry quoting business on Miss Carmichael, he would soon discover that such was the case. Yet, if the Du Plessis liked that sort of thing, he had no right to interfere. He remembered that he had once been just such an ass himself, and wondered how he could have so far strayed from the path of common sense. It was [Pg 244]worse than Tryphosa and Timotheus sitting down to sing with a hymn-book between them.

"What are you doing out in the garden all by yourself, Eugene?" asked a small voice. He looked down and saw Marjorie fingering the barrel of his rifle. "Don't you know," she continued, "that all the people have gone in to dinner?"

"Did the gong sound, Marjorie?"

"To be sure it did. Tell me, what were you thinking about not to hear it?"

"I was thinking about a dear little girl called Marjorie," answered the prevaricating lawyer, picking the child up and bestowing a hearty salute upon her lips.

"You're a very good boy now, Eugene; you get a clean shave every day. Do you go to Collingwood for it in the night time, when I am in bed?"

"No, Marjorie; I get the cat to lick my face," the untruthful man replied.

"What? our pussy Felina that spits at Muggy?"

"The very same."

"Then I'll ask Tryphosa's father if he would like to have the loan of Felina. Don't you think she would do him good."

Coristine laughed, as he thought of Mr. Hill's stubbly countenance, and carried "the darlin'" into the house.

At the dinner table he found himself punished for his day-dreaming. Bangs was on one side of Miss Carmichael, and Bigglethorpe on the other, and he was out in the cold, between the latter gentleman and the minister. Mr. Bigglethorpe resumed the subject of fishing, and interrogated his right hand neighbour as to his success at the River. He laughed over the so-called mullets, and expressed a fisherman's contempt for them as devourers of valuable spawn, relating also the fact that, in the spring, when they swarm up into shallow parts of the stream, the farmers shovel them out with large wooden scoops, and feed them to the pigs or fertilize the land with them. Finding he had more than one auditor, the fishing store-keeper questioned the Squire about the contents of his brook, and, learning that dace, chubs, and crayfish were its only occupants, promised to send Mrs. Carruthers a basket of trout when the season came round. In order to [Pg 245]give a classical turn to the conversation, the dominie mentioned the name of Isaac Walton and referred to his poor opinion of the chub in the river Lea. "I know the Lea like a book," said Mr. Bigglethorpe, "and a dirty, muddy ditch it has got to be since old Isaac's time. When I was a schoolboy I went there fishing one afternoon with some companions, and caught not a single fish, hardly got a nibble. We were going home disappointed, when we saw a man at the reservoir above the river, near the Lea bridge, with some eels in a basket. They were queer looking eels, but

122

we bought them for sixpence, and one of our fellows, called Wickens, put them in his fishing can; then we maide for home. Before we could get there we had to cross a pretty rough part of the Kingsland road. It was pretty dark, but, of course, the shops were all lit up and we sawr a lot of boys, common cads, coming our wy. Just in front of a public house they called out 'Boots, Boots! fish, fish!' and out caime a stout lad of about eighteen to lead the gang. Three of us clubbed our rods over them, briking the top joints, of course, but Wickens wouldn't fall in with us. So Boots ran after him, followed by a crowd. When Wickens sawr he couldn't escype, he opened his can, took out an eel and slapped it over Boots' fyce. The beggar just yelled, 'O, Lawr, water snykes!' and he ran, and Wickens after him like mad, slashing 'em with the water snykes. O dear, O dear, I shall never forget those snykes to my dying dy."

"Are there any water snakes in our rivers in Canada?" enquired Mrs. Du Plessis.

"Oh yes, ma'am," answered the fisherman, "I imagine those lykes we are going to visit this afternoon are pretty full of snykes. Mr. Bulky, whose nyme is known to Mr. Coristine, I'm sure, wears long waterproof boots for wyding in the Beaver River—"

"But, Mr. Bigglethorpe," asked the fair questioner, "how can one ride in a river?"

"Excuse me, ma'am, I did not say riding, I said wyding, walking in the water. Mr. Bulky was wyding, one morning, with rod in hand, when, all of a sudden, he felt something on his leg. Looking down, he sawr a big black water-snyke coiled round his boot, and jabbing awy at his leg. It hung on to him like a boa-constrictor, and[Pg 246]squeezed his leg so tight that it gyve him a bad attack of gout. He had to get on shore and sawr it in two with his knife before the snyke would leave go. Fortunately, the brutes are not venomous, but that beggar's teeth scratched Mr. Bulky's boots up pretty badly, I must sy."

When they rose from the table, Miss Carmichael went up to the lawyer and said: "Please forgive me for punishing myself between Mr. Bangs and Mr. Bigglethorpe. I sigh for good English." The lawyer answered, all unwittingly, of course, in his worst brogue: "Miss Carrmoikle, it's my frind Wilks I'll be aafther gitten' to shtarrt a noight school to tayche me to shpake Inglish in aal its purity." To this there could be but one response: "Go away, you shameful, shameless, bad man!" It pleased the lawyer better than a more elegant and complimentary remark.

CHAPTER XIII.

Walk to the P.O.—Harding's Portrait—The Encampment Besieged—Wilkinson Wounded—Serlizer and Other Prisoners—No Underground Passage Found—Bangs and Guard Remain—The Constable's New Prisoners—Wilkinson a Hero—The Constable and Maguffin—Cards.

There was no room for twenty persons in two waggons, yet twenty proposed to go, seventeen to the seat of war, and three to the post-office. As those three were the young ladies of the house, all the warriors offered to surrender their seats to them. They refused to accept any surrender, preferring to walk, whereupon Messrs. Errol, Wilkinson and Coristine thought an after-dinner walk the height of luxury. Mr. Bangs saw he was not wanted as a fellow pedestrian, and mounted his horse instead of having him trot behind a waggon. The vehicles, or at least one of them, received instructions to wait at the post-office for the three members of squad No. 1. The walk was strictly proper, Mr. Errol taking Miss Carmichael, the dominie Miss Halbert, and the lawyer Miss Du Plessis. "What a goose you are, Mr. Wilkinson," said his fair companion. "What a goose you are to leave Cecile, whose footsteps you fairly worship, and to come and walk with a girl for whose society you don't care a penny."

[Pg 247]"I should care more for Miss Halbert's society if she did not say such unjustifiable things."

"Cecile," called the young lady, "I want to change escorts with you; I like pleasant society."

The dominie felt as if a big school-girl had declined to receive a reprimand from the principal, and coloured with vexation, but Miss Du Plessis calmly turned and said: "If Mr. Wilkinson is tired of you already, Fanny, I suppose I must send Mr. Coristine to comfort you," whereat Mr. Errol and his companion exchanged a smile.

"Did the villain shoot Wordsworth at you, Miss Halbert, or was it Hans Breitmann in the original, or a Spanish *cantinella*, or some such rubbish? If I was Miss Du Plessis I'd wear a signboard over my ears, 'No poetical rubbish shot here;' perhaps that might fix him."

"Cecile is sentimental: she dotes on poetry."

"Pardon me for saying I don't believe it. I offered to recite my original poem on the Grinstun man to her, and she didn't seem to want to hear it."

"How ungrateful and unsympathetic! You will favour me with it, will you not?"

"With the greatest pleasure in the world. You know it's awful balderdash, but here goes."

The original poem was recited with appropriate gestures, intended to imitate the walk of the hero of the piece and his various features. The people in front turned their heads to look at the performance and take in the words. Not to laugh was almost an impossibility, but the dominie succeeded in doing the impossible, and frowned heavily. He felt that his unworthy friend was bringing disgrace upon the causes of poetry and pedestrianism. When her laughter subsided, Miss Halbert said: "There is one thing I want to ask you seriously, Mr. Coristine." "Name it," he answered, "even to the half of my fortune." "It is to look after papa, and see that he does not expose himself too much to danger. I asked Mr. Perrowne too, but he is with the horsemen, you know." This last was said with a peculiarly arch smile, which convinced the lawyer that Perrowne was in deeper than was generally suspected. The first thought that followed in Coristine's mind was what awful cheek he had been guilty of in following Perrowne's precedent in drop [Pg 248]the handkerchief. He managed, however, to assure the lady that he would do his best to watch over the safety of her father and Squire Carruthers, the latter words being spoken loud enough for Miss Carmichael to hear. When the post-office was reached Mr. Bangs dismounted, was ready to receive the ladies; and the three escorts, shaking hands warmly with each of their fair companions, entered the remaining waggon and drove away, the buts of their firearms rattling on the floor, and the suspended bludgeons playfully flogging their shoulders.

It was ghastly work propping up the dead murderer's shoulders in the shell, and placing a rest for his head. The jaw had been tied up, but the eyes would not close; yet, staring though the face was, it was not a repulsive one. The ordinary observer could not read what Bangs saw there, greed and hypocrisy, envy, treachery, murder. While Miss Du Plessis went on calmly sketching, the other girls turned their heads away. No one cared to break the stillness by a word. The detective went out and secured the services of Styles to accompany the ladies home, and remain at Bridesdale till the armed band returned. Then he went over to the shell in which the body of his brother detective lay, and, nobody looking at him, allowed himself the luxury of a few tears, a silent tribute to the man he honoured. When the sketch was completed, he warmly thanked the artist, and told her that he never would have dreamt of proposing such a task, but for his desire to do justice to his dead friend, whom an informer named Flower had greatly injured in the department. The department had faith in his cleverness all along, but suspicions had been cast upon his honesty, which embittered his days, along with troubles that were then only known to himself.

Bangs was not a detective, but a man of warm, brotherly heart, as he told the tale of the outwardly always cheerful, but inwardly sore-hearted, Nash, cut off in the midst of his years and usefulness. Then old Styles appeared, and, with a salute, the detective mounted and rode away to join the forces in front, while the ladies journeyed homeward. Mr. Bangs soliloquized as he rode rapidly on. "Boys read detective stories, and think our life an enviable one. They [Pg 249]dowte on the schemes, the plots and counterplots, the risks, the triumphs, and look beyond to fame and rewerd, but they know nothing of the miserable envies and jealousies, the sespicions, the checks and counterchecks, and the demnable policy of the depertment, encouraging these irresponsible informers, dem 'em, to break up all legitimate business and merder honest men. O Nesh, my pore dead friend, yo're avenged in a wey, bet who's going to avenge yore pore sister, and even this devil of a Flower or Herding, whose death lies at the door of that greater devil of a Rawdon?"

The expedition was waiting for him at Richards', the colonel in command. The scow had departed in charge of the captain, who had orders to do nothing to the barrier till he heard a signal shot; then he was to respond with the unmistakable blunderbuss, and batter down the obstruction. Squire Walker, Mr. Perrowne, and Maguffin had patrolled, without meeting even a passing team or wayfarer; but the colonel judged it best to get off the road without delay. Accordingly the waggons were left in Richards' shed, and the infantry doubled forward after the colonel and Bangs. When the rocky ascent was reached, over which the fugitives of the night before had clambered, a halt was called, and the colonel gave Dr. Halbert instructions. Just where the rock rose out of the swamp, Sergeant Terry's squad entered, and easily wheeled round large trunks of trees resting on stone pivots, revealing a good waggon-track, the masked road. This the cavalry occupied, looking to the priming of their pistols, and bringing their clubs into handy positions. The Squire's squad scaled the height near the road, and Mr. Terry's took ground farther to the right. The doctor led the way in front of and between the two sections. The cavalry moved slowly, keeping pace with the climbers. Soon the crest was reached, and the main body began to descend gradually, when the dominie slipped and his piece went off, the trigger having caught in his red window cord, startling the echoes. Then came the diffusive boom and crackle of the blunderbuss, and the doctor, inwardly anathematizing Wilkinson, hurried his men on. They heard axes at work, as if trees were being felled; it was the Captain and the Richards at the barrier. No enemy appeared on the rocks, [Pg 250]but pistol shots warned them that there was collision on the road, and the doctor called the second squad to wheel towards it. The dominie, on the left of the first, saw what was going on below. Revolvers were emptied and clubs brought into requisition. He could not load his old muzzle-loading piece to save his life, but he knew single stick. Two men were tackling the brave old colonel, while a third lay wounded at his horse's feet. The dominie sped down to the road like a chamois, and threw himself upon the man on the colonel's right, the dissipated farmer. He heard a shot, felt a sharp pain in his left arm, but with his right hit the holder of the pistol a skull cracker over the head, then fainted and fell to the ground. His luckless muzzle-loader was never found. The colonel had floored his antagonist on the left, and turned to behold the dominie's pale face. Leaving the command to the doctor, he dismounted and put a little old Bourbon out of a pocket flask into his lips, and then proceeded to bandage the wound. Wilkinson had saved his life; he was a hero, a grand, cultivated, sympathetic, chivalrous man, whom the colonel loved as his own son. When he came to, were not the very first words he uttered enquiries for Colonel Morton's own safety? Maguffin, having felled his man, held his master's horse.

Squire Walker, Mr. Perrowne, and Bangs galloped on, the latter eager to seize Rawdon. They and the infantry squads came almost simultaneously upon the select encampment, which was simply a large stone-mason's yard, full of grindstones in every state of preparation, and bordered by half-a-dozen frame buildings, one of which, more pretentious than the others, was evidently the dwelling-place of the head of the concern. Two simple-looking men in mason's aprons stood in the doorway of another, having retired thither when they heard the sound of firing. This was evidently the boarding-house of the workmen, and an object of interest to Ben Toner, who, with his friends Sullivan and Timotheus, pushed past the two stonecutters, immediately thereafter arrested by Sergeant Terry, and invaded the structure. Soon Ben reappeared upon the scene, accompanied by a young woman whose proportions were little, if at all, short of his own, and calling aloud to all the company, as if he had accomplished the main object [Pg 251]of the expedition, "It's all raight, boys, I've got Serlizer!" Behind the happy pair came an old woman, gray, wrinkled, and with features that bore unmistakable traces of sorrow and suffering. "Hev they ben good to you, Serlizer?" asked Mr. Toner, after he had in the most public and unblushing manner saluted his long lost sweetheart. The large woman raised her bared arms from the elbow significantly, and replied, with a trace of her father's gruffness, "I didn't arst 'em; 'sides I allers had old Marm Flowers to keep 'em off." The expedition was demoralized. The colonel and his servant were with the dominie on the road. Ben, with Timotheus and Sullivan, was rejoicing in Serlizer; while Mr. Hislop and Rufus were guarding the captured stone-cutters. Sylvanus, not to be outdone by his companions of the second squad, attached himself, partly as a protector, partly as a prisoner's guard, to Mrs. Flower, the keeper of the boarding-house. Sergeant Terry, without a command, followed what remained of the first squad in its search for Rawdon. The first person he came upon, in his way down to the water, was Monsieur

Lajeunesse, who could run no farther, and, perspiring at every pore, sat upon a log, mopping his face with a handkerchief.

"A such coorse 'ave I not med, Meestare Terray, sinsa zat I vas a too ptee garsong." Mr. Terry understood, owing to large experience of foreigners, and could not permit the opportunity of making a philological remark to pass, "D'ye know, Mishter Lashness, that Frinch an' the rale ould Oirish is as loike as two pays? Now, there's garsan is as Oirish a worrud for a young bhoy as ye'll find in Connaught. But juty is juty, moy dare sorr, so, as they say in the arrmy, 'Fag a bealach,' lave the way." The sergeant's next discovery was the doctor, borne in the arms of the lawyer and the dismounted parson. He had sprained his ancle in the rapid descent to which his zeal had impelled him, and had thus been compelled to leave the Squire in command. Mr. Hill had been left behind on the left of the encampment with the horses of the three dismounted cavaliers, Squire Walker, Mr. Perrowne, and the detective, so that Sergeant Carruthers, now acting colonel, had with him a mere corporal's guard, consisting of Messrs. Errol and Bigglethorpe.

The junction of the land forces with those operating [Pg 252]on the water was effected in good order, the latter being intact under command of the captain, but the former exhibiting, by their terribly reduced numbers, the dreadful fatality of war. Squire Walker and Mr. Bangs alone represented the cavalry; Carruthers and his corporal's guard, the first squad, and the veteran all alone, the second squad of the infantry. Even this remnant had its deserter, for, during the conversation between the Squire and the Captain, private Bigglethorpe stole away, and when next seen was standing far out upon a dead hemlock that had fallen into the lake, fishing with great contentment, and a measure of success, for bass. The numbers of the force were soon augmented by the appearance of the doctor and his bearers. The disabled physician was accommodated with a seat on the bottom of the scow, two of the Richards boys being displaced in his favour. The Captain reported a prize in the shape of a handsome varnished skiff, which he found drawn up on some skids or rollers at the foot of a great mass of rock, that seemed as if cut all about in regular form, in readiness for quarrying. The finding of the boat just opposite it, the worn appearance of the ground, the absence of moss or any other growth on the severed edges of the square mass of limestone, led the detective to ask if there was any report of a subterranean passage in connection with this mysterious region. The doctor, whom his former guide had taken by water, and insisted on blindfolding at a certain point, was sure that he had walked some distance on rock, and, although the lamp-lit room, in which he had seen his patients, was lined with wood, and had blinds on apparent windows, he doubted much that it was built in the open air. Then, Coristine remembered how the dissipated farmer had coupled Rawdon's geology with trap rock, as well as with galena, quartz and beryl. Knives were produced and thrust into the seams at the top and on the two sides, as far as the blades would go, but along the bottom there was no horizontal incision answering to that above; it was perpendicular towards the earth, and of no great depth.

It was decided, in the meanwhile, to leave the Captain with Richards senior, his youngest son, and Mr. Bigglethorpe, who declined to leave his sport, as a guard on the [Pg 253]skiff and the adjoining mysterious stone. The rest of the party returned to the encampment, to consult with the colonel and learn the reason of his absence. Pierre Lajeunesse was found where Mr. Terry had left him, and gladly accepted an arm up the hill. Arrived at the stone-yard, the Squire and Coristine learnt with concern of the dominie's wound, but were rejoiced to find it was nothing more serious, and that his was the only casualty, besides the doctor's. Squire Walker and Mr. Bangs accompanied the colonel, whom Coristine relieved in attendance upon the dominie, and Maguffin, to look for the felled accomplices of Rawdon, but, of the four who certainly were knocked insensible by the clubs, not one was to be found, nor was there any sign that the pistols of the cavalry had taken effect on the other three. The whole seven had escaped. Meanwhile Rawdon's house and all the other buildings had been searched by Carruthers, without a single incriminating thing, save a half empty keg of peculiar white spirits, being brought to light. The stables contained many horses; and strong waggons, such as those seen by the pedestrians at the Beaver River, were in the sheds. The stone-cutters and the women professed to know nothing, and, save in the case of the woman called Flower, Bangs was of opinion that they spoke the truth. All the

126

men could tell was that Rawdon paid them good wages, so that they were able to live without work all winter; that six other men worked for him elsewhere and came to the boarding-house for their meals, but did not sleep there; that one of them had got hurt in the back, and was away in the hospital, and that two teamsters had left shortly before the intruders arrived, along with the remaining five. They had also seen Rawdon ride in that morning, but did not know where he had gone. Did they know of any underground vaults or trap doors, or any buildings apart from those in the encampment? No, they had seen none; but, three years ago, before they returned to work in the spring, there must have been quarrymen about, for enormous quantities of stone were lying ready for them, which they had not taken out. Mrs. Flower declined to answer any questions, but did not scruple to ask if the Squire and others had seen anything of a man called Harding. When she learned the man's fate, as she sat in [Pg 254]a low chair, she rocked it to and fro and groaned, but shed no tear nor uttered an articulate syllable.

Bangs would not give up the search, nor would he leave the place. There was food enough in the boarding-house, and he would remain, even if he had to stay alone. Squire Walker had to be home for an engagement early in the morning; the two clergymen had to prepare for Wednesday evening's duty, and had pastoral work before them; the colonel could not leave the man who had saved his life. The doctor and the dominie were incapacitated; Ben Toner was worse than useless over Serlizer; Pierre dreaded his beloved Angelique's ire if he remained away over night; and Sullivan's folks might be kinder anxious about him. Messrs. Hill and Hislop also thought they had better be going. Thus the army melted away. Everybody insisted on the Squire going home, and getting a good night's rest. When, with difficulty, persuaded to do so, he offered to leave Timotheus as his substitute, if that worthy were willing. Timotheus consented, whereupon Sylvanus and Rufus volunteered, it being understood that Ben Toner and Maguffin would do their work about the kitchen and stables, while Serlizer helped the Bridesdale maids. Two other volunteers were Mr. Terry and the lawyer; and two of the Richards offered to watch with Mr. Bigglethorpe on the lake shore. Thereupon, the three members of that gallant family withdrew to the lake, and, while one boarded the scow and helped his father and younger brother, under the Captain's directions, to paddle home, the others hailed the fisherman and asked if he was going to remain. "I'm here for the night, boys," replied the man of the rod. "I'll turn up that skiff against the wind and dew, light a fire by the water, and, early in the morning, have the loveliest bass fishing I've had for many a day. Oh yes, I'm here. D'ye see my gun lying about anywhere?" Mr. Bigglethorpe's gun was found, and deposited in the skiff. While this was going on below, Ben Toner harnessed up a team, hitched them to a waggon, for which he found seats by depriving other waggons of their boxes, and prepared to take the wounded dominie, his affectionate friend, the colonel, with Serlizer and the woman Flower, to Bridesdale. The last named person insisted upon going at once to see the dead body of Hard[Pg 255]ing. The two stone-cutters also asked to be allowed to accompany the two props of the encampment boarding house. Mr. Hill rode the colonel's horse, and the Squire, that of the detective. Along the once masked, but now unmasked, road, the procession of waggon, horsemen, and footmen, passed, waving a farewell to the allies of Mr. Bangs who held the fort. It should be added that Sylvanus accompanied the waggons as far as the Richards' place, to obtain the Captain's permission for his volunteering, and to bring the borrowed waggon back.

At Richards' the waggons were brought out. One was devoted to the two injured men, the dominie and the doctor, with their attendants, the colonel and the Captain, and Barney Sullivan as driver. The other was driven by Ben, with Serlizer beside him. It also contained the woman Flower, Mr. Errol, Mr. Lajeunesse, and Mr. Hislop. The cavalry, consisting of Squire Walker in command, Mr. Perrowne, Carruthers, Hill, and Maguffin, trotted forward, and the infantry and prisoners, comprising Tom Rigby, who turned up at the Lake Settlement, and the two masons, followed in the rear. The constable was angry; he had lost his prisoners of the morning. Having arrived at Mr. Newberry's hospitable house, and being asked to take some refreshments, which, esteeming the objects of his care to be simple souls, he had no hesitation in doing, he was amazed, on his return to the waggon, to find his captives gone. At once he started in pursuit, but, up to the time of his arrival at the Lake Settlement, he had seen no trace of the fugitives. Accordingly, the corporal made the present life of the two stone cutters a burden. He searched them for concealed weapons, and confiscated the innocent pocket knives with which they shred their plug tobacco; he forbade them to smoke; and, finally, tied the left hand of the one to the right of the other to prevent their running away, of which they disclaimed any intention. The cavalry came first to the gate of Bridesdale, and reported the casualties, Perrowne proudly relating that he and Coristine, who was "now end of a good fellow," had carried the doctor to the scow, which he called "the bowt." Ben Toner's waggon came next, having dropped Mrs. Flower at the post office, where, a little later, the constable landed his prisoners. Her companion Serlizer sought the [Pg 256]kitchen with Ben, while Mr. Errol joined his brother divine; but Messrs. Hislop and Lajeunesse, with Mr. Hill, waited only for Sylvanus' appearance to take their homeward journey. At last the ambulance waggon drove slowly up, and tender hands lifted out the disabled and the wounded. Miss Halbert and Miss Carmichael relieved the Captain of his patient, who managed to hop cheerfully into the house, with an arm on each of their shoulders. The Squire and the colonel helped the dominie along, and up to a special single room which was to be his hospital, and which Mrs. and Miss Du Plessis and Mrs. Carruthers were prepared to enter as nurses, so soon as his bearers had put him to bed. Then the doctor came up with his instruments, cut off the colonel's improvised bandage and the shirt sleeve, bathed the wound, found and extracted the bullet, and tied all up tight. The meek dominie bore it all with patience, and apologized to his surgeon for giving him so much trouble while he himself was suffering. The three ladies brought the wounded hero all manner of good things that sick people are supposed to like or to be allowed to eat and drink, and Wilkinson was in a *dolce far niente* elysium. Little Marjorie, having knocked timidly at the door, came in with some square gaudily-covered books under her arm, and asked if Mr. Wilks would like her to read to him. She offered the victim his choice of "Puss in Boots," "Mother Goose," and "Nursery Rhymes"; but Miss Du Plessis, who, at the sufferer's request, was looking up in Wordsworth that cheerful theme, The Churchyard in "The Excursion," interposed, saying, some other day, when Mr. Wilkinson had grown stronger, he might perhaps be able to make a selection from her juvenile library. Marjorie told her cousin that she was sure, if it had been her Eugene who was sick, he would have liked her to stay and read to him. She had told Eugene to marry Cecile, but she would never do so any more; she would give him all to cousin Marjorie.

The three squires sat in council, and agreed to dismiss the nominal captives on condition of their promising to appear when wanted as witnesses. This Serlizer at once agreed to. Mr. Walker rode to the post office and exacted the promise from Mrs. Flower and the masons, thus depriving the constable of his prey. He was compelled to [Pg 257]untie their hands, and restore the confiscated pocket knives. The masons were invited to supper at Bridesdale, as was the woman; but the men proposed to go on to the River, as they had money to pay their way; and Mrs. Flower, who would not leave Harding's body, was given in charge to the post mistress. The supper tables in hall and kitchen were very different from those of the previous night. In the latter, Ben Toner, the constable, and Maguffin had each a lady to talk to. Their superiors missed the company of the lawyer, the detective, and Mr. Bigglethorpe, to say nothing of Mr. Terry. The doctor was stretched out upon a sofa in the office, where his daughter waited on him, assisted by Perrowne, who had to carry the other articles of food while she preceded him with the tea. Miss Du Plessis, similarly helped by the colonel, attended to the wants of the dominie. Consequently, the steady members of the supper circle were the three matrons and Miss Carmichael, with Squires Walker and Carruthers, Mr. Errol, and the Captain. All agreed that Wilkinson had done a very fine thing, and Mrs. Du Plessis was warm in his praise. "The only men that stuck to me," said the Squire, "were Mr. Errol and Bigglethorpe, and even Bigglethorpe went off fishing as soon as he came to the water, so that I may say Mr. Errol was my only faithful adherent." The ladies all looked with much approbation on the blushing minister, and Mrs. Carmichael showed her approval by immediately refilling his cup. Squire Walker whispered in his ear: "Fine woman, Mr. Errol, fine woman, that Mrs. Carmichael! Is she a widow, sir?" Mr. Errol did not like this whispering at table, especially on such a subject, but he replied affirmatively in as brief a way as possible, and went on with his repast. The Captain said that his mill was clean run out of gear with all these starboard and port watches and tacks to every point of the compass; and, when conversation lagged, Carruthers fairly nodded over his plate. Nevertheless, after supper, the occupants of the kitchen were called in and prayers were held, in which Mr. Errol offered petitions for the bereaved, the suffering, and the criminal, and committed the watchers at the post of danger and duty to the care of their Heavenly Father, to all of which Mr. Perrowne responded with a hearty Amen. Then, the parsons insisted [Pg 258]on going home to their boarding houses, and Squire Walker mounted his horse for home. Anxiously, Mrs. Carruthers asked her husband if he anticipated danger where her father was, and Miss Carmichael asked the Captain the same question, without mentioning anyone, but having Coristine in view. Both endeavoured to reassure the minds of the half tearful women, after which they carried the doctor upstairs, and all went to bed. Fearing that the idiot boy might repeat his double attempt to fire the verandah, Mr. Perrowne had told Muggins to lie there and watch it, and there the faithful dog lay the whole night through, to the satisfaction of the inmates of Bridesdale, although happily nothing happened to test his quality as a watch dog.

In the kitchen, Mr. Maguffin considered himself, next to Tryphena and Tryphosa, the representative of the family, as the deputy of Timotheus and the servant of the colonel. Ben Toner was his ally in war, but had no local standing, and the pensioner was simply an intruder. Yet, with cool effrontery, the corporal sat in the place of honour beside Tryphena, and regaled her with narratives of warfare, to which she had listened many times already. Ben and Serlizer were still full of one another's society. He had comforted her heart, if it needed any comforting, over the condition of her father, whom he and Timotheus had treated so cavalierly, and urged her not to go home any more, but to come and help the old woman. With a bad example before her at home, and very far from improving ones at the Select Encampment, Serlizer was yet, though not too cultivated, an honest steady girl, and was pleased to learn that Ben had really turned over a new leaf. She gave her sweetheart to understand that she had kept her own money, not being such a fool as to let the old man get his hands on it, and that it was safe in the bundle she had brought from the boarding-house, whereupon Ben said she had better put that bundle away in a safe place, for you couldn't tell what kind of characters might be about. Mr. Maguffin heard these words, and, taking them to himself, waxed indignant.

"Ef yoh'se diloodin' ter this pressum comperny, Mistah Tonah, I wants ter say I takes the sponsability ob these young ladies on my shouldahs, sah, the shouldahs ob[Pg 259]Mortimah Magrudah Maguffin, sah. Foh what remains ober ob the mascline paht ob it, I ain't no call foh ter spress mysef. It kin speak foh itsef."

The corporal glowered, and smote the table with his fist.

"Pardon my indignation, Miss Hill! This creature, with no military or other standing that I know of, calls me, a retired non-commissioned officer of the British army, it. In India, where I served, I called such things *chakar* and *banda*, the very dust beneath my feet, Miss Tryphena; and it was as much as their life was worth to call me less than *sahib*. And, now that I have retired on a pension, with my medals and clasps, and am an officer of the law, a black man, a *kali*, presumes to *it* me. I have known a *kali chakar* killed, yes killed, for less. 'Corporal,' said the commanding officer to me, 'Corporal Rigby,' said he, many a time, 'order one of your men to call up that black dog of mine!' I assure you he did, Miss Hill."

"I doan' take no erbuse ner nigger talk in this yere house, where I'm takin' Timothis' place, an' where my bawss is mighty high ercount, no, not fom consterbles nor no nuther white tresh. I didn't go foh ter call Mistah Rigby *it*, Miss Tryphosy, I swan ter grashus I didn't. I spressed the pinion as all the comperny as isn't ladies is it and so it is it."

"Ef you go a ittin' of me Maguffin," struck in Ben, "I'm buzz sawed and shingled of I don't hit you back fer what you're ma guvin us." Then he opened up his mouth and laughed, and Serlizer laughed, and the Hill girls. Even Maguffin displayed his ivories, and remarked: "Mistah Tonah, foh a gennelman what ain't trabbled none, yoh'se mighty smaht."

"Oh, Serlizer," said Ben, "we don't go traavellin' much; we ain't like the rollin' stones as don't gaythyer no mawss."

"When the cunnel and me was ridin' ter Tronter, laast Sat'day," continued Mr. Maguffin, "the cunnel he began egspashuatin' on the things he see. 'That there mawss' says he, 'at Hogg's Holler, minds me ob two coloured men was habin' a counterbessy on they

129

bawsses. Says one of the gennelmen, "My bawss," (the cunnel says massa, but that's a name I doan' take to) "my bawss says he ain't like yoh bawss, trabellin' around all the time and [Pg 260]gatherin' no mawss." "No," said the other coloured gennelman, "but my bawss gathers what yoh bawss want mighty bad, and that's a heap ob polish."'"

"For polish," remarked Constable Rigby, turning to Tryphena, "for polish, Miss Hill, commend me to an English army officer."

"My bawss," said Maguffin, "is an officer and a gennelman, and yoh cayn't beat him foh polish nohow."

"There are no officers and no soldiers in America," replied the pensioner.

"Oh, Mr. Rigby," interrupted Tryphosa, "I remember reading in my history that the American soldiers beat the British army many times in the Revolutionary War."

"Flim-flam. Miss Tryphosa Hill, garbled reports! The British army never has been beaten, never can be beaten. I belonged to the British army, Miss Hill, I beg pardon, Miss Tryphosa, and know what I assert from experience."

"Le'ss stop this jaw and have a game o' keerds," suggested Serlizer.

Ben seconded his lady love's proposal, and thought a game of euchre would pass away the time. The constable said euchre was no game. There was only one game at cards, and that was whist. The man or woman who could not play whist was uneducated. Sarah Eliza professed a preference for High, Low, Jack, and the Game; any saphead could play that. She wasn't a saphead herself, but there might be some about. Maguffin regretted that in the Baktis pussuasion cards were not allowed; and the Hill girls had distinctly promised their mother to play no games of chance. As, however, none of the parties owned a pack of cards, nor knew where to find one, further controversy on the subject was useless. Tryphosa, looking intelligent, left the room, and speedily returned with a little cardboard box in her hand, labelled Countries, Cities, Mountains, and Rivers, with which Timotheus had once presented her. She said it was an improving game, and that all could play it. The shuffling and dealing, of course, presented an almost unavoidable chance element, but, apart from that, the game was a matter of science, of geographical knowledge. Now the Hill girls were educated, as Mr. Rigby said; and he, having travelled far as a soldier, was not deficient in geographical lore; but what about the other three?

[Pg 261]"Oh!" ejaculated Miss Newcome, "at them there keerds, I guess we jist are sapheads. Ain't that so, Ben?"

Ben said "I guaiss"; and Mr. Maguffin added: "joggrify, entermoligy, swinetax, and paucity was teached me, but I done clar forgit how they run, it's so long since."

It was, therefore, agreed to play a triangular game, the pair having the most books to be winners, and have the right to shuffle and deal for the following trial of skill. The contending pairs were the pensioner and Serlizer, Ben and Tryphosa, Maguffin and Tryphena, partners were allowed to help each other. While the British Islands, Turkey, Russia, and India were being played, Rigby and Miss Newcome were triumphant, but when it came to any other part of the world, especially to America, with the exception of Canada, where Serlizer scored her one victory, that pair was helpless. Maguffin acquired a book by his own unaided wisdom, that of the Southern United States; otherwise Tryphena inspired him. Ben had an unavailing contest with Miss Newcome over Canada, and saw her make up the book and slam it on the table with mingled feelings of pride in her, and mortification for his own want of success. But, as he said, Tryphosa was "a daisy and parlyzed the hull gang." Laurel after laurel she took from the brow of the travelled pensioner; she swooped down upon Tryphena and Maguffin, and robbed them of books wholesale, till Mr. Toner remarked that she had "quayte a libery"; in her hands the strapping Serlizer was helpless as a child. Magnanimously, she allowed Ben to shuffle and Serlizer to cut, then Ben again to deal.

The second game was more exciting. Mr. Maguffin, naturally quick and possessing a memory cultivated by closely following the prelections of his coloured Baptist religious instructors, rapidly seized the hitherto unknown combinations, and astonished Tryphena with his bold independence of action. The constable's mind worked more conservatively, as became his rank and profession, and Serlizer was worse than useless to him, but, by chance, they had magnificent hands. He piled up India in quick marching time, as he hummed "The British Grenadiers," and accompanied it with a drum beat of his right foot on the floor.

Calcutta, Bombay, and Madras, Indus, Ganges, and Godavery, Himalayas, Ghauts, and Vindhyas, lay cap[Pg 262]tured at his right hand. Ben won Ireland from him, but he annexed England, Scotland, and Turkey. Once more Serlizer took Canada, and, owing to Mr. Toner's imperfect shuffling, laid complete books of Egypt, Australia, and Brazil upon the table. The stars fought against Tryphena and Tryphosa, and, in spite of Mr. Maguffin's gallant struggle against fate, the pensioner took the honours. Then Miss Newcome favoured him with a friendly kick under the table, accompanied by the elegant expression: "Bully for you, old man!" Next, the victorious damsel shuffled, allowed Tryphena to cut, and dealt out the cards for the third game. This time the deal was fair, and Mr. Rigby, glancing over his partner's capacious hand, beheld there no prospect of continued good fortune. Tryphena was on her mettle as a geographer, and Maguffin had stowed away in his all-embracing memory the names of half the globe's prominent features in city, river, and mountain. He wrested half India and all Russia from the pensioner, captured the whole of the United States, Canada, Mexico, and various states of South America. Almost the entire continent of Europe succumbed to Tryphena. Tryphosa fought doggedly, and encouraged Ben to continue the unequal contest, but the constable and Serlizer yielded up card after card with the muteness of despair. Mr. Maguffin was transported with joy, when his partner counted up their united books, amounting to more than those of both the other pairs put together.

"I'se larned moah joggrify this heah bressid night nor I'd git in six mumfs er schoolin'. Hit makes me feel kind er smaht all ober, but not smaht enough foh ter ekal you, Miss Trypheeny, ner yoh pah. Ain't he jest a smaht man, foolin' me on Typernosties and Gasternickle, words I nevah knowed afoah, yah! yah! yah!"

A new game was in progress, when a tap came to the inside door, and, immediately thereafter, a figure in a dressing gown appeared, partly thrust into the half-opened entrance. "Do you know Tryphena," said a pretty voice, "that it is very late, long past midnight, and you two girls have to be up by six o'clock at the latest! Take Sarah with you, and go to bed. Toner, you know Timotheus' room, and had better get some rest, which I am sure you need." As the four parties addressed somewhat sheepishly [Pg 263]departed, Mrs. Carmichael turned to the remaining card players, who were standing, corporal Rigby at military attention, and said, with a somewhat tremulous accent: "There's a large fire out in the Lake Settlement direction, but I cannot bear to awaken Mr. Carruthers or the other two gentlemen, for he is very tired, and they are much older and require rest also. Perhaps, Maguffin, you will be kind enough to saddle a horse quietly, and find out where it is and see that my father and Mr. Coristine are safe."

"I'se ony too pleased ter obey yoh commandemens, marm, wif percision an' dispatches," answered the coloured gentleman, hasting stablewards.

"As constable, ma'am, if I may be allowed to speak," said Corporal Rigby, saluting for the second time, "as constable, it is my duty to be present at all township fires, for the purpose of keeping order and directing operations. I shall, therefore, with your permission, ma'am, respectfully take my leave."

"It is a long way, constable, and you and I are not so young as we once were—"

"Pardon an old soldier's interruption, ma'am, but you are as young as ever you were, the youngest married lady I know."

"Thank you, corporal! What I meant to say was that you had better get Maguffin to saddle a horse for you, as the distance is great."

"You are very good, ma'am, but I never served in the cavalry. I belonged to Her Majesty's Foot Guards, ma'am, and could not possibly insult the memory of my old comrades lying in Crimean graves, by putting the legs, that a merciful Providence furnished me to march with, across the back of a horse. Had I even served in the Artillery or in the Engineers, I might have been able to comply with your kind request. Being what I have been, I must proceed without delay to the seat of the conflagration. I have the honour, ma'am, of saluting you. Good night!"

So Maguffin quietly escaped from the stables, and rode rapidly towards the fire, which shed its lurid light far over the clouded sky; and the pensioner trudged after him on foot, with his official baton under his arm, to make that conflagration acquainted with the law.

131

CHAPTER XIV.

Picnic Supper—Sentries—Sylvanus' Silence—Coristine and Bigglethorpe Hear Sounds—Invaders Repelled—Fire and Explosions—Victims Walled In—Water Retreat in the Rain—The Constable Secures Mark Davis—Walk Home in the Rain—Bangs and Matilda—Into Dry Clothes—Miss Carmichael's Mistake—A Reef in Mr. Bangs—Ben has no Clothes—Three Young Gentlemen in a Bad Way.

Mr. Bangs had no fewer than eight men under his command, Bigglethorpe and the two Richards at the water, and Coristine and the veteran, the two Pilgrims and Rufus, up above. The latter tired themselves out, under the detective's direction, looking for an opening in the ground, but found none, nor anything that in the least resembled one. Some of the searchers wondered why the chimney in Rawdon's house was so unnecessarily large and strong, but no examination about its base revealed any connection between it and an underground passage. The detective, in conference with Mr. Terry and the lawyer, decided on four sentries, namely one each at the house and the lake, as already set, one at the road looking towards the entrance, and the other half way between the lake and the house, to keep up the connection. Some bread and meat and a pot of tea, with dishes, were sent down to the three men on the shore by the hands of Timotheus, but they rejected the cold meat, having already made a fire, and broiled the bass caught by Mr. Bigglethorpe. They had a very jolly time, telling fish stories, till about eight o'clock, and the fisherman of Beaver River was in wonderful spirits over the discovery of a new fishing ground. If those lakes had only contained brook trout he would move his store to the Lakes Settlement; as it was, he thought of setting up a branch establishment, and getting a partner to occupy the two places of business alternately with him. The Richards boys were pleased to think that their new acquaintance was likely to be a permanent one, and made Mr. Bigglethorpe many sincere offers of assistance [Pg 265]in his fishing, and subordinate commercial, ventures. At eight Mr. Bangs came down the hill, and posted one of the Richards as sentry, while the fisherman indulged in his evening smoke, preparatory to turning in under the skiff with his friend Bill. "I went that fire put out, gentlemen," said the detective, "net now, but say efter ten o'clock, as it might help the enemy to spy us out," to which Bill Richards replied: "All right, cap'n; she'll be dead black afore ten." Rufus was placed on the hill side to communicate between the distant posts; Timotheus overlooked the encampment; and Sylvanus was given the station on the road. Mr. Bangs walked about nervously, and the lawyer and Mr. Terry, bringing some clean coverlets out of the boarding-house, spread them on the chip-covered ground, and lay down to smoke their pipes and talk of many things. "Oi tuk to yeez, sorr," said the veteran with warmth, "soon as Oi mit ye in the smokin' carr, and to think what a dale av loife we've seen since, an' here's you an' me, savin' yer prisince, as thick as thaves."

Nothing of any moment occurred till within a quarter of ten, when Sylvanus saw two figures suddenly start up close by him on the right. At first, he thought of challenging them, but seeing one was a woman, and remembering the going over the Squire gave him about capturing Tryphosa, he resolved to await their arrival. Both figures greeted him joyfully by his name, for it was his two proteges, the crazy woman and her son, who had escaped the constable and lain concealed until darkness veiled their movements. "Has Steevy woke up yet?" she asked the sentinel, quietly.

"Not as I know on," responded the elder Pilgrim.

"Then we will slip quietly into the house, and get some supper for Monty, and go to bed. It's tiresome walking about all day," she continued.

"Don't you two go fer to make no noise, 'cos they's sentries out as might charlinge yer with their guns," remarked the compassionate guard.

"No," she whispered back; "we will be still as little mice, won't we, Monty? Good night, Sylvanus!" The boy added, "Good night, Sylvy!" and the sentinel returned the salutation, and muttered to himself: "Pore souls, the sight on 'em breaks me all up."

[Pg 266]Sylvanus should have reported these arrivals, when the detective came to relieve him, and put Mr. Terry in his place, but he did not. He had forgotten all about them, and was wondering if that "kicked-out-of-service old ramrod, the corpular, was foolin' round about Trypheeny." Coristine relieved Timotheus; Bill Richards, Rufus; and Mr. Bigglethorpe,

Harry Richards. The relieved men went to sleep on the quilts and under the skiff. Mr. Bangs came up every quarter of an hour to the lawyer, and asked if he had heard a noise about the house, to which the sentinel replied in the affirmative every time; whereupon the detective would take a lamp and search the building from top to bottom without any result. Once, after such a noise, that sounded like some heavy article being dragged along, Coristine thought he heard the words: "Keep quiet, Tilly," and, "Take it hoff," but he was not sure. The night was cloudy and dark, and the mosquitoes' buzzing sometimes had a human sound, while the snoring of the Pilgrims, and the restless moving of the horses, brought confusion to the ear, which sought to verify suspected articulations. Had he known that Matilda Nagle was about the house, he would not have let Bangs rest until the mystery was solved. He did not know; and, being very tired and sleepy, was inclined to distrust the evidence of his senses and lay it to the charge of imagination.

Down by the water's edge Mr. Bigglethorpe sat on a stone in front of the carved out block, thinking of the best fly for bass, and of a great fishing party to the lakes that should include Mr. Bulky. Standing up to stretch his legs and facing the block of limestone, he thought he saw a narrow line of light along the left perpendicular incision. Moving over, he saw the same perpendicular line on the right. Just then the clouds drifted off the moon, and he convinced himself that the light lines were reflections from the sheen that glimmered over the lake. He also thought he heard a whining noise, such as a sick person or a child might make, and then a rough voice saying: "Stow that now!" but Richards, like the two Pilgrims above, was snoring, and Harry had a slight cold in his head. "What a stoopid, superstitious being I should become," said the fisherman to himself, "if I were out here long all alone." But, hark! the sound of paddles softly dipping came from [Pg 267]the left, and at once the sentry lay down behind the upturned skiff, and, gun in hand, listened. He poked Richards with his foot, and, as he awoke, enjoined silence. Richards crawled out, and quietly replaced the boat in its original position. There were now two on guard instead of one. The boat entered the lake. It was the scow, Richards' scow, and Harry was indignant. There were five men in it, and they were talking in a low tone.

"Quite sure them blarsted Squire folks has all gone home, Pete?"

"Sartin, I seen 'em, the hull gang's scattered and skee-daddled, parsons an' all."

"Where's the blarsted light, then?"

"Seems to me I kin see long, thin streaks. O Lawr, boys, Rodden must ha' been hard put, when he drapped the block into the hole. It's shet up tight. Hev ye got the chisel and mallet?"

"They're all right."

"Then less git ashore and drap the block out, though it's an orful pity to lose it in the drink."

"Carn't we git the blarsted thing back to its place agin?"

"Onpossible; wild horses couldn't do it."

Harry whispered to Bigglethorpe: "What'll we do?" and the fisherman answered: "Our duty is to fire, but we weren't told to kill anybody. Don't you fire till I reload."

Then Bigglethorpe called out: "Surrender in the Queen's name," and fired above the scow. Two or three pistol shots rattled over the sentries' heads, and flattened themselves on the rock behind. "All ready!" said the storekeeper, and Harry let fly his duck shot into the middle of the crowd, who paddled vigorously from the shore. Bill Richards, having alarmed the upper sentries by the discharge of his gun, came running down, with the Pilgrims and Rufus, led by the detective, not far behind him. "Shove out the skiff," called Bigglethorpe. The Richards shoved it off, and Bill rowed, when the two sentries got on board. "Go it, Bill, after the old tub," cried Harry; "we'll soon catch up." The Rawdon gang worked hard to get to the narrows, but found it hopeless. "Give it to them," shouted Bangs from the shore; and in response, the guns rang out again, while Bill strained [Pg 268]every muscle to the utmost. The punt grounded on the shore above the narrows, and four of the men jumped out into the water and fled up the bank, firing their pistols as they retired. The punt was captured, and brought back to the guarded beach, with a wounded man and some tools in the bottom. Only by swimming, or by a long detour of very many miles, could the four fugitives find their way back to the shore they had sought in vain.

133

The wounded man was taken out of the punt and laid on the beach. "Is he dead?" asked Bigglethorpe. "No," answered the detective, feeling the head of the victim, and inspecting him by the aid of matches struck by the smoker Sylvanus; "it's a good thing for him thet yore two gens were louded with deck shot end thet they sketter sow, else he'd a been a dead men. He's got a few pellets in the beck of his head, jest eneugh to sten the scoundrel for a few minutes. Ah, he's hed a creck owver the top of his head with a cleb, the colonel's werk, very likely."

"Do you want him kept?" enquired Mr. Bigglethorpe, as sentry.

"Oh, dear me, yes; he's Rawdon's chief men. I wouldn't lose him fer a hendred dollars. Rufus, do you mind blowing his brains out if he attempts to escaype?"

The good-natured Rufus said he didn't mind watching the prisoner, but he imagined clubbing would be kinder than blowing out his brains.

"All right!" answered the detective, "all right, so long as you keep him safely."

So Mr. Bangs went back to the house, followed by Sylvanus, Timotheus and Bill Richards, the last of whom resumed his post, namely the trunk on which Pierre Lajeunesse had rested.

When the encampment was reached, Mr. Bangs asked Coristine if he had been smoking on guard or lighting matches, but he had not. He asked Mr. Terry the same question, which the old soldier almost took as an insult. "An' is it to me ye come, axin' av Oi shmoke on guarrd, an' shpind my toime loightin' matches loike a choild? Oi've sane sarvice, sorr, and nobody knows betther fwhat his juty is."

"I sincerely beg your pardon, Mr. Terry. Please excuse my enxiety; I smell fire."

[Pg 269]"Don't mintion it, sorr, betune us. Faix, an' it's foire I shmill an' moighty sthrong, too."

The detective came back to the front of the house, and saw the fire that had broken forth in a moment, and was flaming in every room of basement and upper storey, a fire too rapidly advanced to be got under, even had the means been at hand.

"Quick, Sylvanus, Timotheus, get out the horses and any other live stock," he cried; but the lawyer had been before him, and the two Pilgrims and he were already leading the frightened animals past the house and on to the road, where they turned their heads outward and drove them along. Forgetting their watch, Mr. Terry and Bangs himself helped, until every living creature, as they thought, was safely away on the road to the Lake Settlement. Then, two figures, that the guilty Sylvanus knew, came out of the door of the boarding house, and the flames leaped out after them. The woman came up to Coristine, and said: "I know you; you helped to carry poor Steevy, who is not awake yet. He said it was cold down there, so Monty and I have made a fire to keep him warm." The lawyer thought she meant that her dead brother was cold. As to the fire, when he saw Monty, it did not astonish him; but how came they both there through the guard?

The frame buildings, their light clapboards dried by the summer sun, burned furiously, and the flames roared in the rising wind. The sheds and stables caught; the fire ran over the ground, in spite of the dew, catching in shrubs and fallen timber, and even climbing up living trees. Back the beholders were driven, as far as Bill Richards' post, by the terrible glare and heat of the conflagration. Leaving Bigglethorpe on sentry, and Rufus over the prisoner, Harry came running up to learn what was the matter, and to tell of noises like human voices and hammer blows behind the slab of rock. Then, as the fire in the house burned down to the ground, there was an explosion that seemed to shake the earth, and a column of fire sprang up the standing chimney, side by side with another less lofty and more diffused from the right of the building. Report after report followed, and the whole party, half terror-stricken, descended to the beach. Rufus, with Bigglethorpe's help, had considerably transferred his [Pg 270]prisoner to the punt, and guarded him there. The store-keeper, taking chisel and mallet in hand, was striking off chip after chip of rock, in answer to muffled cries from within; and now the big rock had moved half an inch. Still the brave man worked away amid the continued explosions, and in spite of the advancing fire. The block continued to slide, and Bigglethorpe cried: "Take the boats out of the way, and get back from me, or you will all be crushed in a minute." The punt was out of danger, but Bill Richards, with a single movement, shoved off the skiff, and, kneeling on her stern, sent her

134

far out into the lake. Then he rowed the boat rapidly back into a place of safety. The slab was still sliding, and had cleared the rock out of which it had been cut by an inch. A human hand was thrust out, a dumpy, beringed hand, bleeding with the effort; a most audible voice cried "For God's sake, 'urry!" and then there came a perfect Babel of explosions, and the gallant deliverer was forcibly drawn out of a fierce river of liquid fire that streamed down into the lake, and burned even out on the water. The fisherman was badly burnt, hair, beard and eyelashes almost singed off; but still he thought of rescue. "Fire at that miserable little chip that holds it," he cried; "fire, since you can't hit it otherwise. Oh, for an asbestos suit, and I would have styed." They fired pistol and gun with no effect, till the lawyer, out in the skiff with Bill, got his rifle sighted to the point in the blue flame, where he thought the preventing ridge ought to be. He fired at close range, the ball hit the rock projection, and at once the great block slid away into the lake, with a splash that damped the flames with a column of spray, and revealed an awful corridor of fire. No living creature was there, but the detective, dipping his feet in the lake, took a boat hook out of the returning skiff, and then, standing in the flames, hauled out two charred masses, and extinguished them in the shallow water by the shore.

Mr. Terry came running down and crying: "Out on the wather wid yeez, ivery mother's son av yeez; the foire's spreadin' an' the threes is fallin'; fer yer loife, min." Mr. Bangs, still in command, asked:—

"How many will the skiff howld, Bill?"

"Seven, anyway," replied the Richards of that name.

[Pg 271]"Mr. Coristine and Mr. Terry take commend and choose crew."

"Come, Matilda and Monty," said the lawyer.

"Come on, Sylvanus, Timotheus, Rufus," cried Mr. Terry.

"I'll row," said the Irishman.

"And me, too," added Sylvanus.

"Look after my prisoner, Mr. Bangs," cried Rufus; and the skiff went out to sea.

Bill transferred himself to the scow, with his brother Harry and Mr. Bigglethorpe. The detective lifted the two charred masses to the opposite side of the middle thwart from that against which the prisoner lay. Then, Bill and Bigglethorpe having taken the bow, he and Harry took the stern, and the scow followed the skiff. For a time the two boats stood stock still, fascinated by the awful scene. The explosions were over, but the forest was blazing fiercely, and up towards the smouldering buildings, but underground, blazed a vault of blue fire that reached up to the standing brick chimney of Rawdon's house. Hundreds of animals were in the water around them, squirrels and snakes and muskrats, even mice, swimming for dear life. Then, pitter, patter, came the rain, hissing on the flames. It fell more heavily; and the lawyer, having doffed his coat to row, threw it over the woman's shoulders, while Mr. Terry put that of Sylvanus about the boy. "Lead on, Mr. Coristine," cried the detective; and the skiff shot through the narrows, with the punt hard after it. The rain fell in torrents and drenched the occupants of both vessels; but those whose faces were towards the stern could see the bush-fire still raging. "The rain'll stop it spreadin'," Bill called out cheerfully, and the lawyer rejoiced, because the fire was on Miss Du Plessis' land. Long was the journey, tired were the rowers and paddlers, and draggled was the crew, or rather draggled were the crews, that reached the Richards' homestead. The prisoner was awake by this time, had been so all along since he was deposited in the punt, and a paddle had splashed his face. When walked ashore, he had made a dash for liberty, but Mr. Bangs had brought him up short. "Yore in too great a herry, Merk Devis," he had said; "we went you, my men, and we'll hev you, [Pg 272]dead or alive." So Mark Davis, since that was the name of Wilkinson's dissipated farmer, had to fall into line and march to the Richards' place. There the party found Maguffin and the constable.

The colonel's servant had been much closer to the conflagration, but, having seen no sign of any person there, nothing but a number of startled horses, and the fire having taken possession of the sides of the masked road, he had retired to the nearest house. He at once enquired after the safety of Mr. Terry and the lawyer, and, finding that they and all the rest of the party were safe, rode back at his utmost speed to report. The constable, rejoiced at seeing his prisoners again, was about to rearrest them, when Coristine and Sylvanus interposed, the latter threatening to thrash the pipe-clay out of the pensioner's "old putrified jints" if he touched the boy. The Crew meant petrified, but the insult was no less offensive to the corporal on account of the mistake. As a private individual in the Squire's kitchen, Mr. Rigby was disposed to peace and unwilling to engage in a contest with big-boned Sylvanus, but, as a constable on duty, he was prepared to face any number of law-breakers and to fight them to the death. Drawing his baton, he advanced, and only the commands of his legal superior, Mr. Bangs, backed by the expostulations of the pseudo sergeant-major Terry, induced him to refrain from recapturing his former prisoners, and from adding to them the profane Pilgrim who had been guilty of interfering with an officer in the discharge of his duty. Finally he was mollified by being put in possession of a really great criminal, Mark Davis, whom he at once searched and deprived of various articles, including a revolver, all the chambers of which were fortunately empty. Then, producing his own revolver, the corporal gave it to his prisoner to smell, remarking that, if he tried any nonsense, he would have a taste of it that he would remember. Mrs. Richards was busy reducing the inflammation of Mr. Bigglethorpe's burns. She insisted that he should go no farther that night, and the whole Richards family, which had greatly taken to the fisherman, combined to hold him an honoured prisoner. Mr. Bigglethorpe consented to remain, and the Bridesdale contingent bade him and his hosts good night. The constable went first with his pris[Pg 273]oner, followed by Matilda Nagle, between the lawyer and the detective. Monty came next, clinging to Sylvanus and Mr. Terry, while Timotheus and Rufus brought up the rear. Mrs. Richards had furnished the woman and her boy with two shiny waterproofs, called by the young Richards gum coats, so that Coristine and Sylvanus got back their contributions to the wardrobe of the insane, but, save for the look of the thing, they would have been better without them, since they only added a clammy burden to thoroughly water-soaked bodies.

Still the rain fell in torrents. It trickled in many rills off the penthouses of the pedestrians' headgear; from the lapels of coats and from waistcoats it streamed down, concentrating itself upon soggy knees. Broad sheets, like the flow of a water-cart, radiated from coat tails of every description; and rivers descending trouser-legs, turned boots and shoes into lakes, which sodden stockinged feet pumped out in returning fountains. Happily there was no necessity for using gun or pistol, since these weapons shared in the general pervading moisture. Yet the corporal marched erect, with his left hand on his prisoner's shoulder. Poor Matilda was cheerful, though shivering, and, turning round to her boy, said; "It is a good thing, Monty, that we lit the fire when we did, for it would be very hard to light one now;" to which the lad answered, "I hain't a goin' to light no more fires no more." Sylvanus and the veteran had been telling him what a bad thing it was to set houses on fire, and the hypnotized boy, freed apparently from the mesmeric bond by the death of his unnatural father, responded to the counsels of his new friends. The influence lasted longer with Matilda, for as, in spite of the absorbing rain, her companions were able to make a study of her talk, they observed that it was controlled by one or two overmastering ideas, which were evidently the imposition of a superior will. In his dog-Latin, which he presumed the poor woman could not understand, Mr. Bangs said to the lawyer: "*Oportet dicere ad Doctorem dehypnotizere illem feminem.*" To this elegant sentence Mr. Coristine briefly answered, "*Etiam,*" but soon afterwards he asked: "Where did you pick up your Latin, Mr. Bangs."

"I wes at school, you know where, with pore Nesh; [Pg 274]*mulier nescit nomen.* We both took to Letin, because we could talk without being understood by the common crowd. You find velgar criminals thet know some French, German, Spenish or Portegese, bet none thet know Letin. In dealing with higher class criminals we used our own gibberish or artificial shibboleth."

"A sort of Volapuk?"

"Exectly; pore Nesh was ohfelly clever et it."

"I am going to kill Mr. Nash as soon as I can find him," interrupted the woman, in an amiable tone of voice, as if she proposed to discharge some pleasant duty.

The men shuddered, and Mr. Bangs said: "You know, my dear Matilda, what the Bible says, Thou shelt not kill. You surely would not kemmit the sin of merder?"

"I am not to mind what the Bible says, or what Steevy says, or what clergymen or any other people say. I am only to do what he says, and I must."

136

"Did he tell you to light thet fire?"

"Not that fire, but the other said it was cold down there."

"Why did he not come up?"

"Because I covered the trap over with the big stones, and Monty helped me."

"Surely he didn't tell you to dreg the stones on to the trep?"

"Yes, he did, but not then. It was before, when Flower wanted to get up, and crawl away and tell, because he thought he was going to die."

"Was Flower down there with him?"

"Yes; that's why Monty and I put the big stones on the trap."

"Flower was hert, wasn't he, shot in the beck, I think?"

"Yes; he crawled in all the way on his hands and knees, and I helped his wife to tie him up, till the doctor came, the morning that I found Steevy."

"How do you know thet Stephen wes esleep?"

"He told me."

"*Deminus Coristinus, mulier non est responsibilis pro suis ectionibus. Facit et credit omnia qua mendet enimel mertuus.*"

"*Eheu domine!*" replied the lawyer; "*sic est vita dolorosa!*"

[Pg 275]Bridesdale was all lit up, and the front door was open to receive the soaked wayfarers, but no one could be induced to enter it. Mr. Terry asked Honoria to leave his dry suit and a pair of shoes at the kitchen, when he would take them to the carriage house, and change there. The lawyer and the detective had no dry suit, so Mrs. Carruthers brought them some of her husband's clothes, and two umbrellas, under which they carried their bundles, wrapped in bath towels, to the place the veteran had chosen. While the three drawing-room guests stripped, rubbed themselves down with the grateful towels, and put on their dry attire, the kitchen filled up with the humid and steaming Pilgrims, Rufus, the idiot boy, and his mother. Constable Rigby lodged his prisoner on some straw in an empty stall in the stable, and, producing a pair of handcuffs, which he had left there, secured him, fastening also a stall chain round one of his legs with a padlock. The constable was severe, but he had lost two prisoners the previous day, had been abused by Sylvanus Pilgrim, and was very wet and tired. To the credit of Sylvanus be it said, that he came out with Ben Toner's clothes, and lent them to his elderly rival, and actually carried the corporal's wet garments into the kitchens, there to hang with a large assortment of others, drying before the two stoves, in full blast for the purpose. The gum coats had fairly protected the clothes of Matilda and Monty, but their feet needed reclothing, and it took some time to dry their heads. Maguffin had taken off his wet things, and was asleep in the loft bed, keeping one ear open for the safekeeping of the colonel's horses. Tryphena and Tryphosa were both up; and into their hands Rufus consigned the dripping habiliments of their two admirers as well as his own, his fraternal relation allowing him to appear before the ladies of the kitchen in a long white garment with frills that had never been constructed for a man. "Guess it ain't the last time you'll have to dry them clothes, gals," said the sportive Rufus, skipping along in his frilled surplice, when Tryphena chased him out of the apartment with a sounding smack between the shoulders. Tryphena hesitated to send the mad woman into the room in which Serlizer was sleeping, not knowing the nature of their relations at the Select Encampment. Matilda, however,[Pg 276]evidenced no intention of retiring, or feeling of drowsiness. She talked, with the brightness and cheerfulness of other days, and in a gentle, pleasant voice, but on strange wild themes that terrified the two young women. Monty looked at the fire and then at Tryphosa, saying: "I hain't a goin' to light no more fires no more." "Why?" asked Tryphosa, and the answer came, which revealed a genuine working of the intellect: "'Cos Sylvy says hit's wicked." His mother turned, and said: "Monty, you must not mind what Sylvanus says or anybody else; you must mind what he says."

The boy looked his mother full in the face, and replied in a very decided tone, "Hi'm blowed hif I do!"

In the forepart of the house, only the ladies were up. The doctor and the colonel, the captain and the Squire, slept the sleep of tired men with good consciences, and the wounded dominie was enjoying a beautiful succession of rose-coloured dreams, culminating in a service, at which a tall soldierly man in appropriate costume gave away into his hand that of a very elegant and accomplished lady, saying, as he did so, "Can I do less for the heroic saver of her uncle's life?" Mr. Terry's appearance, on entering to salute his daughter, exacted no remark. The lawyer looked somewhat bucolic, but highly respectable. But poor little Mr. Bangs was buried in clothing, and tripped on his overflowing trowser legs, as he vainly strove to put his right hand outside of its coatsleeve, for the purpose of shaking hands with the company. Mrs. Carmichael took pity on him, and turned back his cuffs, and, his hands being thus of use to him, he employed them to do the same with the skirts of his trousers. The usually polite veteran took Coristine to a corner of the room, and, between violent coughs of suppressed laughter, said: "Och, Misther Coristine, it's the dumb aguey I'll be havin' iv his clawthes is not droied soon. It's Bangs by name he is and bangs by natur'. Shure, this bangs Banagher, an' Banagher bangs the world." The young ladies had not yet entered the apartment, and the three night-watchers were busy relating to the three matrons the terrible events of the night. The lawyer was sitting with his back to the door, conversing with Mrs. Carruthers, when Miss Carmichael came tripping in, followed by Miss [Pg 277]Du Plessis and Miss Halbert. The lawyer's hair was brown, and so was her uncle's. The coat was the Squire's, and the white collar above it. So she slipped softly up to the back of the chair, took the brown head between her hands, and administered a salute on the forehead, with the words: "Why, Uncle John!—," then suddenly turned and fled, amid the laughter of the veteran and his daughter, and the amused blushes and smiles of her mother. The other young ladies came forward and joined in the conversation, but Miss Carmichael did not show her face until the family was summoned for prayers. The colonel came down in his usual urbane smiling way, saying that he had taken the liberty of looking in upon his dear friend and prisoner, and was rejoiced to find that he had spent a good night. The captain could be heard descending the staircase, and telling somebody that he was becalmed again with a spell of foul weather. The somebody was the Squire, who insisted that thieves had been through his wardrobe, and then eagerly asked for news from the encampment. All were shocked beyond measure when they heard of the terrible tragedy. "I wished the man no good," said the Squire, with a regretful expression on his manly face, "but, if he had been ten times the deep dyed villain he was, I couldn't have dreamt of such an awful fate for him." The captain remarked that in the midst of life we are in death, that the ways of Providence are mysterious, and that where a man makes his bed he must lie down, all of which he considered to be good Scripture and appropriate to the occasion. "Yoah fohce met with no moah casualties, I hope, Captain Bangs? I do not see our fishing friend, Mr. Bigglethorpe; is he safe, suh?" These questions led to an account of the fisherman's heroic attempt to release the self-imprisoned occupants of the underground passage, of his wounds, and of the subsequent exploits of the lawyer and the detective. Coristine escaped upstairs to put himself in shape for breakfast, and to visit his wounded friend. He found that gentleman progressing very favourably, and perfectly satisfied with his accommodation.

After morning prayers, conducted by the Squire with unusual solemnity, the lawyer asked Miss Carmichael if she alone would not shake hands with him, making no[Pg 278]allusion to any previous encounter. She complied, with a blush, and seemed pleased to infer that the Captain, above all, had not heard of her mistake. The two had no time for explanations, however, as, at the moment, Messrs. Errol and Perrowne, who had been told there was a fire out towards the Lake Settlement, came in to learn about it, and were compelled to sit down and add something substantial to their early cup of coffee. They reported the rain almost over, and the fire, so far as they could judge from the distance, the next thing to extinguished. Once more the trays were in requisition for the invalids, and again the colonel and Mr. Perrowne acted as aids to Miss Du Plessis and Miss Halbert. Just as soon as he could draw her attention away from the minister, Coristine remarked to Miss Carmichael: "I have the worst luck of any man; I never get sick or wounded or any other trouble that needs nursing." The young lady said in a peremptory manner, "Show me your hands;" and the lawyer had to exhibit two not very presentable paws. She turned them palms up, and shuddered at the scorched, blistered and scratched appearance of them. "Where are Mr. Errol's gloves I put on you?"

"In the pocket of my wet coat in the kitchen."

"Why did you dare to take them off when I put them on?"

138

"Because I was like the cat in the proverb, not that I was after mice you know, but I couldn't fire in gloves."

"Well, your firing is done now, and I shall expect you to come to me in the workroom, immediately after breakfast, to have these gloves put on again. Do you hear me, sir?"

"Yes."

"And what else? Do you mean to obey?"

"Oh, yes, Miss Carmichael, of course, always, with the greatest joy in the world."

"Nobody asked you, sir, to obey always."

"I beg your pardon, Miss Carmichael, I'm afraid I'm a little confused."

"Then I hope you will not put me to confusion, as you did this morning."

"I'm awfully sorry," said the mendacious lawyer, "but it was the coat and collar, you know." Then most [Pg 279]illogically, he added, "I'd like to wear this coat and this collar all the time."

"No, you would not; they are not at all becoming to you. Oh, do look at poor Mr. Bangs!"

The detective's sleeves were turned back, thanks to Mrs. Carmichael, but, as he sat at breakfast, the voluminous coat sagged over his shoulder, and down came the eclipsing sleeve over his coffee cup. When he righted matters with his left hand, the coat slewed round to the other side, knocked his fork out of his hand, and fell with violence on his omelet. The Captain looked at him, and bawled: "I say, mate, you've got to have a reef took in your back topsel. You don't mind a bit of reef tackle in the back of your coat, do you, John?" The Squire did not object; so Miss Carmichael was despatched to the sewing room for two large pins, and she and the Captain between them pinched up the back of the coat longitudinally to the proper distance, and pinned the detective up a little more than was necessary.

"Whey," asked he of his nautical ally, "em I consistent es a cherecter in bowth phases of my berrowed cowt?"

"I know," chuckled the Captain; "'cause then you had too much slack on your pins, and now you've got too much pins in your slack, haw! haw!"

"Try egain."

Coristine ventured, "Because then your hands were in your cuffies, but now your coffee's in your hand." This was hooted down as perfectly inadmissible, Miss Carmichael asking him how he dared to make such an exhibition of himself. Mr. Errol was wrestling with something like Toulouse and Toulon, but could not conquer it. Then the detective said: "If the ledies will be kind enough not to listen, I should answer, Before I wes loose in my hebits, end now I em tight."

Of course the Captain applauded, but the lawyer's reprover remarked to him that she did not think that last at all a nice word. He agreed with her that it was abominable, that no language was strong enough to reprobate it, and then they left the table.

There was trouble in the kitchen. Timotheus and Maguffin had each a Sunday suit of clothes, which they had donned. Sylvanus and Rufus having special claims [Pg 280]on Tryphena, she had put their wet garments in a favourable place, and, being quite dry, handed them in to her befrilled brother, early in the morning, through a half open doorway. The constable, attired in the garb presented to him by Sylvanus, having fastened his prisoner securely with a second stall chain, entered the house, and politely but stiffly wished the cook and housemaid "Good morning." Breakfast was ready, and then the trouble began. Ben had no clothes, and the boys enjoyed the joke. The company was again a large one, for Serlizer and Matilda Nagle were added to the feminine part of it, and the constable and the boy brought its male members up to six, exclusive of the prostrate Ben. Mr. Terry had temporarily deserted the kitchen. Mr. Toner's voice could be heard three doors off calling for Sylvanus, Timotheus, Rufus, Mr. Rigby and Mr. Maguffin. These people were all smilingly deaf, enjoying their hot breakfast. Then, in despair, he called Serlizer.

"What's the racket, Ben?"

"My close is sto-ul, Serlizer."

"They's some duds hangin' up here and in the back kitchen to dry. Praps yourn's there."

"No, Serlizer, myuns never got wayt. You don't think I was sech a blame fooul as to go out in that there raiun do you?"

"Didn't know but what yer might."

"Whey's them close, anyway?"

"I don't know nuthun 'bout yer clothes. Most men as ain't marrd looks after they own clothes."

"Is that you Ben?" asked the more refined voice of Tryphena, in a tone of surprise.

"Yaas, Trypheeny, that's jest who it is. Saay, ken you tayl me what's come o' my close?"

"They are here, Ben, close to the table;" whereupon all the company glanced at Mr. Rigby, and choked.

"Cayn't you take 'em off what they're on, and saynd one of the boys in with 'em, Trypheeny?"

The cook coloured up, and laughter could no longer be restrained. The constable laughed, and the contagion spread to Matilda and her boy.

"Dod rot it?" cried Mr. Toner, indignantly; "what are you fools and eejuts a screechin' and yellin' at? [Pg 281]Gimme my close, or, s'haylp me, I'll come right out and bust some low down loafer's thinkin' mill."

"Now, be quiet, Ben," answered Tryphena, "and I will send Rufus in with your breakfast. You shall have your clothes when they are ready."

So, Rufus took in a plentiful breakfast to his friend Toner, who sat up in the big bed to enjoy it. "I'm powerful sorry for you, Ben," remarked the Baby. "You don't think Serlizer could ha' come in and taken your clothes out into the rain, do you?"

"Hev they been out in the rain, Rufus?"

"Why yes, didn't you know that much? If it hadn't been for the constable, they might ha' been out there yet. I'd say thank ye to him if I was you, Ben."

"Consterble Rigby!" shouted Toner.

"At your service, sir," replied the pensioner.

"I'm awful obligated to you, consterble, fer bringin' in my wayt close."

"Do not speak of it, sir," replied Mr. Rigby, with a large piece of toast apparently in his mouth; "I am proud to do you a service, sir."

Ben was a big man, and somewhat erratic in his ways, so the constable retired, and came back in his own garb, which he had carried out with him. "I think, Miss Hill," he said, "that Mr. Toner's clothes are now dry enough for him to wear them with safety. What do you think, Miss Newcome?"

"Guess we kin take them off now," answered Serlizer.

"Serlizer," growled Ben, "you're an old cat, a desprit spiteful chessacat, to go skylarkin' on yer own feller as never did yer no harm. Gerlong with yer!"

Rufus came in for the breakfast things, and deposited Ben's clothes on the bed. "It wasn't Serlizer, Ben, sure; If I was you I'd try the nigger. Them darkies are always up to tricks."

Mr. Toner got into his clothes, resolved to have it out with somebody, even if Rufus himself should prove to be the traitor. When, a few minutes later, Mr. Terry, smoking his morning pipe, foregathered with Ben in the stable yard, and asked him what he was after now, the answer he gave was: "Lookin' araound fer somebody to whayul!" to which the veteran replied: "Bin, my lad, it's aisy talkin'."

[Pg 282]When the men were out of the kitchen, Mrs. Carruthers and her sister-in-law came in to see the mad woman and her boy. The boy they knew already, and had always been kind to, giving him toys and other little presents, as well as occasional food and shelter. They were much taken with the mother's quiet manners, and, having heard that she had been a milliner, invited her to join them in the workroom. But, when they unitedly arrived at the door of that apartment, they speedily retired to the parlour, and there engaged in conversation. Mrs. Du Plessis was upstairs, with the colonel to play propriety, sponging the dominie's face and hands, and brushing his hair, as if he were her own son. Every now and again Colonel Morton came up to the bedside, saying: "Be kind to him, my deah Tehesa, and remembeh that he saved the life of yoah poah sistah Cecilia's widowah." So the stately

140

Spanish lady shook up the wounded man's pillows, while the colonel put his arm around him and held him up; and then, as he sank back again, she asked. "Are you strong enough to have Cecile come up and read to you?" Wilkinson, sly dog, as the Captain called him, said it was too much trouble to put Miss Du Plessis to; but his objections were overruled. Soon a beatific vision came once more on the scene, and Wordsworth was enthroned as the king of poets. Miss Halbert and Mr. Perrowne were in the garden, and the clergyman had a rose in his button hole which he had not plucked himself. If he had not been in holy orders, he would have thought Miss Fanny was awfully jolly. Then he said to himself, that holy orders don't hinder a man being a man, and Miss Fanny was, really was, awfully jolly, and boarding in the houses of uncultivated farmers was an awful bore. But this was nothing to what was going on in the studiously avoided work room. The lawyer's hands were being washed, because a voice from an arch-looking face said that he was a big baby, and didn't know how to wash himself. It was quite a big baby in size and aspect that was soaped and glycerined, and had some other stuff rubbed into his hands by other pretty hands, one of which wore the victim's ring. Corry felt that he could stand it, even to the putting on of the minister's gloves. When she had finished her work, the hospital nurse said, "that silly little Marjorie, angry [Pg 283]because Cecile would not allow her to read fairy stories to Mr. Wilkinson, surrendered you to me."

"O Marjorie, my darlin', and would you throw your lovely self away on a poor, stupid, worthless thing like me?"

CHAPTER XV.

Miss Carmichael Snubs and Thinks—The Constable and the Prisoner—Matilda and the Doctor—The Children Botanize—Pressing Specimens—Nomenclature—The Colonel Makes a Discovery—Miss Carmichael Does Not Fancy Wilks—Mr. Newberry Takes Matilda—Mr. Pawkins Makes Mischief and is Punished—Rounds on Sylvanus—Preparations for Inquest

"Mr. Coristine, I never gave you permission to call me by my Christian name, much less to think that I accepted Marjorie's foolish little charge. I am sorry if I have led you to believe that I acted so bold, so shameless a part."

"Oh, Miss Carmichael, forgive me. I'm stupid, as I said, but, as the Bible has it, I'll try and keep a watch on the door of my lips in future. And you such an angel of mercy, too! Please, Miss Carmichael, pardon a blundering Irishman."

"Nonsense," she answered. "I have nothing to pardon; only, I did not want you to misunderstand me." The gloves were on, and she shook hands with him, and laughed a comical little insincere laugh in his face, and ran away to her own room to have a foolish little cry. She heard her friend Cecile reading poetry to the wounded Wilkinson, and, looking out of her window, saw Mr. Perrowne helping her uncle to lift the doctor's chair out into the garden, and her mother, freed from conversation with the madwoman, plucking a flower for Mr. Errol's coat. There, too, was a young man, his hands encased in black kid gloves, sitting down on a bench with Mr. Terry, and with difficulty filling a meerschaum pipe. She thought he had a quiet, disappointed look, like a man's whose warm, generous impulses have been checked, and she felt guilty. It was true they had not known one another long, but what was she, a teacher in a common school, that was [Pg 284]what people called them, to put on airs before such a man as that? If it had been Mr. Wilkinson, now; but, no; she was afraid of Mr. Wilkinson, the distant, the irreproachable, the autocratic great Mogul. She looked down again, through the blinds of course. Marjorie Thomas was on the lawyer's knee, and Marjorie Carruthers on the veteran's. The Captain's daughter was combing Coristine's brown hair with her fingers, and pointing the ends of his moustache, much to the other Marjorie's amusement and the lawyer's evident satisfaction. Miss Carmichael inwardly called her cousin a saucy little minx, resenting her familiarities with a man who was, of course, nothing to her, in a way that startled herself. Why had he not saved somebody's life and been wounded, instead of that poetic fossil of a Wilkinson? But, no; it was better not, for, had he saved the colonel's life, Cecile would have been with him, and that she could not bear to think of. Then, she remembered what Corry had told her of the advertisement to the next of kin. Perhaps she would be wealthy yet, and more than his equal socially, and then she could condescend, as a great lady, and put a treasure in those poor gloved hands. Where would they all have been without these hands, all scarred and blistered to save them from death? Everybody was very unkind to little Marjorie's Eugene, and failed to recognize his claims upon their gratitude. Oh, that saucy little minx, with her grand assumptions of proprietorship, as if she owned him, forsooth!

Mr. Bangs called the justices to business. There was a prisoner to examine, and two charred masses of humanity for the coroner to sit upon. So a messenger was sent off to summon the long-suffering Johnson, Newberry, and Pawkins, for the coroner's inquest, and the doctor was carried back into the office for the examination of the prisoner, Mark Davis. The two Squires sat in appropriate chairs behind an official table, at one side of which Mr. Bangs took his seat as clerk. Constable Rigby produced his prisoner, loaded with fetters. "Has this man had his breakfast, Rigby?" asked the Squire. "Certainly not, Squire," replied the constable. "Then take him at once to the kitchen, take off these chains and handcuffs, and let him have all that he can eat," replied the J.P., sternly. [Pg 285]The corporal's sense of rectitude was offended. The idea of feeding criminals and releasing them from irons! The next thing would be to present them with a medal and a clasp for each new offence against society. But, orders were orders, and, however iniquitous, had to be obeyed; so Davis was allowed to stretch his limbs, and partake of a bountiful, if somewhat late, morning meal. "To trespass upon your kindness, Miss Hill, with such as this," said the apologetic constable, pointing to his prisoner, "is no act of mine; Squire Carruthers, who, no doubt, thinks he knows best, has given orders that it has to be, and my duty is to carry out his orders to the letter." Breakfast seemed to infuse courage into the dissipated farmer. When it was over, he arose, and, without a note of warning, doubled up the stiff guardian of the peace, and made for the door, where he fell into the arms of the incoming Serlizer. She evidently thought that Mark Davis, smitten with her charms, was about to salute her, for, with the words "Scuse me!" and a double turn of her powerful wrists, she deposited the assailant upon the floor. Sadly, but officially, the constable crawled over and sat upon the prostrate form of the would-be fugitive from justice. The prisoner squirmed, and even struck the doubled-up corporal, but the entrance of Ben Toner put an end to that nonsense, so that, handcuffed and chained once more, the desperate villain was hauled into the presence of the magistrates. In dignified, but subordinate, language, Mr. Rigby related the prisoner's escapade, and, by implication, more than by actual statement, gave the J.P.s to understand that they knew nothing about the management of offenders against the law. They were, therefore, compelled to allow the handcuffs to remain, but summoned sufficient courage to insist on the removal of the stable chains.

"What is your name, prisoner?" asked Squire Carruthers.

"Samuel Wilson," answered the man.

"Oh! kem now," interposed Mr. Bangs, "thet's a lie, you know; yore name is Merk Devis, end yore a brether of Metthew Devis of the Peskiwenchow tevern, end you were Rawdon's right hend men. We know you, my led, so down't you try any alias games on us."

"Ef you know my name so mighty well, what do you want askin' for't?"

[Pg 286]"To see if you can speak the truth," replied Carruthers.

"What other prisoners hev you got asides me?"

"That is none of your business," said the Squire.

"If I might be ellowed to seggest, Squire," whispered the detective, "I think I'd tell him. Whet do you sey?"

"Go on, Mr. Bangs."

"Well, my fine fellow, the Squire ellows me to sey thet the ethers are Newcome, the stowne ketters, and the women."

The name of Newcome disconcerted Mark, but he asked, "Whar's Rawdon and old Flower?"

"Didn't you see?" asked Mr. Bangs.

"I seen the fire all right, but they wasn't such blame fools as to stay there when there was a way out up atop."

"The epper wey wes clowsed," said the detective.

"Was they burned alive then?"

142

"Yes, they were berned to eshes."

"O Lord!" ejaculated the prisoner, and then, wildly: "What do you want along of me anyway?"

The magistrates and Mr. Bangs consulted, after which the doctor answered: "We want information from you on three points: first, as to the attempt of Rawdon's gang to burn this house; second, as to the murder of Detective Nash; and, third, as to the whole secret of Rawdon's business at the Select Encampment. You are not bound to incriminate yourself, as every word of this preliminary examination may be used against you, but, on the other hand, if you make a clean breast of what you know on these questions, your confession will go a long way in your favour with judge and jury."

"Suppose'n I don't confess not a syllabub?"

"Then, we shall commit you, all the same, to the County Gaol, to stand your trial at the assizes."

"That's all right, I'll stand my durned trile. You don't get nawthin out'n me, you misable, interferin', ornary, bushwhackin' jedges!"

"Don't strike him, Rigby!" commanded Carruthers; for the constable, shocked and outraged by such indecorous language in a court of justice, was about to club his man. Then he added: "The colonel's servant, Maguffin, is going to town on business, and will drive you so far, and help [Pg 287]to guard your prisoner. You can tie him up as tight as you like, without being cruel or doing him an injury. We shall have to do without you at the inquest."

Accordingly, while Mr. Maguffin brought round a suitable vehicle, and received his commissions from the colonel, the commitment papers were made out, and Constable Rigby securely fastened the worst criminal that had ever come into his hands. The said criminal did a little hard swearing, which called the long unused baton into active service. Davis was quiet and sullen when the buggy, under the pensioner's command, wheeled away in search of connections for the County Gaol.

The two bodies were still lying in their shells, with ice about them, in the unfinished annex of the post office. It was, therefore, decided to hold the new inquest in the Bridesdale coach house, as also more convenient for the doctor, whose sprain might have been aggravated by driving. While Ben Toner was sent with a waggon to the Richards, to bring the ghastly remains snatched from the flames out of the punt, and to convey three members of that family to the coroner's jury, Mr. Bangs explained to Doctor Halbert his and the lawyer's thought regarding Matilda Nagle. The doctor consented, and the detective went to find the patient, who was busy and cheerful in the sewing room with Mrs. Carruthers. He told her that she was not looking well, and had better come with him to see the doctor; but, with all the cunning of insanity, she refused to go. He had to go after Coristine in the garden, and take him away from Marjorie. With the lawyer she went at once, identifying him, as she did not the detective, with her brother Stevy. Mechanically, she sat down by the kind doctor's chair, and seemed to recognize him, although he did not remember her. After a few enquiries as to her health, he took one of her hands in his, and, with the other, made passes over her face, until she fell into the mesmeric sleep. "Your husband, Mr. Rawdon, is dead," he said; "you remember that he died by his own hand, and left you free." The woman gave a start, and seemed to listen more intently. "You will kill nobody, hurt nobody, not even a fly," he continued. "Do you remember?" Another start of comprehension was made, but nothing more; so he went on: "You will read [Pg 288]your Bible and go to church on Sundays, and take care of your boy, and be just the same to everybody as you were in the old days." Then, with a few counter passes, he released her hand, and the poor woman told him all that he had enjoined upon her, as if they were the resolutions of her own will. She was not sane, but she was free from the vile slavery in which her inhuman keeper had held her. Moreover, she understood perfectly that Rawdon was dead, yet without manifesting either joy or grief in the knowledge. The lawyer led her back to the workroom, where she confided her new state of mind to Mrs. Carruthers, greatly to that tender-hearted lady's delight. The doctor did not think it necessary to practise his art upon the lad Monty, in whom the power of Rawdon's will was already broken, and upon whom his changed mother would, doubtless, exert a salutary influence.

Coristine had nothing to do, and almost dreaded meeting Miss Carmichael, which he probably would do if he remained about the house and grounds. Therefore he got out the improvised vasculum, and invited Marjorie and the older Carruthers children to come with him down to the brook to look for wild flowers. This met with the full approval of the young people, and they prepared at once for the botanizing party. The Captain saw Marjorie putting on her broad-brimmed straw hat, and enquired where she was going. She answered that she was going buttonizing with Eugene, and he said that he guessed he would button too, whatever that was. A very merry little group frisked about the steps of the two seniors, one of whom was explaining to the older, nautical party that he was on the hunt for wild flowers.

"Is it yarbs you're after?" asked the Captain.

"Well, not exactly, although I want to get a specimen of every kind of plant."

"You don't want to make medicine of 'em, Mandrake, Snakeroot, Wild Sassyperilly, Ginsing, Bearberry, Gentian, Cohosh and all that sort o' stuff, eh?"

"No; I want to find out their names, dry and mount them, and classify them according to their kinds."

"What good are they agoin' to do you?"

"They will help me to know Nature better and to admire God's works and His plan."

[Pg 289]"Keep on there, mate, fair sailin' and a good wind to you. No pay in it, though?"

"Not a cent in money, but lots of pleasure and health."

"Like collectin' post stamps and old pennies, and butterflies, and bugs."

"Something, but you see scenery and get healthy exercise, which you don't in stamp and coin collecting, and you inflict no suffering, as you do in entomologizing."

"I can tell trees when they're a growin' and timber when its cut, but I don't know the name of one flower from another, except it's garden ones and common at that. Hullo, little puss, what have you got there?"

Marjorie, who had run on in advance and was not by any means ignorant of the flora of the neighbourhood, had secured three specimens, a late Valerian, an early spotted Touch-me-not, and a little bunch of Blue-eyed-grass. Coristine took them from her with thanks, told her their names and stowed them away in his candle box. The zeal to discover and add to the collection grew upon all the party, the Captain included. Near the water, where the Valerian and the Touch-me-not grew, Marjorie Carruthers found the Snake-head, with its large white flowers on a spike. Another little Carruthers brought to the botanist the purple Monkey flower, but the Captain excelled his youthful nephew by adding to the collection the rarer and smaller yellow one. Then the lawyer himself discovered another yellow flower, the Gratiola or Hedge Hyssop, at the moment when Marjorie rejoiced in the modest little Speedwell. Once more, the Captain distinguished himself by finding in the grass the yellow Wood-Sorrel, with its Shamrock leaves, which, when Marjorie saw, she seemed to recognize in part. Then, crossing the stepping stones of the brook, she ran, far up the hill on the other side, to a patch of shady bush, from which she soon returned victorious, with a bunch of the larger Wood-Sorrel in her hand, to exhibit the identity of its leaves, and its delicate white blossoms with their pinky-purple veins. By the time the other juveniles brought in the blue Vervain, pink Fireweed and tall yellow Mullein, the botanist thought it about time to go home and press his specimens.

Miss Carmichael met the scientists at the door, looking, [Pg 290]of course, for the children and Uncle Thomas, who was never called by his Christian name, Ezekiel. Learning the nature of the work in hand, she volunteered the use of the breakfast-room table. The lawyer brought down his strap press, and, carefully placing oiled paper between the dried specimens and the semi-porous sheets that were to receive the new ones, proceeded to lay them out. The new specimens had all to be examined by the addition to the botanical party, their botanical and vulgar names to be recited to her, and, then, the arranging began. This was too monotonous work for the Captain, who carried the children off for a romp on the verandah. Marjorie stayed for a minute or so after they were gone, and then remembered that she had not given papa his morning button-hole. Coristine was clumsy with the flowers, owing to the gloves he said, so Miss Carmichael had to spread them out on the paper under

144

his direction, and hold them in their place, while he carefully and gradually pressed another sheet over them. Of course his fingers could not help coming into contact with hers. "Confound those gloves!" he thought aloud.

"Mr. Coristine, if you are going to use such language, and to speak so ungratefully of Mr. Errol's gloves, which I put on your hands, I shall have to leave you to put up your specimens the best way you can."

"O Miss Carmichael, now, please let me off this once, and I'll never do it again. You know it's so hard working in gloves. Understand me as saying that botanically, in a Pickwickian sense as it were, and not really at all."

"You must not say that, either botanically or any other way."

"To hear the faintest whisper of your slightest command is to obey."

It was delicate work arranging these little Speedwells, and Gratiolas, the Wood-Sorrels, and the smaller Monkey-flower. Hands had to follow very close on one another, and heads to be bent to examine, and sometimes there was just a little brush of brown and golden hair that, strange to say, sent responsive tingles along the nerves, and warm flushes to cheek and brow. What a hopeless idiot he was not to have foreseen the possibility of this, and to have brought home twice the number of specimens! Alas! [Pg 291]they were all in the press. But, a happy thought struck him: would Miss Carmichael care to look at the dried ones, some of which had kept their colour very well? Yes, she had a few minutes to spare. So, he brought chairs up to the table, and they sat down, side by side, and he told her all about the flowers and how he got them, and the poetry Wilks and he quoted over them. Then the specimens had to be critically examined, so as to let Miss Carmichael learn the distinctive characteristics of the various orders, and this brought the heads close together again, when suddenly their owners were started by the unexpected clang of the dinner gong. "Thank you so much, Mr. Coristine," said the lady, frankly; "you have given me a very pleasant half hour." The lawyer bowed his acknowledgment, but said, beneath his moustache: "Half an hour is it? I thought it was a lifetime rolled up in two minutes, no, one."

What did those deceitful men, Errol and Perrowne, mean, by saying they had to go away to get up their Wednesday evening talk, and to visit their parishioners? There they were, in their old places at the table, Mr. Errol at Mrs. Carmichael's right, and apparently on the best of terms with her, and Mr. Perrowne dancing attendance upon Miss Halbert and her invalid father. Mrs. Du Plessis thought she would take up Mr. Wilkinson's dinner with the colonel's help, as Cecile had been reading to him so long. Accordingly, the Captain talked to that young lady, while Mr. Bangs monopolized Mrs. Carruthers. There was a little commotion, when Mr. Bigglethorpe walked in, and received the sympathetic expressions of the company over his singed face and scorched hands. In spite of these, the sufferer had been up early fishing, just after the rain. Fortunately, he continued, there was no cleared land about the lakes, hence there were very few grasshoppers washed in by the heavy downpour. Had there been, he wouldn't have got a fish. But he had got fish, a big string of them, in splendid condition. He had left some with his kind entertainers, the Richards, but had plenty remaining, which he had left in the kitchen in care of the young woman with the unpronounceable Scripture name. "Now," said the fisherman, "a nime is a very important thing to a man or a woman. [Pg 292]Why do people give their children such awful names? Bigglethorpe is Dinish, they say, but Felix Isidore is as Latin as can be. They called me 'fib' at school."

"'Tis the hoighth av impartance to have a good name, say Oi," added Mr. Terry. "Moy fayther, glory be to his sowl, put a shaint's name an me, an' I put her own mother's name, the Howly Vargin rist her, on Honoria here. 'An', savin' all yer prisinces, there's no foiner Scripcher name than John; how's that, Squoire?"

"It suits me well enough, grandfather," replied Carruthers. The Captain was feeling uneasy. He didn't want Ezekiel to come out, so he asked Miss Du Plessis how her young man was. Such a question would have either roused Miss Carmichael to indignation or have overwhelmed her with confusion, but Miss Du Plessis, calm and unruffled, replied: "I suppose you mean Mr. Wilkinson, Captain Thomas. He has been very much shaken by his wound, but is doing remarkably well."

"Fwhat's Mishter Wilkison's name, Miss Ceshile, iv it's a fair quishtyon to ax at yeez?"

145

"It is Farquhar, is it not, Mr. Coristine?"

Mr. Coristine said it was, and that it was his mother's maiden name. She was a Scotchwoman, he had heard, and a very lovely character. The colonel had just returned from his ministrations. "Did I heah you cohhectly, Mr. Cohistine, when I thought you said that ouah deah young wounded friend's mothah's name was Fahquhah, suh?"

"You did, Colonel Morton."

"And of Scottish pahentage?"

"Yes."

"Do you know if any of her relatives were engaged in the Civil Wahah, our civil wahah?"

"I believe her brother Roderic ran the blockade, and fought for the South, where he fell, in a cavalry regiment."

"Be pleased, suh, to say that again. Rodehic Fahquhah, do you say?"

"His full name, I have seen it among Wilkinson's papers, was Roderic Macdonald Farquhar."

"Tehesa, my deah," said the colonel, his voice and manner full of emotion, as he turned towards his sister-in-law, "you have heard me mention my bosom friend, Captain Fahquhah?"

[Pg 293]"Yes, indeed, many times," replied the lady addressed.

"And ouah deah boy upstairs, the pehsehveh of my pooah life, is his nephew, his sistah's son. I was suah there was something drawing me to him. I shall make that brave boy my heih, my pooah deah comhade Fahquhah's nephew. What a fohtunate discovehy. Kindly excuse me, madam, and you my deah ladies, and you Squiah; I must go and tell my deah boy." So the colonel bowed to Mrs. Carruthers, and went out, with his handkerchief up to his face.

After the colonel left the table, the Captain looked over at his niece, saying: "Too late, Marjorie, my lass, too late! Didn't play your cards right, so you're cut out. Shifted his sheet anchor to the t'other bow, Marjorie."

Miss Carmichael was annoyed with good reason, and, in order to put a stop to such uncalled for and vulgar remarks, said, playfully, but with a spice of malice: "Take care, Uncle Thomas, or, as that funny theological student said to the people who were talking in church, 'I'll call out your name before the haill congregation.'" This terrible threat caused Ezekiel to subside, and carry on a less personal conversation with Miss Du Plessis. Then Mr. Terry came to the fore again.

"My little grandchilders' coushin, Mishter Coristine, do be sayin' yer name is Eujane, an' that's Frinch, isn't it?"

"Yes," replied the lawyer; "my mother was of Huguenot descent, and her name was Du Moulin. Some say that the Irish Mullens were once Du Moulins. That I don't know, but I'm not like the man-servant who applied for a situation, saying: 'Me name is Murphy, sorr, but me family came from France.' Coristine, I think, is good Irish."

The name craze spread over the whole table. Miss Halbert thought Basil a lovely name. It was Greek, wasn't it, and meant a king? Mr. Perrowne thought that the sweetest name in the world was Frances or Fanny. Mr. Errol affected Marjorie, and Mrs. Carmichael knew nothing superior to Hugh.

"What made you so savage with the Captain for coupling your name with Wilks?" asked the lawyer in an undertone.

[Pg 294]"Because he is the last man in the world I should want my name to be coupled with."

"Oh, but that's hard on Wilks; he's a glorious fellow when you get to know his little ways."

"I don't want to know Mr. Wilkinson's little ways. I am sorry for his wound, but otherwise I have not the remotest sympathy with him. He strikes me as a selfish, conceited man."

"Not a kinder soul breathing, Miss Carmichael."

"Yes, there is."

"Who, then?"

146

"Yourself."

"Miss Carmichael, you make me the proudest man in the world, but I'm not fit to black Wilks' boots."

"Well, I will not be so rude as to say I think you are. But, never talk that way to me again, if you want me to like you. I will not have you demeaning yourself, even in speech, before Cecile's friend. Now, remember, not a word!"

The test was a severe one between loyalty to his old friend and devoted obedience to the girl he loved. As all the memories of past friendship came before him, he was inclined to be obdurate. Then, he looked at the golden hair which had brushed his awhile ago, and, as the head straightened up, at the pretty petulant lips and the blue eyes, lustrous with just a moist suspicion of vexation and feeling, and he wavered. He was lost, and was glad to be lost, as he whispered: "May I say it?"

"Yes; speak out, like a man, what you have to say."

"It's a bargain, Marjorie; never again!"

Somehow his right hand met her left, and she did not snatch it away too quickly. Then he said: "You won't hate poor Wilks, my old friend, Marjorie?"

She answered "No," and turned her face away to ask some trivial question of the Squire, who knew a good deal more than he saw any necessity for telling.

The kitchen party still kept up its numbers. True, the absence of the constable and Maguffin left two serious blanks in the diversified talk of the table, but the place of these gentlemen was taken by no fewer than six persons, the three Richards and the three jurors, so that the dinner party numbered fifteen, of whom four were women. Old [Pg 295]whitehaired Mr. Newberry, with the large rosy face, smooth, save for two little white patches of side-whiskers, took possession of Matilda Nagle, and rejoiced in her kindly ways and simple talk. He was a Methodist, and a class-leader and local preacher, but a man against whom no tongue of scandal wagged, and whose genuine piety and kindness of heart were so manifest that nobody dreamt of holding up to ridicule his oft homely utterances in the pulpit. If he could do good to the poor demented woman and her afflicted boy, he would, and he knew that his little quaker-bonneted wife would second him in such an effort. So he tried to gain her confidence and the boy's, and, after a while, found that Matilda would like to help Mrs. Newberry in her household duties, and have Monty learn useful work on the farm. When informed by the fatherly juror, in answer to her own questions, that she would not be expected to hurt a fly, and would be allowed to go to church, read her Bible and take care of her boy, she expressed her readiness to go away with him at once. Mr. Newberry felt a few qualms of conscience in connection with fly killing, but, having made an express stipulation that mosquitos and black flies should not be included in the bond, he became easier in mind, and said that, with Mrs. Carruthers and the Squire's permission, he would drive her home in the afternoon. Mr. Johnson and the elder Richards discussed local politics, and the tragedy calling for the inquest; but Mr. Pawkins attached himself to the boys, and consequently to the girls. This gentleman had brought his six feet of bone and muscle, topped with a humorous face, from which depended a Lincoln beard, from the States, and was now, for many years, as he said, "a nettrelized citizen of Kennidy." This disappointment at the absence of the constable was something pitiful, he did so want "to yank and rile the old Britisher." Still, that was not going to deprive him of his innocent amusement. He looked around the company and sized it up, deciding that he would leave the old folks alone, and mercifully add to them the crazy people; this still left him a constituency of nine, with large possibilities for fun.

"Rufus," remarked Mr. Pawkins, "I seen your gal, Christy Hislop, along o' that spry sot up coon, Barney [Pg 296]Sullivan, daown at the mill. He's a cuttin' you aout for sutten, yes sirree, you see if he ain't."

"What's the use of your nonsense, Mr Pawkins? Barney went home along o' fayther and old man Hislop, and I guess he turned in to say we was all right."

"If Andrew knowed you'd called him old man Hislop, he'd fire you aout o' the back door mighty suddent. When I see a spry, set up, young feller and a likely heifer of a gal a saunterin' through the bush, sort o' poetical like, daown to the mill, it don't take me two shakes to know that suthin's up. You're a poor, rejected, cast off, cut aout strip o' factory cotton."

"What do you mean, Mr. Pawkins?"

"I mean overalls, and it's all over with you, Rufus." Having planted this well-meant thorn in the breast of the younger Hill, and excited the commiseration of his sisters, the lover of innocent amusement turned to Ben, and asked that gentleman, whose attentions to Serlizer were most open and above board, "sence when he got another gal?"

Mr. Toner turned angrily, and asked what Mr. Pawkins was "a givin' him."

"I never see Bridget naow but she's a cryin' and rubbin' her eyes most aout with her cuffs," said the cheerful Pawkins; "she allaowed to me you'd the nighest thing to said the priest was ony waitin' for the word to splice; and here you air, you biggermus delooder, settin' along o' Newcome's gal as if you'd got a mortgage on her. Arter that, the sight ain't to be sawed that'll make me ashamed o' my feller-creeters, no sirree, boss, hull team to boot, and a big dog under the waggin!" Mr. Pawkins sniffed vehemently, and Ben and his affianced bride blushed and drew apart.

"Is that so, Ben?" asked Sarah Eliza in a half whisper.

"S'haylp me, Serlizer," replied the injured Toner in a similar voice, "that there Pawkins is the cussidest, lyinest old puke of a trouble-makin' Yankee as aiver come to Cannidy."

"Are you engaged to Biddy Sullivan, Ben?"

"No, I tell you, naiver said a word to Barney's sister I wouldn't say to any gal."

[Pg 297]"Then, what did Barney come here lookin' for you for?"

"So did the tavern keeper and the store keeper, 'cause mother axed 'em, I suppose; you don't think they want me to marry their wives, do you?"

"Wives an' darters is different things, Ben. Ef I'd thought you had been havin' goins on with Biddy, I'd flog the pair of you."

"S'haylp me, Serlizer, it ain't so. Ef it was, you could whayull me till I was stripy as a chipmunk."

"Talkin' abaout whalins," remarked the mischief-maker, who kept one ear open, "Miss Newcome's paa is jest a waitin' to git up and git araound, to give somebody, as ain't fer off'n this table, the blamedest, kerfoundedest lammin' as ever he knowed. He wants his gal home right straight for to nuss him, so's he kin git araound smart with that rawhide that's singein' its ends off in the oven."

"What's dad got agin you, Ben?" enquired Miss Newcome.

"Oh nawthin'; it's only that Pawkins' double-treed, snaffle-bitted, collar-bladed jaw." Mr. Pawkins smiled, but Ben and Serlizer were more uncomfortable than Rufus and his sisters.

The naturalized Canadian turned his attention else where. "I'm kinder amazed," he remarked, eyeing first Sylvanus and then Timotheus, "to see you two a settin' here, as cam as if you never done nothin' to be sorry for. I s'pose you know, if you don't you had orter, that there's a war'nt aout agin the two Pilgrims for stealin' aout o' the Peskiwanchow tavern, or ho-tel, as Davis calls his haouse. I calclate the constable 'll be back with that war'nt afore night. I'd make myself skeerce if I was in your shoes."

"O Sylvanus!" ejaculated Tryphosa.

"O Timotheus!" added Tryphosa.

"It's a lie!" cried Rufus; "it's a mill dam, boom jam, coffer-dam lie, and I won't believe a word of it."

"Fact all the same," said Mr. Pawkins, calmly, "they air guilty, the two on 'em, of stealin' aout o' the Peskiwanchow ho-tel."

"What did they steal out?" asked the Richards boys.

"Clothes, I guess, boots, some money, books, I don't know all what, and it don't consarn me any; but them [Pg 298]boys had best look spry and git aout o' this." With these words, the gentleman of American extraction finished his last piece of pie.

Sylvanus rose cheerfully. He was so radiant over it that Tryphena thought him really handsome. He whispered to Rufus and to Ben; then remarked to Timotheus that he had perhaps better remain, in case the Squire should send for him. Next, he turned to Mr. Pawkins, and said: "A man mought as well be hung fer a sheep as fer a lamb, Mr. Pawkins, and sence they's a warn't out to 'raist me and Timotheus, we ain't a goin' to put the law to no more trouble 'bout a new one. Ef you'll come outside, I'll show you some o' them things we stoled out'n the Peskiwanchow tav." So Sylvanus took the accuser of the brethren by one arm, and Rufus linked his lovingly in the other, while Ben, with a glance of intelligence at Serlizer, and another at his top boots, followed. Mr. Pawkins, confident in his smartness and in the ignorance of the simple-minded Canucks, went quietly with the courteous criminal and his cut-out friend, till, passing the stables, they led him through a broad gate into the meadow. Then he hesitated.

"The stoled things, leastways some on 'em, 'll be at the foot o' this yere slope soon's we will; so hurry, old man!" said Sylvanus. Mr. Pawkins demurred. "Look here, boys," he said, "a joke's a joke, ain't it? D'ye see, you did, the pair on you, steal aout of the hotel. I didn't go to say you took anythin' as didn't belong to you. I reckon your brother had clothes, and money, and books thar, and so, you and him took 'em aout. Lem me go, boys!"

Sylvanus and Rufus were obdurate. "Boost him, Ben," cried the former: "we ain't no time ter spend foolin' with the likes o' him."

Mr. Toner raised his boot and said, "One fer Serlizer!" which made the joker proceed. He had several other ones, before he was run down to the creek—for Timotheus and Tryphena, and Tryphosa, and Christie Hislop, and Barney and Biddy Sullivan, and old man Newcome. Ben's boot did capital service. With difficulty the executioners found a hole in the creek about two and a-half feet deep, in which, at full length and with great gravity, they deposited the exile from the States. Then, [Pg 299]they guessed the Squire, or the Captain, or somebody, would be wanting them, and skipped lightly back to the house. They knew Mr. Pawkins would follow, since he was the last man in the settlement to miss his juror's fee of one dollar. After their return, there was a good deal of merriment in the kitchen, and the two Richards boys roundly upbraided the elder Pilgrim for depriving them of a share in the fun. "He baygged an' prayed for massy," said Mr. Toner, with a grim smile, "but we was the most onmassifullest craowd you ever see."

Timotheus, still in Sunday garb, took his work-a-day suit, now quite dry, and went to meet Mr. Pawkins. Introducing him to the stable, he soon had that gentleman relieved of his wet toggery, when voices were heard without. It was the colonel, bringing his sister-in-law to see his horse, as a sort of relief to the strain on his feelings, consequent upon his interview with Wilkinson. Mr. Pawkins had only got Timotheus' flannel shirt on, when the stable door opened. "Shin up that ladder into the loft, Mr. Pawkins," cried the benevolent Pilgrim, and the spectacle of a pair of disappearing shanks greeted the visitors on their entrance. Timotheus had escaped into the coach-house, but all the clothes, wet and dry, save the shirt, lay over the sides of an empty stall. Immediately the colonel perceived the vanishing heels of the Yankee, he interposed his person between them and Mrs. Du Plessis. "My deah Tehesa," he said, hastily, "I think we had bettah retiah foh the pehsent, and visit the stables lateh in the day." Mrs. Du Plessis, however, once no mean judge of horseflesh, was scanning the good points of her brother-in-law's purchase, and seemed indisposed to withdraw. Soon a head and a pair of flannel shirted arms appeared, hanging over the loft trap, and a voice hailed the colonel.

"Say, mister, you ain't a goin' to bring no wimmen folks up this here ladder, be you?"

"Cehtainly not, suh!" answered the colonel, with emphasis.

"If it won't hurt you, I wisht you'd sling up them dry paants and things daown there."

The colonel looked at the man, and then at the articles, with impatience. Then he got a pitchfork, on [Pg 300]the prongs of which he collected the garments, one by one, and so handed them up to Mr. Pawkins, who was still minus necktie, socks and boots. Before, however, he was ready for these, the visitors had retired, leaving him to complete his toilet in private. Hearing steps again, he hurriedly picked up his wet clothes and re-ascended the ladder. The colonel had evidently asked Sylvanus to take the place of Maguffin about the two horses, for he was the newcomer. Now, Mr. Pawkins bore no malice, but, when jokes were going, he did not like to be left the chief victim. He had had some fun out of the boys; now he would have some more. The Yankee could mew to perfection. He began, and Sylvanus called the strange cat. It would not come, so he climbed the ladder after it, and had almost reached the top, when, with vicious cries, the animal flew at him, seized him by the back of the neck, and drew blood that he could feel trickling down his back. Tugging ineffectually at the beast, he ran out to the kitchen, calling upon everybody to take off that mad cat that was killing him. The cat was taken off, amid shrieks of laughter, and proved to be Mr. Pawkins' rolled up wet trousers and vest, the water from which was the blood imagined by Sylvanus. The owner of the garments entered immediately behind his victim, and from his banter the elder Pilgrim gladly escaped to resume his stable duties, feeling that he had been demeaned in the eyes of the laughing Tryphena.

Timotheus and Ben were busy cleaning out the coach house, putting tables and seats into it, and generally preparing for the inquest. Mr. Bangs, at the coroner's request, empanelled the jury, consisting of the Squire, the captain, and the two clergymen, the three Richards, the three cited jurors, with old Styles from the post office, and Ben Toner. The charred masses of humanity, pervaded by a sickening smell of spirits, were taken from the waggon, and placed in rough board shells, decently covered over with white cloths. The woman called Flower was brought from the post office, and kept in custody, till she gave her evidence; and Bangs himself, with Messrs. Terry, Coristine, and Bigglethorpe, Sylvanus, Rufus, and Timotheus were cited as witnesses. Some evidence was also expected from Matilda and her son. When the coach house doors [Pg 301]were thrown open, all hilarity ceased—even the children seemed to realize that something very solemn was going on. A weight of trouble and danger was lifted off many hearts by the terrible tragedy, yet in no soul was there the least feeling of exultation. The fate of the victims was too awful, too sudden for anyone to feel aught but horror at the thought of it, and deep sorrow for one at least who had perished in his sins. The light-hearted lawyer took one look at the remains of him, whom, within the past few days, he had seen so often in the full enjoyment of life and health, and resolved that never again, in prose or verse, would he speak of the person, whose crimes and cunning had returned so avengingly upon his own head, as the Grinstun man. Mr. Pawkins joked no more, for, with all his playful untruthfulness, he had a feeling heart. The most unconcerned man outwardly was Mr. Bangs, and even he said that he would willingly have given a hundred dollars to see his prisoner safely in gaol with the chaplain, and afterwards decently hanged. The doctor was carefully carried out, and set in the presiding chair as coroner over the third inquest within two days.

CHAPTER XVI.

Inquest and Consequences—Orther Lom—Coolness—Evening Service—Mr. Pawkins and the Constable—Two Songs—Marjorie, Mr. Biggles and the Crawfish—Coristine Falls Foul of Mr. Lamb—Mr. Lamb Falls Foul of the Whole Company—The Captain's Couplet—Miss Carmichael Feels it Her Duty to Comfort Mr. Lamb.

It is unnecessary to relate the details of the inquest. By various marks, as well as by the testimony of the woman Flower and of Mr. Bangs and his party, the remains were identified as those of Rawdon and his wounded henchman Flower. Some of the jurymen wished to bring in a verdict of "Died from the visitation of God," but this the Squire, who was foreman, would not allow. He called it flat blasphemy; so it was altered to: "Died by the explosion of illicit spirits, through a fire kindled by the wife of the principal victim, Altamont Rawdon." Nobody demanded the arrest of Matilda; hence the Squire [Pg 302]and the doctor did not feel called upon to issue a warrant for that purpose. The widowed and childless Mrs. Flower, for the so-called Harding was her son, claimed his body, and what remained of her husband's; and asked Mr. Perrowne to read the burial service over them in the little graveyard behind his humble church. Mr. Bangs, his work over, got the use of a waggon and the services of Ben Toner, to take his dead comrade's coffin to Collingwood. Nobody claimed the remains of Rawdon, till old Mr. Newberry came forward, and said he would take the shell in his waggon, with the woman and the boy, and give it Christian burial in the plot back of the Wesleyan church. "We can't tell," he said, "what passed between him and his Maker when he was struggling for life. Gie un the bainifit o' the doot." So, Ben and Serlizer rolled away with Bangs, and Nash's coffin; and Matilda and her son accompanied Rawdon's remains, in Mr. Newberry's waggon. At the same time, with the sad, grey-haired woman as chief mourner, and Mrs. Carmichael beside her, a funeral procession passed from Bridesdale to the post office, and thence to the English churchyard, where old Styles and Sylvanus dug

150

the double grave, around which, in deep solemnity, stood the Captain and Mr. Terry, the minister and the lawyer, while Mr. Perrowne read the service, and two victims of Rawdon's crime and treachery were committed, earth to earth, dust to dust, and ashes to ashes. Immediately the grave was covered in, the doubly-bereaved woman slipped away, and was never again heard of. There appeared no evidence, far or near, that she had done away with herself; it was, therefore, concluded that she had a child or children elsewhere, and had gone to hide the rest of her wasted life with them. The two clergymen went their ways to their lodgings, and the Bridesdale party walked silently and sorrowfully home.

Mr. Bigglethorpe wanted to go back with the Richards, so that he might have another morning's fishing; but Mrs. Carruthers thought he had better take Mr. Bangs' room, and nurse his eyes and other burned parts before going home. Marjorie and her young cousins dragged him off, after his green shade was put on, to the creek, and made him rig up rods and lines for them in the shape of light-trimmed willow boughs, to which pieces of thread [Pg 303]were attached with bent pins at the other ends. Fishing with these, baited with breadcrumbs, they secured quite a number of chub and dace, and made the valley musical with their laughter at each success or mishap, by the time the Bridesdale people returned from the impromptu funeral. The Squire was busy in his office, looking over Nash's legacy, preparatory to sending it to Bangs, who had begged him to forward the documents without delay. The only thing of note he found was, that Rawdon did not bank his money; he had no bank account anywhere. Where did he stow away the fortune he must have made? There was a note of the casual conversation of an assumed miser with Rawdon, in which Rawdon was represented as saying: "Dry sandy soil, well drained with two slopes, under a rain-shed, will keep millions in a cigar box." That the Squire noted; then he sealed up the rest of the papers, and addressed them to Hickey Bangs, Esq., D.I.R., ready for the post in the morning. The colonel, Mrs. and Miss Du Plessis were all in Wilkinson's room. The colonel was commenting upon the four poor souls that had gone before God's judgment seat, three of them, probably, with murder on their hands; and thanked God that his boy had died in the war, brave and pure and good, with no stain on his young life. "When my boy was killed, my deah Fahquhah, I felt like the Electoh Palatine of the Rhine, when young Duke Christopheh, his son, fell at Mookerheyde, accohding to Motley: he said "Twas bettah thus than to have passed his time in idleness, which is the devil's pillow.' Suh, I honouh the Electoh Palatine foh that. What melancholy ghaves these pooah creatuhes fill." Then Mrs. Du Plessis wept, mildly, and Miss Du Plessis, and they all had to wipe a few tears out of Wilkinson's eyes. Had Coristine been there, he would have been scandalized. The lawyer's lady-love was engaged in very prosaic work in the sewing-room, with her aunt, running a sewing-machine to make much-needed clothes for the unhappy woman, whom the coroner's jury, by a euphemism, called Rawdon's wife. The two had seen her off in charge of good old Mr. Newberry, and had promised to send her the work, which she herself had begun; and, now, they were toiling with all their might to redeem the promise, as early as possible, in [Pg 304]spite of the tears that would come also into their foolish eyes, blurring their vision and damping their material. Coristine, who longed for a sight of fresh young life after the vision of death, did not know what kept that young life within, and, like an unreasonable man, was inclined to be angry. He was overwrought, poor fellow, sleepless and tired, and emotionally excited, and, therefore, ready for any folly under the sun.

Mrs. Carmichael had entered the house, with the Captain and Mr. Terry. The lawyer remained alone in the garden, waiting for something to turn up. Something did turn up in the shape of the stage on its way to the post office, which dropped its only passenger at the Bridesdale gate. The passenger was a young fellow of about twenty-five, rather over than under middle height, of good figure, and becomingly dressed. His features were good enough, but lacked individuality, as did his combined moustache and side whiskers, that formed a sort of imperfect W across his face. He held his nose well up in the air, spoke what, in his ignorance, he fondly imagined to be aristocratic English, and carried, with an apologetic and depressed air, a small Gladstone bag. The newcomer dusted his trouser legs with a cane utterly useless for walking purposes; then, adjusting his eye-glass, he elevated it towards the solitary occupant of the garden, as he entered the gate. "Haw, you sir," he called out to him; "is this, haw, Mr. Corrothers' plaice?" Coristine was nettled at the style of address, but commanded himself to reply as briefly as possible that it was. "Miss Morjorie Cormichael stoying here?" continued the stage passenger. "Miss Carmichael is here," responded the lawyer. "Haw, I thort so. Just you run in now, will you, ond tell Miss Morjorie thot on old friend wonts to speak to her." The lawyer was getting furious, in spite of himself. Taking his pipe out of his pocket, and proceeding to fill it with all apparent deliberation and calmness, he replied: "So far as I have the honour of Miss Carmichael's acquaintance, she is not in the habit of receiving visitors out of doors. There are both bell and knocker on the door before you, which servants will probably answer; but, if that door doesn't suit you, you will probably find others at the back." With this ungracious speech, he turned on his heel, lit his pipe, [Pg 305]and puffed vigorously along the path towards the meadow gate. Then, he strolled down the hill and met the returning fishers, the two youngest in Mr. Bigglethorpe's arms, and with their arms about his neck. Coristine indulged in a kissing bee with the rest of them, so as to assure himself that he was the true old friend, the genuine Codlin, while the other man was Short. "Marjorie," he said, as that fishing young lady clung to him, "there's a duffer of a dude, with an eye-glass, up at the house, who says he's an old friend of your cousin Marjorie; do you know any old friend of hers?" Marjorie stopped to think, and, after a little pause, said: "It can't be Huggins." "Who is Huggins, Marjorie?" asked the lawyer. "He's the caretaker of Marjorie's school."

"Oh no, this dude is too young and gorgeous for a caretaker."

"Then, I think I know; its Orther Lom."

"Who is Orther Lom?"

"I don't know; only Auntie Marjorie said, she wouldn't be astonished if Orther Lom was to come and find cousin Marjorie out, even away up here. It must be Orther Lom."

This was all the information the lawyer could obtain; so he and Marjorie joined Mr. Bigglethorpe and the other anglers, and talked about making domestic sardines and smelts of the chub and dace they had caught.

The summons to tea greeted the wanderers before they had had time to cleanse their hands of fishy odours; consequently Mr. Bigglethorpe and the lawyer were a minute or two late. They found the man of the eye-glass seated on one side of Miss Carmichael, and, as she beckoned the fisherman to the other, she introduced her protegé to him as Mr. Arthur Lamb, a very old friend. Miss Halbert made way for Coristine beside her, and he congratulated her on the doctor's reappearance at the table.

"Mr. Coristine," said Miss Carmichael, and the lawyer, with a somewhat worn society face, looked across.

"Mr. Lamb, who is an old friend of ours, tells me he met you in the garden, but you did not introduce yourself. Let me introduce you, Mr. Lamb, Mr. Coristine."

Coristine gave the merest nod of recognition, and went on talking to Miss Halbert. He thought Perrowne was [Pg 306]right; there was some satisfaction conversing with a girl like that, a girl with no nonsense about her. The minister's gloves had got fishy, handling Marjorie's catch, so he had taken them off when preparing himself for tea, and had left them in his room. Miss Carmichael looked at the burnt hands, and felt disposed to scold him, but did not dare. Perhaps, he had taken the gloves off intentionally. She wished that ring of his were not on her finger. Between Mr. Lamb and Miss Halbert, she felt very uncomfortable, and knew that Eugene, no, Mr. Coristine, was behaving abominably. The colonel and his belongings had been so much about the wounded dominie all afternoon, that Mrs. Carruthers insisted on her right, as a hostess, to minister to him, while her sister-in law presided in her stead. Coristine at once rose to help the hostess, and regained his spirits, while rallying his old friend over the many attentions he was receiving at the hands of the fair sex. He could hardly believe his eyes and ears when he beheld the meek and helpless creature who had once been the redoubtable Wilkinson. How had the mighty fallen! "We'll put you in a glass case, Wilks, like the old gray horse that was jined to the Methodis, and kicked so high they put him in the museum."

"Corry," interrupted the still correct dominie, "I have no sympathy with that rude song; but if you will quote it, please adhere to the original. It was 'my old aunt Sal that was joined to the Methodists,' not the old gray horse."

"Thanks, Wilks, thanks, I'll try and remember. Any more toast or jam, old boy?"

152

"No, I have a superabundance of good things."

"Well, see you again, sometime when I have a chance. You're pretty well guarded you know. Au revoir."

Coristine followed Mrs. Carruthers down stairs; while the dominie sighed, and said: "It seems as if nothing will give that boy stability of character and staidness of demeanour."

"Who is going to service to-night?" asked the Squire. Mrs. Carruthers could not, because of the children; the doctor was unfit to walk; and the colonel and Mrs. Du Plessis had so much to say to each other over their dear boy that they desired to be excused. Mr. Bigglethorpe [Pg 307]said he was a church-going man, but hardly cared to air his green shade in public; whereupon Mr. Terry volunteered to remain and smoke a pipe with him. Mrs. Carmichael and her daughter signified their intention of accompanying the Squire, and Mr. Lamb at once asked permission to join them. Miss Halbert stated that she would like to go to week service, if anybody else was going. Of course, the lawyer offered his escort, and Miss Du Plessis and the Captain begged to be included. Thus, four of the party set out for Mr. Perrowne's mid-week service, and four to Mr. Errol's prayer meeting. Mr. Lamb did not get much out of Miss Carmichael on the way, and Miss Halbert thought her escort unusually absent-minded. Coming home, Mr. Perrowne deprived Coristine of his fair charge, and Mr. Errol relieved the Squire of his sister. Accordingly, the freed cavaliers drew together and conversed upon the events of the day. Good Mr. Carruthers was startled, when the lawyer expressed his intention of leaving in the morning, as he could be of no further use, and felt he had already trespassed too long upon his generous hospitality.

"Noo, Coristine," he said, falling into his doric, "what ails ye, man, at the lassie?"

"My dear Squire, I have none but the kindest and most grateful thoughts towards all the ladies."

"Weel, weel, it's no for me to be spierin', but ye maun na gang awa frae's on accoont o' yon daft haveral o' a Lamb."

"Who is this Mr. Lamb?"

"I ken naething aboot him, foreby that he's a moothin' cratur frae the Croon Lans Depairtment, wi' no owre muckle brains."

Dropping the subject, the Squire proceeded to tell what he had found in Nash's papers, and proposed an expedition, ostensibly for fishing, in which the two of them, providing themselves with tools, should prospect for the hidden treasure of the former master of the Select Encampment. As it was unlikely that any claimant for Rawdon's property would appear, all that they found would belong to Matilda and her boy, unless it were judged right to indemnify Miss Du Plessis for any injury done to her land. There was no reason for the lawyer's [Pg 308]departure. He had another week of leave, which he did not know how to put in. True, he could not remain until Wilkinson was perfectly well, but it would seem heartless to desert him so soon after he had received his wound. He had thought of writing the Squire about Miss Carmichael's position as her deceased father's next of kin, but it would save trouble to talk it over. All things considered, Mr. Carruthers did not find it a difficult task to make his pleasant new acquaintance reconsider his decision and commit himself to an indefinite prolongation of Bridesdale hospitality. Yet, as he entered the gate, he almost repented his weakness, on hearing the eye-glassed Lamb say: "What ohfully jawlly times we hod, Morjorie, when you and I were sweethorts." He wished that he could recall some frightfully injurious and profane expression in a foreign tongue, with which to anathematize the wretched, familiar, conceited Crown Lands Department cad. While the Squire joined the doctor and the Captain in the office, he went over to a corner in which the pipes of the veteran and Mr. Bigglethorpe were still glowing, and, lighting his own, listened to their military and piscatorial yarns.

Rufus had remained at Bridesdale, at the urgent entreaty of his sisters and the Pilgrims; but the sight of the people going to prayer meeting smote his conscience. He knew his father and mother would be at meetin' in their own church, and that there would be a good deal of work to do. Besides he hadn't brought home the team from Mr. Hislop's since the bee. Nothing would stop him, therefore; he shouldered his gun, and, bidding all good bye, started for home. Nobody was left in the kitchen but the two maids and the two Pilgrims. Yes, there was one more, namely Mr. Pawkins, who was afeard his duds warn't dry.

The nettrelized citizen of Kennidy was telling stories, that kept the company in peals and roars of laughter, about an applicant for a place in a paper mill, who was set to chewing a blue blanket into pulp, who was given a bottle of vinegar to sharpen his teeth with, and who was ignominiously expelled from the premises because he didn't "chaw it dry"; about a bunting billy goat; and a powerful team of oxen, that got beyond the control of their barn-moving driver, and planted the [Pg 309]barn on the top of an almost inaccessible hill. Mr. Pawkins complimented the young women, and drew wonderful depths of knowledge out of Sylvanus and Timotheus. But, when a vehicle rolled into the stable yard that brought the constable and Maguffin to join the party, the quondam American citizen waxed jubilant, and beheld endless possibilities of amusement. "Good evenin', consterble," said Mr. Pawkins, blandly.

"Good evening, sir, at your service," replied the pensioner.

"Pawkins is my naum, consterble, kyind er Scotch, I reckin. They say pawky means sorter cute an' cunnin', like in Scotch. Never was thar myself, to speak on, but hev seed 'em."

"The Scotch make good soldiers," said Mr Rigby.

"Yaas; I reckin the oatmeal sorter stiffens 'em up."

"There are military authorities who assert that the Scotch are the only troops that can reform under fire; but that is a mistake. In that respect, sir, the Guards are equal to any other Household Troops."

"Fer haousehold trooeps and reformin' under fire, you had orter ha seen aour fellers at Bull Run. When the shooten' begun, all the Bowery plug uglies, bred to cussin' and drinkin' and wuss, dropped ther guns and fell on ther knees a reformin'; then, when they faound they couldn't reform so suddent, they up on ther two feet and started fer the haousehold. Eurrup ain't got nuthin' ter ekal aour household trooeps."

"You mistake me, Mr. Pawkins; the Household Troops in infantry are the Guards and Highlanders, whose special duty it is to guard the royal household."

"Is it big?"

"Is what big, sir?"

"Why, the household! How many storeys is ther to it besides the attic and basement? Hev it got a mansard?"

"The Household, sir, dwells in royal palaces of great dimensions. It is the royal family and their attendants over whom the Guards watch."

"That's the Black Guards, ain't it?"

"No, sir; you are thinking of the Black Watch, a name of the Forty-second Highlanders."

"D'ye hear that, you Sambo? You orter go and git [Pg 310]draafted inter that corpse, and go araound breakin' the wimmin's hyearts in a cullud flannel petticut."

"There are no negroes, sir, in the Black Watch," interposed the corporal.

"See heah, yoh Yankee Canajiun," answered Mr. Maguffin with feeling, "fo' de law ob this yeah kintry I'se jess es good a man as yoh is. So yoh jess keep yoh Samboo in yoh mouf atter this. Specks yoh'se got a mighty low down name yohsef if t'was only knowed by respeckable pussons."

"My name, Mr. Julius Sneezer Disgustus Quackenboss, my name is Pawkins, great grandson of Hercules Leonidas Pawkins, as was briggidier ginral and aijicamp to George Washington, when he drummed the haousehold trooeps, and the hull o' the derned British army, out'n Noo Yohk to the toon o' 'Yankee Doodle.'"

The constable turned pale, shivered all over, and swayed about in his chair, almost frightening the mendacious Yankee by the sight of the mischief his words had wrought. Tryphena, however, quickly filled the shocked corporal a hot cup of tea, and mutely pressed him to drink it. He took off the tea at a gulp, set down the cup with a steady hand, and, looking Mr. Pawkins in the face, said: "I regret, sir, to have to say the word; but, sir, you are a liar."

"That's true as death, consterble," remarked Timotheus, who did not share the hostile feelings of Sylvanus towards Corporal Rigby; "true as death, and the boys, they ducked him in the crick for't, but they's no washin' the lies out'n his jaws."

154

Mr. Pawkins looked as fierce as it was possible for a man with a merry twinkle in his eyes to look, and roared, "Consterble, did you mean that, or did you only say it fer fun like?"

Mr Rigby, glaring defiance, answered, "I meant it."

"Oh waall," responded the Yankee Canadian, mildly, "that's all right; because I want you to know that I don't allaow folks to joke with me that way. If you meant it, that's a different thing."

"What your general character may be, I do not know. As for your remarks on the British army, they are lies."

"I guess, consterble, you ain't up in the histry of the United States of Ameriky, or you'd know as your Ginral [Pg 311]Clinton was drummed aout o' Noo Yohk to the toon o' 'Yankee Doodle.'"

"I know, sir, that a mob of Hanoverians and Hessians, whom the Americans could not drive out, evacuated New York, in consequence of a treaty of peace. If your general, as you call him, Washington, had the bad taste to play his ugly tune after them, it was just what might be expected from such a quarter."

"My history," said Tryphosa, "says that the American army was driven out of Canada by a few regulars and some French-Canadians at the same time."

"Brayvo, Phosy!" cried Timotheus.

"I assert now, as I have asserted before," continued Corporal Rigby, "that the British army never has been defeated, and never can be defeated. I belong to the British army, and know whereof I speak."

"Were you in the American war, Mr. Pawkins?" asked Tryphena.

"Yaas, I was thar, like the consterble, in the haouse hold trooeps. When they come araound a draaftin', I skit aout to Kennidy. I've only got one thing agin the war, and that is makin' every common nigger so sassy he thinks he's the ekal of a white man. Soon's I think of that, the war makes me sick."

"It is the boast of our Empire," remarked the pensioner, grandly, "that wherever its flag floats, the slave is free."

"It's a derned pity," said Mr. Pawkins; "that there boy, Julius Sneezer Disgustus Quackenboss, ud be wuth heaps more'n he is, if his boss jest had the right to lick him straight along."

"Who," shrieked Maguffin; "who'se yar Squackenbawsin' an' gibbin' nigger lip ter? My name's Mortimah Magrudah Maguffin, an' what's yourn? Pawkins! Oh massy! Pawkins, nex' thing ter punkins. I cud get er punkin, an' cut a hole er two in it an' make a bettah face nor yourn, Mistah Pawkins, candaberus, lantun jaw, down east, Yankee white tresh. What you doin' roun' this house, anyway?"

"Arrah, hush now, childher!" said Mr. Terry, entering from the hall. "The aivenin's the time to make up aall dishputes, an' quoiet aal yer angry faylins afore yeez say yer worruds an' go to shlape, wid the howly angels gyardin' yeez. Good aivenin', Corporal."

[Pg 312]"Good evening, Sergeant-Major."

"Mr. Terry," asked Tryphosa, timidly, "will you play a game at Cities, Rivers and Mountains? We were waiting for even numbers to begin." The veteran, who knew the game, agreed. Gallantly, the gentlemen asked the two ladies to choose sides, whereupon Tryphena selected Mr. Pawkins, Maguffin and Sylvanus; Mr. Terry, the constable, and Timotheus fell to Tryphosa. Peace once more reigned, save when the great-grandson of the brigadier general was detected in looking over his opponent's cards and otherwise acting illegally.

Bigglethorpe and the lawyer entered the house, not far from bed time. The company was in the drawing-room, and a lady was at the piano singing, and playing her own accompaniment, while Mr. Lamb was standing beside her, pretending to turn over the music, of which he had as little knowledge as the animal whose name he bore. The song was that beautiful one of Burns,

O wert thou in the cauld blast
On yonder lea, on yonder lea,

and, though a gentleman's song, it was rendered with exquisite taste and feeling. The singer looked up appealingly at Mr. Lamb twice, solely to invoke his aid in turning the music leaf. But, to Coristine's jealous soul, it was a glance of tenderness and mutual understanding.

Four long days he had known her, and she had never sung for him; and now, just as soon as the Crown Land idiot comes along, she must favour him with her very best. He would not be rude, and talk while the singing was going on, but he would let Lamb do all the thanking; he wasn't going shares with that affected dude. The music ceased, and he turned to see whom he could talk to. Mrs. Carmichael and Miss Halbert were busy with their clerical adorers. The colonel and Mrs. Du Plessis had evidently bid their dear boy good night, for they were engaged in earnest conversation, in which he called her Terésa, and she called him Paul as often as colonel. Miss Du Plessis was turning over the leaves of an album. He went up to her, and asked if she would not favour the company with some music. "Instrumental or vocal, Mr. Coristine?" she asked. "Oh, vocal, if you please, Miss Du Plessis; [Pg 313]do you sing, 'Shall I wasting in despair,' or anything of that kind?" Miss Du Plessis did not, but would like to hear Mr. Coristine sing it. He objected that he had no music, and was a poor accompanyist. Before the unhappy man knew where he was, Miss Du Plessis was by Miss Carmichael's side, begging her dear friend Marjorie to accompany Mr. Coristine. She agreed, for she knew the song, and the music was in the stand. Like a condemned criminal, Coristine was conducted to the piano; but the first few bars put vigour into him, and he sang the piece through with credit. He was compelled, of course, to return thanks for the excellent accompaniment, but this he did in a stiff formal way, as if the musician was an entire stranger. Then they had prayers, for the gentlemen had come in out of the office, and, afterwards, the clergymen went home. As the inmates of Bridesdale separated for the night, Miss Carmichael handed the lawyer his ring, saying that since his hands were fit to dispense with gloves, they must also be strong enough to bear its weight. He accepted the ring with a sigh, and silently retired to his chamber. Before turning in for the night, he looked in upon Wilkinson, whom he found awake. After enquiries as to his arm and general health, he said: "Wilks, my boy, congratulate me on being an ass; I've lost the finest woman in all the world by my own stupidity." His friend smiled at him, and answered: "Do not be down-hearted, Corry; I will speak to Ceci—Miss Du Plessis I mean, and she will arrange matters for you." The lawyer fervently exclaimed: "God bless you, Wilks!" and withdrew, not a little comforted. We cannot intrude into the apartment of the young ladies, but there was large comfort in their conversation for a person whose Christian name was Eugene. If he only had known it!

By the constable, Ben Toner, and other messengers, Mr. Bigglethorpe had acquainted his somewhat tyrannical spouse that he was staying for a while at the Flanders lakes to enjoy the fishing. Mr. Rigby had brought from the store his best rods and lines and his fly-book. He was, therefore, up early on Thursday morning, lamenting that he was not at Richards, whence he could have visited the first lake and secured a mess of fish before breakfast. [Pg 314]He was sorting out his tackle in the office, when Marjorie, an early riser, came in to see if Uncle John was there. When she found out the occupant, she said: "Come along, Mr. Biggles, and let us go fishing, it's so long before breakfast." Fishing children could do anything with Bigglethorpe; he would even help them to catch cat-fish and suckers. But he had an eye to business. "Marjorie," he asked, "do you think you could find me a pickle bottle, an empty one, you know?" She thought she could, and at once engaged 'Phosa and 'Phena in the search for one. A Crosse and Blackwell wide-mouthed bottle, bearing the label "mixed pickles," which really means gherkins, was borne triumphantly into the office. Mr. Bigglethorpe handled it affectionately, and said: "Put on your hat, Marjorie, and we'll go crawfish hunting." Without rod or line, the fisherman, holding the pickle bottle in his left hand, and taking Marjorie by the right, walked down to the creek. On its bank he sat down, and took off his shoes and socks, an example quickly and joyfully followed by his young companion. Then he splashed a little water on his head, and she did the same; after which they waded in the shallow brook, and turned up flat stones in its bed. Sometimes the crawfish lay quite still, when Mr. Bigglethorpe, getting his right hand, with extended thumb and forefinger, slily behind it, grasped the unsuspecting crustacean at the back of his great nippers, and landed him in the bottle filled with sparkling water. Sometimes a "craw," as Marjorie called them, darted away backward in a great hurry, and had to be looked for under another stone, and these were generally young active fellows, which, the fisherman said, made the best bait for bass. It was wild, exciting work, with a spice of danger in it from the chance of a nip from those terrible claws. Marjorie enjoyed it to the full. She laughed and shrieked, and clapped her hands over every new addition to the pickle bottle, and Mr. Biggles was every bit as enthusiastic as she was. Soon they were aware of a third figure on the scene. It was the sleepless lawyer. "Come in, Eugene," cried Marjorie; "take off your shoes and stockings, and help us to catch these lovely craws." He had to obey, and was soon as excited as the others over this novel kind of sport.

[Pg 315]Coristine looked up after securing his twelfth victim, and saw four figures sauntering down the hill. Three were young ladies in print morning gowns; the fourth was the ineffable dude, Lamb. At once he went back, and put himself into socks and boots, turning down his trouser legs, as if innocent of the childish amusement. "Haw," brayed Mr. Lamb, "is thot you, Cawrstine? Been poddling in the wotter, to remind yoursolf of the doys when you used to run round in your bare feet?" Outwardly calm, the lawyer advanced to meet the invaders. Bowing somewhat too ceremoniously to the three ladies, who looked delightfully fresh and cool in their morning toilets, he answered his interlocutor. "I am sure, Mr. Lamb, that it would afford Mr. Bigglethorpe and Marjorie additional satisfaction, to know that their wading after crawfish brought up memories of your barefooted youth. Unfortunately, I have no such blissful period to recall." Mr. Lamb blushed, and stammered some incoherencies, and Miss Carmichael, running past the lawyer towards Marjorie, whispered as she flitted before him, "you rude, unkind man!" This did not tend to make him more amiable. He snubbed the Crown Land gentleman at every turn, and, more than usually brilliant in talk, effectually kept his adversary out of conversation with the remaining ladies. "Look, Cecile!" said Miss Halbert; "Marjorie is actually joining the waders. "Mr. Lamb stroked his whisker-moustache and remarked: "Haw, you know, thot's nothing new for Morjorie; when we were children together, we awften went poddling about in creeks for crowfish and minnows." Then he had the impertinence to stroll down to the brook, and rally the new addition to the crawfishing party. To Coristine the whole thing was gall and wormwood. The only satisfaction he had was, that Mr. Lamb could not summon courage enough to divest himself of shoes and stockings and take part in the sport personally. But what an insufferable ass he, Coristine, must be to keep on wading, in view of such glorious company! What was the use of complaining: had he been there she would never have gone in, trust her for that! Wilkinson and he were right in their old compact: the female sex is a delusion and a snare. Thank heaven! there's the prayer gong, but will [Pg 316]that staring, flat-footed, hawhawing, Civil Service idiot be looking on while she reattires herself! He had half a mind to descend and brain him on the spot, if he had any brains, so as to render impossible the woeful calamity. But the fates were merciful, sending Mr. Lamb up with Marjorie and Mr. Bigglethorpe. Now was the angry man's chance, and a rare one, but, like an angry man, he did not seize it. The other two ladies remarked to each other that it was not very polite of three gentlemen to allow a lady, the last of the party, to come up the hill alone. What did he care?

At breakfast, Miss Carmichael sat between Messrs. Bigglethorpe and Lamb, and the lawyer between Miss Halbert and the veteran. "Who are going fishing to the lakes," asked the Squire, to which question the doctor replied, regretting his inability; and the colonel declined the invitation on account of his dear boy. Mr. Lamb intimated that he had business with Miss Du Plessis on Crown Land matters, as the department wished to get back into its possession the land owned by her. This was a bombshell in the camp. Miss Du Plessis declined to have any conference on the subject, referring the civil servant to her uncle, to Squire Carruthers, and to her solicitor, Mr. Coristine. The lawyer was disposed to be liberal in politics, although his friend Wilkinson was a strong Conservative; but the contemptible meanness of a Government department attempting to retire property deeded and paid for in order to gain a few hundred dollars or a new constituent, aroused his vehement indignation, and his determination to fight Lamb and his masters to the bitter end of the Privy Council.

"Mr. Lamb," said the colonel, "is yoar business with my niece complicated, or is it capable of being stated bhiefly?"

"I can put it in a very few words, Colonel," replied the civil service official; "the deportment hos received on awffer for Miss Du Plessis' lond which it would be fawlly to refuse."

"But," interposed the Squire, "the department has naething to dae wi' Miss Cecile's land: it's her ain, every fit o't."

"You don't know the deportment, Squire. It con [Pg 317]take bock lond of its own deed, especially wild lond, by the awffer of a reasonable equivolent or indemnity. It proposes to return the purchase money, with five per cent. interest to date, and the amount of municipal toxes attested by receipts. Thot is regorded os a fair odjustment, ond on Miss Du Plessis surrendering her deed to me, the deportment will settle the claim within twelve months, if press of business ollows."

"Such abominable, thieving iniquity, on the pairt o' a Government ca'ain' itself leeberal, I never hard o' in aa my life," said the indignant Squire.

"Do you mean to say, Arthur," asked Mrs. Carmichael, "that your department can take away Cecile's property in that cavalier fashion, and without any regard to the rise in values?"

"I'm ofraid so, Mrs. Cormichael."

"What have you to say to that, Mr. Coristine, from a legal standpoint?" enquired Mrs. Carruthers.

"A deed of land made by the Government, or by a private individual, conveys, when, as in this case, all provisions have been complied with, an inalienable title."

"There is such a thing as expropriation," suggested Mr. Lamb, rather annoyed to find a lawyer there.

"Expropriation is a municipal affair in cities and towns, or it may be national and provincial in the case of chartered railways or national parks, in all which cases remuneration is by arbitration, not by the will of any expropriating body."

"The deportment may regord this as a provincial offair. Ot any rate, it hos octed in this way before with success."

"I know that the department has induced people to surrender their rights for the sake of its popularity, but by wheedling, not by law or justice, and, generally, there has been some condition of payment, or something else, not complied with."

"Thot's simple enough. A few lines in the bookkeeping awffice con involidate the deed."

"One or two words, Mr. Lamb, and I have done; the quicker you answer, the sooner Miss Du Plessis' decision is reached. Do you represent the commissioner, the minister?"

[Pg 318]"Well, not exoctly."

"Were you sent by his deputy, the head of the department?"

"Not the head exoctly."

"Is the name of the man, for whom your friend wants to expropriate Miss Du Plessis' land, called Rawdon, Altamont Rawdon?"

"How did you know thot? Ore you one of the deportment outriggers?"

"No; I have nothing to do with any kind of dirty work. You go back, and tell your man, first, that Rawdon is dead, and that in life he was a notorious criminal; second, that Miss Du Plessis' land has been devastated by the fire in which he perished; and, third, that if he, or you, or any other contemptible swindler, moves a finger in this direction, either above board or below, I'll have you up for foul conspiracy, and make the department only too happy to send you about your business to save its reputation before the country."

As Ben Toner and his friends in the kitchen would have said, Mr. Lamb was paralyzed. While the lawyer had spoken with animation, there was something quite judicial in his manner. Miss Carmichael looked up at him from under her long lashes with an admiration it would have done him good to see, and a hum of approving remarks went all round the table. Then, in an evil moment, the young lady felt it her duty to comfort the heart of poor Orther Lom, whom everybody else regarded with something akin to contempt. She talked to him of old times, until the man's inflated English was forgotten, as well as his by no means reputable errand. The young man was quite incapable of any deep-laid scheme of wrong-doing, as he was of any high or generous impulse. He was a mere machine, educated up to a certain point, able to write a good hand, and express himself grammatically, but thinking more of his dress and his spurious English than of any learning or accomplishment, and the unreasoning tool of his official superiors. He had been checkmated by Coristine, and

158

felt terribly disappointed at the failure of his mission; but the thought that he had been engaged in a most dishonest attempt did not trouble him in the least. Yet, had he been offered a large bribe to commit robbery [Pg 319]in the usual ways, he would have rejected the proposition with scorn. Miss Carmichael, knowing his character, was sorry for him, little thinking that his returning vivacity under her genial influence smote Coristine's heart, as the evidence of double disloyalty on the lady's part, to her friend, Miss Du Plessis, and to him. Tiring of her single-handed work, she turned to Mr. Bigglethorpe, saying: "You know Mr. Lamb, do you not!" The fisherman answered: "You were kind enough to introduce us last night, Miss Carmichael, but you will, I hope, pardon me for saying that I do not approve of Mr. Lamb." Then he turned away, and conversed with the Captain. When the company rose, the only person who approached the civil servant was the colonel, who said: "I pehsume, suh, aftah what my kind friend, Mr. Cohistine, has spoken so well, you will not annoy my niece with any moah remahks about her propehty. It would please that lady and me, as her guahdian, if you will fohget Miss Du Plessis' existence, suh, so fah as you are concehned." This was chilling, but chill did not hurt Mr. Lamb. The little Carruthers, headed by Marjorie, were in front of the verandah when Miss Carmichael and he went out. Marjorie had evidently been schooling them, for, at her word of command, they began to sing, to the tune of "Little Bo Peep," the original words:—

Poor Orther Lom,
He looks so glom.

Miss Carmichael seized her namesake and shook her. "You naughty, wicked little girl, how dare you? Who taught you these shameful words?" she asked, boiling with indignation. Marjorie cried a little for vexation, but would not reveal the name of the author. Some said it was the doctor, and others, that it was his daughter Fanny; but Miss Carmichael was sure that the lawyer, Marjorie's great friend, Eugene, was the guilty party, that he ought to be ashamed of himself, and that the sooner he left Bridesdale the better. Coristine was completely innocent of the awful crime, which lay in the skirts of Marjorie's father, the Captain, as might have been suspected from the beauty of the couplet. The consequence of the poetic surprise was the exclusive attachment of Miss Carmichael to [Pg 320]the Crown Lands man, in a long walk in the garden, a confidential talk, and the present of a perfectly beautiful button-hole pinned in by her own hands.

CHAPTER XVII.

The Picnic—Treasure Trove—A Substantial Ghost Captured—Coristine's Farewell—Ride to Collingwood—Bangs Secures Rawdon—Off to Toronto—Coristine Meets the Captain—Grief at Bridesdale—Marjorie and Mr. Biggles—Miss Du Plessis Frightens Mr. Lamb—The Minister's Smoke—Fishing Picnic.

After his Parthian shot, the Captain ordered Sylvanus to get out the gig, as he was going home. Leaving Marjorie in the hands of her aunt Carmichael, he saluted his daughter, his niece, and his two sisters in law, and took their messages for Susan. There was grief in the kitchen at the departure of Sylvanus, who expected to be on the rolling deep before the end of the week. Mr. Pawkins and Constable Rigby had already taken leave, travelling homeward in an amicable way. Then, Doctor Halbert insisted on his vehicle being brought round, as there must be work waiting for him at home; so a box with a cushion was placed for his sprained leg, and he and Miss Fanny were just on the eve of starting, when Mr. Perrowne came running up in great haste, and begged to be allowed to drive the doctor over. With a little squeezing he got in, and, amid much waving of handkerchiefs, the doctor's buggy drove away. Mr. Lamb exhibited no desire to leave, and Miss Carmichael was compelled to devote herself to him, a somewhat monotonous task, in spite of his garrulous egotism. Timotheus, by the Squire's orders, harnessed the horses to the waggonette, and deposited therein a pickaxe and a spade. Mr. Bigglethorpe brought out his fishing tackle, joyous over the prospect of a day's fishing, and Mr. Terry lugged along a huge basket, prepared by his daughter in the kitchen, with all manner of eatables and drinkables for the picnic. The lawyer made the fourth of the party, exclusive of Timotheus, who gave instructions to Maguffin how to behave in his absence. The colonel was with Wilkinson, but the ladies and Mr. Lamb came [Pg 321]to see the expedition under way. It was arranged that

Timotheus should drive the Squire and the lawyer to the masked road and leave them there, after which he was to take the others to Richards place, put up the horses, and help them to propel the scow through the lakes and channels. Accordingly, the treasure seekers got out the pick and shovel, and trudged along to the scene of the late fire. As they neared the Encampment, their road became a difficult and painful one, over fallen trees blackened with fire, and through beds of sodden ashes. At the Encampment, the ground, save where the buildings had stood, was comparatively bare. The lofty and enormously strong brick chimney was still standing in spite of the many explosions, and, here and there, a horse appeared, looking wistfully at the ruins of its former home. There, the intending diggers stood, gazing mutely for a while on the scene of desolation.

"'Sandy soil, draining both ways, and undercover,' is what we want, Coristine," said the Squire. The two walked back and forward along the ridge, rejecting rock and depression and timbered land. They searched the foundations of houses and sheds, found the trap under Rawdon's own house that led to the now utterly caved-in tunnel, and tried likely spots where once the stables stood, only to find accumulations of rubbish. A steel square such as carpenters use, was found among the chips in the stone-yard, and of this Coristine made a primitive surveyor's implement by which he sought to take the level of the ground. "Bring your eye down here, Mr. Carruthers," he said. "I see," answered the Squire; "but, man, yon's just a conglomeration o' muckle stanes." The lawyer replied, "That's true, Squire, but it's the height of land, and that top stone lies almost too squarely to be natural. Let us try them at least. It will do no harm, and the day is young yet." They went forward to a spot beyond the stone yard, on the opposite side from the burnt stables, which they saw had once been railed off, for the blackened stumps of the posts were still in the ground. It was a picturesque mass of confusion, apparently an outcrop of the limestone, not uncommon in that region. But the lawyer probed the ground all about it. It was light dry soil, with no trace of a rocky bottom. Without a lever, [Pg 322]their work was hard, but they succeeded in throwing off the large flat protecting slab, and in scattering its rocky supports. "Man, Coristine, I believe you're richt." ejaculated the perspiring Carruthers. Then he took the pick and loosened the ground, while the lawyer removed the earth with his spade. "There's no' a root nor a muckle stane in the haill o't, Coristine; this groond's been wrocht afore, my lad." So they kept on, till at last the pick rebounded with a metallic clang. "Let me clear it, Squire," asked the lawyer, and, at once, his spade sent the sand flying, and revealed a box of japanned tin, the counterpart of that discovered by Muggins, which had only contained samples of grindstones. A little more picking, and a little more spading, and the box came easily out. It was heavy, wonderfully heavy, and it was padlocked. The sharp edge of the spade loosened the lid sufficiently to admit the point of the pick, and, while Coristine hung on to the box, the Squire wrenched it open. The tin box was full of notes and gold.

"There's thoosands an' thoosands here, Coristine, eneuch to keep yon puir body o' a Matilda in comfort aa' her days. Man, it's a graun' discovery, an' you're the chiel that's fund it," cried the Squire, with exultation. The lawyer peered in too, when, suddenly, he heard a shot, a bullet whizzed past his ear, and, the next moment, with a sickening thud, Carruthers fell to the ground. Coristine rose to his feet like lightning, and faced an apparition; the Grinstun man, with pistol in one hand and life preserver in the other, was before him. Without a moment's hesitation he regained his grasp of his spade, and stretched the ghost at his feet, mercifully with the flat of it, and then relieved his victim of pistol and loaded skull-cracker. He heard voices hailing, and recognized them as those of the veteran and the fisherman. He replied with a loud cry of "Hurry, hurry, help!" which roused the prostrate spectre. It arose and made a dash for the tin box, but Coristine threw himself upon the substantial ghost, and a struggle for life began. They clasped, they wrestled, they fell over the poor unconscious Squire, and upset the tin box. They clasped each other by the throat, the hair; they kicked with their feet, and pounded with their knees. It was Grinstun's last ditch, [Pg 323]and he was game to hold it; but the lawyer was game too. Sometimes he was up and had his hand on his opponent's throat, and again, he could not tell how, he was turned over, and the heavy squat form of Rawdon fell like an awful nightmare on his chest. But he would not give in. He saw his antagonist reach for a weapon, pistol, skull-cracker, he knew not what it was, but that reach released one hand from his throat. With a tremendous

160

effort, he turned, and lay side to side with his enemy, when Timotheus dashed in, and, bodily picking up the Grinstun man in his arms, hammered his head on the big flat stone, till the breathless lawyer begged him to stop. Up came Mr. Bigglethorpe and Mr. Terry in great consternation, and gazed with wonder upon the lately active ghost. "Make him fast," cried Coristine with difficulty, "while I look after the poor Squire." So, Timotheus and the fisher took off Rawdon's coat and braces, and bound him hand and foot with his own belongings. But the veteran had already looked to his son-in-law, and, from the picnic stores, had poured some spirits into his lips. "Rouse up, John, avic," he cried piteously, "rouse up, my darlint, or Honoria 'ull be breakin' her poor heart. It's good min is scarce thim toimes, an' the good God'll niver be takin' away the bist son iver an ould man had." The Squire came to, although the dark blood oozed out of an ugly wound in the back of his head, and the amount of liquor his affectionate father-in law had poured into him made him light-headed. "Glory be to God!" said the old man, and all the others gratefully answered "Amen."

The lawyer explained the circumstances, the excavation, the money, the assault, to his deliverers; but the resurrection of the Grinstun man was a mystery which he could not explain. Without being told, Timotheus, whose arrival had been so opportune, ran all the way to Richards, and brought from thence the waggon, along with Harry Richards, who volunteered to accompany him, and Mr. Errol, who was visiting in the neighbourhood. Young Richards brought an axe with him, and cleared some of the obstructions of the once masked road, so that the vehicle was able to get up within reasonable distance of the encampment. It was desirable to get the Squire home, lest his injuries should be greater than they supposed, and [Pg 324]the prisoner ought to be in Mr. Bangs' hands at once. Accordingly, Mr. Errol and Harry Richards offered to stay with Mr. Bigglethorpe and carry out the original picnic, it being understood that Timotheus would either call or send for them about four o'clock.

"Gin I'm gaun to be oot on the splore, I maun hae a bit smokie. Wha's gotten a bit pipe he's no usin'?" asked the usually sedate minister. Coristine handed over to him his smoking materials, penknife included; and Mr. Errol, taking off his coat, sat down on a stone to fill the pipe, saying, "Nae mair pastoral veesitation for me the day. Gin any body spiers whaur I am, just tell them I'm renewin' my youth." Timotheus and Harry carried the prisoner to the waggon, while the veteran and the lawyer followed, leading the Squire, and carrying the box of treasure. The fishermen came to see them off, and, then, they descended to the lake shore and began the sport of the day. Timotheus drove, and the Squire sat up between him and his affectionate father-in-law. The lawyer was in the rear seat with the prisoner, who, for greater security, was lashed to the back of it. Rawdon's revolver was in his captor's hand, and his skull-cracker in a handy place. Several times, shamming insensibility, the prince of tricksters endeavoured to throw his solitary warder off his guard, but the party reached Bridesdale without his succeeding in loosening a single thong. There was great consternation when Timotheus drove up to the gate. The children had been at their old game of the handkerchief, and Miss Carmichael was actually chasing Orther Lom, to their great glee, and to Coristine's intense disgust. Of course, they stopped when they saw the waggon and the Squire's pale face. The colonel, who had been smoking his morning cigar on the verandah, came forward rapidly, and, with Mr. Terry, helped the master of Bridesdale to alight. Then, his wife and sister took the wounded man in charge, and led him into the house, for he was thoroughly dazed and incapable of attending to any business. "If you will allow me, colonel," said the lawyer, "I will take charge of legal matters in this case," to which Colonel Morton answered, "Most cehtainly, my deah suh, no one moah competent."

Maguffin had come round to see if his services would [Pg 325]be required, and appointed to mount guard over the prisoner in company with Timotheus. To Mr. Terry the lawyer gave the heavy cash box, with orders to put it in a safe place in the Squire's office. Then, Coristine went up-stairs, washed and brushed away the traces of conflict, and knocked at Wilkinson's door. A lady's voice told him to enter, and, on his complying with the invitation, he beheld Miss Du Plessis sitting by the bedside of his friend, with a book, which was not Wordsworth, in her hand. "Please to pardon my intrusion, Miss Du Plessis; the Squire is hurt, and we have captured Grinstuns, who was not burnt up after all. I must see the prisoner safely caged, and have other business to attend to, so that I have come to say good-bye. I am sure that you will take every care of my dear friend here." After this little speech, hard to utter, the lawyer shook his friend by the well hand, saying: "Good-bye, Wilks, old boy, and keep up your heart; any messages for town?" Before he had time to receive any such commissions, he shook hands warmly with the lady, and vanished. Replacing Maguffin over Rawdon, he told him to saddle a horse, and bring it round. His orders to Mr. Terry and Timotheus were to secure their prisoner between them in some lighter vehicle, and bring him with all speed to Collingwood, whither he would precede them on horseback. He found the Squire in an easy chair in the sitting room with three lady attendants. Shaking hands with the half-unconscious man, he assured him that he would attend to the business of the day, and then, with a few words of grateful recognition to Mrs. Carruthers, bade all the ladies good-bye. "Hasten back," they all said, and the kind hostess added: "We will think long till we see you again." Walking back into the kitchen, he bestowed a trifle in his most gracious manner, on Tryphena and Tryphosa, and then went forth to look for Marjorie. As he kissed her an affectionate farewell in the garden, the little girl intuitively guessed his absence to be no common one, and begged her Eugene to stay, with tears in her eyes. But he was obdurate with her and all the little Carruthers, on whom he showered quarters to buy candy at the post office. Maguffin was there with the horse, and, near the gate, was Miss Carmichael with that ineffable ass Lamb. Looking at the latter as if he would [Pg 326]dearly love to kick him, he raised his hat to his companion, and extended his hand with the simple words "Good-bye." Miss Carmichael did not offer hers in return; she said: "It is hardly worth while being so formal over an absence of a few hours." Coristine turned as if a serpent had bitten him, slipped some money into Maguffin's hand, as that worthy held open the gate for him, and vaulted on his horse, nor did he turn to look round so long as the eyes of Bridesdale were on his retreating figure.

The lawyer rode hard, for he was excited. He went by Talfourd's house like a flash, and away through the woods he had traversed on Nash's beast that last pleasant Sunday morning. At the Beaver River he watered his horse, and exchanged a word with Pierre and Batiste bidding the former look out that no attempt at rescuing the prisoner should be made in that quarter. Away he went, with madame's eyes watching him from afar, up the ascent, and along the road to where the Hills dwelt at the foot of the Blue Mountains. He doffed his hat to the old lady as he passed, then breasted the mountain side. For a moment, he stood on the summit to take in the view once more, then clattered down the other side, and away full pelt for the town. Soon he entered Collingwood, and sought the police headquarters without delay. Where was Mr. Bangs? He was told, to his great delight, that the detective was in town, and would report at four o'clock. It was now half-past three. Putting up his horse at the hotel, the lawyer partook of a hasty meal at a restaurant, and returned in time to meet Bangs on the very threshold. "Whet ere you doing here, Lawyer Coristine?" he asked.

"You will never guess, Mr. Bangs."

"Any more trebble et Bridesdele?"

"No, but I'll tell you; we've caught Rawdon."

"Why, the men's dead, berned to a cinder, you know."

"No, he is not; that was some other man."

"Ere you shore, Mr. Coristine?"

"Perfectly. Mr. Terry and Timotheus are bringing him here now."

"Whet, only the two of them, and kemming pest the Beaver too?"

"Yes; there were no more to send. I warned Pierre Lajeunesse to be on the lookout."

[Pg 327]"Is your beast fit to trevel eny more?"

"I think so; it seems a strong animal."

"Then get on hersebeck quick! Here, kensteble, hend me two betons, and a kerbine!"

When the lawyer returned with his hard-ridden steed, he found Mr. Bangs mounted, with a baton by his side and a carbine slung behind him. Off they went along the shore and up the hill. Descending, they saw the buggy approaching slowly in the neighbourhood of the Hills' log shanty, attended by four persons who seemed to be armed. Hastening down the slope, they came up to it, and found the prisoner safe but awfully profane. The foot guards were Ben Toner, Barney Sullivan, and Rufus Hill, under the command of Monsieur Lajeunesse. They were relieved of their self-imposed duty with many thanks, and Coristine

162

shook hands with the honest fellows, as he and the detective replaced them in escort duty. Then Timotheus whipped up his horse, and they drove and rode into town, an imposing spectacle for the eyes of the youth of Collingwood.

Bangs could hardly believe his eyes, and could not conceal his delight, on beholding the murderer of his now buried friend. No pains were spared for the safe-keeping of the notorious criminal. In the presence of a magistrate, Coristine and Mr. Terry made affidavit as to his crimes and capture. The latter and Timotheus also related his attempts to bribe them into giving him his liberty, offering large sums and promising to leave the country. "Now, Mishter Corstine," says the veteran, "it's hoigh toime we was gettin' home. The good payple 'ull be gettin' onaisy about yeez, 'an spashly Miss Carrmoichael that was gravin' sore to think she niver said good-boye to yeez. Come, now, come away, an' lave the baste in the shtable, for it's toired roidin' ye must be."

"I am not going back, Mr. Terry. I said good-bye to them all at Bridesdale, and must hurry away to business. Perhaps Timotheus will ride the horse, while you drive."

"Thet pore enimel isn't fit fer eny more werk to-night, Mr. Coristine. I'll tell you, Mr. Terry, whet I'll do. I shell be beck here to-morrow evening, end will ride the horse to Bridesdele. I've got a weggon and team of the Squire's here, which yeng Hill will drive beck for me. [Pg 328]Then he ken ride pore Nesh's horse, and I ken get my own. Strenge they didn't give you one of thowse beasts instead of the colonel's, Mr. Coristine."

"Is this the colonel's horse?"

"I should sey it is. You down't think eny ether enimel could hev brought you elong so fest, do you?"

"God bless the kind old man!" ejaculated the lawyer.

"Mishter Corstine, dear, it'll be breakin' aall the poor childer's hearts an' some that's growed up too if you 'll be affther lavin' us this way," continued Mr. Terry; and Timotheus, whom his Peskiwanchow friend rewarded, added his appeal: "I wisht you wouldn't go fer to go home jess' yet. Mister." But all entreaties were unavailing. He and Mr. Bangs saw the buggy off, and then retired to the hotel to get some supper. On the way thither, he invested in a briar root pipe and some tobacco to replace those he had given to Mr. Errol. They would be home from fishing long ago, and perhaps good Bigglethorpe would take Miss Carmichael away from that miserable Orther Lom. After supper, the two sat over their pipes and a decoction of some kind in the reading-room, talking over the sad and wonderful events of the past few days. Mr. Bangs took very kindly to the lawyer, and promised to look him up whenever he came to town. He advised him to keep silent about the discovery of Rawdon's money, as the crown might claim it, and thus deprive poor Matilda Nagle of her only chance of independence. He said also that he would instruct the Squire in the same direction on the morrow.

That night, two gaol guards armed to the teeth arrived in police quarters to take charge of Davis, but the bigger criminal was placed in their care. Early in the morning there was a stir in the railway station, when the handcuffed prisoners were marched down under strong escort, and securely boxed up with their guards and Mr. Bangs. Many rough characters were there, among whom the lawyer recognized Matt of the tavern, and Bangs and he could have sworn to the identity of others, whom the former had met in the cavalry charge on the masked road and whom Coristine had seen and heard in the Richards' scow the night of the catastrophe. They scowled, but [Pg 329]attempted no rescue. Thanks to the lawyer's generalship, things had been pushed through too quickly for them to combine. For some time, Coristine travelled alone. There were other people in the car, but he did not know them, nor did he care to make any new acquaintances. All his friends were at Bridesdale, and he was a homeless exile going back to Mrs. Marsh's boarding-house. At Dromore, however, he caught sight of the wide-mouthed barrel of a blunderbuss, and knew the Captain could not be far off. Soon that naval gentleman got on board, helping Mrs. Thomas up to the platform, followed by Sylvanus with the saluting weapon. They were to be his companions as far as Barrie, and much the lawyer enjoyed their society. Marjorie was the great subject of conversation, although, of course, the Captain had to be enlightened in many points of recent history. He still thought Wilkinson a sly dog, but wondered greatly at Coristine's going away. Mrs. Thomas explained the relationship of Orther Lom. He had been a poor neglected boy, when Marjorie Carmichael was a little girl, whom her father, the member, had interested himself in, giving him an education, and supporting him in part while at the Normal School in Toronto. Just before he died, he exerted his influence to obtain a Government berth for him, and that was the whole story. The lawyer saw it all now, and learned too late what a foolish fellow he had been. Of course, there were old times, and they had much to talk of, and she could not help being civil to him, and being angry when he had reminded her father's protegé of his early poverty. Coristine sighed, and felt that, if Lamb had been present, he would have apologized to him. To cheer him up, the Captain invited him to join Mrs. Thomas and himself on a cruise in the *Susan*. He would have enjoyed it immensely he said, but, having made so many assertions of pressing business in the city, he had to be consistent and miserable. At Barrie, he bade his last friends adieu, parted affectionately with The Crew, and then gazed longingly at the spars of the *Susan Thomas* in Kempenfeldt Bay. If only the Captain had brought the two Marjories for a cruise, he would have shipped with him for a month, and have let business go to the dogs. There were no more objects of interest till he arrived in Toronto, took a street[Pg 330]car, and deposited himself, much to that lady's astonishment, in his bachelor's quarters at Mrs. Marsh's boarding-house. After a special lunch, he sat down to smoke and read a little Browning.

It was very late when Mr. Terry and Timotheus arrived at Bridesdale. All the ladies had retired, with the exception of Mrs. Carruthers, who had staid up to await her father's arrival. The gentlemen of the party were the Squire, quite clear in head and not much the worse of his crack on the skull, Mr. Bigglethorpe, and Mr. Errol, who had been induced to continue his splore in the office. He was still renewing his youth, when the veteran entered all alone, and said he didn't mind if he did help Mr. Bigglethorpe with that decanter, for it was tiresome work driving.

"Where is Mr. Coristine, grandfather?" asked the Squire.

"It's in Collinwud he is an his way to Teranty."

"What! do you mean to say he has left us, gone for good?"

"That's fwhat it is. Oi prished 'em, an' porshwaded 'em, an' towld 'em it was desprut anggery an' graved yeez wud aall be. Says he Oi've bud 'em aall good-boye an' Oi'm goin' home to bishness. It was lucky for you, Squoire, that it wasn't lasht noight he wint."

"It is that, grandfather. I'd have been a dead man. He maun hae focht yon deevil like a wild cat tae get oot o' the way o's pistols and things."

"'Twas Timawtheus as kim up furrust an' tuk the thafe av a Rawdon out av his arrums, for he grupped 'em good an' toight."

"Well done, Timotheus!" said Mr. Errol. "He's a fine lad, Mr. Bigglethorpe, though a bit clumsy in his ways."

"We can't all be handsome, sir," answered that gentleman. "If he's got the good principle in him, that's the mine thing, so I always say."

Mrs. Carruthers put her head into the smoke, coughed a little, and said: "Come, father, supper is waiting for you in the breakfast room." The veteran followed his daughter, and, over his evening meal, gave her a detailed account of the proceedings of the afternoon. "And to go away without a bite to eat, and ride all that distance, and [Pg 331]leave his knapsack and his flowers and I don't know what else behind him, what is the meaning of it, father?"

"Honoria, my dear, I aalways thought women's eyes was cliverer nor min's. There's a little gyurl they call Marjorie, an' she's not so little as aall that, if she isn't quoite the hoighth av Miss Ceshile. That bhoy was jist dishtracted wid the crool paice, that goes aff philanderin wid the Shivel Sharvice shape av a Lamb. He didn't say it moind in wurruds, but I see it was the killin' av 'em, an' he jist coulden' shtand it no langer. Smaal blame to him say Oi!"

So grandfather got his supper, and went back to the office to finish his pipe and his tumbler, while Timotheus was entertaining Tryphosa in the kitchen. Mrs. Carruthers retired, but, first, she visited the young ladies' apartment, and said, in a tone which she meant to be reproachful as well as regretful: "Mr. Coristine has left us never to return." The kindest-hearted woman in the world, having thrown this drop of bitterness into her niece's cup, left her to drink it to the dregs. Meanwhile Orther Lom was dreaming that he could not do better than marry the Marjorie of his youth and begin housekeeping, in spite of tailors' bills.

The sun rose bright on Friday morning, and, peeping in upon Mr. Bigglethorpe in his room and upon Marjorie in the nursery bedroom, awoke these two early birds. They met on the stairs and came down together. The fisherman said he thought he would get his things bundled up, meaning his gun and rods, and walk home to breakfast, but Marjorie said he just wouldn't, for Eugene was gone, and, if he were to go, she would have nobody. Well broken in to respect for feminine authority, save when the fishing fit was on, Mr. Bigglethorpe had to succumb, and travel down to the creek after crawfish, chub and dace. He told his youthful companion fishing stories which amused her; and confided to her that he was going to train up his little boy to be a great fisherman. "Have you got a little boy, Mr. Biggles?" she asked, and then added: "How funny!" as if her friend ought to have been content with other people's children, and fish.

"What is his name, Mr. Biggles?" she enquired.

"He hasn't been christened yet, but I think I'll call [Pg 332]him Isaac Walton, or Charles Cotton, or Piscator. Don't you think these are nice nimes?"

"No, I don't. Woollen and Cotton and what Mr. Perrowne belongs to are not pretty. Eugene is pretty."

Mr. Bigglethorpe laughed, and said: "I didn't say Woollen but Walton, and I said Piscator, which is the Latin for fisher, not Episcopalian, which Mr. Perrowne is."

"Why do you want to call him a fisher? It is like a Sunday School story Marjorie read me, a Yankee book, about a little baby boy that was left on a doorstep, and the doorstep man's name was Fish, and he had him baptized Preserved because he was preserved, and he grew up to be a good man and was called Preserved Fish. Wasn't that awful?"

"Oh very streinge! If my boy had been a little girl, I would have nimed her Marjorie."

"See, Mr. Biggles, here she comes again, and Cecile, and, O horrors! Orther Lom."

It was too true. The young ladies had come out to enjoy the morning air, and, after a turn in the garden, had rushed to the hill meadow to escape the Departmental gentleman, whose elegant morocco slippers they had heard on the stairs. Spite of the morning dew he had pursued them, well pleased with himself, and doubtful whom to conquer with his charms.

"O Mr. Biggles," continued Marjorie, "that horrid man got me a naughty, cruel shaking, and he's sent my dear Eugene away never to come back any more. I know, because I went into aunty's room when I got up; and she told me."

"It's too bad, Marjorie. Who mide that little song on Mr. Lamb?"

"You'll never tell?"

"No."

"'Pon your honour?"

"'Pon my honour."

"It was papa, you old goosey."

"Not Mr. Coristine?"

"No, of course not."

"My I sy that it wasn't Mr. Coristine?"

"O yes, don't let them think any bad things about Eugene, poor boy."

[Pg 333]"Good morning, Miss Carmichael," said Mr. Bigglethorpe, or rather he bawled it; "will you come here a minute, please?"

Miss Carmichael gladly skipped down, leaving her companion a prey to the gentleman of the morocco slippers.

"I want to clear our friend, Mr. Coristine, of a suspicion which you may not have shired," said the fisherman. "He didn't mike that little piece of poetry on Mr. Lamb that Marjorie and the other children sang yesterday morning."

"Thank you, Mr. Bigglethorpe; I am very glad to hear it."

"Nasty pig!" said Marjorie to herself; "she drove Eugene away all the same."

Meanwhile, Mr. Lamb was conversing with Miss Du Plessis.

"You don't seem to mind the doo, Miss Cecile."

"Oh, but I do," she answered.

"Your shoes are parfectly wat, sowking I should think."

"No, they are not wet through; they are thicker than you imagine."

"By the bye, where is his high mightiness, the lawyer, this mawrning?"

"Mr. Coristine has returned to the city."

"Haw, cawlled oway to some pettifogging jawb I suppowse?"

"Such as your Crown Lands case."

"Naw, you down't say, Miss Cecile, thot he's awff ofter thot jawb?"

"I cannot tell what Mr. Coristine may have to do in addition to that. He did not confide his business to me."

"I wonder whot time the stage goes awff at!"

"It will pass the gate," said Miss Du Plessis, consulting her watch, "in ten minutes."

"Haw, ofally onnoying you know, but I'll hov to pock up and leave before breakfost. Please remember me to Morjorie, will you Cecile, if I shont hov time to see her before I gow."

Mr. Lamb took his morocco slippers back to the house, and soon reappeared at the gate, Gladstone bag and cane in hand, looking at the approaching stage. It was filled [Pg 334]up with a roughish crowd, all except one seat in the back, into which he jumped. The driver flicked his horses, and Bridesdale was relieved of the presence of Orther Lom.

"Marjorie," said Miss Du Plessis, "I have bad news for you."

"What is it, Cecile?"

"Your young man has called me by my Christian name, without even putting Miss before it."

"Have you killed him and dug his grave with those eyes of yours?"

"No, I simply told him that Mr. Coristine had returned to Toronto, perhaps on Crown Land business."

"Well?"

"It terrified him so, that he packed his valise forthwith and is gone."

"But how?"

"By the stage. Did you not hear the horn just now?

"No, I was too busy with that delightful Mr. Bigglethorpe. But do you mean to tell me that Arthur has left without a farewell word to anybody?"

"He said, 'Please remember me to Marjorie, will you, Cecile?' What do you think of that?"

"What odious impertinence! I am glad the silly creature has gone, and, were it not for the safety of your land, I wish he had never come."

"It was not he who saved my land, Marjorie."

"Oh, don't I know? Don't talk to me any more! You are hateful, Cecile!"

"If you can forget fifty acts of disinterested kindness, Marjorie, it does not follow that I am to do the same." By which it will appear that Miss Du Plessis had her orders to rub it in pretty hot to her friend, and was rubbing it in accordingly, even though it did smart. Miss Carmichael broke away from her, and ran to the house, leaving her once dear Cecile to follow with Marjorie and Mr. Bigglethorpe.

At breakfast the Squire appeared quite picturesque, with a silk handkerchief tied over his head to conceal and hold on what Marjorie called a plaster of vinegar and brown paper, having reference to the mishaps of Jack and Jill.

"Marjorie," said Mr. Carruthers, "ye ken what Jill got for lauchin' at Jock's heed and the plaister."

[Pg 335]"Yes, Uncle John, but mother isn't here to do it."

"Papa said I was to be your mother now, Marjorie," said Mrs. Carmichael.

"You've got a Marjorie of your own, Auntie, that needs to be punished worse than me."

The colonel looked round the table anxiously, and then addressed the hostess: "I fail to pehceive my deah friend, Mr. Cohistine, Mrs. Cahhuthehs; I sincehely trust he is not unwell afteh his gallant fight?"

"I am sorry to say, Colonel, that Mr. Coristine has left us, and has gone back to Toronto."

"O deah, that is a great loss; he was the life of our happy pahty, always so cheehful, so considehate, ready to sacrifice himself and lend a hand to anything. I expected him back on my hohse."

"Timotheus tells me that Mr. Bangs is going to bring your horse over this evening."

"I'm gey and gled to hear 't, gudewife. I'd like weel tae hae anither crack wi' Bangs. But it's an awfu' shame aboot Coristine; had it no' been for his magneeficent pluck, fleein' on yon scoundrel like a lion, I'd hae been brocht hame as deed as a red herrin'. Isna that true, granther?"

"It's thrue, ivery worrud av it. Savin' the company, there's not a jantleman I iver tuk to the way I tuk to that foine man, and as simple-harrted and condiscindin' as iv he wor a choild."

"Where is that lazy boy Arthur, I wonder?" asked Mrs. Carmichael; whereupon Miss Du Plessis told her story, and all joined in a hearty laugh at Mr. Lamb's fright and sudden retreat.

Mr. Errol, feeling none the worse of the previous day's splore, and still renewing his youth over the fish he and Mr. Bigglethorpe had caught, suddenly remembered and confessed: "Dear me, Mrs. Carmichael, I forgot that I had Mr. Coristine's merschaum, and his tobacco and penknife. Puir lad, what'll he dae withoot his pipe?"

"You naughty man, Mr. Errol, is it possible that you smoke?"

"Whiles, mem, whiles."

"How many pipes a day, now, Mr. Errol?"

"Oh, it depends. When I'm in smoking company, I can take a good many, eh Mr. Bigglethorpe?"

[Pg 336]"Yesterday was a very special occaision, Mr. Errol. You called it renewing your youth, you know, and nimed the picnic a splore."

"I felt like a laddie again at the fishing, Mrs. Carmichael, just as light-hearted and happy as if I were a callant on the hills."

"And what do you generally feel like? Not an old man, I hope?"

"I'll never be a young one again, Mrs. Carmichael."

"Perfect nonsense, Mr. Errol! Don't let me hear you talk like that again."

"Hearin's obeyin'," meekly replied the minister, showing that he was making some progress in his mature wooing.

After breakfast, the company sat out on the verandah. The colonel had to smoke his morning cigar, and courteously offered his cigar case to all the gentlemen, who declined with thanks. "If it were not that I might trouble the ladies," said the minister, "I might take a draw out of poor Coristine's meerschaum." Mrs. Carmichael at once said: "Please do so, Mr. Errol; the doctor smoked, so that I am quite used to it. I like to see a good man enjoying his pipe."

"You are quite sure, Mrs. Carmichael, that it will not be offensive? I would cut off my right hand rather than be a smoking nuisance to any lady."

"Quite sure, Mr. Errol; go on and fill your pipe, unless you want me to fill it for you. I know how to do it."

So, Mr. Errol continued the splore, and smoked the Turk's head. Mr. Terry lit his dudheen, and Mr. Bigglethorpe, his briar. The Squire's head was too sore for smoking, but he said he liked the smell o' the reek. While thus engaged, a buggy drove up, and Miss Halbert and Mr. Perrowne alighted from it, while Maguffin, always watchful, took the horse round to the stable yard. The doctor had heard of Rawdon's capture, and had sent these two innocents to see that all was right at Bridesdale. Miss Halbert sat down by Miss Du Plessis, and the parson accepting one of the colonel's cigars, joined the smokers. He also regretted the absence of Coristine, a splendid fellow, he said, a perfect trump, the girl will be lucky who gets a [Pg 337]man like that, expressions that were not calculated to make Miss Carmichael happy. Mr. Perrowne had proposed and had been accepted. He was in wild spirits, when Mr. Bigglethorpe startled the company by saying, "I've got an idear!"

"Howld on to it, Bigglethorpe, howld on; you may never get another," cried the parson.

"What is it?" asked Mrs. Carruthers, who was shooing the children away to Tryphosa.

"It's a united picnic to the likes. Who's got to sty at home?"

"I have for one," answered the Squire; "yon deevil o' a Rawdon has gien me a scunner at picnics."

"I cannot go," said his wife, "for I have him and the children to keep me."

"Paul, you must go, and Cecile also," interposed Mrs. Du Plessis; "I will attend to the wants of our patient."

"Then," spoke up the fisherman, "we shall have Mrs. Carmichael and Mr. Errol, Miss Halbert and Mr. Perrowne, the colonel and Miss Carruthers, Mr. Terry and Miss Du Plessis, and, please Mrs. Carmichael, Marjorie and me. Can ten get into one waggon?"

"O aye," replied the Squire, "the waggon'll haud nine, and Marjorie can sit on Mr. Bigglethorpe's knees. Hi, Timotheus, get oot the biggest waggon wi' three seats, quick, man!"

Once more, the mighty ham was carved into sandwiches, and others were made of sardines and marmalade. Chickens were hastily roasted, and pies and cakes, meant for dinner and tea, stowed away in baskets, with bottles of ale and cider and milk, and materials for tea-making, and a huge chunk of ice out of the ice-house, and a black bottle that Mr. Terry eyed affectionately. "This is for you old men, grandpapa," said Mrs. Carmichael to the veteran; "now, remember, none for these boys, Errol and Perrowne." Mr. Terry replied: "To be sure, ma'am," but thought in his heart, would it be him that would deprive the boys of a bit of innocent recreation at such a time. Such a looking out there was of hats and wraps, of guns and fishing tackle. The colonel was to drive in person. Mr. Terry was to be chief of the commissariat under Mrs. Carmichael. Mr. Bigglethorpe was to direct fishing oper[Pg 338]ations, and bring, with the assistance of Mr. Terry, the scow and Rawdon's boat to the Encampment lake. Marjorie was wild with delight, and insisted on going with the grandfather and dear Mr Biggles. It was ten o'clock when all the preparations were concluded, and Timotheus brought round the capacious waggon. All the household assembled to see the picnic party off, and the young Carruthers lifted up their voices and wept. The whole ten got in, but there was no free rollicking Irish voice to sing:—

Wait for the waggon.
And we'll all take a ride.

CHAPTER XVIII.

At the Encampment—Botany—Fishing—Matilda—The New Lake—Tillycot—Luncheon—After Recreation—New Visitors to Tillycot—Edifying Talk—Songs on the Way Home—Mr. Bigglethorpe's Departure—Uncle and Niece—Mr. Bangs and Rufus—Ladies Catch a Burglar—The Constable Secures Him—Muggins' Death—Burglars Repulsed—Rebecca Toner—The Clergy Hilarious—A Young Lady Finds a Poem.

Mr. Bigglethorpe, Mr. Terry and Marjorie, with part of the picnic material, got off the waggon at the Richards' place, and proceeded to the lake. They found the punt there, but saw no sign of the skiff. Marjorie inherited her father's love of the water, and greatly enjoyed even the slow progress made by the paddles of her boatmen in the unwieldy craft. Meanwhile, the waggon arrived as near the encampment as it was possible to get; the company descended to the blackened ground; and Mr. Perrowne found a path for the ladies up to the ruins. The horses, sedate, well-behaved animals, were unhitched, and allowed to pick about where they pleased, after which the three gentlemen carried the wraps and picnic baskets and pails to where the ladies stood, inspecting the ravages of the fire. Muggins had come with Mr. Perrowne, and sniffed about, rediscovering the treasure hole which had so nearly proved fatal to the Squire. It was agreed to go down to the water's edge, and encamp upon some green spot, near good fishing, over which the bush fire had not run. Such [Pg 339]a place was found to the right of the caved-in tunnel, a broad patch of fine-leaved native grass, shaded by oaks and maples of second growth. There the provisions were deposited, and, the rugs being spread over the grass, the ladies sat down to await the arrival of the boat party. A good three-quarters of an hour passed before they heard the splash of the paddles, and Muggins ran barking to meet the intruders upon the sabbath stillness of the scene. While waiting, Mrs. Carmichael and Mr. Errol took a stroll in the dark woods adjoining, and brought back some floral specimens in the shape of Prince's Pines, Pyrolas, and Indian Pipes, which were deposited in the lap of the finder's daughter, with a suggestiveness that young lady felt disposed to resent. However, Marjorie's voice was heard just then, and thoughts and conversation were turned into other channels. "Where is the skiff?" asked the fisherman, but nobody could enlighten him; they simply answered that it was not there. The colonel remarked that its absence looked suspicious, and bade them be on their guard. He, accordingly, inspected the arms of the expedition, and finding them to consist of two fowling pieces, those of Messrs. Perrowne and Bigglethorpe, and two pistols borne by Mr. Terry and himself, was comforted. As the fisherman had inaugurated the picnic, it was obviously his duty to act as master of ceremonies. He proposed making two fishing parties, one off the scow, and another off a pier, which he and the gentlemen were about to build out from the shore below the picnic ground.

A large pine had been felled many years before, probably by lumbermen, and two lengths of it, each about eight feet, had been rejected as unsound. These the gentlemen, colonel included, got behind, and rolled down into the water. Mr. Perrowne and the fisherman doffed their shoes and socks, rolled up their trouser legs, and waded in to get the logs in position as sleepers. Three spars of driftwood, bleached white, were found along the bank, and were laid over the logs at right angles, and kept in their places, as were the logs, by stakes hammered into the lake bottom. Mr. Errol and Mr. Terry produced some planks, saved from the fire that devoured the stables, and laid them over the erection, making a substantial pier, that would have been the better of a few [Pg 340]spikes to steady the boards. Mr. Bigglethorpe provided rods and lines, and baited the hooks for the ladies, with grasshoppers, frogs, crawfish and minnows. The last were provided by Marjorie. At the fisherman's suggestion, she had got from Tryphena a useless wire dish-cover that had lost its handle, a parcel of oatmeal, and a two-quart tin pail. Mr. Bigglethorpe had fastened a handle cut out of the bush to the dish cover, thus converting it into a scoop-net. Barefooted, Marjorie stood in the shallow water, scattering a little oatmeal, when up came a shoal of minnows eager for the food thus provided. At one fell swoop, the young fisherwoman netted a dozen of the shiny little creatures, and transferred them all alive to the tin pail. Mr. Errol had a great mind to join her in this exciting sport, but was not sure what Mrs. Carmichael would think of it. The possibility that he might have become Mr. Coristine's father-in-law also tended to sober the renewer of his youth. As Marjorie had practically deserted her friend for the minnows, Mr. Bigglethorpe invited her cousin to accompany him, with Miss Halbert and Mr. Perrowne, in the scow, which paddled off to try how the fishing was at the narrows. The colonel did not care to fish; it was too dirty work for him. Neither did the remaining ladies show any appetite for it; but Mr. Errol and the veteran manned the lately constructed pier, and beguiled some bass that came seeking shelter from the sun beneath it. While the gentlemen were thus engaged, the colonel lying on his back near Marjorie's fishing ground, indulging in a second cigar, the two ladies strolled away, followed by Muggins, to look for more flowers. After they had gone about a hundred yards to the right, the dog ran on before them, barking furiously. Mrs. Carmichael clutched her companion's arm and stood still. "It may be a wild beast, Cecile, or some of those terrible men. Let us go back at once." But Miss Du Plessis calmly answered, "It may be only a bird or a squirrel; dogs often make a great fuss over very little." So they stood and waited.

Muggins' barking ceased. The reason was apparent in the sound of a gentle voice they both knew, saying, "Poor Muggins, good doggie, has he come back again to his old friends?" It was the voice of Matilda Nagle, and she [Pg 341]seemed to be alone. Taking heart, the two ladies went in its direction, and, guided by Muggins, who came back to lead them, they descended to a little bay with a sandy beach, where, in the skiff, sat the woman they sought. She was neatly dressed, and wore a large straw hat. When they greeted her, she showed no astonishment, but invited them to enter the skiff and see the pretty place she had back there. Miss Du Plessis hardly cared to accept the invitation, but the curiosity of the older lady was aroused and she pressed her companion to comply. Bringing the bow of the skiff into the shore, Matilda told them to enter the boat and walk back to the stern. When they had taken their seats, the stern was depressed, and the bow floated clear of the sand. Then, with every motion of an accomplished oarswoman, she rowed the skiff along the shore, altogether out of sight of the other picnickers in scow and on pier. After a few strokes, she told her companions to lower their heads, and, ducking her own, shot the boat through what had

169

seemed a solid bank of foliage, but which was a naturally concealed channel, out into one of the loveliest little lakes eye ever rested upon. No fire had touched its shores, which were wooded down to the sandy margin, the bright green foliage of the hardwood in the foreground contrasting with the more sombre hues of the pines and hemlocks beyond. In little bays there were patches of white and yellow water lilies, alternating their orbed blossoms with the showy blue spikes of the Pickerel weed, and, beyond them, on the bank itself, grew many a crimson banner of the Cardinal flower. Another little bay was passed with its last rocky point, and then a clearing stood revealed, void of stump or stone or mark of fire, covered with grass and clover, save where, in the midst of a little neglected garden, stood the model of a Swiss chalet. "Do not be afraid!" said the woman, catching sight of Mrs. Carmichael's apprehensive look; "there is nobody in it or anywhere near. We are all alone; even Monty would not leave his work to come with me." Thus reassured, the party landed, gathered a few late roses and early sweet peas, and then proceeded to inspect the chalet. The whole building and everything in it was in admirable taste, even to the library smoking-room, which was only disfigured by ugly spittoons and half-burned cigars. Many [Pg 342]books were there, chiefly on chemistry, geology and mineralogy, and there was a large cabinet full of geological specimens, betokening much research and abundant labour in their preparation and classification.

The whole thing was so unexpected, so surprising, that the picnic ladies had to rub their eyes to be sure that it was not a dream; but their astonishment was increased when the woman turned to the younger one and said, "I know you are Miss Du Plessis, for I heard you called so at Bridesdale." Miss Du Plessis answered that she was right. Then Matilda said, "This is all your land, and of course, the land carries the buildings with it. I have forgotten a great many things, but I remember that, you see. So Tillycot is yours too; besides I do not want to stay here any more. Good-bye, I am going home to Monty." At first, the two ladies were afraid she was going to take the skiff away and leave them in the house, but she did not. In spite of their entreaties, she walked quickly up the grassy slope at the back, and disappeared in the forest beyond. "Is it not wonderful?" asked Miss Du Plessis. "Come, Cecile, hasten back, or those poor people will be starving," answered the more practical Mrs. Carmichael.

On their return to the skiff, the presiding matron, while Miss Du Plessis rowed, unfolded a long piece of yellow leno she had picked up in one of the rooms. The channel was quite visible from, what may now be called, the Tillycot end, but when the passengers ducked their heads and emerged, they saw there would be difficulty in finding it from the other side. Accordingly, Mrs. Carmichael bade her companion keep the boat steady, while she stood up, and fastened the strip of gauze to two saplings, one on either side of the opening, making a landmark visible immediately the point was passed that intercepted the picnic party from their view. Rowing round this point, the two travellers appeared, to the astonishment of the fishers on punt and pier. The colonel was stretched out on the grass asleep, and Marjorie, having deserted her minnows, was tickling him about the ears with a long blade, greatly enjoying his occasional slaps at the parts affected, and his muttered anathemas on the flies.

"Oi'm thinkin', Mishtress Carrmoikle, it's gettin' toime fer the aitin' an' drhinkin', wid your lave, mum; but fwhere [Pg 343]did yez foind the skifft?" Brief explanations followed to the veteran and Mr. Errol, who were at once put under orders, the one to light a fire and produce the tea-kettle, the other to fill two pails with clean water, and put a piece of ice in one of them. Soon the colonel and Marjorie came to help, the cloth was laid, the sandwiches, chickens, pies and cakes, placed upon it, and everything got in readiness for the home-coming of the punt. "O Aunty," said Marjorie, "this would be so lovely, if only poor Eugene were here too."

"So it would, dear," answered the sympathetic aunt and mother, "but we must try to make the best of it without him."

The kettle boiled under Mr. Terry's superintendence, the tea was infused in the little Japanese tea-pot, and the colonel, taking from his waistcoat pocket a silver whistle that had done duty for a cavalry trumpet in former days, blew a signal for the information of the punters. In a minute they arrived, bearing two grand strings of fish, only the strings that went through the gills of the bass were hazel twigs. Then there was washing of hands without soap, Mr. Bigglethorpe showing his companions how to improvise a substitute for Pears' by pulling up the pretty little water-lobelia and using the unctuous clay about its spreading roots for the purpose. All sat about the table-cloth, Mr. Perrowne said, "For what we are about to receive," and the *al fresco* repast began. Mrs. Carmichael dispensed the tea, and was displeased with Mr. Errol for declining a cup just then, because he was busy with a corkscrew and an ale bottle. Mr. Perrowne joined him with another; but the fisherman said ale made him bilious and his name was not William. So Mr. Terry produced his special charge, and treated the colonel first, then Mr. Bigglethorpe, and finally his honoured self. The boys, as the matron had termed the two clergymen, seemed to be happy with their beer, somewhat to his sorrow. "It takes moighty little, cornel, to shatishfy some payple, but there's aall the more av it for the risht av us."

Miss Halbert said that Basil had eaten ten sandwiches, two plates of chicken, and an extra drumstick in his hand, a whole pie, and she couldn't count the cake. There were also some empty beer bottles at his feet. He said he was [Pg 344]perfectly ashamed of Fanny's appetite, and would have to petition the Bishop for an allowance from the mission fund, if she was going through life at the same rate.

"If we only had ouah deah boy with us, Cecile, what a pleasuhe it would be," remarked the colonel in a personal way, that caused even the stately Miss Du Plessis to blush.

"Eugene would be better than the whole lot," added Marjorie, with an injured air, and added: "If some people I know hadn't been pigs, he would have been here, too." Mrs. Carmichael called her niece to order, and told the gentlemen they might go away to their pipes and cigars, while she and the young ladies put away the things. The black bottle trio adjourned to a shady nook by the shore, and carried three tumblers and a pail of iced water with them. The bottle revealed its neck from Mr. Terry's side pocket. The colonel handed his cigar case again to Mr. Perrowne, who selected a weed, but could not be prevailed upon to fetch a tumbler. Mr. Errol also declined the latter, having the fear of Mrs. Carmichael before his eyes, but, withdrawing a short distance in his brother clergyman's company, he filled the Turk's head, and said he felt twenty years younger. All sorts of banter and pleasant talk went on between the smoking gentlemen and the working ladies. Mr. Errol distinguished himself above his brethren by bringing up water from the lake and by carrying pailfuls of dishes down to it, for which he received great commendation. Mr. Perrowne had his ears boxed twice by Miss Halbert, it was said, for cheek. Mr. Terry was called upon to deliver up his sacred charge, but demurred. When the ladies made a raid upon his party to recover it, he fled, but Marjorie caught him by the coat-tails, and the spoil was wrested from him, although not before he had poured himself out a final three fingers in his tumbler. Filling it up with ice-water, he drank to the success of the picnic, and especially to absent friends. Mr. Bigglethorpe had been so long fishing in the sun that he thought a rest would do him good. Accordingly, he lay down on his back with his hat drawn over his eyes, and composed himself to sleep. Finally, the clergymen went over to where Mrs. Carmichael was sitting with Miss Halbert and Marjorie, while Miss Du Plessis, having had a [Pg 345]chat with Miss Carmichael, invited her uncle and the veteran to go for a row in the skiff. At first, these gentlemen were disposed to decline, but, when they learned that there was something to be seen, they changed their minds, and accompanied her and Miss Carmichael to the shore.

The colonel was entranced with the little lake, the clearing, and the chalet, as were Miss Carmichael and Mr. Terry. It was decided that a guard, in the form of a caretaker, should be put over the place as soon as possible, and it was suggested that Timotheus and Tryphena would make an ideal pair of guardians. While much of the land round about might be cleared to advantage, it was agreed that the wood around Tillycot lake should be left intact, save the breadth of a road to the main highway. Then they fell to discussing Rawdon, a man plainly of extensive reading, of scientific attainments, of taste in architecture and house-furnishing, and yet an utterly unprincipled and unscrupulous villain. "One would think," said Miss Carmichael, "that the natural beauties of a place like this would be a check upon evil passions and the baser part of one's nature." But the colonel answered, "In the wahah, Miss Cahmichael, I have seen soldiehs, even owah own soldiehs, wilfully and

171

maliciously destyoying the most chahming spots of scenehy, without the least pohfit to themselves or matehial injuhy to the enemy. The love of destyuction is natuhal to ouah fallen human natuhe." Mr. Terry corroborated this statement, and added, "Faix, it sames to me there's jist two sarts an koinds av payple in the wurruld, thim as builds up an' thim as batthers down. For moy paart, I'd lafer build a log shanty an' clane a bit land nor pull a palish to paces." Miss Du Plessis assented, but drew attention to the fact that Rawdon had cleared, built up, and beautified the place, and improved his mind on the one hand, while he was warring against society and law, robbing and even murdering, on the other. "Mr. Errol said once," rejoined Miss Carmichael, "that there are two opposite natures, an old man and a new, in all human beings, as well as in those who are converted, and that no contradiction of the kind is too absurd for human nature." "Mistah Ehhol is quite right, my deah Miss Mahjohie, as all expehience attests. Bret Hahte has shewn it from a Califohnian [Pg 346]standpoint. I have seen it in times of wanah and of peace, bad men, the bent of whose lives was destyuction, risking evehything to save some little memohial of a dead motheh or of a sweetheaht, and good men, the regular couhse of whose cahheah was to do good, guilty of an occasional outbuhst of vandalism."

"Thrue fer yez, cornel, ivery bit. There was a little whipper-snapper av a Shunday Shcool shuperintindent out in a lake, about a hundrid moiles frum the city, wid some dacent lads; and, afore they knowed where they was, the cratur had sit a foine grane oisland a foire for the fun, he sid, av sayin' the blaze. Oi'd loike to have had the shuperintindin' av him fer foive minutes."

The explorers were making their way back to the skiff when the colonel, who had gone back for his handkerchief which he had dropped, said: "There is a pehson coming down towahds the house, a woman appahently." Miss Du Plessis looked up the hill, and saw who it was. "It is Matilda Nagle," she said; "see, she is going back again." At once Miss Carmichael ran up the hill after the retreating figure, and, as she was a good runner, and the poor wanderer was tired, she soon overtook her. Taking both her hands in her own, and kissing the woman, she said: "Come with us, Matilda, and we will drive you home." The half-witted creature responded to the caress, and allowed herself to be led to the boat. "I lost my way," she said. "It is a new road I had never been on before, and I got turned round and came back here three times, and I am very tired." The colonel and Mr. Terry made her enter the boat before them, and then Miss Du Plessis and the veteran rowed the party back to the picnic ground, Miss Carmichael, at her friend's suggestion, removing the landmark put up by her mother as they passed out of the channel. At once Matilda was taken to the shady retreat where Mrs. Carmichael and Miss Halbert were, and all the ladies waited upon her with what was left of the eatables and drinkables, in spite of Mr. Perrowne's appetite. Then, Mr. Terry and Mr. Bigglethorpe went after the horses, and harnessed them to the waggon. The fisherman came back to summon the party and help to carry the baskets. Mr. Errol and Mr. Perrowne agreed to row the punt back to the Richards, and walk the rest [Pg 347]of the way, as the addition of Matilda to the company would make riding uncomfortable if they did otherwise. The picnickers were safely seated, the baskets and the strings of fish stowed away, and the Colonel again took the reins for his party of nine. The two clergymen returned to the scow and paddled home, singing songs, one of which Mr. Perrowne gave in genuine cockney style to a Primitive Methodist hymn tune

"Oh we was rich and 'appy once,
And we paid all we was due,
But we've sold our bed to buhy some bread,
And we hain't, got nowt to do;
We're all the way from Manchesteher.
And we hain't got nowt to do.
"Oh him as hoppresses the pooer man
Is a livin on humin' lives,
An I will be sarved in tohother land
Like Lazarius and Dives,
And will be sarved in tohother land
Like Lazarius and Dives."

Mr. Errol applauded the song, but thought it was hardly right to put a hymn tune to it. He said he "minded an auld Scotch song aboot the barrin' o' the door." So he sang:—

"It fell aboot the Martimas time,
And a gay time it was then O,
When our gude wife got puddins to mak',
And she biled them in the pan O.
The barrin' o' oor door weel, weel, weel.
And the barrin' o' oor door, weel."

Thus, lightening the journey, they arrived at the last lake, said how-d'ye-do to the Richards, and tramped home. "How are you feeling now, Mr. Errol?" asked his comrade. "Man, it's just as I tellt ye, I'm renewin' my youth."

It was just about six when the pedestrians arrived at Bridesdale. Mr. Newberry had been there, anxious about his charge, and had joyfully hailed her appearance in the waggon. Mr. Bigglethorpe insisted on going home; so, after a whispered consultation with Miss Halbert, Mr. Perrowne offered him the doctor's carriage, if he would call in and tell Dr. Halbert that his daughter and all the Bridesdale people were safe, which he agreed to do. The colonel and Miss Du Plessis were up with the dear boy, whose name and virtues Miss Carmichael could hardly hear[Pg 348]mentioned with civility. Marjorie fairly wept over the leave-taking of Mr. Biggles, but commanded herself sufficiently to beg that he would not christen that baby Woollens, Cottons or Piscopalian. He said emphatically that he would not, and then departed, taking home a string of bass to propitiate Mrs. Bigglethorpe. The tea party, spite of Miss Du Plessis' marvellous story of Tillycot, was very slow. The newly engaged couple were full of each other. Mrs. Du Plessis, her daughter and the colonel had Wilkinson on the brain, Mrs. Carmichael and the minister were self-sufficient, and Mr. Terry was discoorsin' to his daughter, Honoria. The only free person for Miss Carmichael was the Squire, and happily she sat at his left.

"Marjorie, lassie," said Uncle John, "you're no lookin' weel."

"That's not very complimentary, uncle; but I am quite well."

"Yon block o' a Lamb has been wearin' ye, I'm thinkin'."

"Not at all, uncle; his gifts and graces are not adequate to that."

"Did Coristine tell ye o' that adverteesment in the Barrie paper?"

"Yes."

"Did he say he had dune onything aboot it?"

"Yes, he said he had written to the Edinburgh lawyer and to other people about it."

"That was unco gude o' the lad, Marjorie."

"Yes, it was very kind."

"What garred the laddie gang awa before the time, lassie?"

"How should I know, uncle?"

"Wha sud ken were it no you, Marjorie, my pet?"

"I am not in Mr. Coristine's confidence."

"I'se warrant ye, Marjorie, he's just bitin's nails to the quick at yon Mrs. Swamp's that's he no here the nicht."

"Oh nonsense, uncle, why should he be so foolish? If he wanted to stay, there was no one to hinder him."

"Weel, weel, lassie, we'll hear frae him sometime aboot yon neist o' kin business. Aiblins, ye'll be a braw leddy wi' a gran' fortune yet, and turn up your bonnie bit nose at puir lawyer chappies."

[Pg 349]"I don't want to turn up my nose at Mr. Coristine, uncle. I think it was very splendid of him to fight for you as he did; but I knew nothing about that when he said good-bye, and I wouldn't shake hands with him."

The Squire put up his hand and stroked his niece's hair. "Puir lassie!" he said, "it's a gran' peety, but ye're no feelin' half as bad as he is the noo, gin I ken the lad, and I think I dae."

It was ten when Mr. Bangs brought home the colonel's horse, and Rufus rattled the missing waggon and team into the stable yard. The latter joyfully saluted his sisters, shook hands with Timotheus, and courteously responded to the greeting of Maguffin. Mr. Bangs, declining any solid refreshment, entered the office, where, besides the Squire, Mr. Errol and the veteran were established. The picnic ladies were tired and had gone to rest, and the colonel was relating the events of the day to the wakeful dominie. Mr. Bangs gave his company an account of the safe lodgment of Rawdon and Davis, and mentioned incidentally that he had seen Mr. Coristine alight from the train at Toronto and go up town. He also cautioned the Squire against divulging the secret of the exhumed box of money, if he wished to save it for Matilda Nagle.

"Squire," he said, "I don't went to elerm you, bet I'm efreid there's gowing to be more trebble to-night; I saw thet tevern-keeper from Peskiwenchow, Devis' brether, et the stetion this merning, with sem of the fellows we fought et the Enkempment. They're not in Kellingwood now, end yeng Hill tells me he saw strenge men kemming this way in the efternoon. I towld yeng Hill to bring his gen, and I brought my mounted petrol kerbine."

"This is terribly vexatious, Mr. Bangs, just as we thought all our troubles were over."

"It is, bet I think it will be their lest ettempt, a final effort to get meney and revenge. We must wound es many ef them es we ken, end ellow the survivors to kerry off the dead end wounded. Thet will be the end of it. I met Toner, end he tells me old Newcome is ep and eway. Toner kent come, for Newcome hes threatened to bern down his house."

A gentle rap at the door interrupted the conversation. The Squire went to open it, and saw his niece in night [Pg 350]attire, with a pale, scared face, hardly able to speak. "What is the matter, Marjorie?"

"There's a man in Mr. Coristine's room, either in the cupboard-wardrobe or under the bed," she answered, and slipped quietly upstairs to her own apartment.

Quickly the information was imparted, and the detective at once took command.

"Mr. Terry, I know you are a good shot. Tek my kerbine which is loaded, and wetch the windows of Mr. Coristine's room outside. Give Mr. Errol a pistol, Squire, and kem on. Ah, Mr. Perrowne, we went you, sir; bring that lemp end follow us."

All obeyed, and slipped up stairs with as little noise as possible. Mr. Bangs opened the door and listened. Intuitively, he knew that Miss Carmichael was right; somebody was in that room. Whispering to Mr. Errol to guard the door, and to the Squire to stand by the wardrobe, he took the lamp from Mr. Perrowne and flashed it under and over the bed. There was nobody there. In a moment, however, the wardrobe door burst open, the Squire was overturned, the light kicked over and extinguished, and Mr. Errol pushed aside, when three feminine voices called: "Help, quick!" and, tumbling over one another into the hall, the clever lookers for burglars found their man in the grasp of three picturesque figures in dressing gowns. They were at once relieved of their capture, and many anxious enquiries were made as to whether they had received any injuries from the felonious intruder. It appeared that they had not received any of importance, and that Miss Carmichael was the first to arrest the flight of the robber.

The household was aroused. The colonel came down with his pistols. Timotheus, Rufus and Maguffin awaited orders, so he ordered them to arm, and posted them as sentries, relieving Mr. Terry from his watch on the windows. Then the examination of the prisoner began. He was the youth who had driven the buckboard over for the doctor on the eventful Monday morning. His name was Rawdon, but he was not the son of Altamont Rawdon. His father's name was Reginald, who was Altamont's brother.

"Where is your fether?" asked Mr. Bangs.

[Pg 351]"I dunno," he answered, sulkily.

"Then I ken tell you. He is dead, berned to death by yore precious encle Eltemont."

"O my God!" exclaimed the youth; "is that so?"

"Esk any of these gentlemen, end they will tell you that yore fether end old Flower were berned to death, end thet a keroner's jury set on their remains, which are buried."

"You say as 'ow my huncle Haltamont did that?"

"Yes, I do, end, whet's more, you know it."

Having terrorized his victim, and antagonized him to Rawdon, the detective drew from him the information that five men, three of Rawdon's old employees, the tavern-keeper Matt, and Newcome, were coming at midnight to burglarize the house and get possession of the dug-up treasure. He confessed that he had slipped into the house while the party was away picnicking, and, knowing that Coristine had left without his knapsack, had looked round till he found a room with knapsacks in it. There he intended to remain till his confederates should require his services to open the house to them.

"Who towld you thet awful lie ebout Rawdon's meney being in this house?"

"Matt knew. Uncle Monty guv it 'im by signs, I guess. Oh, he's O.K., he is."

"Well, sir, yore a prisoner here, end if things don't turn out es you sey, I'll blow yore brains out."

"For goodness sake don't be aisty, mister. I've told you the 'ole truth, I swear."

Mr. Bangs next found out that the robbers were coming in a waggon, which would halt some distance to the left of the house, and that their plan was to set one man at the end of the hall to hinder communication with the servants' quarters, and two on the upper landing to command the front and back stairs, while the remaining burglars ransacked the office and any other rooms in which plunder might be found. The youth's appointed mission was to fire the house, when the search was completed. Hardly had this information been received when Maguffin's challenge was heard, and a well-known voice in military accents replied "A friend." The colonel went out, and brought in Corporal Rigby, panting for want of breath.

[Pg 352]"You've been running, Rigby," said the astonished Squire.

"Duty required it, sir," replied the constable, saluting; "I have come at the double, with trailed arms, all the way from Squire Halbert's. This is his rifle I am carrying. The enemy is on the move, sir, in waggon transport." "You are jest in time, kenstable," remarked Mr. Bangs. "Miss Kermichael and the ether ledies hev jest keptured an impertent prisoner. Hev you yore hendkeffs?"

"I have, sir, and everything else the law requires." Mr. Terry handed a glass to the breathless constable, who bowed his respects to the company generally, smacked his lips as a public token of satisfaction, and proceeded to handcuff and search his prisoner. Several blasting cartridges with long fuses, and other incendiary material, were the results of the last operation.

"If I had my way with him, sergeant-major," the constable remarked, while taking his man under the veteran's command, to the stable, "I would borrow an old chair from the back kitchen, not the front, sergeant-major, tie him to it, and set off all these cattridges under him. He would not go to heaven, sergeant-major, but they would help him a bit in that direction. The man that would cattridge a house with ladies in it should be made a targate out of, sergeant-major."

"Poor, deluded crathur!" replied Mr. Terry, "it's but a shlip av a bhoy, it is, wid a burnt up father, that's been shet on to mischief by thim as knows better. Kape him toight, Corporal Rigby, but be tindher wid the benoighted gossoon." Mr. Bangs ordered all lights out, save one in the thoroughly darkened office, and another in the closet back in the hall, which had no window. He called in the three sentries, ordered the constable to maintain silence in the stable, and slipped out to reconnoitre. The colonel, the Squire and Maguffin prepared their pistols for the first volley on the housebreakers. The clergymen, with Timotheus and Rufus, got their guns in order for the second. It was almost on the stroke of midnight when the detective slipped in and closed the door after him. "They are here," he whispered; "wait for me to ect! Now, not another word." Silent, as if themselves [Pg 353]conspirators, the eight men crouched in the darkened hall, listening to steps on the soft grass of the lawn. There was the low growl of a dog, a short bark, and then a muttered oath, a thud, and a groan that was not human. Poor Basil Perrowne ground his teeth, for he had heard the last gasp of the faithful Muggins. A hand was on the outside knob of the door. Mr. Bangs turned the key and drew back the catch of the lock, when two men thrust themselves in. "Ware's the lights, you blarsted fool?" one of the ruffians asked. The detective drew back, and the others with him, till all five had entered. Then Mr. Perrowne threw open the office door, and Timotheus that of the linen closet. In the sudden light cast on the scene the pistol men fired and the burglars tumbled back, two hanging on to three. "Don't shoot," cried Mr. Bangs to the gunners, "but kem on, fellow them up." After the fugitives they went, not too quickly, although the bereaved parson was longing for a shot at the murderer of Muggins. The burglars were on the road, and the waggon, driven by a woman, was coming to meet them. "Now then," said the detective, as a couple of revolver shots whizzed past him, "give the scoundrels thet velley, before there's any denger of hitting the woman." The four guns were emptied with terrible effect, for the woman had to descend in order to get her load of villainy on. The detective gave but one minute for that purpose, and then ordered a pursuit; but the waggon had turned, and, spite of screams and oaths that made hideous the night air, the woman drove furiously, all unconscious, apparently, that her course betrayed itself by a trail of human blood. "Nen ere killed outright," remarked Mr. Bangs, "bet I downt believe a single mether's sen of them escaped without a good big merk of recognition."

"Do you think we have seen the last of them, Bangs?" asked the Squire.

"Certainly! This wes a lest desperate effort of a broken-up geng."

"I wonder who that woman can have been," said Mr. Errol. "I know most of the people about here by sight."

"She's a very clever yeng woman," Mr. Bangs answered, evasively.

[Pg 354]"It'll no be Newcome's daughter?" half asked the Squire.

The detective drew Mr. Carruthers aside, and said: "It wes to hev been Serlizer, bet she wouldn't gow, even if Ben hed ellowed her; bet a nice gel from wey beck, a cousin of Ben's, whom he had never seen before, end who hed just called on Mrs. Towner in the efternoon, offered to take her place. Her neme is Rebecca Towner, a very nice young person."

"Losh me, Bangs, you're an awfu' man! What deevilment is this ye've been at?"

"I didn't went you to shoot Rebecca Towner, because, next to pore Nesh, she is our best female personater, end her name, when she takes off these clowthes, is Cherley Verley."

"So, you brocht thae villains here by deputy?"

"Yes; they hed to kem, you know, bet I didn't know anything ebout thet boy end their plans, except in a general way. Rebecca woun't leave the pore fellows till they're pretty sick."

Bridesdale was lit up again, for nobody cared to go to bed. The ladies came down to see that the belligerents were safe, and Miss Carmichael and her brave companions received the meed of praise and thanks their splendid services deserved. Sorry for the injuries of the would-be robbers, and perhaps murderers, the Squire was nevertheless relieved in mind by the success of the night's work. In his satisfaction he entered the kitchen, and ordered late supper for his allies in that quarter. Then he summoned Constable Rigby from the stable, bidding him bring his prisoner with him, and give him something to eat. The constable declined to sit in a prisoner's presence in an unofficial capacity, but had no objection to feeding him. When, therefore, the young intruder had eaten his supper, his gaoler standing by, he was reconducted to the separate stable, handcuffed, chained, and locked in, the key being deposited in the constable's pocket. Then, and only then, did Mr. Rigby unbend, and, after supper, indulge with his five companions, male and female, in the improving geographical game of cards. The dining room bell occasionally called Tryphosa away, when, as a matter of course, Timotheus played for her. The colonel, with a [Pg 355]cigar in his lips, and a substitute for fine old Bourbon in his hand, went up-stairs to enlighten his dear boy as to the doings of the night, and, especially as to dear Cecile's magnificent courage. The dominie was terribly concerned about that lady's single-handed contest with the desperate robber, and would not be satisfied until she came in person to let him know she was not hurt in the least, that Marjorie deserved all the credit of the capture, and that the unhappy youth had seemed so taken aback by the character of his hall assailants as to be almost incapable of resistance. The colonel smoked, and sipped, and smiled incredulously, as much as to say, You may believe this young person if you like, my dear boy, but there is somebody who knows better, and can make allowance for a young lady's charming self-depreciation. Mrs. Carruthers, grateful for the safety of her husband and her father, and Mrs. Carmichael, for that of her brother and Mr. Errol, were prepared to be hospitable to a degree. The minister had another opportunity of praising the toddy which the latter lady brewed, and Mr. Perrowne said: "It isn't half bad, you know, but I down't know what Miss Crimmage's Band of Howpe would think of it, if she knew the two temperance champions were imbibing at three o'clock in the morning." The minister remarked that he didn't care for all the Crimmages in the world, nor the Crummages either, whatever he meant by that, for there was no such name in the neighbourhood. "Basil," said Miss Halbert, "you had better take care. I shall not allow you any toddy, remember, but shall subscribe for the Montreal *Weekly Witness*". Mr. Perrowne put a little out of the decanter into his tumbler, with a practised air very unlike that of a Band of Hope patron, saying: "Drowned the miller, Fanny! Must take time by the forelock, if you are going to carry out your threats. But I think I'll drop you, and ask Mrs. Carmichael to have compassion on me. She wouldn't deprive a poor man of his toddy, would you now, Mrs. Carmichael?"

"Mrs. Carmichael," said Mr. Errol, answering for that lady, "would hae mair sense," which shut the parson effectually out of conversation in that quarter.

Miss Carmichael listened to the conversation, and beheld the minister renewing his youth. She heard Mr. [Pg 356]Bangs entertain her uncle with stories about a certain Charley Varley, and Mr. Terry say to Mrs Du Plessis, "Whin I was in Sout Ameriky wid the cornel, God save him." She saw her friend Fanny exciting the lighter vein in the affianced Perrowne, and knew that Cecile was upstairs, the light of the dominie's eyes. There was a blank in the company, so she retired to the room in which she had found the burglar, and looked at the knapsacks there. She knew his; would it be wrong to look inside? She would not touch Mr. Wilkinson's for wealth untold. If he had not wanted his knapsack opened, he should not have left it behind him. But it was open; not a strap was buckled over it. The strap press was there, and a little prayer-book, and a pocket volume of Browning, some cartridges and tobacco, and an empty flask, and a pair of socks and some collars. What was that? A sheet of paper that must have fallen out of Browning. It had fluttered to the floor, whence she picked it up, and it was poetry; perhaps the much-talked-of poem on the Grinstun man. No, it was another, and this was how it ran, as she read it, and hot and cold shivers ran alternately down her neck:—

> The while my lonely watch I keep,
> Dear heart that wak'st though senses sleep
> To thee my heart turns gratefully.
> All it can give to thee is given.
> From all besides, its heartstrings riven.
> Could ne'er be reft more fatefully.
> For thou art all in all to me,
> My life, my love, my Marjorie,
> Dow'ring each day increasingly
> With wealth of thy dear self. I swear
> I'll love thee false, I'll love thee fair.
> World without end, unceasingly.

"O, Eugene, Eugene," she sobbed to herself, "why would you go away, when everybody wanted you, and I most of all?" Then she put the things back into the knapsack, all but the sheet of paper, which she carried away, and thrust into the bosom of her dress, as she saw Miss Du Plessis approaching. In common with the other ladies of the house, they retired to their rooms and to bed, leaving the gentlemen to tell stories and smoke, and otherwise prepare themselves for an unsatisfactory breakfast [Pg 357]and a general disinclination for work in the morning. In the back of the house, geographical studies continued to flourish, the corporal and Maguffin contending with the ladies for educational honours, now being lifted up to the seventh heaven of success, and, now, depressed beneath the load of many adverse books. All the time, a little bird was singing in Miss Carmichael's sleeping ear, or rather in that which really does the hearing, certain words like, "My life, my love, my Marjorie," and then again "I'll love thee false, I'll love thee fair, world without end, unceasingly." When she awoke in the morning, the girls told her she had been crying in her sleep, and saying "O Eugene!" which she indignantly denied, and forbade them to repeat.

CHAPTER XIX.

The Glory Departed—The Mail—Coristine's Letters to Miss Carmichael, Mrs. Carruthers and the Dominie—Sylvanus to Tryphena—Burying Muggins—A Dull Week—A Letter From Coristine and Four to Him—Marjorie's Letter and Book—Telegram—Mr. Douglas and Miss Graves—Reception Parties—The Colonel and Marjorie.

After breakfast on Saturday morning, Mr. Bangs departed, riding his own horse, while Rufus bestrode that of his late friend Nash. As the colonel had no need for the services of Maguffin, that gentleman drove the constable and his prisoner in a cart between these two mounted guards. The clergymen went home to look over their sermons for the morrow, and to make good resolutions for pastoral duty in the week to come, not that either of them was disposed to be negligent in the discharge of such duty, but a week of almost unavoidable arrears had to be overtaken. The Squire was busy all day looking after his farm hands, and laying out work to be commenced on Monday morning; and Mr. Terry went the rounds with him. The colonel's time was spent largely in conversation, divided between his dear Farquhar and his dearer Teresa. When not engaged in helping the hostess and her sister in-law in the press of Saturday's household [Pg 358]work, the young ladies were in consultation over the new engagement, the ring, the day, the bridesmaids, the trousseau, and other like matters of great importance. Marjorie took her young cousins botanizing in honour of Eugene, and crawfishing in memory of Mr. Biggles; then she formed them into a Sunday school class, and instructed them feelingly in the vanity of human wishes, and the fleeting nature of all sublunary things. Even Timotheus could not be with Tryphosa as much as he would have desired, and had to console himself with thoughts of the morrow, and visions of two people in a ferny hollow singing hymns out of one hymn-book. The glory seemed to have departed from Bridesdale, the romance to have gone out of its existence on that humdrum Saturday. The morning passed in drudgery, the dinner table in prosaic talk, and the hot afternoon was a weariness of the flesh and spirit. Just about tea time the mail waggon passed the gate; there was nobody in it for Bridesdale. When the quiet tea was over, the veteran lit his pipe, and he and Marjorie went to the post office to enquire for letters, and invest some of Eugene's parting donations in candy. Half the mail bag and more was for the Squire, the post-mistress said, and it made a large bundle, so that she had to tie it up in a huge circus poster, which, being a very religious woman, she had declined to tack up on the post-office wall. "Marjorie," whispered Mr. Terry, so that the post-mistress could not hear, "I wudn't buoy any swates now, for I belave there's a howll box iv thim in the mail for yeez." Accordingly, they left without a purchase, to the loss of the candy account at the store.

The circus poster and contents were deposited on the office table, and Mr. Carruthers called big Marjorie to sort the mail. So Miss Carmichael appeared, and gave him his own letters and papers. There were two from India for Mr. Terry, that had been forwarded from Toronto, and one from the same quarter for aunt Honoria. Some United States documents were the colonel's property, and a hotel envelope, with a Barrie postmark, bore the name of Miss Tryphena Hill. The bulk of the mail was in one handwriting, which the Bridesdale post-mistress had seen before. Only two letters were there, a thick one for aunt Honoria, and one of ordinary size for Mr Wilkinson, [Pg 359]but there were several papers and magazines for that invalid, and at least half a dozen illustrated papers and as many magazines or paper-bound books for herself, which she knew contained material of some kind in which she had expressed an interest. Then came three large thick packages, one marked "Misses Marjorie, Susan, and Honoria Carruthers," another "Masters John and Michael Carruthers," and the third "Miss Marjorie C. Thomas and Co." The young lady with the Co. laid violent hands upon her own property; but that of the young Carruthers was given to their mother, along with her letters. Miss Du Plessis, failing to receive anything of her own, carried the dominie's spoil to him, and found that some of the magazines, though sent to his name, were really meant for her, at least dear Farquhar said so. Mrs. Carruthers opened her Toronto letter and read it over with amusement. Then she held up an enclosure between forefinger and thumb, saying, "You see, Marjorie, it is unsealed, so I think I must read it, or give it to your mother to read first, in case it should not be right for you to receive it." But Miss Carmichael made a dash at the document, and bore it off triumphantly to her own room, along with her literary pabulum. It was dated Friday afternoon, so that he could not have been long in the city when he wrote it, and ran thus:—

My Dear Miss Carmichael,—I wish to apologize to you very humbly, and, through you, but not so humbly, to Mr. Lamb, for any harsh, and apparently cruel, things I said to or about him. Your aunt, Mrs. Thomas, whom I met, with the Captain and Sylvanus, on their way to the schooner, enlightened me regarding Mr. Lamb's history, of which I was entirely ignorant while at Bridesdale. I should be sorry to think I had been guilty of wilfully wounding the feelings of anyone in whom you take the slightest interest, and I trust you will pardon me for writing that, apart from my natural gratitude for your patience with me and your kindness to me, a mere stranger, there is no one in the world I should be more sorry to offend than yourself.

Believe me,

My dear Miss Carmichael,

Ever yours faithfully,

EUGENE CORISTINE.

P.S.—I have taken the liberty of addressing to you some trifles I thought might interest the kind friends at Bridesdale.   E.C.

The note was satisfactory so far as it went, but there was not enough of it; no word about the gloves, the ring, the half confession, the promise, no word about coming[Pg 360]back. Still, it was better than nothing. Eugene could be dignified too; she would let everybody see that letter.

"I hope you had a nice letter, Marjorie?" asked Mrs. Carruthers. "You would like, perhaps, to read what Mr. Coristine has to say to me." Her niece replied that the letter was quite satisfactory, and the ladies exchanged documents. That of Mrs. Carruthers read:—

Dear Mrs. Carruthers,—Since I left your hospitable mansion I have been like a boy that has lost his mother, not to speak of the rest of the family. I look at myself like the poor newsboy, who was questioned about his parents and friends, and who, to put an end to the enquiries, answered: "Say, mister, when you seen me, you seen all there is on us." Please tell Marjorie Thomas, and your own little ones, that, perhaps, if I am good and am allowed, I may run up before the end of next month, to see if the fall flowers are out, and if they have left any crawfish and shiners in the creek. Will you kindly give the inclosure to Miss Carmichael, with whom, through my foolishness, I had an awkward misunderstanding that still troubles me a good deal. If I had known I was offending her, I would not have done it for the world. I cannot sufficiently thank you for your great kindness to my friend Wilkinson and me, nor shall I soon forget the happiest days of my life in your delightful home. Please make my sincere apologies to the Squire, and any other dear friends whom I may have left abruptly, under the peculiar circumstances of my departure. Remember me gratefully to Mrs. Carmichael, Mrs. Du Plessis, and the young ladies, and give my love to all the children.

I am, dear Mrs. Carruthers,

Very sincerely and thankfully yours,

EUGENE CORISTINE.

P.S.—Please forgive me for sending a few bonbons for the children by this mail.   E.C.

"That's a very nice gentlemanly letter, Marjorie," said Mrs. Carruthers, returning it.

"I like yours better, Aunty; it is not so stiff."

"Nonsense, you silly girl. I am only 'dear' and you are 'my dear.' He thinks of me as a mother, and of you as the chief person in the world. I think you are getting vain and greedy, Marjorie. Well, I must put these bonbons away, or the children will see them, and will be making themselves too ill to go to church. Where is cousin Marjorie?"

"Oh, she is off with her box. Very likely she is giving some to uncle and grandpa. It's a great pity the Captain is not here; he has a sweet tooth. Do you know Tryphena has a letter from Sylvanus?"

"That accounts for her delay with the dishes. What other letters did you get?"

[Pg 361]"None; only a lot of books, magazines, and illustrated papers from Mr. Coristine for the family."

"For the family, Marjorie?"

"Yes; did you not read the postscript?"

"To be sure I did; but you know better than to take that literally,—Marjorie, I think you're deep, deep."

"Do you think he will come here next month?"

"I am going to command my niece, Marjorie Carmichael, or to ask Marjorie's mother, to answer his letter for me, and to insist upon his coming back as soon as possible."

179

The aunt and niece had a kissing match, after which the latter said: "Thank you, aunt Honoria," and went out of the room, ready for the congratulations of the Bridesdale world.

Meanwhile Miss Du Plessis, having laid the dominie's wealth of postal matter before his eyes, at his request read the solitary letter.

My Dear Wilks,—I hope that, under your excellent corps of nurses and guardian angels, you are gradually recovering from your Falstaffian encounter with Ancient Pistol. Don't let Miss Du Plessis see this or she'll faint. I had a toughish ride to Collingwood, and part of the way back, the latter at the suggestion of Hickey Bangs. If I were as plucky for my size as that little fellow is, I could face a regiment. He got the prisoner safely caged, which is the proper thing to say about gaol birds. I came down with him and his select party this morning, meeting Captain and Mrs. Thomas and The Crew on the way. They wanted me to go on a cruise. The kindness of the whole Carruthers family is like the widow's curse; it's inexhaustible. Having been badly sold, however, over a Lamb, and cheap, too, I was not eligible for more sail. I write this, Wilks, more in sorrow than in anger, but I do hanker after those jolly Bridesdale days. Mrs. Marsh received me cordially, but not in character; she was the reverse of martial.——

"Really, Farquhar, this is very terrible," said Miss Du Plessis, laughing; "I hardly know whether to go on. Who knows what dreadful things may be before us?"

"The taste, Cecile, is shocking; otherwise any child might read his letters."

"I left off at 'martial.'"

I went to the office, very unlike the Squire's, and pulled White *off his* stool before he knew I was there. He told me I had just come in the nick of time, for he wants to go to some forsaken watering place down the Gulf—as Madame Lajeunesse said "Law baw"—and that immediately. So, I get my two weeks next month, by which time I hope to have got that next of kin matter straightened out. Then, if I'm let, I'll go up and have my *golf* with Mr. Errol on his links. How are [Pg 362]his links matrimonial progressing, and Perrowne's, not to mention those of Ben Toner, Timotheus, yourself, and other minor personages? Will you commission me to buy the ring?——

"Really, dear, I think I must stop."

"Please do not, dear; there is not much more, is there?"

"Not much, but it is so personal!"

The York Pioneers are having an exhibition of antiques; couldn't you get somebody to send down our two knapsacks, it seems such an age since we started them? Ask Miss Du Plessis and Miss Carmichael what they meant giggling at them at the Brock Street station and on the train that Tuesday morning.——

"Farquhar, did he, did you think it was Marjorie and I who did that, what he calls giggling?"

"I certainly never thought you did, and I think it is only his banter."

"Neither Marjorie nor I could have so disgraced ourselves. Did you not see the school-girls behind us? I was ashamed of my sex."

"When you write Corry for me, you must give him a talking to for that."

"Very well; where was I, oh, yes, 'Tuesday morning.'"

I send a few lines by post. If there is anything in the world I can do for you, Wilks, let me know. If my presence can help you at all, I'll run up at a moment's warning. Love to all at Bridesdale. Sorry I made an ass of myself running away. Mail closes and must stop.

Your affectionate friend,

EUGENE CORISTINE.

P.S.—Tell Errol to keep that pipe as a memorial of a poor deluded wretch who had hoped one day to call him by the paternal name. Fancy having the good minister for a step father-in-law! No such luck, as Toner would say. Adieu   E.C.

"Is she fond of him, Cecile?"

"Yes, very much so."

"Is it not a pity, when they think so much of one another, that a mere trifle should keep them apart, perhaps for ever?"

"Yes it is, but I am not sorry for Marjorie. Kind heart and all, she ought to have had more sense and more forbearance than to have openly preferred that selfish creature, Mr. Lamb, to your warm-hearted friend."

"Corry is the soul of honour and generosity, Cecile, in spite of his hideous taste in language."

[Pg 363]"That is a mere eccentricity, and does not affect his sterling qualities. I shall make it my duty to speak to Marjorie again. Good night, Farquhar dear!"

"Good night, Cecile, my darling, my guardian angel, as Corry rightly says."

Miss Tryphena Hill was reading Sylvanus' letter in the kitchen, first to herself. It ran as follows:—

A Board THE SUSAN THOMAS

Friday noon.

My ever of thee I'm fondly dreaming, Tryphena,—U sed my spelins was caple of beterment so I got the tittle out of a song buk in the cars and wrot it down in the end lefe of the litel testymint you giv me wile the capen and the nusboy was int lukin on. How duz it tak yor i. The capen he brung Mrs. T long for a sale. I see Mr. Corstoene in the cars lukin poekit lik wat is the mater of him. He wooden cum long on the skuner. Giv my luv to Tryphosa and Timotheus i can get there names all rite out of the testymint NEW TESTAMENT Now my ever of thee Tryphena I am orf wunc more on the oshin waive and the hevin depe and If i never more cum bak but the blew waives role over yor Silvanus, the TESTAMENT dont spel it with a why, i left my wil at farthys in the yaler spelin buk on the sheluff nere the side windy levin all my property to my saley Tryphena. I wud of kist u of i had dard beefor I leff wen I am more prospuz i wil dar of I get slaped for it The capen has fyred the blungeybush and i must go ashore with the dingy and get the tavun boy to get ma a nenblope out of the orfis

Yore onley luving afekshunit saler boy

SYLVANUS PILGRIM.

Just as Tryphena had finished this touching epistle, a knock came to the kitchen door. She opened it, and Mr. Perrowne appeared. "Is Timotheus here?" he asked. Timotheus himself answered, "Yaas sir!" when the parson said, "Would you mind bringing a spaide to help me to bury my poor dawg?" The willing Pilgrim rose, and went in quest of the implement, while Mr. Perrowne walked round to the verandah, under which lay the inanimate form of his long lost canine friend, over which he mourned sincerely. The Squire and Miss Halbert came out to assist at the obsequies, and were soon joined by Miss Carmichael and Mr. Terry, all of whom regretted the loss of poor Muggins, the children's friend.

"Do you think you will ever see your dog again, Basil?" asked the doctor's daughter.

"I down't know," replied the parson. "He was part of the creation that St. Paul says is growning and waiting for the redemption of the body from pain and disease and[Pg 364]death. It used to be said that man ownly is naturally and necessarily immortal, but that is rubbish, built up on a pantheistic idea of Platow. If God continues the life of man beyond this world, I see no reason why He should not continue that of a dawg which has shared man's fight here below. There are some such good dawgs, don't you know, moral, kind, faithful dawgs!"

"Is it not the poor Indian who thinks his faithful dog shall bear him company in another world?" asked Miss Carmichael.

"Yes, it is Low; but really, in the great Sanscrit epic of the Bharatan war, King Yoodistheer is represented as refusing immortality, unless the god Indra will let him take his dawg to heaven along with him."

"And left his wife behind, did he not? He did not even hold her something better than his dog, a little dearer than his horse."

"Ow, now, I think Draupadee died before him. Still, it is a strange fact though that some people do love animals better than human beings."

"D'ye ken why?" asked the Squire, with a glance at his niece. "It's because they're no as exacting and fashious as beass."

"Well, there's a lesson for you, Fanny. Good-night. I must gow to my sermon and the hymns." So Mr. Perrowne departed, and the mourners returned to the house.

On Sunday it rained; nevertheless all went to their respective churches, except the Carruthers children, whom Tryphena kept in order, and the colonel, who sat with Wilkinson. Both clergymen preached impressively with reference to the events of the past week, and, at the close of the services, they both repaired to Bridesdale for dinner. In the afternoon they rode to their respective stations, but the Squire stayed at home to teach the children and read to them, while they devoured the contents of the lawyer's elaborate boxes. Tryphosa and Timotheus had to do their singing in the kitchen, in which they were joined by Tryphena and Maguffin. The latter had a very soft rich voice, and made a great addition to the musical performance. The colonel smoked an after dinner cigar, and Mr. Terry a pipe, on a dry part of the verandah. The young ladies overhauled the entire collection of literature [Pg 365]sent to Miss Carmichael and to Wilkinson, and read a good many things that were not for Sunday. As to the three matrons, it is nobody's business what they did with their afternoon. Mr. Perrowne came back to his Fanny in the evening, and Mr. Errol, to have "a crack" with Mrs. Carmichael. Monday was fair enough to permit of a game of golf between the parsons, with the colonel and the veteran for spectators. Miss Halbert went home in the evening, and so, except for the wounded dominie upstairs and the colonel, things went on in the usual jog-trot way, for Miss Du Plessis had been at Bridesdale before. Letters and papers came from Coristine to the bedridden dominie, and another package for Marjorie, before Saturday night, but none for anybody else, for the reason that Miss Du Plessis had written him simply at Wilkinson's dictation, and Mrs. Carruthers and Miss Carmichael had not written at all. In her round of household duties and the care of a young family, the former had forgotten all about her letter, and the latter did not know what to say for herself, and did not feel disposed to humiliate her sense of self-respect by reminding her aunt of her promise. Another Sunday passed without other incident than Mr. Errol's visit. Mr. Perrowne spent most of his spare time at the Halbert's. But, Monday night's post brought an official envelope, type-written, from the offices of Tylor, Woodruff and White for Miss M. Carmichael. She opened it, with a feeling of irritation against somebody, and read the wretched type-writing:—

Dear Madam,—I have the honour to inform you that I have received a cable message from Mr. P.R. Mac Smaill, W.S., of Edinburgh, to the effect, that, as very large interests are involved in the case which I had the honour to claim on your behalf as next of kin, his nephew, Mr. Douglas, sailed to-day (Saturday) for Montreal, vested with full powers to act in concert with your solicitors. As my firm has no written instructions from you to act in the matter, I am prepared to hand over the documents and information in my possession to the solicitors whom you and your guardians may be pleased to appoint to deal with Mr. Douglas on his arrival. Awaiting your instructions, I have the honour to remain,

Dear madam,

Your obedient servant,

EUGENE CORISTINE.

Nothing but the signature was in his writing; this was terrible, the worst blow of all.

[Pg 366]She took the letter to uncle John in the office and laid it down before him. He read it gravely, and then bestowed a kiss of congratulation on his niece. "I aye kennt your fayther was weel conneckit, Marjorie, but lairge interests in the cen o' writers to the signet like Mac Smaill means a graun' fortune, a muckle tocher, lassie. We maun caa' your mither doon to talk it owre." So Mrs. Carmichael came to join the party. Her daughter wished to appoint some other firm of lawyers in Toronto, or else to leave all in the hands of Mac Smaill, but the Squire and Mrs. Carruthers would not hear of either alternative. They knew Coristine, and could trust him to work in the matter like one of themselves; so the young lady's scruples were outwardly silenced, and the Squire was duly authorized to conduct the correspondence with the lawyer. This he did in twofold fashion. First he wrote:—

EUGENE CORISTINE, ESQ.,

Messrs. Tylor, Woodruff and White.

Dear Sir, Although my niece, Marjorie Carmichael, is of legal age, it is her desire and that of her mother that I, in the capacity of guardian, should authorize you or your firm, as I

182

hereby do in her name, to prosecute her claim as the heir of the late Dr. James Douglas Carmichael, M.P., to the fortune advertised by P.R. Mac Smaill, W.S., of Edinburgh as falling her late father, and to conduct all necessary negotiations with Mr. Mac Smaill and his clients in the case. Kindly notify me at once of your acceptance of the trust, and make any necessary demands for funds and documents as they may be required.

Yours,

JOHN CARRUTHERS, J.P.

The other letter was:—

My Dear Coristine, What do you mean, you scamp, by frightening the wits out of my poor lassie with that typewritten bit of legal formality? I have a great mind to issue a warrant for your arrest, and send Rigby down with it, to bring you before me and Halbert and Walker. Man, we would put you through better than Osgoode Hall! But, seriously, we all want you to stick to this next of kin case. Spare no expense travelling about, especially if your travel is in this direction. I think you are not judging Marjorie fairly, not that I would throw my bonnie niece at the head of a prince of the blood, but I have taken a great liking to you, and I know that you have more than a great liking for her. So, no more nonsense. Honoria and Marjorie (Mrs. Carmichael), and all the rest of Bridesdale, send kind love and say "come back soon."

Yours affectionately,

JOHN CARRUTHERS.

Mrs. Carruthers also wrote a note that will explain itself:—

Dear Mr. Coristine,—Please to overlook my long delay in replying to your kind letter and in thanking you for your goodness to the chil[Pg 367]dren, who miss you very much, I intended to get Marjorie or her mother to write for me, but in the bustle of housework, preserving, and so on, forgot, which was not kind of me. Father desires me to remember him to you, and says he longs for another smoke and talk. The others have a delicacy in writing, so I am compelled to do it myself, though a very poor correspondent. John has told me about Mr. Douglas coming out to see about Marjorie's fortune. As I suppose he will want to see her and her mother, will you please bring him up yourself, and arrange to give us a long visit. Marjorie Thomas says there are many new flowers out, and that she and my little ones have hardly touched the creek since you left us.

With kind regards,

Your very sincere friend,

HONORIA CARRUTHERS.

Coristine came home jaded on Wednesday evening. The day had been hot, and in the absence of all the other principals, the work had been heavy. He had interested himself, also, in lady typewriters since his return, and had compelled some to take a much-needed holiday. Four unopened letters from Bridesdale were in his pocket, which he had saved for after dinner. At that meal, the young men of Mrs. Marsh's grown-up family rallied him on his lack of appetite and general depression. He had not made a pun for four days running, a thing unprecedented. Dinner over, he slipped away to his rooms, lit a pipe, and read the letters, the contents of two of which, three including the Squire's formal one, are already known. Another, in a fine clerkly hand, was from Mr. Errol.

My Dear Mr. Coristine,—A thousand thanks for the bonny pipe, which I fear you must have missed. I shall take great care of it as a memorial of pleasant, though exciting, days. I wish you were here to help Perrowne and me at our cricket and golf, and to have a little chat now and then on practical theology. My ministerial friend is that infatuated with Miss Halbert (they are engaged, you know) I can get very little out of him. Mrs. Carmichael sends her kind regards. Her daughter Marjorie is looking pale and lifeless, I do trust the dear lassie is not going like her poor father. We all love to hear her sing, but she has got that Garden of Gethsemane poem of his set to music. It is very beautiful but far too sad for her young life. I have been visiting your friend Mr. Wilkinson, pastorally, and am just delighted with him. He is a man of a very fine mind and most devout spirit. Miss Cecile and he will suit one another admirably. Colonel Morton is wearying for your society, and so is the good old grandfather. If it will not be putting you to too much trouble, will you ask your bookseller to get me a cheap Leipsic edition of Augustine's "De Civitate Dei," as I wish to polish up my patristic

183

Latin, in spite of the trash written in it, that still defiles our theological teaching. I have been visiting Matilda Nagle, and even that old reprobate, Newcome, who got a terrible shaking in his last nefarious adventure. [Pg 368]Matilda is doing remarkably well, and her boy is quite bright and intelligent. Half a dozen cases of sickness in my two charges have kept me from writing, especially as one was a case of infection. Haste ye back to all your warm friends here.

Yours very faithfully,

HUGH ERROL.

The last was a stuffy envelope addressed correctly to Mister Eugene Coristine, in the hand of a domestic, Tryphosa probably, and contained some half dried flowers, among which a blue Lobelia and a Pentstemon were recognizable, along with a scrap of a letter in large irregular characters.

Derest Eugene—Wat makes you stay sew long a way. This is meter as Pol sed to Petre put on the gridel and take of the heter. A lot more flours are out in bloome like the ones I send with my love so dear fete have been in the creke sints you went a way I think that pig is sory she made you go now the chilren granpa sed to me to rite you to come back for a smok. Dere mister Bigls has gone too and no nice one is left give my love to Tyler and say he must let you go for the house is sew quite their is no more fun in it. Feena got a funy leter from old Sil with moste orfle speling the pusy is well but pore Mug in ded. It was verry good of you to send me candes but I like to have you beter

Your litel love

MARJORIE.

The lawyer put this letter reverently away in a special drawer which contained his peculiar treasures, but registered a vow to reprove his little love for applying the word pig to a young lady. He did not know whether to be glad or sorry that Miss Carmichael's case was left in his hands. Of course he could not refuse it. If this man Douglas had to go up to Bridesdale, he supposed he would have to introduce him, and watch him on behalf of his client. A great heiress, perhaps with a title for all he knew, would be very unlikely to take more than a passing interest in her solicitor. Still, it cut him to the heart that the girl was as Mr. Errol represented her. Doubtless she was quite right in not acknowledging his business note in person. Then he laid down his pipe, put his elbows on his knees and his face in his hands, exclaiming bitterly, "O Marjorie, Marjorie."

Before the end of the week, the Squire received answers to his official and non-official letters, accepting the trust confided to him, and regretting that Miss Carmichael had given the writer no opportunity of more fully explaining himself. The non-official letter also stated [Pg 369]that the lady's position was so much changed by the prospect of a large fortune as to make it little less than dishonourable in him to press his suit, at least in the meantime. Mrs. Carruthers also received a promise that the lawyer would, if practicable, accompany Mr. Douglas to Bridesdale. Mr. Errol reported a nice letter received by him from the same quarter, along with the "Civitate Dei" and some reviews. Wilkinson was in clover so far as papers and magazines were concerned, and both Miss Carmichael and Miss Du Plessis were remembered with appropriate literary pabulum of the same nature. More bonbons for the juveniles arrived by Saturday night, and a letter for Marjorie.

My Dear Little Love, Marjorie.—It was very kind of you to remember your poor boy in his exile from home in the big, hot, dusty city. I liked your dear little letter very much, all except that one word about you know who. I am sure you did not think, or you would never have written so of one so good and kind to you and me. You will not say that any more I am sure. I have put your letter and the flowers you were so kind as to pick and dry for me in my best drawer where I keep my treasures. I send you a new picture book just out, with many coloured plates of flowers in it. When I come up you must tell me if you know their names. Please tell your cousins' grandpapa that I would like very much if he were here, or I were there, that we might have a nice quiet smoke and talk together. I am sorry poor old Muggins is dead. You did not tell me what killed him. Tryphena ought to make Sylvanus buy a spelling book to study while he is on watch in your papa's ship. Your papa and mamma asked me to go for a sail with them, but I had to go to town. Now, my little love, be very kind and nice to everybody, and above all to your dear cousins, big and little, and when I come up and hear how good you have been, we will fish in the creek on week days and sing

184

some of those pretty hymns on Sunday. Do you ever go to see my poor sick friend Wilks? I think he would like to see a little girl some times. Try him with a bonbon and with the poetry under the pictures of flowers in your new book. Give my love to all the kind friends, and keep a great lot for your dear little self.

From your own

EUGENE.

"Where is the book?" asked Marjorie, when the letter was read to her by the lady whom she had written so slightingly of. Miss Carmichael looked over her own mail matter, and found a large flat volume addressed Miss Marjorie Carmichael, while the other packages bore simply Miss Carmichael. She opened it up, and found the book demanded. The lawyer had been so full of the name that he had written it mechanically, instead of Miss Marjorie Thomas. Marjorie was not well pleased that her cousin [Pg 370]should have usurped her book, but loyalty to Eugene made her suppress any expression of indignation. Mr. Terry had to read that letter through his spectacles, and Tryphosa; and on Sunday she proposed to invade the sanctity of Mr. Wilks' chamber and interest him in both letter and book.

The Sunday came and went, and then the slow week dragged along. Whoever would have thought that, a short time ago, they had been so cheerful, so merry, even with danger threatening and death at their door. The dominie was out of his room at last, walking about with his arm in a sling, rejoicing in changes of raiment which Coristine had sent from his boarding house by express and the mail waggon. The city clothes suited him better than his pedestrian suit, and made him the fashionable man of the neighbourhood. In conversation over his friend, he remarked that he was pleased to find Corry toning down, writing quiet sensible letters, without a single odious pun. "Puir laddie!" said the Squire, "if it wad mak him blither, I could stan' a haill foolscap sheet o' them. I'm feard the city's no' agreein' wi' him." Before noon on Friday there came a hard rider to the Bridesdale gate, a special telegraph messenger from Collingwood, with a telegram for Mrs. Carruthers. She took it hastily from Timotheus and, breaking the seal, read to the group gathered about her: "If agreeable, Douglas and I will be with you by Saturday's stage. Please answer by bearer. Eugene Coristine." The Squire, home a little sooner than usual, said: "Let me answer that, Honoria," and retired to his office. When he came out, it was with a written paper in his hand, which he read for approval. "You and Douglas heartily welcome—will meet you at station, so do not disappoint." This was accepted by a unanimous vote; after which the messenger partook of a hasty meal, as did his horse, and then galloped back to town. "The waggonette will hold six," said the Squire; "that's Coristine, Mr. Douglas and me. Who are the other three? Will you no come, Marjorie? The ride'll dae ye guid, lass."

No, Miss Carmichael declined, and the Squire was inwardly wroth. Mrs. Carmichael took the place offered to her daughter, and Marjorie Thomas and Mr. Terry volunteered to make up the required number. It seemed [Pg 371]such a long time till Saturday morning, but Marjorie tried to shorten it, by running everywhere and telling everybody that Eugene was coming. The whole house caught the infection. Tryphena and Tryphosa were kept busy, preparing already for a late six o'clock dinner on the morrow. There was a putting of rooms in order for the coming guests, during which Miss Carmichael, conscience stricken, returned the lawyer's verses to the leaves of Browning. She dreaded meeting the author of them, and found comfort in the fact that he was not coming alone. If she had not been, in her own estimation, such a coward, she would have gone on a visit to Fanny, but she dared not thus offend her uncle and aunt, and desert her mother and Cecile. What was he coming for? She had not sent for him. Why did she not want him to come? She did not know, and it was the right of nobody to question her on the subject. She only knew that she was very unhappy, and hoped she would not act stupidly before the stranger from Edinburgh.

That night the Squire received a letter from Coristine, written on Thursday, saying that Mr. Douglas had arrived, and was a very fine fellow; and that, as soon as he had made up his mind to go to Bridesdale, a telegram would be sent. He also requested Mr. Carruthers, if it was not trespassing too far upon his kindness, to secure the rooms, which the postmistress had told him she had to let, for Miss Graves, a young lady in his firm's offices, who needed complete rest and change of scene, and who would either go up by the stage on Saturday or accompany Mr. Douglas and him at a later date. The letter was read at the tea

185

table, and Miss Du Plessis said she knew Marion Graves very well, and was glad to think she would be so near, as she was a lovely girl; but what a strange thing for Mr. Coristine to recommend her to come to Flanders! "Oi'm thinkin'," remarked Mr. Terry, "that av the young lady in dilikit loike, it 'ud be a marcy to kape her aff that rough stage; so, iv yer willin', Squoire, I'll shtay at home an' lave my place to put the poor lady in inshtid av me." Mrs. Carruthers would not hear of the veteran's losing the drive, and resigned her seat. Honoria would probably want her at any rate, so it was very foolish and selfish in her to have thought of going. "There maun be some one [Pg 372]o' the female persuasion, as good old Newberry calls it, to invite Miss Graves and to keep her company, especially if she's an invalid," said the Squire. "I will go, uncle," said Miss Carmichael, quietly. The uncle was amazed at this new turn things were taking, and arranged in his mind to have Miss Graves and Mr. Douglas with him in the front seat, and Coristine between the two Marjories behind. After tea, Timotheus and Maguffin were sent to invite Miss Halbert and the two clergymen to the Saturday evening dinner, but, by Mrs. Carruthers' directions, the postmistress was not notified that her rooms were wanted. If Miss Graves were all that Cecile said of her, she had remarked, she would be better at Bridesdale, and would also be an acceptable addition to the number of their guests.

Saturday morning was a time of wild excitement for Marjorie. She went to the brook by anticipation, to look at the sportive fish, and turned up a flat stone or two, to be sure the crawfish, which the ignorant Timotheus called crabs, were still there. She was prepared to report favourably on the creek. Then she journeyed along the banks, looking for new flowers, and over the stepping stones to the opposite shore, and up the hill to the strip of brush, returning with a handful of showy wild blossoms. Next, she visited the stable yard, and watched Timotheus and Maguffin polishing up the waggonette and the harness of the horses. The colonel was there, and, in answer to Marjorie's enquiry regarding his interest in the scene, said: "You are not going to leave me behind, you little puss, although you did not invite me. I have invited myself, and am going to accompany you on hohseback."

"Are you going to take Guff too, colonel?"

"Who is Guff, my deah?"

"Don't you know Guff?"

"No; I am not awahe that I do."

"Oh Guffee am de niggah
Wif de tah on his heel;
He done trabble roun' so libely
Dat he's wuff a mighty deal."

"You do not shuhly mean Maguffin?"

"Of course I do; who else could be Guff?"

"No, I shall not take Maguffin, seeing we come right [Pg 373]back. Had we been going to put up anywheah, of couhse, he would have been indispensable."

"What a funny name! Do you mean the waggonette?"

"By what, Mahjohie?"

"By this fencepail?"

"Silly child, I did not say that. I said indispensable, which means, cannot be done without."

"Oh!" answered Marjorie; "it's a long word, is it?"

There was no necessity for starting before ten, at which hour Timotheus brought round the waggonette, and Maguffin the colonel's horse. The Squire assisted the two Marjories to the front seat, and took his place beside the younger. The colonel chivalrously bowed to the ladies while on foot; then, he mounted his horse with a bound, and the transport and escort trotted away. Mr. Terry, alone and neglected, betook himself to the Carruthers children, who soon found many uses to which a good-natured grandfather could be put, to the advantage and pleasure of his grandchildren.

CHAPTER XX.

The Collingwood Arrivals—Coristine Goes to the Post Office—Mr. Perrowne is Funny—Bang's Note and the Lawyer's Fall—Coristine in Hospital—Miss Carmichael

Relents—Bangs on the Hunt—The Barber—Mr. Rigby on Wounds—Berry-Picking with the New Arrivals—The Lawyer's Crisis—Matilda's—Miss Carmichael in Charge.

The train had just come in when Squire Carruthers' party arrived at the station, so nicely had he timed his driving. As there was nobody to hold the horses, he kept his seat, while Coristine, looking faultlessly neat in his town dress, came forward and assisted Miss Carmichael and Marjorie to alight. Having asked the former's permission, the lawyer introduced Miss Graves, a young lady not unlike Miss Du Plessis in stature and carriage, but with larger, though handsome, features and lighter complexion. Then, Mr. Douglas, a fine-looking blonde man of masculine Scottish type, was made acquainted with his [Pg 374]fair client, and with her nominal guardian on the box. Finally, the colonel, standing by his horse's head, bowed with genial dignity to the new arrivals, and warmly pressed the hand of his dear boy's friend. The Squire's little scheme was frustrated. His niece, without asking advice or permission from anybody, placed Miss Graves beside the driver, and established herself on the same seat, leaving Marjorie between the two gentlemen on the one behind, after they had bestowed their valises and Miss Graves' portmanteau in their rear. Beyond a ceremonious handshake, Miss Carmichael gave Coristine no recognition, although she could not have failed to perceive his delight at once more meeting her. To Miss Graves, however, she was all that could be desired, cheerful, even animated, and full of pleasant conversation. Marjorie kept her Eugene and the new gentleman busy. She reported on the creek, and presented her faded bouquet of wild flowers, which Eugene received with all the semblance of lively satisfaction. She made many enquiries regarding the big girl in front, and insisted especially on knowing if she was nice. Then she turned to Mr. Douglas and asked his name.

"My name is Douglas," he answered.

"Oh, I know that, even Timotheus himself knows that. I mean what's your real name, your very own, the name your mamma calls you?"

"She used to call me James."

"Oh; have you got a brother called John?"

"Yes; how did you know that?"

"Oh, I know. Then your papa's name is Zebedee, and your mamma's is Salome."

"No, we are not those two James and Johns; they are dead."

"They are the only James and John I know."

"I don't think so. Your uncle, Dr. Carmichael, was called James Douglas, like me."

"Marjorie's dead papa?"

"Yes; your cousin is a sort of far-away cousin of mine; so you must be one of my cousins, too. What do you think of that?"

"I think it's nice to have a growed-up man cousin. I'll call you Jim."

"Marjorie!" said a reproving voice from the front [Pg 375]seat; "you must not talk to Mr. Douglas in that pert way."

"If my cousin lets me call him Jim, it's none of your business, cousin Marjorie. You will let me, won't you, cousin Jim?"

"To be sure, if Miss Carmichael will allow me."

"I don't think it's fair to let her boss the whole show."

Mr. Douglas laughed loud and long over this expression, so novel to his British ears.

"Where did you learn that, Marjorie?" asked Coristine.

"Oh, from Guff; there's heaps of fun in Guff."

Her companions occasionally took advantage of silent intervals to discuss the scenery, and the Canadian lawyer pointed out spots, memorable in the great pedestrian tour, to his Scottish compeer. Miss Carmichael never turned, nor did she give Miss Graves a chance to do so; but the Squire managed to sit sideways, without at all incommoding the ladies, and, keeping one eye on his horses, at the same time engaged in conversation with Marjorie's captives. The colonel also kept close to the vehicle, and furnished Coristine with new information concerning his wounded friend. Miss Graves was informed that she was not to be allowed to go to the post office, and her protests were imperiously silenced by Marjorie's "boss of the whole show." The horses, having come out quietly, went home at a rattling pace, and, a good hour before dinner time, the party arrived at Bridesdale, there to be greeted by Miss Halbert and the parsons, in addition to the occupants of the house.

187

Wilkinson and Mr. Terry received Coristine with enthusiasm, but all the ladies bore down upon the latest arrival of their sex and carried her away, leaving the man, in whom they had expressed so much interest, to feel as if there were a plot on foot to ignore him.

"It must be very pleasant for you, Corry, to find all the ladies so attentive to your lady friend," remarked the Dominie.

"Very pleasant for Miss Graves, no doubt; I can't say the same about myself."

"I should have thought you would have regarded a compliment to her as more gratifying than one to yourself."

[Pg 376]"Haven't reached that heavenly stage of Christian self-abnegation yet, Wilks."

"Perhaps I am mistaken in supposing you take a great interest in the lady?"

"Interest, yes; great, more than doubtful. She's the third girl I've had to send away for the good of her health. The other two knew where to go, and went. She didn't; so I thought of establishing her at the post office. I never dreamt the Squire would come for us till I got his message. I meant to accompany her in the stage, and land her in the arms of Mrs. Tibbs; but here we are, like a bridal party, with Marjorie for bridesmaid and Douglas for best man."

"Thank you, Corry; you have relieved me from a great anxiety. Miss Du Plessis thinks very highly of your —— travelling companion."

"Douglas, do you mean?"

"No, the lady."

"Oh, bother the lady! Wilks, it's a doubly grave situation. If it wasn't for Mr. Terry and Marjorie, I'd cut my stick. As it is, I'll run and engage that post-office room for myself, and be back in time for dinner or whatever else is up. Au revoir." With a bound he was off the verandah, valise in hand, and away on to the road.

When Coristine returned, he was just in time for dinner. He had not been missed; the entire interest of the feminine part of the community was centred in Miss Graves. The Squire took her in, as the latest lady arrival, while Mr. Douglas escorted the hostess. To his infinite annoyance, Coristine, who had brought in Mrs. Du Plessis, was ostentatiously set down by the side of his invalided type-writer, to whom he was the next thing to uncivil. Miss Carmichael, between Mr. Douglas and Mr. Errol, was more than usually animated and conversational, to the worthy minister's great delight. The amusing man of the table was Mr. Perrowne. His people were building him a house, which Miss Halbert and he had inspected in the morning, with a view to the addition of many cupboards, which the lady deemed indispensable to proper housekeeping. Mr. Perrowne thought he would call the place Cubbyholes; but Miss Du Plessis asked what it would really be, the rectory, the vicarage or the parsonage? [Pg 377]Miss Halbert suggested the basilica, to which he replied that, while a good Catholic, he was neither Fannytic nor a Franciscan. He derided his intended bride's taste in architecture, and maintained that the income of a bishop would be insufficient to stock half the storerooms and wardrobes, leaving all the rest of the house unfurnished. As it was, he feared that the charming Fanny would be in the predicament of old Mother Hubbard, while he, unfortunately, would be in that of the dog. "In that case, Basil," said Miss Halbert, "you would be like an inclined plane."

"How so?" enquired Mr. Perrowne.

"An inclined plane is a slope up, you know," answered the mischievous bride elect.

"Talking about dawgs," remarked the victim of the terrible conundrum, "I asked a little girl belonging to one of my parishoners what kind her dawg was. She said it had been given to her as a spanuel, but she thought it was only a currier."

"When I was at the school," said the Edinburgh gentleman, "a boy whom I had offended some way, offered to make the like of me with a street cur and an old gun. He said he could make 'one dowg less' in the time it took to fire the gun."

"What did you do to that boy, Mr. Douglas?" asked Miss Carmichael.

"I left him alone, for he was a good deal bigger than me."

"You were not a Boanerges then?"

"No, I was James the Less."

"What are you dreaming about, Mr. Coristine," called the Squire, "to let all this wild talk go on without a word?"

"I am sorry to say I did not hear it, Squire," replied the moody lawyer, whose little conversation had been wholly devoted to Mrs. Du Plessis.

After dinner, the lawyer repaired to the Squire's office, and briefly informed him, that the fortune in funds and property to which his niece had fallen heir was valued at 80,000 pounds sterling, and that, fortunately, there was no sign of any contest or opposition in the matter. He also explained that, under the circumstances, he felt constrained [Pg 378]to take a brief lodging at the post office, and begged Mr. Carruthers to apologize to his wife for the desertion of Bridesdale. Then, he sought out Mr Terry in the garden and smoked a pipe with him, while his new friend, Mr. Douglas, was chatting on the verandah between Miss Carmichael and Miss Graves. Nobody else seemed to want him or care for him; he had even lost his old friend Wilks, who was absorbed in his beloved Cecile. The colonel was as bad with Cecile's mother, and Mr. Errol with Mrs. Carmichael. The Squire was busy, so the veteran and he were left alone. For a time, they smoked and talked, listening all the while, as they could not fail, to the merry badinage of the party on the verandah. At last he could stand it no longer. He rose, bade his companion good-night, and strolled away on to the road. Once out of observation from the house, he walked rapidly to his new quarters. "Is that you, Styles?" asked Mrs. Tibbs, as he entered. He assured the postmistress that he was not Styles, and asked if there was anything he could do for her. "There is a letter here for Squire Carruthers, marked 'immediate,' and they have not been for their mail," she answered. So, sorely against the grain, the lawyer had to take the letter and return with it to Bridesdale. Mr. Carruthers was still in his office. He opened the envelope and read:—

COLLINGWOOD, Saturday, 12 m.

My Dear Squire,—

Rawdon and his nephew have broken gaol and escaped. Be on your guard. Will go to you as soon as possible.

Yours truly,

J. HICKEY BANGS.

"This is bad news, Coristine. It seems as if we're never to hear the last o' yon villain."

"I'm at your service, Squire."

"I canna thole to ask the colonel, puir man, to lose his nicht's rest, an' I'm no ower sure o' his man. Sae, the granther an' I'll watch till it's twal', if you wi' Timotheus 'll relieve us till two i' the mornin'. What say ye to thon?"

"All right, I'll be here at midnight. Could you get me the cartridges out of my knapsack upstairs?"

The Squire produced the cartridges, and the lawyer went back to his post-office quarters.

[Pg 379]Punctually at midnight he returned, and relieved Mr. Carruthers in front of the house, while Timotheus took Mr. Terry's place behind. It was after one when he saw a figure, which he did not recognize as belonging to any one in the house, steal out of the front door with a heavy burden. He ran towards the figure, and it stole, as rapidly as possible, down the garden to the hill meadow. He knew it now, outlined against the heavens, and fired his revolver. He knew that he had hit his man, and that Rawdon was wounded in the body or in the upper part of a leg. Hurriedly he pursued, entering the strip of woodland towards the brook, when something fell upon him, and two keen qualms of pain shot through his breast. Then he lay insensible. Meanwhile, a lithe active form, leaving a horse tethered at the gate, had sprung to meet a second intruder, issuing from the front door of Bridesdale. The opposing forces met, and Mr. Bangs had his hands upon the younger gaol breaker. A loud shout brought Timotheus on the scene, and the prisoner was secured. The household was aroused. The Squire found his office a scene of confusion, his safe broken open, the hidden treasure and many of his papers gone. Inwardly he muttered maledictions on the sentry of the watch, little knowing that the burglars had entered the house while he was himself on guard. In his vexation, and the general excitement, with the presence of Miss Graves and Messrs. Douglas and Bangs, the unhappy lawyer's absence was overlooked. His shot apparently had not been heard. The vicinity of the house was scoured for Rawdon, but without effect. He had got away with his own money and many incriminating papers, to be a continued source of annoyance and danger. Those who gave any thought to Coristine imagined him asleep at the post office, and wondered at his indifference. Chief among them were the dominie and Miss Carmichael. There was little more rest that night in Bridesdale. One villain at large was sufficient to keep the whole company in a state of uncomfortable disquiet and apprehension. It was still dark, when old Styles came to the gate and asked for Mr. Coristine, as he said the crazy woman was at the post office, and Mrs. Tibbs wanted to know if she could have the use of the spare room for the rest of the night. Then the Squire was [Pg 380]alarmed, and a great revulsion of feeling took place. The man almost entirely ignored was now in everybody's mind, his name on all lips but those which had been more to him than all the rest.

Stable lanterns were got out, and an active search began. Mr. Terry's practiced ear caught the sound of voices down the hillside, and he descended rapidly towards them. Soon, he came running back, tearing at his long iron grey hair, and the tears streaming from his eyes, to the place where his son-in law was standing. "Get a shate or a quilt or something, John, till we take it out av that Och, sorra, sorra, the foine, brave boy!" At once, Mr. Douglas and Timotheus accompanied the Squire to the little wood, and beheld the owners of the voices, Mr. Newcome and his intending son-in-law, Ben Toner.

"Aw niver tetched un, Ben. Aw wor jest goan troo t' bush, when aw stoombled laike over's carkidge and fall, and got t' blood on ma claws," said the former to his captor.

"S'haylp me," replied Ben, "ef I thunk it was you as killed the doctor, I'd put the barl o' this here gun to your hayd and blow out your braiuns."

"Don't let that man go," said the Squire to Toner.

"Ain't that what I come all this way fer?" answered the lover of Serlizer.

The Squire and the veteran, with terrible mental upbraidings, raised the body from its bed of leaves and wood-mould and placed it reverently upon the sheet, which it stained with blood at once. Then, while the colonel held one lantern and Wilkinson the other, Mr. Douglas and Timotheus took the other corners of the simple ambulance, and bore their burden to the house. In his own room they laid Rawdon's victim, removed the clothing from his wounds, washed away the clotted blood, only to despair over the flow that still continued, and rejoiced in the fact that life was not altogether extinct, when they handed him over to the care of the three matrons. While the colonel was sending Maguffin in search of the doctor, the voice of Squire Halbert was heard in the hall, saying he thought it must have been Miss Carmichael who had summoned him, at any rate it was a young lady from Bridesdale. He stanched the bleeding, administered stimulants, and [Pg 381]ordered constant watching. "The body has suffered terribly," he said, "and has hardly any hold upon the soul, which may slip away from us at any moment." The good doctor professed his willingness to stay until the immediate crisis from loss of blood was overpast. To all enquiries he answered that he had very little hope, but he sent the kind ladies away from the death-like chamber, and established himself there with Wilkinson, who would not leave his friend.

The light of a beautiful Sunday morning found Miss Du Plessis, Miss Halbert, and Miss Graves in bitter sorrow, and little Marjorie beside herself with grief. The very kitchen was full of lamentation; but one young woman went about, silent and serious indeed, yet tearless. This was Miss Carmichael. The doctor had come down to breakfast, leaving the dominie alone with the patient, when she took a tray from Tryphena, and carried up the morning repast of the watcher. Then, for the first time, she got a sight of the wounded man, whose eyes the doctor had closed, and whose jaw by gentle pressure he had brought back, till the lips were only half parted. She could hardly speak, as she laid a timid hand on her late principal's shoulder, directing his attention to the breakfast tray. "Look away, please, for Cecile's sake if not for mine," she managed to stammer, and, as he turned his head aside, she flung herself upon her knees beside the bed, and took the apparently dead man's hand in her own, covered it with tears and kisses, and transferred the ring she had once worn back to her own hand, replacing it with one of her own that would hardly slip down over the bloodless emaciated finger. Quietly she arose, and noiselessly left the room, when the dominie returned to his watching and administration of stimulants. When she came down stairs, outwardly calm but looking as if she had seen a ghost, everybody, who was in the secret of past days, knew, and respected her silence. Even Mr. Douglas, who had thought to improve his distant cousinship, read there the vanity of all his hopes, and bestowed a double share of attention upon Miss Graves, charming in her genuine sorrow over her considerate employer. Nobody cared to go to church, but the good Squire pointed out that few could be of any service at home, and that, if ever they had [Pg 382]need of the comforts of religion, it was at such a time. So Mr. Perrowne and Mr. Errol each received a quota of grief-stricken worshippers from Bridesdale, and, at the close of their respective services, mingled heartfelt expressions of sorrow with theirs. The clergymen declined to intrude upon the saddened household, until they could be of some service, so the worshippers returned as they went.

Mr. Bangs and the doctor were the lights of the dinner table, their professional acquaintance with all sorts of trouble hindering them from being overcome by anything of the kind. The former had sent for Mr. Rigby, and had placed the two prisoners in his charge, thus releasing Timotheus and Ben Toner. The latter reported that his patient was restored to animation, but this restoration was accompanied with fear and delirium, the effects of which on a rapidly enfeebled body he greatly dreaded. If he could keep down the cerebral excitement, all might be well, and for this he depended much on the presence with the sufferer of his friend, Mr. Wilkinson. Just as he said this, the dominie's voice was heard calling for assistance, and the doctor and the Squire sprang upstairs. The patient had broken his bandages, and was sitting up fighting with his attendant, whom in his delirium he identified with Rawdon. It was almost ludicrous to hear him cry, as he clutched at Wilkinson's throat: "Ah, Grinstuns, you double-dyed villain, I've got you now. No more free circus for you, Grinstuns!" With difficulty the three men got him down, and bandaged him again; but his struggles were so violent that they feared for his life. He recognized none of them. Little Marjorie heard his loud shouts, and ran to save her friend from his murderers, as she thought them to be. The Squire would have repelled her intrusion angrily, but Doctor Halbert said: "Come, little girl, and tell your poor friend he must be quiet, if he wants to live for you and the rest of us." It is hard to say what prompted her, but she took out a little tear-soaked handkerchief and laid it on Coristine's shoulder, calling, "Eugene, you silly boy". The silly boy closed his staring eyes, and then opened them again upon the child. "Is that you, pet Marjorie?" he asked feebly; and she sobbed out: "Yes, Eugene dear, it's me; I've come to help you to get well."

[Pg 383]"Thank you, Marjorie; have I been sick long?"

"No, just a little while; but the doctor says you must be very very still, and do just what you're told. Will you, Eugene?"

"Yes; where's your cousin, Marjorie?"

"Can you turn your head? If you can, put it down, and I'll whisper something in your very own ear. Now listen! don't say a word till I come back. I'm going to bring cousin Marjorie to you." Then she slipped away out of the room.

"Doctor," said the Squire in a shaky voice, "we had aa better gang awa oot o' the room till the meetin's owre." So the three men withdrew to the hall as the two Marjories entered.

"Eugene," whispered little Marjorie, "have you been good while I was away, and not spoken?"

"Not a word, Marjorie," breathed rather than spoke the enfeebled lawyer.

"I have brought cousin Marjorie to you. You must be very good, and do all she says. Give me your hand." She took the limp hand, with the ring on the little finger, and placed it in her cousin's; then, with a touching little sigh, departed, leaving the two alone. Their hands lay clasped in one another, but they could not speak. His eyes were upon her, all the fierce light of delirium out of them, in spite of the fever that was burning in every limb, resting upon her face in a silly wistful way, as if he feared the vision was deceptive, or his prize might vanish at any moment. At last she asked: "Do you know me, Mr. Coristine?" and he murmured: "How could I help knowing you?" But, in a minute, he commanded himself, and said: "It is very kind of you to leave your friends and come to a stupid sick man. It is too much trouble, it is not right, please go away."

"Look me straight in the face, Eugene," said Miss Carmichael, with an effort. "Now, tell me, yes or no, nothing more, mind! Am I to go away?" As she asked the question, her face bent towards that of the sufferer, over which there passed a feeble flush, poor insufficient index of the great joy within, and then, as they met, his half-breathed answer was

191

"No." She commanded silence, shook up his pillows, bathed his forehead, and in many [Pg 384]ways displayed the stolen ring. He saw it, and, for the first time, perceived the change on his own hand. Then, she ordered him to go to sleep, as if he were a child, smoothing his hair and chanting in a low tone a baby's lullaby, until tired nature, with a heart at peace, became unconscious of the outer world and slumbered sweetly. On tiptoe, she stole to the door, and found many waiting in the hall for news. Proudly, she called the doctor in and showed him his patient, in his right mind and resting. "Thank God!" said the good man, "he is saved. We must come and relieve you now, Miss Carmichael." But she answered: "No, my place is here. If I want assistance I will call my uncle or Mr. Wilkinson." Doctor Halbert told the joyful news to the Squire and the assembled company. The clergymen would not arrive till tea time, so Mr. Carruthers, as the priest of the family, gathered the household together, and, in simple language but full of heart, thanked God for the young life preserved. The doctor went away home, but without Miss Fanny, and, as he drove off, remarked to the Squire, significantly: "There is no medicine in the world like love," a sentiment with which the Squire thoroughly agreed.

The evening was a very pleasant one. Messrs. Errol and Perrowne rejoiced to hear the good news from the sick room, and Mrs. Carmichael gave the former to understand, in a vague, yet to his intelligence perfectly comprehensible, way, that the assurance of her daughter's future happiness would remove a large obstacle in the way of her becoming the mistress of the manse. Mr. Perrowne appreciated Dr. Halbert's consideration in leaving his daughter at Bridesdale. The Du Plessis quartette were even farther advanced than the Carmichael four; and consequently Miss Graves was left to the entertainment of Mr. Douglas. The patient upstairs awoke, feeling very stiff and sore, but quite rational, and almost too happy to speak, which was a good thing, as his strength was that of a baby. He had to be lifted and turned, and propped up and let down, which the Squire generally did for him, under the head nurse's instructions, received from the doctor. Then he had to be fed, and begged to have his moustache curtailed, so as to facilitate the task. Two little hands, a comb, and a pair of scissors went to work, and, without annihilating [Pg 385]the hirsute adornment, so trimmed it as to reveal a well-curved upper lip, hitherto almost invisible. It is astonishing what a sense of proprietorship this "barberous operation," as she termed it, developed in the heiress, who thought more of it than of her prospective thousands. It was past ten o'clock before she consented to yield her post to the devoted Wilkinson, who already began to look upon her as a sister, and to whom she gave directions, with all the gravity and superior dignity of an experienced nurse. The colonel would willingly have taken his turn in the sick room, but Mr. Terry, Mr. Douglas, and the Squire insisted on relieving him. Mr. Bangs was away with Ben Toner and two guns hunting for the Grinstun man. The watchers got along very well through the night, with the exception of the veteran, who was a little too liberal in the application of stimulants, which led to a reappearance of fever, and necessitated his calling in the aid of the ever-willing and kindly Honoria. Both the clergymen had volunteered to sit up with him, whom they were proud to call their friend, but it was not considered fair to impose upon them after the labours of their hardest day.

The morning saw Miss Carmichael in the sick room again, putting things to rights, purifying and beautifying it, as only a woman can, with the romantic and tearful, Shakespeare loving Tryphosa in her train. Poor little neglected Marjorie, who had performed for her young self an art of heroic sacrifice in handing over her own Eugene to her unworthy cousin, was allowed, a great and hitherto unheard of reward, to bring the patient an armful of flowers from the garden, gathering any blossoms she chose, to fill vases and slender button-hole glasses in every corner. She was even permitted to kiss Eugene, although she protested against the removal of that lovely moustache. She offered to bring Felina to lick off the stubble on her friend's chin, but that friend, in a wheezy whistling voice, begged that Maguffin might be substituted for the cat, in case pussy might scratch him. Maguffin came with the colonel's razors, and Marjorie looked on, while he gave the author of his present fortunes a clean shave, and made ironical remarks about moustache trimming. "Guess the man what trimmed yoh mustash fought he was a bahbah, sah?" The patient smiled seraphically, and whistled in [Pg 386]his throat. "Never want to have a better, Maguffin."

192

"It's awful, Guff, isn't it?" asked Miss Thomas, and continued, "it quite gives me the horrows!"

"Dey's bahbahs and dey's bahbahs," replied the coloured gentlemen, "and I doan want ter blame a gennelum as cayn't help hisself."

The barbering completed, Marjorie junior was dismissed with her ally Guff, and the senior lady of that name reigned supreme. The eyes of the feeble invalid, whose heart had been hungering and thirsting for love during a month that had seemed a lifetime, followed her all over the room, and almost stopped beating when she went near the door. But she came back, and held that hot fevered hand on which her modest ring glistened, and cooled his brow, and made him take his sloppy food, and answered back in soft but cheery tones his deprecating whispers. She had him now safe, and would tyrannize over him, she said; till, spite of the weakness and the sharp pains, his eye began to twinkle with something of the old happy light that seemed to be of so long ago, and, smilingly, he murmured: "We are not ready for our graves yet." Miss Carmichael looked severe, and held up a warning finger. "Repeat that, Eugene, and I will send her to take care of you at once," she said; "that is, if she will leave her dear Mr. Douglas for a poor bed-ridden creature like you." As an affectionate salute followed these words, it may be presumed they were not so harsh as they sounded. The doctor came in time for breakfast, but, before partaking of that meal, he visited his patient, eased his bandages, looked to the wounds, and praised the nurse. "He could not be doing better," he said, as he cheerfully descended to the breakfast table.

The constable had respected the sanctity of the Sabbath, and was still in the kitchen, while his prisoners languished in the stables. Tryphena presided over the morning meal, at which Timotheus and Ben sat; and Tryphosa, who had just descended from her labours in the sick room, was giving them so touching and poetical an account of the invalid and his nurses that Timotheus began seriously to consider the propriety of having some frightful injury inflicted upon his own person. Mr. Toner related for the tenth time how the spurious doctor had cured him, and [Pg 387]then proceeded to tell of Serlizer's wonderful skill in pulling through her shot-riddled old reprobate of a father, till "he was eenamost as good as new and a mighty sight heavier 'n he was, along o' the leaud in his old carkidge." Constable Rigby laughed at the wounds of the day, and characterized them as mere scratches, unworthy of mention in casualty despatches. "There was a man of ours, an acting corporal, called Brattles, in the melee at Inkerman, who broke the tip of his bagginet off in one Rooshian, and the butt of it in another. Then he had nothing to do but to club with what the French call the crosse. He forgot that he had not emptied his gun of the last charge so, just as he had floored his fourth Rooshian, the piece went off into his left breast, and the bullet ran clear down him and came out of his boot under the hollow of the left foot. Captain Clarkson thought he was done for; but Brattles asked him for two champagne corks, plugged up the incoming and the outgoing wounds with them, and stuck to it till the Rooshian bugles sounded the retreat. That I call a wound to speak of." Tryphena, who had listened to this story of her elderly admirer with becoming gravity, ventured to ask: "Do officers carry champagne corks about with them on the battle-field, Corporal Rigby?"

"Not all officers, Miss Hill. I never heard that Lord Raglan or Sir Colin did. But the young fellows, of course. How else could they blacken each other's faces?"

"Do they do that?"

"Regular. There was a subaltern they called Baby Appleby, he was so white-skinned and light-haired. Well, one night we had to turn out for an alarm in the dark, and charged two miles up to the rifle pits of the first line. When we came back, the colonel halted us for inspection before dismiss. When he came to Mr. Appleby, he turns to his captain and says: 'Where did you get this nigger in uniform, Ford?' The captain looked at him and roared, for poor Mr. Appleby was as black as Maguffin. The gentlemen had amused themselves corking him when he was asleep."

"Yoh finds it mighty easy, consterble, ter say disrespeckshus remahks on cullud folks," said the temporary barber, entering at that moment. "Ef the Lawd made [Pg 388]as dahk complected, I specks the Lawd knowed what He was a doin', and didn't go foh ter set white folks a-sneezin' at 'em. I'se flissertaten myself ebery day yoh cayn't cohk me inter a white folks."

"They's whitewaush, Maguffin," interpolated Ben "A good heavy coaut o' whitewaush 'ud make a gashly Corkashun of you."

"Yah! yah! yah! I'se got a brudder as perfesses whitewashin' an' colourin'. When he's done got a job, he looks moh like the consterble's brudder nor myuns, yah! yah! yah!"

The corporal frowned, and went on with his breakfast, while Mr. Maguffin gave an account of his shaving adventure, and of the sight of that poor man whose moustache had been trimmed by a non-professional.

Ben was soon after called by the detective to re-engage in the hunt for Rawdon, who was now known to be wounded, and, therefore, to be lurking somewhere in the neighbourhood. Mrs. Carmichael accompanied Mr. Errol on a visit to Matilda Nagle at the post office. The absence of the minister made the morning game of golf impossible, so that Mr. Perrowne had to surrender himself to the care of Miss Halbert, which he did with a fine grace of cheerful resignation. Mr. Douglas expressed a desire to take a walk in the surrounding country, and the dominie echoed it, with the condition that the ladies should share in the excursion. The Squire and Mrs. Carruthers were busy; the doctor had his patient to look after, and expected to be summoned to the other at the post office; and Mr. Terry occupied himself with the children. But Mrs. Du Plessis and her daughter, Miss Graves, Miss Halbert, and, of course the colonel and Mr. Perrowne, were willing to be pedestrians, if the proposers of the tramp promised not to walk too fast. There was a pretty hillside, beyond Talfourds on the road towards the Beaver River, from which the timber had once been removed, and which was now covered, but not too thickly, with young second growth; and thither the party determined to wend their way. Marjorie had intended to stay at home, in the hope of being allowed to see Eugene again, but the doctor had begged her to leave him alone for a day or two, and now the prospect of blackberry and thimbleberry picking on [Pg 389]the hillside was too much for her to resist. Gaining permission from her aunt, she loaded Jim with baskets and little tin pails, and led him away to the road between herself and Miss Graves. The other gentlemen relieved the burdened Edinburghian of portions of his load, and fell into natural pairs with the ladies, Miss Du Plessis and Wilkinson bringing up the rear. There was a pleasant lake breeze to temper the heat of the fine August morning, which gave the dominie license to quote his favourite poet:—

And now I call the pathway by thy name,
And love the fir-grove with a perfect love.
Thither do I withdraw when cloudless suns
Shine hot, or wind blows troublesome and strong.

Anticipating the thimbleberries, he recited:—

Thy luscious fruit the boy well knows,
Wild bramble of the brake.

Miss Du Plessis liked that sort of thing. It was a blessed relief from type-written legal business letters. So she responded in the lines of Lamartine:—

Mon cœur à ce réveil du jour que Dieu renvoie,
Vers un ciel qui sourit s'éleve sar sa joie,
Et de ces dons nouveaux rendant grace au Seigneur,
Murmure en s'éveillant son hymne intérieur,
Demande un jour de paix, de bonheur, d'innocence,
Un jour qui pèse entier dans la sainte balance,
Quand la main qui les pèse à ses poids infinis
Retranchera du temps ceux qu'il n'a pas bénis!

By this it will appear that the two were admirably suited to each other, finding in their companion peculiar excellences they might have vainly sought among a thousand on Canadian soil. "This is a morning of unalloyed happiness, Farquhar," remarked Miss Du Plessis in prose, and, in the same humble style of composition, he answered: "Thank God, Cecile! Think what it might have been had the worst happened to poor Corry!"

"As it is," replied that lady, archly, "the worst has turned out for the best."

"As it was with me," the dominie humbly responded, and relapsed into silence.

Meanwhile, Marjorie trotted on ahead, and, her eyes, made observant by former botanical expeditions on a small scale, found the purplish blue five-flowered Gentian [Pg

194

390]by the open roadside, the tall orange Asclepias or Butterfly Weed, and the purple and yellow oak leaved Gerardias or False Foxgloves in grassy stretches among the second growth. These she bestowed on Jim, who begged to be allowed to present the most perfect specimens to Miss Graves. The walkers were now on the top of the hill, and strayed off into the overgrown clearing. A shout from Marjorie declared that the berries had been reached, and within five minutes the whole party was engaged in gathering, what Mr. Douglas hailed with delight as "brammles." Marjorie accused the colonel of picking for his own mouth, but this was a libel. He picked for Mrs. Du Plessis, whom he established under the shade of a straggling striped maple of tender growth. That lady received the tribute of brother Paul very gracefully, and darkened her lips with the ripe berries, much to the colonel's amusement and their mutual gratification. Miss Halbert stood over Basil, and so punished him with a sunshade, whenever he abstracted fruit for personal consumption, that the man became infatuated and persisted in his career of wrong doing, till he was deprived of his basket, which he only received back after an abject apology delivered on his knees, and a solemn promise to have regard to the general weal. Miss Du Plessis and the dominie would have done well, had not the worship of nature and human nature, in prose and in verse, withheld their hands from labour, and fortunately, as Mr. Perrowne remarked, from picking and stealing. Mr. Douglas was absorbed in admiration for Miss Graves, who, thinking nothing of the handsome picture she made, attended strictly to business, and roused him to emulation in basket filling. Marjorie, with her oft-replenished tin can, aided them time about impartially, as the only honest workers worthy of recognition. Steadily, they toiled away, until the rising sun and shortening shadows, to say nothing of stooped backs and flushed faces, warned them to cease their labours, and prepare to take their treasures home. Then they compared baskets, to the exultation of some and the confusion of others. Miss Graves and Mr. Douglas were bracketed first with a good six quarts a piece. Miss Halbert came next, with Mr. Perrowne a little behind. Miss Du Plessis and Mr. Wilkinson had not six [Pg 391]quarts between them; and, when Marjorie saw the colonel's little pail only half full, she exclaimed: "O horrows!" and said it was a lasting disgrace. But Mrs. Du Plessis smiled sweetly with her empurpled lips, and the colonel did not mind the disgrace a particle. They all went home very merry and full of innocent jocularity.

"Cecile," said the dominie, "I trust you will excuse the adjective, but I should dearly love to hear Corry's jolly laugh just now. Poor fellow, I think I could almost bear a pun."

The audacious Mr. Perrowne overheard the last words, and, with great exuberance of feeling, propounded a conundrum.

"Mr. Wilkinson, why is a pun of our friend Coristine's like your sling? D'ye give it up? Because there's now arm in it now. Ha! ha!"

They had only been a few hours away, but, when they returned to Bridesdale, it did not require clever eyes to see that a great change had taken place. The people were in the house, even the children, but they were all very quiet. Neither the doctor nor the Squire was visible, and instinctively the berry-pickers feared the worst. Mrs. Carruthers told them that excitement had been too much for the enfeebled patient. Happily, he was not strong enough to be delirious, but he seemed sinking, and had fallen into unconsciousness, only muttering little incoherences in his attenuated voice. Doctor Halbert hoped much from a strong constitution, but work and worry had reduced its vitality before the dreadful drain came on the life blood. Soon, he came down stairs with the Squire, both looking very solemn. "Let me go to my friend, Doctor," pleaded Wilkinson, and many other offers of service were made, but the doctor shook his head. "Miss Marjorie is there and will not leave him," he answered; "and, if she cannot pull him through, nobody else can. When she wants help, she will summon you." Then, turning to Mr. Errol, he said: "I will go with you now, and see to that poor woman at the post office." The minister took the good doctor's arm, and they went away dinnerless to attend to the wants of Matilda Nagle, suddenly smitten down with fever while on the way to obey the imperious infelt summons of the unseen Rawdon. Mr. [Pg 392]Newberry was with her, having been driven over by that strange mixture of humanity, Yankee Pawkins, and Mrs. Tibbs was acting as the soul of kindness. The woman's case was a remarkable combination of natural and mesmeric causes, but presented no reason for serious apprehension. The doctor prescribed, and Pawkins drove off at breakneck speed to get the prescription filled by the medical student at his dispensary. Then, he and the minister returned to the sobered and melancholy company at Bridesdale. "Resting, but hardly breathing," was the bulletin that greeted them, when they enquired after the solitary battler for life in the upper chamber. Yet he was not alone; one sad stricken woman's heart was bound to that poor shadow of former vital wealth forever.

CHAPTER XXI.

Matilda Free—The Constable Captured—The Thunderstorm—Rawdon Found—The Lawyer Revives—Inquest—Mr. Pawkins Again—Expeditions—Greek—Committee of the Whole—Miss Graves and Mr. Douglas—Weddings—The Colonel, Wilkinson and Perrowne Off—Arrival of Saul—Errol, Douglas and Coristine Wedded—Festivities in Hall and Kitchen—Europe—Home—Two Knapsacks—Envoi.

That was a dreary Monday afternoon inside Bridesdale, in spite of the beautiful weather without, for the shadow of death fell heavy and black on every heart. Those who had shared in the morning's merriment felt as if they had been guilty of sacrilege. Even Mr. Rigby exhibited his share in the general concern by being more than usually harsh towards his prisoners. About four o'clock there was an incident that made a little break in the monotony of waiting for the death warrant. Old Styles arrived, to say that the crazy woman was no longer crazy. Half an hour before she sat up in bed and cried "Free at last!" and since then, though the fever was still on her, her mind was quite clear. Doctor Halbert took a note of the time, and wondered what the sudden and beneficial change meant. Mrs. Carmichael and Mr. Errol sympathized with [Pg 393]him, rejoicing for the poor woman's sake. The detective and Ben Toner came home, very tired and disgusted with their want of success. When night came, the dominie again offered to stay with his friend, and, in his anxiety, even forced himself into the sick room. Miss Carmichael was very pale, but very quiet and resolute. "He is your dear friend, I know," she said, calmly, "but he belongs to me as he does not to anybody else in the world. I may not have him long, so please don't grudge me the comfort of watching." Wilkinson had to go away, more pained at heart for the sad eyed watcher awaiting the impending blow than for the unconscious friend on whom it was to fall more mercifully. Mr. Bangs took charge of the outside guard that night, in which the clergymen had volunteered to serve. Mr. Rigby took a grey blanket out to the stables, and lay down near his prisoners, with baton and pistol close at hand. About eleven o'clock Ben Toner, on guard before the house, saw a female figure approaching, and challenged. "Squit yer sojer foolins, Ben, and leave me pass," came from the well known voice of Serlizer. "Is the gals up in the kitchen?"

"They is," replied Mr. Toner, humbly and laconically; and his ladylove proceeded thitherward. Miss Newcome looked in upon Tryphena, Tryphosa, and Timotheus, Mr. Maguffin being asleep, and, after a little conversation, guessed she'd go and see Ben. She had found out that the constable had two prisoners in charge, quite incidentally, and listened to the news as something that did not concern her. Instead of going to see Ben, however, she visited the stables. The corporal was evidently tired of lying in front of his captives, and probably proposed to himself an improving game of geography over a mug of cider in the kitchen, for he had risen and unlocked the door. Serlizer stood by it with a stout handkerchief in her hand, in the middle of which was knotted a somewhat soft and unsavoury potato. As Mr. Rigby slipped out, after a glance at his shackled charges, that potato went across his mouth, and was fastened in its place by the handkerchief, firmly, though quickly, knotted at the back of his neck. The terror of Russians and Sepoys struggled for liberty, but he was a child in the arms of the encampment cook. Halters, ropes, and chains of many kinds were [Pg 394]hanging up, and with some of these the Amazon secured her prisoner in a stall. Then she searched him, retaliating upon the constable the indignities he had practised on his former victims. Handcuff and padlock keys were found in his pockets, and with these she silently freed her venerable father, who, in his turn, delivered young Rawdon from his bonds. "Now, you two," said the rescuer, quietly, "go round the end of the stables, cross the road into the bush beyont, and leg out fast as ye can. I'm a-goin' ter foller, and, ef I see ye take a step 'campment way, I'll have ye both hung, sure pop." Mr. Newcome gave the prostrate constable two parting kicks in the ribs, and obeyed orders,

196

while his affectionate daughter followed, until she saw the fugitives safely on the homeward road. Then she strayed back to the kitchen, and guessed, seeing Ben was all safe, she'd go home, as the night was fine. She put in half an hour's irrelevant talk with Mr. Toner after this, and, thereafter, left him, suggesting, as she departed, that, when his watch was over, he might look into the stables, where the horses seemed to be restless.

Simple-hearted Ben informed Mr. Bangs that he had heard noises in the stables, which was not true. Proceeding thither with a lantern he found only one prisoner, who, on examination, proved to be the constable. He had attacked the unsavoury potato with his teeth as far as the tightness of his gag allowed, and was now able to make an audible groan, which sounded slushy through the moist vegetable medium. When released, he was speechless with indignation, disappointment, and shame. Ben flashed the lantern on the handkerchief, and recognized it as the property of a young woman of his acquaintance, whereupon he registered an inward vow to throw off a Newcome and take on a Sullivan. Bridget was better looking than Serlizer anyway, and wasn't so powerful headstrong like. Mr. Bangs came to see the disconsolate corporal, and Mr. Terry sought in vain to comfort him. The detective was not sorry, save for the possibility of the fugitives effecting a junction with Rawdon, who would thus be at the head of a gang again. Otherwise, Newcome was not at all likely to leave the country, and could be had any time, if wanted. As for the unhappy lad, he had suffered enough, and if there were any chance of his [Pg 395]amending his company, Mr. Bangs was not the man to put stumbling blocks in his way. But the demented constable, having recovered his baton, began searching. He explored the stables, the lofts, the coach-house, the sheds, examined every manger, and thrust a pitchfork into every truss of hay and heap of straw. He came outside and scrutinized the angle of every fence, poked every bush, peered under verandahs, and, according to the untruthful and unsympathetic Timotheus, rammed twigs down woodchucks' holes for fear the jail breakers had taken refuge in the bowels of the earth. Ben and Maguffin brought him in by force, lest in his despair he should do himself an injury, and sat him down in an easy chair with the wished-for cider mug before him. He had sense enough left to attach himself to the mug, and draw comfort from its depths. Then he murmured: "Thomas Rigby, eighteen years in service, promoted corporal for valour before the enemy, Crimean and Indian medals and clasps, captured by a female young woman, bound and imprisoned by the same, Attention! no, as you were!" Addressing Mr. Terry he continued: "Sergeant Major, that woman, unless I find her, will bring my grey hairs with sorrow to the grave."

"Come, come, now, corporal dear! shure it isn't the firsht toime a foine lukin' owld sowljer has been captivated boy the ladies. Honoria's blissed mother, rist her sowl in heaven, tuk me prishner wid a luk av her broight black eyes, an', iv she wor livin', she cud do it agin."

With the morning came a thunderstorm, altogether unexpected, for Monday's north-western breeze had promised fine and cooler weather. But the south wind had conquered for a time, and now the two blasts were contending in the clouds above and on the waters of the distant great lake below. The rain fell in torrents, like hail upon the shingled roof; the blue-forked lightning flashed viciously, followed instantaneously by peals of thunder that rattled every casement, and made the dishes dance on the breakfast table. The doctor had been with his patient; and as the clergymen were about to conduct family worship, he whispered to them that the soul might slip away during the terrors of the storm, as he had often seen before. It was a very solemn and awful [Pg 396]time. In vain Mrs. Carmichael, aided by the other ladies, sought to make her daughter rest or even partake of food. How could she? The storm outside was nothing to that which raged in her own breast, calm as was her outward demeanour. Marjorie crouched on the mat outside the bed-room door, and quietly sobbed herself to sleep amid the crash of the elements. But, when another sad dinner was over, the colonel and Mr. Terry bethought them of asking the detective if he knew of the inner lake on the shore of which Tillycot stood. He did not, but saw the importance of searching there. As the last of the rain had ceased, he proposed to explore it, but told the Squire, with whom he communicated, that the skiff his informants had mentioned was not at the place where first found, or anywhere on that lake. Therefore Mr. Perrowne and Mr. Douglas proposed to go with Ben Toner to get the Richards' scow, and meet Mr. Bangs with the colonel and Mr. Terry at the encampment. The two parties armed and drove away. One of the Richards boys, namely Bill, joined the three watermen, and together they propelled the punt to the extent of a punt's travelling capacity; but it was between four and five when the explorers of Tillycot, leaving Ben, Timotheus and Richards on the shore, entered with difficulty through the veiled channel, into the beautiful hidden lake. They saw the skiff on the shore near the house, and soon perceived the numerous blood stains in it. They ran up the bank, entered the chalet, and, at last, in the library, beheld him whom they sought, extended upon the floor. He had died by his own hand, his fingers being still upon the pistol whose bullet had pierced his brain. Mr. Bangs seized a scrap of writing lying on the table, which ran thus:—

"Curse you, Tilly, for leaving me to die like a rat in a hole. I have stood the pains of hell for thirty-eight hours, and can't stand them any longer. They shan't take me alive. Box and that hound Carruthers' papers are covered with brush and leaves under the last birch in the bush, where I finished that meddlesome fool of a lawyer. You know why you ought to give a lot to Regy's boy. It's all over. Curse the lot of you. Here goes, but mind you kill that damnable Squire, or I'll come when I'm dead and torture the life out of you."

[Pg 397]No compassion could follow the reading of this document. There was nothing of legal importance in the chalet, so Mr. Bangs, aided by Mr. Terry and Mr. Douglas, carried the dead man to the punt, and the party in it and in the skiff returned to the Encampment lake. Richards, Ben Toner, and Timotheus carried the body up the hill to the waggon on the masked road. Then they returned to the scow, while Mr. Bangs drove to the post office annex, with the colonel and Mr. Terry, Mr. Perrowne and Mr. Douglas. Ben Toner and Timotheus arrived in the other waggon, soon after the ghastly burden had been deposited in the unfinished hall, and were left in charge, while the others went home to inform the Squire and the doctor. Having done this, the detective took the former to the little wood, and, after a little searching, found the concealed box, which held the incriminating papers as well as the original treasure. But for Coristine's fatal shot, these would have been carried away. On their return, Doctor Halbert said, after consulting Mr. Bang's paper: "He took his life the very hour Matilda exclaimed 'Free at last.' The neighbourhood and the whole country may breathe more freely now that he is gone. Your poor friend upstairs, John, has not died in vain."

"But he's not dead, Halbert!" almost sobbed the Squire.

"Not yet," replied the doctor, gravely.

Coristine had survived the thunderstorm and the finding of Rawdon's remains; and, now that all sympathy in the latter was forfeited, many a one would gladly have gone to the sinking man who fired the shot to tell him, in his own vernacular, that Grinstuns had ceased from troubling. But few dared intrude upon the stillness of his chamber, from the door of which Marjorie had to be carried bodily away. The villain dead, the treasure and papers recovered, Matilda Nagle in her right mind, confidence was restored in Bridesdale, and only one absorbing thought filled all minds. Yet, while the colonel shared his cigar case with Mr. Douglas, and Mr. Terry smoked his dudeen, Mr. Bangs wrote to Toronto an account of the escaped prisoner's death, Miss Du Plessis resigned her type writership to Messrs. Tylor, Woodruff, and White, Mr. Wilkinson sent in to the Board of School Trustees his[Pg 398]resignation of the Sacheverell Street School, and the Squire, on behalf of his niece, signified that her position in the same was vacant, and informed the legal firm of the serious illness of their junior partner. The clergymen returned to their lodgings and their duties, and the constable, having no living criminal to watch over, relieved Timotheus and Ben Toner of their care of the dead. Maguffin had summoned Messrs. Newberry, Pawkins, and Johnson for the coroner's jury in the morning, and no excitement was left at Bridesdale. When night came, all retired to rest, except the one watcher by the bedside of despair. Early in the morning, when the sun began to shine upon the night dews and peep through the casements, a tap came to the dominie's door. He was awake, he had not even undressed, and, therefore, answered it at once. He knew the pale figure in the dressing gown. "Put on your pedestrian suit," she said with eagerness, "and bring your knapsack with you as quickly as possible." He put it on, although the arms of coat and shirt were ripped up for former surgical reasons, and he objected to the blood marks on the sleeves. Then he took up his knapsack, and went hastily to the sick room. His friend was lying on his side, and looking very deathly, but he was speaking, and a wan smile flitted over his lips. "Two knapsacks," he

198

murmured, and, "Dear old Wilks," and, "rum start." Miss Carmichael said: "Put yours here on the table above his, where he can see them," and he obeyed. "Now, stand beside them, and say 'Corry,' gently." The dominie could hardly do it for a queer choking in his throat, but at last he succeeded in pronouncing the abbreviation in an interrogative tone. "Wilks," wheezed the sick man, "O Wilks, she called them pads!" and his eyes rested on the knapsacks. "Stay with him," the nurse whispered, "while I call Fanny." Soon Miss Halbert came, and, walking boldly but quietly up to the bedside, asked: "Who are you calling she, you naughty boy that want to leave us all?" With an effort, he answered: "I beg your pardon, Miss Halbert, but you know you did call them pads." "Well, so they are, you poor dear," she replied, bending over and kissing the white forehead, for which it is to be hoped Mr. Perrowne absolved her; "but you must stay here, for see, I have brought [Pg 399]Marjorie to nurse you till you are fit to carry a knapsack again." Then Miss Carmichael came forward, and the patient became ceremoniously polite in a wheezing way, and was ashamed of himself to be ill and give so much trouble; but he allowed himself to be shaken up and receive his strengthening mixtures, and behaved like a very feeble rational man with a little, but real, hold on life. That was the turning point in the lawyer's career; and, when the doctor descended from seeing him later in the morning, he announced that the crisis was past, and that, with proper care, the Squire's prospective nephew would live. Joy reigned once more in Bridesdale, from Mr. Terry to Marjorie, and from the stately Mrs. Du Plessis to Maguffin in the kitchen.

The only thing to mar the pleasure of that day was the inquest, and even that brought an agreeable surprise. When Matilda Nagle was called, she refused to acknowledge the name, insisting that she was Matilda Rawdon, and producing from her pocket a much crumpled marriage certificate, bearing the signature of a well-known clergyman who had exercised his sacred office in a town within thirty miles of Toronto. This she had taken from the library on the occasion of her last visit to Tillycot. Old Mr. Newberry's face beamed with delight, and that of Mr. Bangs was a curious study, revealing a mind which had joyfully come to a decision it had been struggling after in the face of serious difficulties. When the verdict of suicide was given, the jury dismissed, and he prepared, along with the constable, to deliver over the body of the escaped prisoner into the gaoler's hands, he bade Mrs. Rawdon an almost affectionate goodbye, and made touching enquiries after the welfare of her son Monty. As an honourable woman, she was received, in spite of her late husband's character, and her own unconscious crimes, into the Bridesdale circle, which, however, she soon left in the company of her benevolent host. The Squire informed her that he had a large sum of money in keeping for her and her son, and that Miss Du Plessis would either send her all the furniture of Tillycot, when she was prepared to receive it, or take it from her at an equitable valuation, to either alternative of which she strongly objectd. Before Mr. Rigby finished his midday meal, without which [Pg 400]it was impossible that he, at his age, could travel, Mr. Pawkins twisted the British lion's tail several times, to which the corporal replied sadly: "Had I still been in the British army, sir, I should have been degraded for losing prisoners committed to my guard, but any man who allows himself to speak as you do, sir, of what you are too ignorant to judge of, is degraded already." The cautious Yankee was equally unsuccessful with Ben, who met him with: "Don't give me no more lip about Serlizer and old man Newcome, but jist you tell 'em I've waushed the bilin' of 'em clear off'n my hands fer a gayul as Serlizer ain't a patch on." Then Mr. Pawkins amused himself asking Tryphosa if it was Maguffin or Timotheus was her young man, giving as his private opinion that the nigger was the smarter man of the two. When Tryphena playfully ordered him out of the house, he expressed intense sorrow for Sylvanus' future, but was glad to hear he was getting a present rest, paddling his mud barge round the Simcoe pond. Mr. Pawkins was offensively personal, but kept the table lively, and parted with them, regretting that, having left his catechism at home, he was unable to favour his dear children with a little much-needed religious instruction. The door was slammed behind him, and Mr. Rigby remarked with animation: "Very properly done, Miss Hill, a very timely rebuke of unpardonable American insolence!"

When evening came, the Squire and Mrs. Carmichael mastered courage, and took Coristine's pale-faced nurse away from him with gentle force, the mother taking the daughter's place for a time. After this, Miss Carmichael was allowed no night duty, Wilkinson and the Squire, the clergymen, Mr. Terry, and Mr. Douglas attending to it in turns, while all the ladies, in the same way, relieved her during part of each day. Very slowly, but silently and patiently, the invalid regained his lost strength. He was grateful, sometimes with a few words of thanks, but oftener mutely, with a deprecating look, to all who ministered to his comfort. One day Marjorie was allowed in, and, among other wise remarks, informed her Eugene that "cousin Marjorie wasn't you know what any more." "My little love," he answered, "she's an angel, and always was"; Marjorie was not at all sure of this, but did not like to cross a sick [Pg 401]man. During his progress towards health, there were walks and drives, picnics to Tillycot and the Beaver River, expeditions to town, fishing expeditions with Mr. Bigglethorpe, for whom the lawyer had brought a bundle of new flies, which in his anxious state of mind he had forgotten to deliver, and a four days' trip on the *Susan Thomas*, which pleased Miss Graves and Mr. Douglas immensely. Only two days were actually spent on the water, but, as Tryphena was there in the capacity of cook, and a coloured lady of Maguffin's acquaintance was temporarily engaged for Mrs. Du Plessis, the crew and the manservant were in the seventh heaven of delight. Marjorie, of course, was present, and shared the command of the schooner with her father. She also attached herself a good deal to Jim, and, although resenting the attentions he bestowed upon the big girl, carefully abstained from porcine epithets, a result of Eugene's epistolary instructions. The great Mr. Tylor came up to Bridesdale in person to see his junior, and was duly informed of the engagement between him and the heiress, Miss Carmichael, "Ah, Coristine, my dear fellow, we shall be losing you for the law, now, and, the first thing we know, you will be in Parliament. If not, I may say White is going out of the firm, and Woodruff and I had resolved on Tylor, Woodruff and Coristine for the new style. Your servant, Miss Carmichael! I congratulate my friend and partner on a friend and prospective partner, in life as well as law, so infinitely superior, and I trust you will allow an oldish man to congratulate you on being won by as fine a young fellow as ever lived." When the good Q.C. left the room, the patient remarked: "Everybody shows me so much kindness, now, Marjorie, when I have all I want in yours."

"Is it kindness, Eugene, only kindness?"

"No, no, it is love, Marjorie, isn't it, undying love? Would you think me very foolish if I were to go back for once to Wilks' and my habit of reciting all sorts of poetry?"

"I could not stand all sorts, Eugene. There are some that Marjorie quotes which are simply awful. She says she gets them from Guff."

"Oh, this isn't that kind. It is Greek, Modern Greek:—
[Pg 402]
Ὦ Ἔρωτ' ἀνθηρότατε
Γλυκὲ καὶ ἱλαρώτατε,
Τοῦ κόσμου κυβερνήτη.
Ἔσεν ὁ νοῦς, τὸ σῶμά μου,
Τὸ στῆθος, καὶ τὸ στόμα μου,
Λατρεύει καὶ κηρύττει.
Ô Erôt' anthêrotate,
Glyke kai hilarôtate,
Tou kosmou kybernêtê.
Esen ho nous, to sôma mou,
To stêthos, kai to stoma mou,
Latreuei kai kêryttei.

"That is very pretty, Eugene, for love in a general kind of way—love in the aibstrac', as the metaphysical Scotch girl said."

"What! Marjorie, you know Greek!"

"Yes; my father taught me to read the Greek Testament, and I have read some of it with Mr. Errol."

"Oh, you are a treasure! But I mean your love, and my mind and body, heart and voice."

"That will do, you silly boy. Now lie down, and do not excite yourself any more." But she said in her heart that she did not believe Mr. Wilkinson could quote Greek, and, if he did, Cecile, she was sure, could not understand him.

One evening, by general agreement, a committee of the whole sat in the office, the Squire in the chair. The chairman jocularly asked the colonel, as the senior of the meeting, his intentions. "My intentions, Misteh Chaihman, orratheh ouah intentions, those of my deah Tehesa and me, are to be mahhied heah, if you will pehmit, by Misteh Pehhowne, whom we also wish to unite in holy matymony ouah daughteh Cecile to ouah deah boy Fahquhah. Also, with yoah pehmission, we will place Timotheus and Tryphosa, when mahhied, in chahge of Tillycot and Cecile's fahm heah; and will then jouhney westwahd to the Mississippi, and so southwahd, to show ouah deah childyen theih futuhe inhehitance, and save Misteh Wilkinson's ahm the rigouhs of yoah Canadian winteh. That is all, Misteh Chaihman, three weddings, a meeah tyifle, suh." The colonel laughed, took a little imaginary Bourbon, and whiffed his cigar, while Mrs. Du Plessis, her daughter, and the dominie blushed, but also smiled, to think that explanations had been frankly made and the coast was clear. "I suppose," said the Squire, "it will be my turn next to explain for self and freens. The doctor says my nephew that's to be maun tak' a sea voyage for the guid o's health, [Pg 403]and Marjorie, wha sud be here by richts to speak for hersel', is gaun tae kill twa birds wi' ane stane, tak care o' her husband, and spier aifter her graun' fortune. But the meenister's wantin' tae take her mither wi' him; sae the gudewife and me, we're thinkin' o' sendin' aa the weans tae Susan at Dromore, and makin' a pairty o't. We canna leave Bridesdale unprotreckit, that means Sylvanus and Tryphena 'll be pit in chairge till we're back, and they gang to Sylvanus' ain fairm. Ony mair intentions?" Mr. Perrowne sought the chairman's eye, and addressed him. "Mr. Chairman, unaccustomed as I am to public speaking (derisive cheers), and unwilling as we are to obtrude our private affairs upon what Virgil calls the *ignobile vulgus* (hisses from Messrs. Errol and Bangs and the doctor), nevertheless, on this festive occasion, we owvercome our natural modesty and spirit of self-effacement (more derision) sow far as to remark that Cubbyholes (a dig from Miss Halbert) will be ready for our occupation in the second week of September, about which time the Bishop will make a visitation, including the office of howly matrimony. Meanwhile the bride elect will look forward with pleasant expectation to those precious tyings of the nuptial knot, which will enrich her housekeeping account with liberal marriage fees." Here the parson was compelled to stop, since one of the indignant Miss Fanny's hands was over his mouth, and the other actively engaged in boxing his mercenary ears. "Ony mair intentions?" cried the Squire again, warming to his work. "Pahdon me, Misteh Chaihman, foh rising a second time, but I am given to undehstand by Madame Du Plessis that Maguffin, who accompanies us, has matyimonial intentions towahds her new maid, Sophronia Ann Trelawny Tolliveh; that is all, suh." "I see Maister Bangs has a word for the chair," said the Squire, when the colonel ended. The detective, for the first time in his life, looked uneasy. "I owly wented to sey, Mr. Chairman, thet, within a year, when you are all beck frem yore visit, Mrs. Metilda Rawdon hes premised to bekem Mrs. Bengs. I may also edd thet, frem kenversation with Ben Towner, I hev learned thet the priest is soon to selemnize his union with Miss Bridget Sellivan." The company was aghast, and cried out as one man, "What is to become of Serlizer?" Mr. Bangs [Pg 404]responded: "The yeng weman, Sarah Eliza Newcome, wes the person who rebbed kenstable Rigby of his prisoners. When he kem to know the fect, he conceived sow high a degree of respect fer her kerrage end skill, thet he et wence propowsed to her, end hes been eccepted. Mr. Perrowne hes been esked, I believe, to merry them; is it net sow, Mr. Perrowne?"

"Yes, the corporal bespowke me, as he said; but that wretched Maguffin insists on being married by the Baktis. I'm ashamed of you, colonel, allowing so unhallowed a marriage tie in your household."

"I leave religion, Misteh Pehhowne, to evehy man's conscience." The meeting then adjourned.

Two young people had been sitting on the verandah while the matrimonial congress was going on, and were much amused by what they occasionally heard of the proceedings. Next morning, Marjorie carried off one of this pair by the name of Jim to look for crawfish and shiners in the creek. Under her able tuition, Mr Douglas was making rapid progress in Canadian slang, and treasured in his memory many choice extracts from the words of supposed coloured poets, contributed originally by Guff. The scraps of doleful ballads, taken from the stores of the Pilgrim brothers, Marjorie objected that he did not seem to take stock in. While up to the bared elbows in the crawfishery, the twain heard voices, those of Miss Graves and Mr. Terry, but they kept on turning over stones and shouting all the same. Marjorie had never had the veteran really interested in that creek, so she ran to secure him, while her friend pulled down his sleeves and went to meet the lady. It was a pretty place, the bank of that creek, an ideal spot for a morning stroll, and they were soon out of earshot of the fishers. Mr. Douglas remarked, in allusion to the previous night's committee of the whole, that Bridesdale was going to be Bridesdale indeed, and would soon be no place for single people, like himself and his companion. "But I suppose we will both be gone before then," she answered. "I should have been back a week ago, had not Mr. Tylor kindly lengthened my holiday. It is hard to have to leave this place."

"Very," replied Mr. Douglas, "and harder to leave [Pg 405]the people. I haven't known you very long Miss Graves."

"No, only a few weeks, but very pleasant weeks."

"They have been so to me, and the more I see of you, the more I dislike going away."

"Yes, the people gathered here are delightful, almost a unique party."

"I did not mean the people in general. I meant Miss Graves. I hope that blunt speech doesn't offend you."

"Not at all. It is blunt, as you say, but complimentary."

"I don't want to make compliments, Miss Graves, until I have the right. I want you to come home with me to Edinburgh as my wife."

"This is very sudden and very kind, Mr. Douglas. What do you know of me, a poor girl working for my living?"

"I know more than you think, and honour you for your work and independent spirit. I am not going to say I want to take you away from drudgery, and put you in a better position, because I want you to take me for myself, if I am worth taking, as a man."

Miss Graves looked upon his manly honest face with eyes as honest, yet with the merest shade of coquetry in them, and said: "You are worth taking as a man."

"Then, take me, Marion, and all I have."

"You are not a bit like my picture of a Scotch wooer. You give a poor girl no chance to hold you back."

"But I don't want to be held back. Shall we report ourselves to the matrimonial congress?"

"Oh no, not yet, Mr. Douglas; you take wonderful liberties with a new acquaintance."

Some distance off, Mr. Terry was trying to still the voice of Marjorie. "I saw him, granpa, I saw Jim with my very own eyes. Oh, these men will break my heart!"

The first parties to perpetrate matrimony were Ben Toner and Biddy Sullivan. Mr. Toner, to use his own expressive language, was afraid Serlizer might round on him if he delayed. Therefore, Father McNaughton was called in, and, with the aid of Rufus Hill and Barney Sullivan, groomsmen, Norah Sullivan and Christie Hislop,[Pg 406]bridesmaids, and the Bigglethorpes and Lajeunesses, spectators, the knot was tied. A honeymoon trip of two days to Toronto, where, in their new clothes and white cotton gloves, they were the admired of all beholders, rounded off the affair, and delivered Ben from all fear of the redoubtable Serlizer. Next Sunday morning there was a great commotion in the Church of St. Cuthbert's in the Fields. Miss Newcome, gorgeous of attire, supported by Tryphena in her very best, first marched proudly up the aisle, and then came the corporal, in full uniform, even to his stock, and adorned with medals and clasps which told of his warlike achievements, backed by Mr. Terry in an unostentatious suit of black broadcloth. Shortly before the close of the service, Mr. Perrowne, in his most ecclesiastical manner, called the parties up, and put them through their catechism. The corporal answered with military precision and dignity, and Serlizer, glancing at his martial magnificence, was so proud of the bridegroom that she felt equal to answering a bench of bishops. Mrs. Newcome, who had given her daughter away, remarked, as all the bridal party retired from the vestry to receive their friends' congratulations, that the constable, for a widower, was a very proper man, and Serlizer might have done much worse. To his best man, Mr. Terry, the corporal said: "Sergeant-major, I have got my guard. A prisoner may slip from me, Sergeant-major, but when that strapping woman puts her arms round him, he'll be as helpless as a child. I shall apply to the Council for an increase of pay." Soon afterwards, Maguffin got a holiday, went to Dromore, where Miss Tolliver was sojourning with Mrs. Thomas, took that lady to Collingwood, the coloured Baptist preacher of which united them, and came home triumphantly in the stage with his bride. They received a great ovation in the kitchen, and, Mr. Terry having joined the party, played the geographical game till midnight, as a sober, improving, and semi-religious way of celebrating the event. Mr. Maguffin remarked that the Baktis preacher had promised, out of the two-dollar fee, to insert a notice of the marriage in a leading paper, adding the words, "No Cards," but, said Tobias, "he warn't nebber moah leff in all hees life, 'kase here's the keerds and heaps on 'em. Yah! yah! yah!"

[Pg 407]The colonel was getting anxious to start for the Mississippi, and begged his deceased wife's sister to confer with her daughter, and name the day. The dominie was also consulted, and, seeing it was vain to hope for his friend's restoration to the extent of performing groomsman's duty, he acquiesced in whatever decision should be reached. Mr. Douglas took Coristine's place, and Miss Graves that of Miss Carmichael, and, for both of them, the Edinburgh lawyer ordered from the city handsome wedding presents to bestow upon the two couples, a little proof of generosity gratifying to the lady whom he now regularly called Marion. The said Marion had definitely resigned her situation with Messrs. Tylor, Woodruff, and White. On Thursday morning, St. Cuthbert's in the Fields was a scene of wonder to the assembled rustics, with flowers and favours and lighted candles. Miss Du Plessis, stately and lace bedight, was led in by her uncle, and followed by Miss Graves and Marjorie, while Wilkinson, in elegant morning dress, preceded Mr. Douglas and Mr. Bangs. The colonel, with much emotion, gave his niece away, and Mr. Perrowne made them one. Then came Mrs. Du Plessis, arm in arm with her former husband's faithful servant, Mr. Terry, and behind her followed Miss Halbert, training for her own approaching celebration. Mr. Errol was the colonel's right hand man. The second couple was united, and, amid the strains of the wedding march on the parlour organ, there went on salutes, congratulations, and hysterical little weepings, until the serious business of affixing signatures in the vestry called the contracting and witnessing parties to order. Then they retired to Bridesdale, where there was a wedding breakfast, at which Mr. Perrowne, elated with liberal fees, was the soul of jocularity, and Mr. Douglas let the cat out of the bag as to his relations with Miss Graves. Mr. Bangs sang "He's a jolly good fellow" to every toast indiscriminately. The Squire was felicitous in his presidential remarks; but Mr. Terry broke down at the thought of parting with Madame and with Miss Ceshile that was. Mr. Errol made a good common-sense speech, and alluded roguishly to the colonel's setting a good example that even ministers were not too good to follow. Marjorie, in the dignity of a bridesmaid, slipped away to bring Cousin Marjorie down, [Pg 408]and was accompanied by the new brides, who hugged Miss Carmichael, and implanted motherly and sisterly kisses on the cheek of the only man who was left out of the festivities. Lastly, Wilkinson appeared on the scene with the colonel, and took a most affectionate leave of his friend. "You will not forget me, Corry?" said the late dominie. "Never, Wilks, never, nor you me I hope. I'll tell you, let us each carry away our knapsacks, and, when we look at them, think of each other, and the happy chance that brought us here together." The Squire's voice rung out: "Come, come, good people, pack up quick, for the carriage is at the door." The valises were got down by Timotheus, who received large tips. The two ladies and Wilkinson got in with the Squire, and the new Mrs. Maguffin occupied the hind seat, while the colonel and his servant rode away amid much throwing of old shoes and rice, and waving of handkerchiefs, to make steamboat connections at Collingwood. The departure of so large a company left quite a blank at Bridesdale.

The Bishop, a gentlemanly cleric in orthodox hat and gaiters, arrived on Saturday with his examining chaplain. Mr. Perrowne conducted them to Dr. Halbert's, where the Squire, Mr. Douglas and Mr. Errol, with the ladies, were invited to meet them. The Bishop turned out to be much more liberal and evangelical in his views than the clergyman under visitation.

203

On Sunday, there was a confirmation service, and, on the following Monday, St. Cuthbert's put on its festal robes once more. Mr. Douglas and Mr. Errol stood by Mr. Perrowne, and Miss Graves and Miss Carmichael by Miss Fanny, whom the doctor gave away in person. The Bishop did his duty well, and afterwards honoured the wedding breakfast with his presence. The sight of his diocesan kept Mr. Perrowne in order, and devolved the jocularity on the Squire and the doctor. Mr. Terry was at home with Coristine, describing the ceremony; and somebody at the Halbert's hospitable table was longing for a chance to replace him. This, however, she could not effect without its being noticed. The examining chaplain fell foul of Mr. Errol by remarking that, when Scotch Presbyterians came into the church, they generally did well, both in England and in Canada, several of them having risen to the episcopate. "That minds me," [Pg 409]answered the minister, intentionally putting on his broad Scotch, "that minds me o' Jockey Strachan, that was Bishop o' Toronto. He met a Kirk man aince, frae Markham, I'm thinkin', that had a threadbare coat. 'Man,' said he till's auld freend, 'yon's a shockin' worn-out coat. Can yer freens i' the Kirk no dae better than that by ye?' 'Toot, toot, Jockey,' said the Kirk man, 'what ails ye at the coat? It's no turned yet.'" The sensible Bishop saw that the chaplain, who was preparing to reply, would probably put his foot farther in, and turned the conversation into other channels. Then the wedding presents were re-examined, the bride donned her travelling costume, and, amid affectionate leave takings, the doctor drove off his daughter and son-in-law, with the clerics, toward the distant railway station, en route for Ottawa, Montreal and Lake George. The Bridesdale party went home, and, while Mrs. Carmichael and Miss Graves were attended by their respective cavaliers, Miss Carmichael flew to the bedside where Mr. Terry kept cheerful guard.

Everything hinged now upon the sick man's health. "He must be got away, John, before the winter comes," the doctor had said to the Squire, and all wrought with this end in view. Some time before Maguffin left, he had determined, with his Marjorie's permission, to give up being shaved and let his beard grow, and now the beard was there, long, brown and silky, a very respectable beard. But the face above it was very pale yet, and the cruel knife wounds were still sore, and the whole man enfeebled in limb by long bed-keeping. One pleasant day, far on in September, the doctor allowed him to rise, and, between the Squire and Mr. Terry, he was raised up and dressed. Then they carried the wasted form out into the autumn sun, and laid him on a couch on the verandah. Marjorie and all the little Carruthers came to see him, with bouquets of garden flowers. Timotheus ventured to pay his respects, and even Tryphena came round to congratulate him on his recovery. "Shall I read Wordsworth to you, dear?" asked Miss Carmichael, ironically.

"Marjorie," answered a beard-muffled voice, "your single word's worth more than all in that old duffer's poems," which the lady took as an indication that her patient was improving.

[Pg 410]"They are all depending on us to fix the day, Eugene; when will you be strong enough?"

"Any time, Marjorie; what's to-day?"

"Saturday, you foolish man, don't you smell the preparations for Sunday?"

"And the New York steamer sails on Saturday?"

"Yes."

"Well, if we are all married next Wednesday, we shall have time to get to New York easily on Saturday morning."

"Then I will get uncle to arrange with papa Errol, and to summon the Captain and auntie and Sylvanus."

"Oh yes, and Bigglethorpe and Bangs, and old Mrs. Hill. I would like to have Ben here, too, if you wouldn't mind, Marjorie."

"We shall have everybody, and leave here on Thursday morning, to get you well on the sea."

Mr. Terry came to ask if Mr. Coristine didn't think the least draw of a pipe would do him good. The invalid thought it would, and, while the veteran went upstairs to fetch the lawyer's long-unused briar, Miss Carmichael left him, ostensibly offended that he preferred a pipe to her society, yet inwardly glad that he was strong enough to relish tobacco again. Mr. Douglas joined the smokers, and they had a very jolly time. "What will you do, Mr. Terry, when we are all gone!" asked the Edinburgh lawyer. "It 'ull be gone too Oi will mysilf by that toime," replied the veteran.

"I mean, when we are on the Atlantic."

"Plaze God, Oi'll be an the Atlantic mysilf."

"What, are you coming with us?"

"Av coorse! D'ye think the departmint cud ha done so long wit'out me iv Oi hadn't shint in my risignaation?"

"Then you are really going across for a holiday?"

"Oi'm goin' to lit Honoria git a shmill av the Oirish cloimate, an' a peep at the ould shod, fwhere her anshisters is slapin' it's many a long year."

"What a glorious time we're going to have!"

"Troth for you, sor, an' we'll sit this bhoy on his pins agin."

Many letters were despatched that afternoon, and Timotheus was kept busy, inviting parties whom the post [Pg 411]was slow in reaching. On Sunday, there being no service at St. Cuthbert's in the Fields, the Kirk was crowded, and Mr. Errol announced a service of special interest on Wednesday morning at 11 o'clock, when his co-presbyter, the Rev. Dr. MacPhun, would officiate. His own text was "It is not good that the man should be alone," and towards the close of the service he stated that the Presbytery had given him leave of absence for three months, which he intended to spend in Britain, during which time his people would have an opportunity of hearing many profitable preachers, under Dr. MacPhun's moderatorship *pro tem*. Monday was a day of trunk packing and other preparations, connected with all sorts of boxes and parcels brought by the stage during the previous week. The next day the guests arrived. Dr. Halbert came first, excusing his early appearance by saying he felt lonely, and wanted to see young faces again. Then the Captain drove up in grand style, having on board Mrs. Thomas, her domestic, Malvina McGlashan, Sylvanus, and his strict parent, Saul. Malvina was received by the maids with great effusion, while the paternal Pilgrim eyed Timotheus, who had come forward to shake hands with his father. "What is the chief end of man, Timotheus?" The son answered correctly. "What is sin?" was appropriately solved, and "What is the reason annexed to the fifth commandment?" Then came, "What is repentance unto life," and on the answer to this Mr. Pilgrim preached a brief homily. "With grief and hatred of his sin, turns from it, with full purpose of, and endeavour after, new obedience. Is that you, Timotheus?" "Yes, fayther."

"Young women," said Saul, addressing the maids, "has the walk and conversation of Timotheus been according to his lights, or according to his whilom lammentable and ungodly profession?"

Tryphena could not reply, for the audacious Sylvanus, unaffected by the propinquity of his venerable relative, had whispered in her ear, "he's a livyer' 'cordin' to his lights, he is;" but Tryphosa spoke up and said that nobody, not even a minister, could have behaved better than Timotheus. Then Saul shook hands with his repentant son, solemnly, and producing a well-worn catechism from his tail pocket, placed it with reverence in the [Pg 412]shaken hand. Looking upon Tryphosa, he remarked: "Remember, Timotheus, the words of wisdom, 'Favour is deceitful and beauty is vain, but whoso findeth a wife findeth a good thing.' Go thou and do likewise, Amen." Further improvement of the occasion was checked by the arrival of a well-laden waggon, driven by Rufus, and containing his parents, Christie Hislop, Mr. Bigglethorpe and Ben. Mr. Bigglethorpe was hailed with delight by Marjorie, who immediately carried off "dear Mr. Biggles" to see the creek, and tell her about his little boy, who was not yet christened, because, in the face of Marjorie's opposition, he could not call him Walton, Cotton or Piscator, and he could not think of any other name. She had objected to Felix as too catty like, and Isadore she had said was as bad as Is-a-window. However, he enjoyed the creek for a few minutes before dinner. Mrs. Hill was installed as the mother of the kitchen. With her great conversational powers and large knowledge of scripture, she rather overawed father Pilgrim, and her own and her husband's abundant cheerfulness revived a company, ready to droop under the austerities of Saul's genuine but unpleasant religion. Ben, as a sedate married man, gave himself largely to Mr. Hill's society, until Mr. Terry came in to see his friend from the north, and unfold his plans of an Irish tour. Later in the day Mr. Bangs rode over, and made excuses for Matilda, who thought it wrong to go into society so soon after her husband's death. Finally, the constable appeared in full regimentals, with the stalwart Mrs. Rigby on his arm. That lady bestowed on the faithless Ben a glance of withering contempt, but the constable shook hands with him, as if he had been his greatest earthly benefactor.

It would take chapters to recite the goings on of that evening in either end of the house, the jokes of father Hill, and the homilies of father Pilgrim. Sylvanus dared and was slapped; and Timotheus followed his example, but was more gently dealt with. Christie and Malvina, as bridesmaids, had to inspect the trousseaus with Mrs. Hill. In spite of Saul's protest against worldly amusements, the geographical cards were produced, and the lady of the third-class county certificate swept the board,[Pg 413]although the constable maintained his right to Russia and India, and Pilgrim pater easily secured all Palestine and Syria, owing to his extensive study of Josephus, which he recommended to Mr. Hill as a valuable commentar on the Old Testament Scriptures. Nor were the occupants of the drawing-room less jolly. The Squire and the doctor, Mr. Bangs and Mr. Bigglethorpe, kept the conversation lively, and would have hurt the feelings of Orther Lom, who arrived by the stage, if he had had any to hurt. The contracting parties were grave and self-contained, as became their position; and, to look at Mr. Errol, no one could have dreamt of his ever having gone on the splore. Dr. MacPhun came late, in his own buggy, accompanied by his daughter Maggie, a pretty girl of seventeen, who was just what the feminine community wanted. The reverend doctor warmly congratulated his co-presbyter, and jocularly quoted words to the effect that hope's blest dominion never ends, and the greatest sinner may return, which Mrs. Carmichael regarded as an unworthy reflection upon her intended's antiquity. Wednesday came at last, and the Kirk was decked at morning tide, but, unlike St. Cuthbert's, the tapers did not glimmer fair. The concourse was great, and the organ and choir were at their best. Mrs. Carmichael was attended by Miss Graves and Miss MacPhun, and Mr. Errol by Mr. Douglas and Mr. Lamb. When Dr. MacPhun had united them, and spoken a few felicitous words, he retired to the vestry, and yielded the gown and bands to the new bridegroom, before whose bar appeared Miss Graves, supported by the two Marjories, and Mr. Douglas with Mr. Bangs and Mr. Lamb. When little Marjorie saw herself paired off with Orther Lom, she thought of the Captain's couplet, and burst into a fit of laughter, which drew down upon the culprit her cousin's reproof. The Squire had given away his sister, and Miss Graves was handed over to Mr. Douglas by the doctor, for the reason that her late lamented father had been a distinguished medical man. When the wedded pairs passed out of the church, there was great cheering, in which Mr. Terry and Mr. Bigglethorpe seemed to be rival fuglemen. At Bridesdale, a pale young man with a long brown beard was reclining on a couch, and looking eagerly out of a window. His dark blue frock coat, light grey trousers, [Pg 414]and white silk necktie, meant business, too. It would never do for little Marjorie to be three times a bridesmaid, for that was unlucky; so Miss MacPhun stood by Marjorie the greater, and Bangs helped Coristine to his feet. The two divines mercifully made the service brief, and two well mated souls obtained each its chief desire. Mr. Errol and the Squire were very patronizing towards their new made son and nephew. The Captain was satisfied. "I thought all along it was that sly dog Will-kiss-em was after the old man's niece, the sly dog; but he's off, and a good riddance to poor stuck-up rubbish, say I." The table speeches were marvellous. Dr. MacPhun exhausted Dean Ramsay's anecdotes, Mr. Bigglethorpe allegorized marriage as fishing in all its branches, Doctor Halbert said the great trouble with female nurses always was that they would go and marry their patients, and Mr. Bangs remarked that, if he could run down somebody who was wanted as quickly as Mr. Douglas had done, he would make his fortune. Mr. Lamb lavished himself on Maggie MacPhun, and, as she was young, semi-rural, and unused to the masculine production of cities, his attentions were agreeable, much to his satisfaction; his peace of mind with himself nothing could disturb.

In the evening, Mr. Errol put on his gown once more, and Dr. MacPhun stood by his side, while in front of them there was a small table on which lay a Bible, and, a short distance off, a larger one with a marriage register, pen and ink, and duly filled certificates. At a given signal, Mr. Hill appeared, leading his daughter Tryphena, followed by Christie Hislop and Malvina McGlashan. Next came Sylvanus in the grasp of Saul Pilgrim, attended by Rufus, and the ubiquitous Mr. Bangs. Without being asked, Mr. Pilgrim senior ostentatiously stated, after Mr. Hill had bestowed his oldest daughter, that he gave his son to be that woman's husband, and trusted they would bring up their family, as he had done his, in the nurture and admonition of the Lord. This bombshell excited some merriment in the rear of the procession, where Mrs. Rigby was pushing the corporal forward to exhibit his uniform and medals. When the ceremony was over, the bride and bridegroom remained, but the fathers and the assistants returned to the kitchen. Tryphosa now hung [Pg 415]upon her father's arm, and Timotheus was hauled in by Saul, receiving admonitions on the way. The groomsmen and bridesmaids were as before. Mrs. Hill, who stood by Mrs. Carruthers, wept copiously, when her favourite daughter's turn came, and Hill senior gave her away with a qualm, especially as the parent of Timotheus presented him as the prodigy's son come back from the swine husks. So the last ceremony was over. "Siccan a thing as five waddins in ae day was never heard o' in Flanders before," said the Squire, with a sigh of relief. Of course, the people ought all to have gone away somewhere, according to all the rules that govern civilized marriage. Mr. Errol went to his lodgings to pack up, and took Mr. Douglas with him. As for the rest of the married people, they simply went on with their ordinary tasks and amusements as if nothing personal had happened. Before these two gentlemen retired, however, they had to take part in a dance in the coach-house, at which old Styles played the fiddle, and the constable called out the figures, while Mr. Pilgrim groaned in the ears of Mrs. Hill over the worldly spirit that was sapping the foundations of spiritual life. When the drawing-room people left the festive coach-house, the ladies divested themselves of the day's finery, and the gentlemen retired to the office, where Mr. Errol smoked three pipes and renewed his youth. Dr. MacPhun told more stories, as did Messrs. Bigglethorpe and Bangs, and at last they all became so happy, that a deputation of the Squire and the minister was sent to produce their new relative Coristine, and make him drink a bumper of champagne to his bride's health. As the relatives crossed arms, and, on this improvised chair, carried the bridegroom round the table in triumph, the Captain roared: "Pour it down his scuppers, boys, for he's the A1 clipper; and that sly dog thought he'd have the old man's niece, with no more fun in his calf's hide than a basswood figure head!"

Next morning early, Messrs. Errol and Douglas appeared to claim their brides at the Dale, and found them packed, and ready to start after breakfast. Mrs. Thomas was left mistress of the house, with directions to hand it over to Sylvanus and Mrs. S. Pilgrim when she wished to return home. Timotheus and Mrs. T. Pilgrim were told to go and take possession of Tillycot, [Pg 416]and put in a winter of judicious clearing. Good bye was said all round. Coristine was lifted into the second seat, between Mrs. Carruthers and his new made wife, who looked her loveliest. Mrs. and Mr. Errol sat by the Squire, and Mr. Bigglethorpe intruded himself as far as the bridge on Mr. and Mrs. Douglas. Ben Toner, tired of being haughtily glared at by Mrs. Rigby, offered to drive the trunks in a separate vehicle, but, to the great delight of the junior Pilgrims, the Captain ordered Saul to perform that duty. Nevertheless, Ben accompanied Saul part of the way, and got off with Mr. Bigglethorpe. The patient was tired when Collingwood was reached, but recovered in the parlour car and arrived in Toronto in good condition, and able to introduce his bride to Mrs. Marsh. Mr. Douglas and he got together their portable effects, and Mrs. Douglas increased her travelling impedimenta. The party then left in time to see the glorious fall scenery of the Hudson in the morning, and reached New York in abundance of leisure. Coristine's imperious wife insisted that he should begin at once to spend her fortune, saying that was the only reason for her marrying him; but the invalid, otherwise so biddable, was very firm on this point, and represented that his bank account was far from exhausted. They were hardly on the steamer, when Mrs. Carruthers ran forward and fell into an old man's arms. It was Mr. Terry, who had bidden them an affectionate farewell at Bridesdale, and had then taken the stage in their wake to give them all a grand surprise. The weather was fine, the equinoctials all past, and the sea gently flowing. Rugs and pillows were laid on the deck, between camp chairs and stools, and, while the bearded lawyer lay propped on the former, with the most beautiful woman on board kneeling beside him, the rest of the company occupied the higher seats. The ladies worked away at airy nothings, and the gentlemen, Squire included, smoked cigars and pipes, all talking of the stirring events of the past, and forecasting the pleasures of the near future. Somehow they all seemed to miss little Marjorie, and wondered what sort of time she and the rest of them were having at Bridesdale.

Three months soon passed away. Mrs. Coristine's fortune was secured, and transformed into Canadian [Pg 417]securities by her legal husband, half being made over to Mrs. Errol. The minister took his bride to Perth, and introduced her to his friends, who received her as graciously as the Edinburgh people did Mr. Douglas' queenly wife from Canada. On Princess Street many a pedestrian stopped to look at the well-matched pair. Mr. Carruthers looked up his Scotch relations, and then crossed the Irish Sea to inspect the "owld shod," under Mr. Terry's proud guidance. But the great doctors said Mrs. Coristine must take her husband away to the south of France, to the Riviera, perhaps even to Algeria, for the winter. Mr. Douglas, who was like a brother, saw them safely established at Mentone, and returned to England in time to see the Flanders' five on board their steamer at Liverpool, laden with presents for the children and the servants, the Thomases and the Perrownes, not forgetting Mr. Bigglethorpe and Mr. Bangs. Three more months of winter passed at Bridesdale, then the brief spring, and at length summer came round in all its glory. Timotheus and his men had cleared the encampment of its scorched trees, had put many acres into crop, and had built the farm house on the site of the burnt buildings, into which he and his blooming wife had moved, because the Wilkinsons and the Mortons were coming to the chalet in July. The Bridesdale people heard that the former dominie had not been idle, but, by means of his geological knowledge, had discovered iron and lead mines, which were already yielding him a revenue. Mrs. Errol brought them a letter from Marjorie, saying that Eugene was quite restored, and that they would be home early in July, bringing that dear old lady, Eugene's mother, with them. Correspondence had also been going on between the Wilkinsons and the Coristines on both sides of the houses, and Mr. Terry seemed to be included in the circle. One fine July morning he asked for the loan of the waggonette and set off to town, whence he returned in the afternoon, with three ladies and a coloured ladies' maid, attended by a gentleman and his servant on horseback. Strange to say, the Errols, the Perrownes, the newly-married Bangs, and Mr. Bigglethorpe, were at Bridesdale. Marjorie's terrier, a new Muggins given her by Mr. Perrowne, but which she called Guff, ran barking to meet the[Pg 418]approaching party, and the animal's mistress, following it, was soon in the arms of long absent friends. "Where is Eugene?" she cried, in a tone of disappointment. "Where is Mr. Wilkinson?" asked Mrs. Carruthers, in concern. "We have lost them for a little while," replied the ladies, cheerfully. So they changed their things, unpacked their trunks, dispensed many gifts, brought through all sorts of custom houses, and assembled in the drawing-room to await the stated six o'clock tea. The clock was on the stroke, when they all heard singing, on the road, of two male voices:—

For, be it early morning,
Or be it late at night,
Cheerily ring our footsteps,
Right, left, right!

Then two jovial pedestrians came swinging through the gate, with the old knapsacks on their backs, and newly cut staves in their hands. They responded heartily to the varied salutations of the company, and, as each bowed himself over the woman he loved best, they said: "God has been very good to us, and has sent us more than a marshal's baton through these two knapsacks."

Pleasant were the two summer months at Bridesdale and Tillycot, with visits to the Manse and Cubbyholes, to Bangslea and the Beaver River. Two little Pilgrim girls and a Toner boy appeared before the visitors went home; and, soon after their arrival at their homes, they learned that Basil primus was marching Basil secondus in his arms, clad in a nocturnal surplice. Mr. Bigglethorpe had had his baby christened Felix Marjoram, regarding the latter botanical word as a masculine equivalent of Marjorie. When, next year, the welcome visitors came to Flanders from Toronto and the far south, they brought each a maid and a warm little bundle. The bundle of Mrs. Coristine was called James Farquhar, and that of Mrs. Wilkinson was Marjorie Carruthers. When they cried, Mr. Coristine, M.P., and Dr. Wilkinson, if they were about, carried them round, singing outlandish songs; when they were good, the parents laid two knapsacks over a rag on the lawn, put pillows on top, and the babies [Pg 419]against the pillows, betting quarters as to which would kick the highest.

The culprits were all set free or left unmolested. The two Davis brothers disappeared, evidently across the lines. Old man Newcome is said to have been converted by Father Newberry and to be living a life in keeping with the exalted station of his daughter Serlizer. Reginald Rawdon's son was looked up by Mr. Bangs, and started in business in a new town, as a country store-keeper, on part of his uncle's ill-gotten money. Monty, growing a big lad, has charge of the farm at Bangslea, and, to see him and his grey-haired, but otherwise young-looking, mother, none would think they had ever been deprived of their reason. The character of Nagle, alias Nash, has been amply cleared by his friend, who has erected a suitable memorial to him at Collingwood cemetery. Peskiwanchow is hardly recognizable in its reformed condition, and the Beaver River, like the Flanders' lakes, is safer to visit, though otherwise as delightful as ever, than when the Maple Inn was invaded by two knapsacks. Mr. Bulky is still its hero, and Wilkinson, who does not smoke, has had him up to Tillycot with Mr. Bigglethorpe and without his fishing coat.

Made in the USA
Columbia, SC
16 June 2022